Llove the Llama

Mel Conner

Dedication

This is pretty much a work of fiction.

I would like to thank the following people for reading early manuscripts of my novel and offering invaluable advice: Chuck Woolfolk, Gene Openshaw, Lydia Moland, Mike O'Neal, Frost Freeman, Jim Conner, David Conner, Cheyenne Cordell, Rebecca Kim, Ellen Bradley, Jeremey Bedford, Risa Laib, Bruce Ramsey, Theresa Harrington and Dave McElhaney.

Thank you to Liam Quinn for the cover photo. By the way, I did not meet Liam until after I completed <u>Llove the Llama.</u> Is it happenstance that he shares his last name with three characters from this novel? I can guess what Gracie Quinn would say: "Not a chance." Whereas her husband Cole would likely consider it a "Quincidence."

Thank you to Frances Dayee and my fellow mischief-makers at the Lake Forest Park Writers Workshop.

Thank you to Gene Openshaw and Mike McGregor for your inspiration and years of companionship as fellow Miners of Light.

Many thanks to my lovely wife Donna, who read and critiqued my manuscript, and who has supported me as a writer for all these years.

copyright © 2015
all rights reserved

Contents

    Prologue
1 Get Lost
2 Sacrificial Llama
3 God or Gaudy
4 Blue Muña
5 Stalemate
6 Moby's Trip
7 Anatomically Confused
8 Our Native Tongue
9 Return to Earth
10 The Devil's Harlot
11 Band o' Leer
12 One Too Many Zeroes
13 Sidestep Death
14 The Source of All
15 Those Few Who Are Blessed
16 Dry as a Bone
17 He Sacrificed Himself
18 Better Than Hell
19 Your Daddy Ain't Your Daddy
20 Juan Dunbar
21 Buddha Would Agree
22 Set For Life
23 Call That Fair?
24 Bogeyman
    Epilog

Prologue – January 1992

I gotta get outta here.

My tickets came today. I fly out of Tucson for Peru on March 1st. Truth is, I'm ready to go now. Dad is deaf, and Mom's not around anymore, so the Duncan family's lunacy tends to get channeled through me, though I am the youngest of four. Get any two of us together, and we generate a wicked vortex, drawing us together as we fall. Here's what I mean:

Phil dropped by on New Year's Day. "Theo, I'm a little short this month; could I borrow five hundred bucks? I promise to pay you back this time." I "loaned" him ten bucks, for which he was, pathetically, grateful.

My sister Claire asked for help moving last week. "Could you swing by after work and pick up a few things? I have a date, but there's a key under the mat. I'm sure Dad will let you use his pickup." Phil and I were fool enough to move a truckload of her stuff; she was displeased that we didn't hang up her shoes.

And here's Rowan: "I credit Billy Graham with saving my first marriage." When Claire asked who saved her third marriage, Ro cried all day.

Claire called later that night. "I *know* it's midnight, Theo, but Phil says Dad thinks Ro cut herself. Again. You're.... what, twenty-one? Oh, twenty-five. Huh...? No, *you* talk to her; you're the least damaged of us."

Still, when Claire is feeling charitable, we have enjoyable moments: "Theo, you got your guitar with you? Remember the song you wrote about the cripple and his pet crocodile? We worked up harmony parts."

This past month I've tried acting as the Duncan family peacemaker or counselor or loan officer, as need dictates. It didn't hit me how ineffectually I play these roles until Phil borrowed my beloved twelve-string and hocked it to buy art supplies – easel, beret and camel hair brushes.

"Got 'em on sale," he told me, pumping his fist. "I saved a bundle."

It was all I could do not to punch him. It finally dawned on me that I've been playing the sucker. And while we're on the subject of sucking, my siblings are moving ever closer to being sucked down the drain, and it would be easy to follow them on in. Things have been spinning out of control lately.

But now that I listen to myself, my family has been headed downhill for a long time.

I've wanted to see Machu Picchu ever since coming across those National Geographic pictures in sixth grade. It's time to put my history degree to use. I've got six weeks to bone up on the Incas.

Oh, damn! My phone's ringing. I mean it, I gotta get outta here.

Chapter 1: Get Lost

As in all Peruvian cities, Cusco's main square is called Plaza de Armas, literally, the Town Square of Weaponry. The plaza is dominated by a pair of cathedrals, built atop the ruins of Incan temples that were leveled by the Spanish shortly after they arrived in 1534. Before entering the larger of the cathedrals, I gaze up at the muted Christmas colors, the green bronzed doors and massive twin towers of red granite.

To my left, an American man reads in mumbled monotone. "The altar is constructed of solid silver; it weighs 884 pounds."

"Yep, it's easy to build 'em this big if you pillage and plunder." A husky young man is doing the pontificating. "The pope may speak of paradise in the next life, but it's power he wants in this one." With his shaggy blond hair and week-old beard, my sister Rowan would have described him as "rugged."

His denunciation of the pope draws a sharp response from a plain-looking blonde with steel-grey eyes and angular facial features. "The Spaniards were no angels, brother, but they did bring the love of Christ to the New World."

I don't want to eavesdrop, or at least I don't want to be obvious about it. Looking back toward the cathedral, I take a few stealthy steps toward them.

The first man drops his monotone. "Not so, Fiona. The Spaniards were Catholics, not Christians, and—"

Shaggy interrupts. "Just so I understand, are you saying there were no Christians prior to Martin Luther? CHEEE-ses! The Incas were doing just fine until the Spaniards showed up."

Having heard enough squabbling from my siblings to last a lifetime, I turn to leave, but at this moment a new voice halts the dispute. "However you look at it, it's a lovely building." This comes from a wisp of a woman with straight black hair and bangs, wearing a long white skirt with angels embroidered on the hem. My sisters would have pegged her as a hippie chick.

She continues, "It's built in the shape of a cross, the Christian symbol for death, sacrifice and re-birth. It's also an

Incan icon for the Tree of Life."

This woman emanates a joyful serenity, but her companions signal annoyance at her comments, which seems odd, given that she's made an effort to accommodate each of their beliefs. Shaggy catches me staring at her, and I look away. They enter the cathedral, and I don't want it to appear as if I'm tailing them, so before going in, I pause to take in my surroundings.

Brick pathways slice through the spacious plaza at oblique angles, creating a patchwork of manicured lawns and luxuriant gardens. On steps leading up to a multi-tiered, octagonal fountain, women are preparing children for a play, the boys strutting around with pomp and purpose, the girls giggling over their make-up and costumes. Their smiles accentuate high cheekbones, signifying Incan ancestry. The audience numbers about twenty, some dressed in modern clothing, others in the traditional, brightly colored garb of the Andes.

After twenty hours in airplanes and airports, I stand in awe of my surroundings; Cusco was once the heart of the Incan Empire.

I'm here! I want to shout it. I'm really here!

Until the mid-1400s, Incan rule was limited to the valley in which Cusco sits. Employing a pragmatic mix of savvy diplomacy and brutal warfare, the Incas expanded their domain at such a dizzying pace that by the time an illiterate Spanish pig farmer named Francisco Pizarro showed up seventy years later, the Incan Empire stretched from present day Columbia through Ecuador, Peru, Bolivia and down into parts of Argentina and Chile. Harsh administrators, the Incas collected taxes and oversaw an efficient means of growing and distributing food. Brilliant engineers paved a 10,000-mile network of roads.

It was here – right *here*, in this square – that Pizarro, thousands of miles from the nearest outpost in the Caribbean, completed his conquest of Peru. I picture him riding into town, full of audacity, full of himself. Clad in steel, sitting astride horses, the bearded Spaniard and his band of mercenaries would have seemed like gods. Pizarro, with 106 infantrymen and 62 horsemen, faced down 80,000 Incan soldiers, and through bravery and treachery, he prevailed.

This is my first time travelling alone, and I glory in the freedom of going where I want, when I want. My life is simple.

No sooner has this thought settled in my mind than a pre-teen boy shambles up to me. Clad in tatters, he holds out a pitiable hand and fixes me with big black crystalline eyes. It's troubling to encounter a beggar in the shadow of the two largest cathedrals I've ever seen.

I wrestle with the issue of giving him money, just as I've wrestled with "loaning" my brother Phil money to fix his car so he can get to an art fair in Santa Fe. In either case, the question is: Am I helping too much, or not enough?

Two more urchins sneak up on my flank, so I hustle away, shamed by my indecision and miserliness. The first kid chastises the other two for spooking his mark.

An elderly Ecuadorian man, standing maybe five foot five, approaches me. He's dressed in a plum-colored suit with matching tie and white shirt. "You are American?"

"Si. And you? Do you live here? Work here?"

"I am retired professor, history."

"Oh! I studied history in college. I'm Theo."

"Tayo? Hello, I am Sancho." He reaches out to shake. "What state you are from?"

"Arizona. Es muy caliente." Very hot.

He seems appreciative of my fledgling attempt to speak his language. "You have seen city? No? You want me show you?"

Oh man, this is why we travel! "Well, sure! Si!"

Leaving the square, we enter an alley, bordered on one side by a twelve-foot wall constructed of irregularly shaped stones. "Five hundred years old," says Sancho, pointing out a twelve-sided stone imbedded in the wall. He grins and adds, "No mortar." It's easy to imagine how he looked as a boy. "Earthquake 1650, Spanish buildings fall, old stones shake, then settle."

"Is there a lot of this stonework left?"

"Some, but Spaniards destroy much. Come. I show more."

Ten minutes later, we leave the city limits and climb a dusty, rutted road. Sancho points out the crumbling remains of a tiny stone house. "Manco Capac's home, first king of Cusco, 800 years ago, son of Sun God."

Son of Sun God, huh? It sounds like a deity you'd concoct to one-up Jesus.

Wheezing, I look out over the red-tiled roofs of Cusco. At

eleven thousand feet, the air is crisp, cool, impossibly clear.

"Manco sure had a nice view."

"You are tired by altitude?" asks Sancho.

"Yeah, poco." A little. How embarrassing; here's this old man, not even breathing hard, while I'm about to keel over.

"Uno momento." He disappears around a caved-in wall and returns with a leafy stalk. What's this? He gonna brew me up a pot of tea?

"Muña," he says, rhyming it with "ruin ya." He motions to a stone slab. "Lie down."

What is *this*? Oh well, if things get weird, I have twenty pounds and forty years on him. Besides, he's a professor dressed in suit and tie; how much more respectable can you get? I lie down.

Sancho lifts my shirt and rubs leaves on my chest. "Muña, help you breathe." Then, quick as a prairie dog, he sticks a few leaves down my shorts. "There," he says. "Feel alert?"

Why, yes, I certainly do! But is that because of the muña, or because of I just got groped? I pop to my feet, incensed. But he prattles on about Cusco, acting like his prairie dog fingers have been above ground the whole time. So maybe a little muña-to-the-manhood is how tourists acclimate to the altitude.

Yeah, right.

"Need to go now," he says. "Wife expecting me."

We head back downhill, and I thank him for the tour. He ambles off along the outskirts of town, waving goodbye over his shoulder. The mix of muña and adrenalin has cleared my head. But here I am, three thousand miles from home, my life still on the verge of spinning out of control. Maybe I'll write a song about being felt up by a Peruvian geezer. Let's see, what else rhymes with "muña"? Suin' ya? Doin' ya?

Crossing the sparsely furnished hotel lobby in late afternoon, I hear a familiar voice. Shaggy is asking the clerk if there's a bank nearby.

The man behind the desk replies, "No Inglés."

Shaggy turns and scans the lobby. Meeting his eyes, I ask if he needs a hand.

"Be my guest." He waves me up to the desk.

I ask, "Donde esta el banco mas proxima?" Where is the closest bank?

The clerk replies with a supersonic brand of Español bearing no resemblance to anything I learned in Miss McCready's class. There's a map on the counter, and he points out a spot ten blocks away.

"Gracias," I tell him.

Shaggy says to me, "Gracias yourself." His forehead scrunches up, bringing to mind my brother's bulldog. "Hey, I saw you in the square today."

"Oh, yeah, sorry if I was eavesdropping."

"That's okay. I talk too loud. It's a problem."

"No, it was an interesting debate. Who won?"

An attractive, mischievous face with dark bangs appears next to his head. "Nobody ever wins The Endless Debate. Where ya from?" The hippie chick is standing on tiptoes, peering at me over his shoulder.

"Tucson. You?"

"Seattle." She steps sideways and announces, "I'm Gracie; this is my hubby Cole." Her hair reaches past her shoulders, partially obscuring her gold lame' shawl.

Cole tells her, "Theo got the clerk to show us where a bank is."

"But there's a closer one by the plaza," I say. "Want me to show you?"

"You bet," says Cole. "Hey, we're meeting some people later, but until then we're gonna go exploring. Wanna come?"

Gracie chirps, "The more the merrier."

We step out onto the darkening street. This close to the equator, in the Andes, the sun sets around five-thirty, regardless of the month. The air has cooled ten degrees in the past hour.

Cole holds out his arm. "Shall we, Slick?"

Seeing my confusion, she explains, "I grew up in San Francisco. Mom named me after a singer."

"Oh, right, Grace Slick, from The Jefferson Airplane. Amazing voice, and you look like her, sort of."

Cole sings the opening to "Somebody to Love" in a voice that is both raspy and smooth. "When the truth is found...."

I add a harmony: ".... to be lies."

"Hey, that's good!" says Gracie.

Cole asks, "How do you even know that song? It's twenty-five years old."

"My sisters are older. I grew up with that stuff. What's your excuse?"

"Growing up in the 80s was hell on us drummers; all you heard were those damn drum machines. I listened to the old guys – Ringo, Moon, Bonzo."

"I know what you mean. But it was different for us guitar players; we had Van Halen and Stevie Ray Vaughn. Hey, you're from Seattle; are you Nirvana fans?"

Gracie skips sideways. "We saw 'em at The Crocodile in January! Three bucks! That was one butt-rockin' show!"

"Three guys in that band," says Cole. "You cannot believe how much racket they make."

I lead him and Gracie over to the bank I'd seen earlier, but it's closed. So we enter Plaza de Armas, where two unkempt men are splashing around in the fountain. One man, wearing a tattered baseball cap, is dunking the other.

Cole asks, "He's not drowning him, is he?"

"It's a baptism," I say. "I think. But there's a fine line…."

The baptist lets the other man up for air and delivers a shivery benediction. The scene brings to mind my own botched consecration at age six. My father insisted that we kids be baptized, and our church leaders didn't put much stock in that sprinkle-a-couple-drops-on-the-forehead routine. No sir, we went the full immersion route.

I had only the faintest memory of Phil's baptism two years prior, so Dad explained how the whole thing would work. It seemed like a sweet deal – dunk my head, pray to Jesus, wash away my badness. Mom went along with it, just as she'd gone along with my dad's edict that we attend Sunday school, which, she'd told me half-heartedly, would be good for me."

On the appointed day, Dad dressed me in a white baptismal gown, then I descended four steps into a creamy white fountain, where Pastor Pete waited in the cold, chest-deep, chlorinated water. Pete was a kind, pink-skinned man who smelled minty fresh. He said some Jesus words, then set his hand gently behind my head and advised me to close my eyes. He pinched my nose shut with doughy fingers and leaned me backwards into the water. As Rowan told me later, Pete apparently lost his footing, and he and I both went under. I was not a swimmer, so I panicked and opened my mouth to scream.

There are undoubtedly countless ways to die that are horrible, but I refuse to entertain the notion that any of them are as awful as drowning. The need to inhale is our single most basic impulse, and the inability to do so overrides all other cares. Baptismal water forced its way down my convulsing throat, leaving no doubt that Death had found me. I was alone. Though my ordeal lasted no more than four seconds – Pastor Pete found his footing and lifted my thrashing body clear of the water – the horror has stuck with me. To make matters worse, I came up choking and gagging, which struck many in the congregation as hilarious: Oh, look at that cute little asphyxiated boy!

I imagine they laughed for any number of reasons. Some wished to lighten my load, some chuckled nervously, and some will laugh at absolutely anything. Later on, Mom assured me they were laughing at Pete's embarrassment. But on that morning, I believed they were laughing at me. I also assumed Pastor Pete had not finished my baptism, so I'd be going back under.

It didn't seem fair.

I looked to my family for salvation. Their reactions are etched in my mind. Rowan is horrified, Phil looks confused, and Claire is cackling and clapping. Dad oozes compassion but he's disinclined to stop the show, and Mom.... well, Mom, bless her heart, becomes an enraged lioness. She comes roaring up the aisle, descends the four steps and yanks me out of Pastor Pete's hands, then she slings me over her shoulder, climbs out of the fountain and heads for the door. We're sloshing water all over hell and gone, making splatting noises on the slate floor. Claire is hooting and howling like a maniac, and Mom yells, "Whoever has ears, let him hear: Ho-ly shit!"

I did not understand until later that this vulgarity was aimed at my deaf Dad.

"Baptized by a beggar in a baseball cap," I say, pleased with my alliteration.

Cole gestures back at the Cathedral. "Built with God, guns

and guilt."

Gracie outdoes both of us. "Wise woman with wise guys watching Juan the Baptist." She dashes up to the fountain, scoops up a palmful of water and splashes it on her face, explaining that it symbolizes purity.

Cole is irked. "Hold on, last week you said it symbolized tranquility."

"That's right too." She flicks her dripping fingers at him.

A deep voice behind us yells, "Vamanos!" Get lost! A gruff young soldier is motioning with his machine gun for the bedraggled men to get out of the fountain. The soldier then regards us with a scowl.

Cole shrugs. "Let's get lost."

We wander away from the plaza, marveling at the unpronounceable street signs, like Q'aphchik'ijllu. At the next intersection, Cole says, "Now I know why Peruvians talk so fast; if you tell your cabbie to hang a right on Malampata Ccochirihuaylla Avenida, you better be quick about it or you'll be across town with a half dozen syllables to go."

The brick streets are fairly clean, and the homes well-kept, but away from the plaza, the neighborhoods become increasingly rundown. Women cook over open fires beside ramshackle houses.

Cole says, "Pretty bleak."

"Yeah, but look," says Gracie. "People are still talking, and eating and singing."

Cole points out a cluster of little kids laughing and chasing each other. "And screwin', apparently."

When the children see us, their merriment dissolves and they transform their faces into masks of misery. I'm ready to make a run for it, but Gracie crouches and speaks to them in Spanish. She takes off a turquoise bracelet and hands it to a particularly sad-looking boy. He hugs her around the neck, then runs off with his playmates in tow.

Cole smiles triumphantly. "See why I married her?"

Yes, I do. "How long have you two been together?"

"We got hitched last summer," says Gracie. "We met at the zoo; that's where I work. I was minding my own business, feeding the sea lions, and two of them were—"

Cole finishes for her. "Doin' the waterbed waltz."

She smacks him in the stomach. "A voice beside me said, 'Looks like true love to me.' I wondered who let this baboon out of his cage – see how long his arms are?"

Cole makes kissie noises, and says, "I, on the other hand, was enchanted."

She smacks him again. "It got him all hot, watchin' sea lions make sweet sea lion love."

He winces. "Actually, it looked kinda painful."

Back in Plaza de Armas, three teenage boys are tossing out come-ons to girls and insults to younger kids. Hungry for trouble, they spot us and head our way. I audition ways of dealing with the looming confrontation: Go around 'em, go over 'em, joke, bluster, run. Their leader, a stocky kid of maybe fifteen, stops us, and his stooges fan out to either side. So much for going around them. With puffed up chest, the boy rubs his bare chin with one hand and points up at Cole's blond stubble with the other. The kid says something I'm unable to follow, but he's laying down a challenge. His pals crack up.

"Leave it alone, hubby." Gracie tugs on Cole's arm. "I don't want them getting hurt."

I've been in exactly one fight in my life. Here's how it happened: Phil blames our parents for his chronic misery, so he's always looking for a little compensation. He "borrowed" Mom's ancient Ford Fairlane last Thanksgiving, then had the audacity to sell it to back to Dad at Christmas. Phil only charged him a hundred bucks, but that's beside the point. In an effort to shield Dad from this incessant mooching, I told Phil to get a job. He told me to butt out, I called him a butthead, and the slugfest was on. It was a savage exchange, all offense and no defense.

I'm not a warrior by nature, but I've been surly these past few months, so when Cole steps forward to engage these boys, I stand beside him. He then makes a move that no one saw coming; he pretends to snip off a bit of his beard and stick it on the leader's chin.

"No, no, no!" The boy bats at Cole's hand, like he'd walked into a spider's web.

Following Cole's lead, I pretend to cut off his beard and put it on my chin.

The boys cry out, "Si, si, si!" The leader says something that Gracie translates as: "Yes, cover up his face!"

Cole lifts his arm, cuts off an imaginary sprig of armpit hair, and shakes it at the boys. They erupt in high-speed Spanish that not even Gracie can follow. I cut a nonexistent lock of hair from Cole's armpit and stuff it in his ear. Spurred on by their taunts and laughter, he looks around like he's under surveillance, then digs the hair out of his ear and lowers it to his crotch.

The boys hoot and howl and crowd around us, wanting to know our names. One kid touches Cole's beard, then jerks his hand away, like he'll get cooties. I am not fluent in Spanish, but with patience and miming, we all manage to discuss soccer, drums and guitars. Gracie stands back, grinning as we muddle through. A kid shares a candy bar with us. Gracie takes out a ballpoint pen and hands it to him. He thanks her repeatedly.

Eventually, Cole points at his watch, indicating it's time to go, and we all shake hands. Cole pretends to snip off his beard and tosses it in their direction.

"No, no, no!" the boys say, retreating and laughing.

Gracie reaches her thin arms around Cole's middle. "See why I married him?"

Yes, I do. Cole is all smiles as we walk the perimeter of the plaza. He asks, "Theo, you wanna have dinner with us?"

Gracie nods enthusiastically, so I say, "Count me in."

"Cole's sis and her fiancé are coming too," she says.

"Not fiancé," he says. "Boyfriend." To me, he adds, "I'm looking forward to reconnecting with Fiona. She just graduated from WSU. After four years in the wheat fields, she's moving back to civilization."

We're standing in front of a tavern now, and Gracie says, "We just met Barry a few days ago at the airport. He seems...." Cole has his hand on the door, but he waits to see how she will finish. "....stable."

Cole snorts and opens the door. Most of the aged wooden tables are occupied by locals, which I take as a good sign. An unamplified band is tuning up in the corner. Cole leads us to a window table and introduces me to his sister Fiona, the woman with angular features. Except for the shaggy hair, they bear no resemblance to one another. She's the one who sang the praises of the Spaniards for bringing the Word of God to the New World. Barry stands to greet us. He's a bit stiff, but friendly enough. I take a seat between him and Cole.

Gracie looks around and points out the dimly lit amber lampshades. "I like this lighting; it warms up the room."

To which Barry responds, "They keep the lights low so you can't see the roaches and dirt." His lips scarcely move, as if he's practicing to be a ventriloquist.

Cole grinds his teeth, but remains silent until the waiter arrives. Barry orders a chili relleno, while the rest of us order Trucha al Horno – literally, "trout to the furnace." To irk Barry, I suspect, Cole calls it "trout to hell." I agree to share a bottle of Merlot with him and Gracie.

The band opens with an upbeat instrumental number. The percussionist thumps a leather-skinned drum, and the guitarist strums a beat-up six-string. A man plays panpipes, constructed of bamboo tubes bound with strips of brightly dyed cloth; playing a higher pitch simply means blowing through a shorter pipe.

But what catches and holds my attention is the charango, a ten-stringed, ukulele-sized instrument with a curved back. Though the panpipe player fronts the band, it's the diminutive man with the charango that drives them. With a remarkably supple right wrist, he unleashes a stuttering torrent of chords.

Cole is having a tough time sitting still. We give each other a look that says: I *know*!

I catch Fiona staring at the side of my head, and she turns away. What? Is my hair sticking up? I run a hand over my scalp. Or is it my ears? They're sizable, and when I was six, Claire referred to them as "elephantine." For years afterward, I slept on my side, trying to get them to lay flat.

The next song is a peppy little number that never gets off the ground. To my ear, it's too fast, over-caffeinated, like they have some place to get to.

Barry asks, "Theo, what have you been up to?"

"I met a retired history professor. He showed me the home of Cusco's first emperor, well, what's left of it. And then...." I hesitate, not knowing how the muña story will play.

Cole says, "What?"

"Oh nothin'." But now I'm grinning and grimacing.

"No no, you don't get away that easy. I know a raunchy tale when I smell one."

So I tell them about Sancho taking me up to Manco Capac's view property. By the time we get to the hand-down-the-trousers part, I'm referring to Sancho as "Professor Plum."

Cole and Gracie are giggling and clapping, which enables me to see my encounter with Sancho for what it was – comical, weird, harmless.

Cole asks, "Did he get a rise out of you?"

Barry huffs disdainfully, while Fiona shuts her eyes and shakes her head. They make no effort to hide their distaste, though it's hard to tell if they're bothered by the incident itself, or my telling of it, or because Cole and Gracie are egging me on.

At one point I pause, and Cole says, "Oh ho, there's more!"

"Still got twigs down my shorts," I say, "and they're kinda itchy." I get up and circle the table, while gyrating my hips.

Gracie says, "Ah, the muña walk."

I shimmy backward, doing a lousy imitation of Michael Jackson's moon walk. Fiona turns away to hide a smile. Embarrassed, Barry dips his head and looks around to see if I'm attracting attention. Gracie, who can actually do the moon walk, gets up and glides across the room. Cole and Fiona applaud.

I look at Fiona anew. The act of smiling has transformed her face, as if her skeletal structure has been reconfigured, or her musculature recontoured. Gone are the harsh angles; her countenance is now one of warmth and vibrancy. Her grey eyes have taken on a silver cast.

The waiter brings us our trout to hell, stuffed with onions and tomatoes, baked and served with potatoes au gratin. It's fresh, hot, delicious. I order another bottle of Merlot, and Fiona asks for a wine glass. Gracie asks the man how to say 'muña' in Inglés.

Eyes wide, he calls over another waiter and rattles off something in Spanish. They burst out laughing and slap each other on the back. Our waiter forces the grin from his face and tells Gracie, "Lo siento, no se." Sorry, I don't know.

He scurries away, and seconds later we hear a burst of hilarity from the kitchen.

"Most of that wasn't repeatable," says Gracie, "but the word 'aphrodisiac' is pretty much the same in Spanish. Muña is apparently a stimulant." This gets an awkward chuckle out of me and laughs from my companions.

The band eases into an instrumental number in a minor key. The drummer lays down an undulating rhythm by shaking a handful of seashells, beaded on a string. The urgency of the chord changes hold me spellbound, while the man with the panpipes blows a mournful melody. I am unnerved by the song's simple beauty, an arrow through my heart.

Fiona's eyes ping-pong back and forth between my temples. She furrows her brow, and I brush my hair back again.

The waiter returns with wine and an extra glass. He does his best to keep a straight face as he pours.

Gracie raises her glass. "To Cusco. I love this town."

"Me too," says Barry, "except for the beggars. If you ignore them, they stick a hand in your crotch." When Barry encounters one of those letters that requires moving the lips, like an "m" or a "b," he mumbles through it or leaves it out altogether. Is he on the lookout for a dummy through which to speak?

Cole says, "I don't like it either, but Señor Muña here...." He lays a chummy arm across my shoulders. "I bet he gets a thrill from a little paw in his crotch."

Barry's eyes narrow.

"Keep it up," I tell Cole, "and that's what I'm gonna do: I'm gonna moon ya."

"Pass, but I bet Professor Plum would go for it." The waiter brings the bill and Cole picks it up. "31 soles."

Barry snatches it away. "My treat; you bought last night."

I shove a wad of bills across the table, but Barry pushes them back. "Put 'em away; you can buy another time."

Fiona picks up one of my bills. "These aren't soles. Whoa! This says 'ten million.'"

"Those are intis," I say. "When the exchange rate got to be a million intis to the dollar, they lopped off six zeroes and printed a new currency, the sol."

Fiona asks, "Isn't it a mess, having two currencies in circulation?"

"The sol and inti aren't really different," I say. "Their exchange rate is tied together, like the dime and dollar."

Gracie says, "Like we have two gods in circulation.... well, more than two."

Barry growls, "Yeah, and look how well that's goin'."

"Where does the word 'inti' come from?" asks Fiona.

I say, "Inti was the Incan sun god – Manco Capac's father."

"Hold on," says Barry. "I thought that Manco guy was human. How could he have a god for a father?"

"Funny you should put it that way," says Cole, his grin dripping with glee and scorn.

Chapter 2: Sacrificial Llama

The next morning I hike up to the Incan fortress of Sacsayhuaman, overlooking Cusco. Three gargantuan, parallel walls zigzag across the hillside for four hundred yards. According to my guide book, the stones used to build the ramparts weigh as much as a half million pounds each. Standing thirty feet tall, these limestone blocks were carved with hammers and chisels. How did the Incas do this?

No effort had been made to standardize the shape or size of these stones, yet they fit together seamlessly. I take a guitar pick out of my wallet and try unsuccessfully to insert it between the boulders. How did they do this?

The Incas transported these stones up and down precipitous inclines from quarries twenty miles away, using log rollers, ropes and strong backs, but without the benefit of iron or wheels.

How.... did they do.... that?

The stones lean against one another in such a way that allows earthquakes to pass without inflicting damage. Incredible. Sacsayhuaman – pronounced "Sexy Woman" by tourists – stood intact until the Spanish arrived and began dismantling it to build cathedrals down in the valley. As recently as the 1950s, trucks were hauling away stones for new construction.

An Ecuadorian man calls out to me, speaking so quickly as to suggest he's an auctioneer.

I say, "Hablo Español poco." Speak Spanish little.

He switches to English. "Sir, I think you buy postcard."

Annoyed, I turn away. "No, thank you."

He holds up a card to my face. "You buy this one."

I brush his hand away, and order him, "Vamanos! You ass cactus." I picked that one up from Claire. I'm not sure what it means, exactly, but it doesn't sound real complimentary.

But still this guy persists. "Sir, you recognize this man?"

The postcard features four local tourist attractions, in the middle of which is glued a photo of.... me, in the jacket I wore at the airport yesterday. With a beguiling smile, he flips through a stack of cards. Attached to the center of each is, presumably, a picture of a foreigner.

"Four million intis," he says.

I have to admire his resourcefulness. Although, if you consider the perseverance it took his ancestors to build these walls, this man's gimmick is nothing. I take the postcard and give him a five million inti bill.

"Lo siento, no cambio." Sorry, no change.

Not knowing the word for "liar," I say, "Okay."

He wanders off in search of other prey. The spell cast by Sexy Woman is broken, and I start back to town, in the general direction of the twin towers of La Catedral.

Once inside the city, the cobblestone streets meander past homes and shops. From what I remember of my map, Plaza de Armas lies due south of Sacsayhuaman. Consulting the sun is no help; for hours a day, it will pretty much be directly overhead. This close to the equator, getting around will be trickier than it was in Arizona, where the sun acted as a compass.

I try out my marginal Spanish on a passerby. "Donde es norte?" Where is north? He regards me blankly. I say, "Donde esta La Catedral?"

Eager to help, he points back the way I came and smothers me in a blizzard of Español; the only words I understand are "tres" and "derecha." Three, right. I backtrack three blocks, turn a corner, and there, fronting a small plaza, stands a magnificent cathedral. But it isn't the specific cathedral I'm looking for.

This stone edifice bears no likeness to the church I attended growing up, with its white wooden walls and modest steeple. Our congregation was nondenominational: Catholic this, Baptist that, c'mon on in, sing your heart out. I took my first communion on Easter at age ten. Dad told me the crackers and wine become the body and blood of Jesus once we swallow them, which struck me as cool and gory. I was surprised to discover that wine tastes remarkably like Welchade grape juice.

When I pointed this out to Claire, she told me, "It's make-believe, dummy."

"But some people believe it. Dad does."

"Yeah, well, Dad's a dumb ass. We don't even know Jesus's blood type. And how can wine change to blood if it's not wine to begin with?"

"So, if you used real wine, would it change to blood?"

"Maybe," said Claire, "if you're a vampire or a dumb ass or somethin'."

On the plaza is a dilapidated music store, a tenth the size of Saguaro Music in Tucson, where I sell guitars. I enter and pick a charango off its hanger. The nylon strings, grouped in pairs, are meant to be played two at a time. The frets are haphazardly embedded in the neck; some are noticeably non-parallel, rendering the instrument untunable. I imagine its maker at work: Let's see, we'll put in a fret right.... about.... *here*. Bash!

The other charangos are also poorly crafted, so I leave.

"Tayo! Tayo!" Sancho, wearing his plum-colored suit, scurries across the plaza. He shakes my hand with both of his. "How you are doing?"

"Sancho, hi. I'm fine.... well, no, I'm not. I'm looking for a charango, but the ones they sell here aren't well made."

"Oh, don't buy here." He gives the store a dismissive wave. "You want see fine shop? Follow." He leads me down a side street that veers left, then tapers to one lane. I look around, suspicious. Battered doors offer access to weathered three-story buildings. Eyes peer out from behind dingy curtains. Our passage startles a flock of pigeons perched overhead. Looking up, I watch them beat a noisy retreat into the narrow strip of dazzling blue sky.

There's a crash behind me, and I jump two inches off the ground. Turning, I find a shattered red tile – a bird must have knocked it loose. Theo, calm the hell down.

Sancho gives me his little boy grin. "Master craftsman. Best in city."

The alley constricts further, enabling me to reach out and touch both walls. Sancho is ahead of me now, and I am no longer concerned about anything as innocuous as muña bushes. Turning another corner, the alley dead-ends. When Sancho turns around, I half expect him to be brandishing a meat cleaver. I am ready for battle. He opens a well-worn door and waves me in.

"Why put a store down here where nobody can find it?"

"Local musicians. They all know is here."

With twitchy eyes and fingers, I enter the shop and....

Oh my! Check out these charangos – there must be fifty of

'em. One instrument in particular catches my eye; the soundhole is bordered by inlayed iridescent shells, and the fingerboard is laid out precisely. I lift it off its wall hanger, and plunk out a scale. The strings are set low enough to play smoothly, high enough to eliminate buzz. But it's not until I turn the charango over that I realize just how well-crafted it is. The contoured back is stained and buffed to a glossy, light chocolate. The grain of the wood is gnarly in places and straight in others, infusing the surface with a cohesive mix of chaos and order.

Sancho says, "Beautiful, no?"

"Beautiful, si," I gush. Then, remembering that prices here are negotiable, I hang the charango on its hanger and walk away with feigned disinterest. I try out other fine instruments, but keep returning to that first one. I bring it up to the sleepy-eyed luthier and ask him to play it.

He looks up from the piece of wood he's sanding, and says, "No Inglés."

"Por favor?" I mime a strumming motion.

He sets down his sandpaper and nestles the charango in close. He strums a simple chord progression in an offbeat, fluid motion.

"Quanto cuesta?" How much?

"Ciento treinta millónes." Let's see, 130,000,000 intis, divide by 1.2, knock off six zeroes. A hundred ten bucks. Damn! He saw me caressing it. No, I fondled it. There's no way a local would pay more than thirty bucks for it.

I work on him for five minutes, after which we settle on 90,000,000 intis – seventy-five bucks. He tosses in a soft shell case and shows me some chords.

Sancho congratulates me as we leave. "Good deal!"

Is it? I probably paid double what a native would. And it still seems odd to locate your store back here, where nobody can find it. Oh well, if you have a good enough product, it sells itself.

I ask Sancho about the schools in Cusco.

"Come," he says, "I introduce you principal." We set off, and he asks what kind of women I like.

Is he asking what kind I like in general? Or is he offering to set me up? If so, are we talking about dinner? Or what?

I say, "Smart, pretty, funny, not skinny."

"Oh, you liking big woman?" His expression is no longer that of a little boy's.

"I like athletic women."

"You like gymnast?"

"Yeah, I guess. How about you? What kind of women do you like?"

"I am married, Tayo."

I don't have the slightest idea what we're talking about.

Three blocks on, we enter a crumbling brick building. The principal's office is outfitted with a beat-up desk, a high-backed leather chair with a missing wheel, and a 1985 wall calendar featuring July's girlie-of-the-month.

The principal is out, so we tour the school, stopping in at an all-girl math class with thirty eighth graders, clad in grey. Without prompting, they stand to greet us. The teacher, a stout woman of strict bearing, obviously knows and respects Sancho, and she invites us in. When instructed to sit, the students do so with military precision, and they resume the lesson. The teacher poses a question about decimals and the girls answer in unison, as she writes on a gouged-up chalkboard. Broken floor tiles are heaped in the corner beneath a shattered window. Outside, boys play soccer on cement.

Yawn. The teacher should brew up a pot of muña tea and pass it around. When Sancho sees me nodding off, he stands and thanks the woman.

Strolling the halls, we pass an unsupervised classroom. Sancho says the teacher must be in el baño. We peek into a science class where students are taking an exam. It's a surprise to see them chatting.

Sancho's pride is evident. "Peruvian school – you like?"

"Oh, yes," I lie.

We leave, and Sancho shows me a stone wall that had once formed the foundation of an Incan temple. He draws my attention to a hole in the wall. "Blood flow, offer llama as sacrifice." I grimace at the vision of a sacrificial llama, and he shrugs. "Not so bad. In other place Inca bring sons of distant ruler. Child pure, death is gift to mountain gods, guarantee eternal life in spirit world." Seeing my consternation, he says, "Life better now, yes? Okay, Tayo, I go now. Wife expecting me."

"Sancho, wait!" I don't know where I am, where I've been, or how to get where I'm going.

Back in my hotel room, I run through the chords the luthier taught me, and lurch through "Losing My Religion," by REM. Not bad for a first effort. "With or Without You," by U2 doesn't work at all; the charango, having no real bass notes, sounds thin, as does my playing. I figure out enough chords to try some Beatles songs. "Nowhere Man" comes out okay.

I'm surprised by a knock on my door, and open it just as Gracie whacks Cole in the stomach with the back of her hand. "See?" she tells him smugly. "Told ya so."

"Hey, hey! C'mon in!"

Cole slaps a million intis into her waiting palm. "Slick bet she'd be able to weasel your room number out of the desk clerk. I was fool enough to bet against her."

"But you don't even know my last name. It's Duncan, by the way."

Gracie says, "I told him we were looking for a handsome American with a big smile and big ears. I said we had...." Her face turns grave. ".... an important message for you."

"What's the message?"

She hops toward me. "You're coming to dinner with us!" Cole was right; only a fool would bet against her. "It was Barry's turn to choose the restaurant, so we're having pizza."

Cole is scornful. "Pizza, in Peru. CHEEE-ses!"

Gracie spots my charango. "Whoa, what do we got here?"

"I just bought it."

She cradles the instrument like a newborn. "Wow," she whispers, and hands it to me. "Can you play a song?"

"Not really."

Cole says, "Show me a chord, would you?"

I strum a C major, and hand him the charango. He flips it around and fingers the chord with his right hand. "It's a pain sometimes, being a lefty," he says. "Both grandparents on the Quinn side were left-handed. Crampy Q.... Grandpa Quinn – see, Fiona couldn't say her g's when she was young – he claimed that being a southpaw gave him an edge; said right-handed batters couldn't hit his curve. But Grandma griped about her left-handed banjo costing twice as much. You can't just turn a right-handed banjo around and string it backwards."

"As soon as you can play a song," says Gracie, "we want to hear it. But right now, we're meeting Fiona and Barry at the Inka Museum. Hey, you wanna come?"

Thirty minutes later, the five of us are standing before a five-hundred-year-old skull with half-dollar-sized holes in it. According to the accompanying explanation, the holes were cut by Incan brain surgeons.

I ask, "How do we know the holes weren't made during autopsy?"

"Because the skull had begun to heal," says Fiona.

"Please tell me they used anesthetics."

"Maybe. The Incas knew how to make alcohol out of maize, so they might have combined that with coca, cacti and datura." Seeing my confusion, she adds, "I just graduated from nursing school; pharmacology was part of the curriculum."

I shudder. "So the doctor slipped his patient a mickey and started drilling away. Why?"

"It was a brutal world," says Barry. "They fought with clubs and spears, so head wounds were common."

Reading from a guide book, Gracie says, "There's evidence they performed surgery for religious reasons, to let out evil spirits."

Cole folds his thick arms. "I'm fond of my evil spirits; just as soon keep 'em."

We come across a mummy propped up in a glass cage with his knees shoved up inside his chest. Fiona shivers and says, "I hope he wasn't alive when they did that."

Barry says, "Those who present the Incan regime as a civilized society are—"

Cole breaks in. "Yeah, it's a good thing Pizarro liberated 'em. And hey, while we're here, we might as well liberate their gold."

"Question," says Barry. "Are these natives better off than if Europeans had not crossed the Atlantic?" He doesn't wait for a response. "You'd have to say yes." Somewhere along the way, he ditched that ventriloquism bit. His words are now articulated precisely.

"Really?" asks Cole. "Yesterday I saw a woman on the street selling Chicklets. And what about the four million Indians who used to live in the Amazon? Now there's twenty thousand. Here it is, 1992, the five hundredth anniversary of Columbus' arrival in America, and most Peruvians live in squalor."

"Agreed," I say. "They don't have it great. But Incas used to sacrifice children to appease their gods."

"See? There you go," says Barry, as if my statement trumps Cole's remarks regarding genocide. "Let me ask you this," he says, "who is happier: believer, or non-believers?"

"Probably believers." I say this with envy. Though I'm reasonably sure that nobody can ever know whether a deity exists, it must be comforting to believe.

Cole disagrees. "Believers are more content, more docile, but happy? I don't buy it. As Karl Marx put it, 'Religion is the opiate of the masses.'"

"He certainly did," Barry says, "but look at communism's track record. Marx has been thoroughly discredited."

He has a point. A few months ago, on Christmas, Gorbachev resigned as General Secretary of the USSR, and the Soviet flag was lowered for the last time. I've followed the dissolution of the Soviet Union these past several years with a stomach-churning combination of hope and trepidation.

"And don't get me started on Peruvian communists," says Barry.

Sendero Luminoso, or Shining Path, has been sowing discord here for the past decade, burning ballot boxes, bombing government buildings and murdering peasants who won't buy into their Marxist philosophy. Though their influence isn't widespread, they've disrupted commerce and terrorized communities.

Keeping her voice low, Gracie tells me that Barry didn't want to make this trip while the Shining Path guerillas were active, whereas Cole maintained that this is the perfect time to travel – there won't be many tourists here, and security will be stepped up.

Gracie smiles. "See why I married him?"

I'm nursing an Inca Kola in the brightly lit pizzeria when my acquaintances show up. "Muña Man," says Cole, giving my shoulders a friendly squeeze. "Sorry we're late."

Gracie hugs me from behind, wrenching my neck as she does so. She takes a seat beside me, saying, "I'm a Pisces." It takes me a minute to understand this was offered as justification for being late.

Barry says hello without moving his lips; they look like they've had a shot of Novocaine. Fiona is wearing wrinkled khakis and a baggy sweater. She looks at my ears and grins.

A waiter greets us, and Gracie orders a pitcher of beer and a large pizza with goat cheese and onions. Barry opts for one with pepperoni and mushrooms. Each pizza runs about six soles – five bucks.

"Why are they called soles?" asks Fiona.

Gracie says, "The Incas revered Inti, the Sun God, and 'sol' means 'sun' in Spanish. Money is god here."

"You cannot serve both God and money," says Barry. "Matthew 6:24. In the words of a well-known evangelist—"

Cole interrupts. "If you read a lot, you're considered well-read. But just because you're well-known doesn't mean you know a lot."

Fiona smiles at Cole. "Graham McHugh."

Barry is annoyed. "Who's that?"

Cole says, "We're related to him by…. how, sis? Is he an uncle?"

"Maybe. Or a cousin?"

"Got me. I guess we know him from family reunions, before Mom took off. But I don't really remember him." She tells Barry, "He sends books for birthdays, or for no reason. Do you still get presents, Cole?"

"Yeah, I've got two of his books in my backpack. I'd love to meet the guy. Again."

I ask, "What does your dad say about him?"

"Says he must be from Mom's side. She lives in Ohio."

"How strange. Where's he live?"

"He moves around," says Fiona. "Anyway, whenever he sends a book, he inscribes that saying about being well-known on the inside cover."

Barry is anxious to get back to The Issues. "Why are you not a Christian, Cole?" It's a jarring question.

Cole sizes him up, gauging what sort of answer to give: one

that rankles, one that's conciliatory, or one that will spark a lively debate. "If you start asking questions like that, you'll never stop. Why are you not a Buddhist? Or a dentist? Why not a redheaded dentist with a Daffy Duck tattoo?"

"This is not a game, Cole."

"Sure it is. It's a very strange game."

"Seriously, why don't you believe in God?"

"Same reason I don't believe in Santa. And why put such emphasis on belief, anyway? Let's define ourselves by what we do. Let's emphasize kindness and singing, and eating our veggies. Barry, there are a bunch of gods that neither of us believe in: Ra, Allah, the Easter Bunny, the Cocoa-breathing Dragon.... I just go one god further – I don't believe in yours."

"But you can't equate all those deities. Allah, for example, is a false god."

"That's what a Muslim might say about your god."

"And he'd be wrong."

"That's what a Muslim might say about you."

"But Islam doesn't lead to salvation."

"That's what a Muslim might say about Christianity."

"But we can't both be right."

"A Muslim might agree. See? You have a lot in common."

Having grown up with siblings who skirmish at every opportunity, I grow tired of Barry's bellicosity and Cole's provocative smirks. Their bickering makes me want to plug my agnostic ears. I tune them out until Barry asks Gracie, "How 'bout you? What do you believe?"

"I believe...." She turns her face up and deliberately places an index finger on her chin. "I believe I'll have another beer. Waiter!" This is the kind of response I've always wanted to toss out while attempting to defuse a Duncan family quarrel.

Gracie orders another pitcher, then tells Barry, "If you're asking whether I want to be born again, I do." He's licking his chops, until she says, "I want to be born again and again. I want to be reborn every day, every hour of every day, every minute—"

The waiter brings our pizzas, and Gracie asks, "Who wants what?" When I hesitate, she picks up a gob of goat cheese and says, "Open!"

I catch it in my mouth and manage to choke it down, then I

take a swig of Inca Kola and swirl it around like mouthwash. "I'll have the pepperoni."

Barry slides a piece of pizza onto my plate, while telling Gracie. "Jesus is calling. Why don't you answer?"

Cole eyes him with scorn, and just like *that*, the skirmish is on again. "Barry, you've placed your life in the care of a dead man whose language you don't even speak. And your question implies that my wife needs a reason to believe something other than what you were taught when you were five, or two."

"Just because I learned it at a young age doesn't make it untrue."

"But it doesn't make it true either. And the onus of proof lies with the believer."

"But that's just it; I don't need proof. I *know*. Jesus died for my sins."

Barry does not submit this as conjecture, as I would say: Goat cheese might be made from the milk of the devil. Nor does he state it as a preference: I like mozzarella better, and studies show that 97% of goat cheese lovers were abused as children. Or a vow: I will never again ingest goat cheese, unless my 'nads are in a vice. Or advice: Take goat cheese off the menu and replace it with food. Finally, Barry does not deliver it as an exclamation: CHEEE-ses! No, he delivers it as an incontrovertible fact.

Fiona says, "That's not to say our faith doesn't get tested."

Barry adds, "But God never gives us more than we can handle."

"Easy for you to say," says Cole. "If you were a starving eight-year-old Rwandan orphan with AIDS who eats bugs and bark for breakfast, you might think differently."

"It sounds like cold comfort, I know, but God reaches out to everyone."

I say, "Barry, you talked about God testing us. What's been your biggest test?" Gracie looks at me appreciatively.

He answers unsurely. "A guy broke into our house when I was fourteen. He didn't know my brother and I were home. We caught him sneaking in a window, and I yelled at him to beat it. He knocked Tony out with a crowbar and took off. I called 911. Tony was unconscious for two days." Blinking wildly, Barry says, "He would have gone to Heaven, so I shouldn't have been afraid, but I was." This is a difficult admission for him, and all of us lean forward to encourage him. Barry goes on, "The burglar sped away, and crashed into a tree. He was paralyzed from the waist down. That was the first time I realized how powerful and just is Our Lord."

Cole gives him a now-hold-on-a-minute squint, and looks around to see if anyone is going to challenge this. I'm appalled by the insouciance with which Barry rendered his verdict, but it's not my place to speak up. Gracie shrinks into herself, and Fiona seems torn – I imagine she agrees with him, in theory.

Cole is outraged. "So you think it was God's.... uh, God's *intent* to break this guy's spine?"

"It's not for me to judge," says Barry.

"But that's exactly what you just did."

"How about the rest of you?" asks Fiona, anxious to move on. "Biggest test?"

Gracie answers immediately. "When I was sixteen...." She looks undecidedly at Cole, who is still livid, but he nods with gentle certainty. "I had an abortion." The vitality oozes out of her. Barry starts to comment, but Fiona grips his arm, and Gracie continues, "Oh, it was the right thing to do, but there's not a day passes when I don't think about having a seven-year-old child. But everything happens for a reason."

I am set to challenge that remark, but Barry bails her out: "I'd agree; everything does happen for a reason, as part of God's plan."

"Yes," says Gracie. "Cole and I were meant to be together. If I'd had a child back then, I wouldn't have moved to Seattle and gotten a job at the zoo." She brightens. "I wouldn't have met this big oaf. I can't wait to have kids with my hubba-hubba-hubby. But let's hope Cole Jr. doesn't inherit his daddy's wrinkly ol' forehead." Caressing his scalp, she grows serious. "My father almost disowned me – he's Italian Catholic. He told me I was not welcome at Mass, and he stopped speaking to me. Dinner was a real picnic – if my sisters talked to me, they'd get the silent treatment too." She sounds more defiant than sad. "He only spoke to me twice that year, once while doing his taxes, to let me know he didn't claim me as an exemption, and the other time to say he had misnamed me at birth."

"He was so wrong about that," says Barry. "How do you and he get along now?"

"Better. I got in a motorcycle accident a year later and ended up in the hospital. Here, have a look." She hikes up her ankle-length skirt and shows us an angry-looking scar slicing across the outside of her calf. "Dad took one look at me, tube in my arms, face looking like a plate of lasagna – he wept and begged forgiveness, and he invited me to attend Mass, but I declined. Haven't been back since." Gracie looks to her sister-in-law.

Fiona takes a breath. "Our folks split up when I was nine. Mom visits every few years, but she's mean, especially to Dad. And she's immoral, because.... Well, let's leave it at that. It's hard to think of her as a mother." We wait, but she says, "That's it. Cole?"

"Biggest test – after Mom left, Fi wanted Dad to teach her to cook. He asked why the sudden interest. Sis, you said, 'Mom left, and if you and Cole leave, I wanna know how to take care of myself.' You were so matter-of-fact about it, cheerful almost. I was only ten, and a young ten at that, but it broke my heart."

She gazes at him fondly. "Odd, I have no memory of that. But I do remember the day I found out she was leaving; I asked Dad, 'If I keep my room clean, will Mommy stay?'"

We leave at midnight. As we approach our hotel, an old man trips on the cobblestone street, and he falls, spilling a sack of canned goods. Barry helps him up, while the rest of us chase after the cans rolling and bouncing down the street. We're a bit tipsy, so we stumble and flail around, cackling like cartoon characters.

We return the cans, and Gracie asks the man if he's hurt. The two of them speak in Spanish, then she translates for us. "He says, 'Bless us all.'"

Barry beams. "Well, bless him too!" To himself he recites, "Bear one another's burdens, and so fulfill the law of Christ."

The man thanks us and continues on his way.

Cole asks, "Theo, do you know about the Bridge of Qeswachaka? It spans the Apurimac River at 13,000 feet. It's made of rope, and gets rebuilt every year or two by locals."

Gracie adds, "Construction know-how has been passed down for five hundred years. We're heading up there tomorrow morning and comin' back the next afternoon. Wanna come, Theo? Forty bucks. We get picked up here at the hotel at six-thirty." Fiona nods amiably; Barry nods amiably enough.

"Sure," I say. "Thanks."

Gracie hugs me, nearly ripping off my ear in the process. She says, "Hasta mañana." See you tomorrow.

"Hasta muñana," I reply.

Cole, Gracie and Fiona yell, "Safety blitz!" Then they tackle me. It's a gentle takedown – the women each grab an arm, and Cole picks me up by my ankles and lowers me to the street. Barry stands off to the side, as befuddled as I.

Fiona explains, "In the Quinn family, whenever somebody cracks a truly awful joke, we tackle 'em. Crampy Q was a football fanatic; he started safety blitzing us when we were little."

As she and Gracie help me up, I say, "Sounds fair to me."

Chapter 3: God or Gaudy?

By the time I haul my backpack downstairs at dawn, I'm gasping for breath. The thin air of the Andes has caught up with me. And we haven't even left the hotel yet.

My companions show up a minute later. Gracie is wearing a Beatles sweatshirt with "All You Need Is L♥VE" printed on the front. Fiona begins singing the chorus, and Gracie joins in.

Barry says, "Love is good, but what we need is God."

While humming the melody, Cole asks with a hillbilly inflection, "Fer whut?"

"Ethics. We need God's Word to guide us. Otherwise we'd have lawlessness."

"Whoa. So, if not for Jesus, you'd be out lootin' and torchin' homes?"

"Well, no, I wouldn't, but some would."

"Lesser people than you?" Cole waits for a response, but doesn't get one. "Look, it's not God that keeps people in line. It's cops we need."

I add, "And fair laws."

"But whose laws?" asks Barry. "Yours or God's?"

"Neither. Societies develop laws."

"But laws change."

Cole says, "Yep, they do. They evolve." He sings, "All you need are cops," and Gracie answers with the roo-da-doodle-doo horn part by blowing into her fist.

Piped-in music begins playing in the lobby; apparently the management would like us to keep it down. The intercom is playing an Andean folk song that gallops along in 6/8, sounding both wistful and uplifting. As it fades out, Fiona is watching me, ready to crack up.

"What?"

"Oh, nothing," she says, blushing.

"C'mon, what's so funny?" I'm not offended, just curious.

"Well, it's your ears." Okay, now should I be offended? She says, "I can tell when you like a song. Your ears stand up and out and back, like they're trying to collect more sound."

"You mean like a dog's?"

"No, I don't mean that." She's back-pedaling, apologetic. "No, more like a.... a...."

"A llama," says Cole.

"Right," she says. "But I like llamas! I do!"

"Well, so do I. And all is forgiven." I've seen her smile before, but this is the first time she's aimed it at me. Every cell in my body is given a shock of infinitesimal voltage, toasting me from the inside out.

A battered VW van rumbles up to the curb, and we haul our belongings outside. The side door opens and a somber-looking man hops out. He takes one look at my labored breathing and shakes his head. "13,000 feet would be dangerous for you. I will not take you."

I want to swap addresses with my fellow travelers, but the driver barks at them to get moving. They stow their gear in the back of the van and climb in the side.

I call out, "Have a great trip."

Their good-byes are cut off by the slam of the sliding door. Hands wave at me through the gritty back window as the van pulls away, and it's only now that I realize how much I've enjoyed their company. Waving back, I must look a sorry figure, panting and shivering in the Peruvian dawn, with my backpack leaning against my leg, as the only people I know on this continent depart. The van backfires as it rounds a corner, leaving silence and long shadows in its wake.

It's time to move on. Having paid my hotel fare the night before, I hoist my pack onto my shoulders and set off for the train station a half mile away. The streets are devoid of people; the air lacks warmth and oxygen.

Passing through Plaza de Armas, I face La Catedral and recall the debate between Cole and the others: Impressive or oppressive? Breathtaking or just big? God or gaudy? A sanctuary for the spiritually inclined or a brutish manifestation of the Catholic Church?

I've not yet seen the interior of the cathedral, so I enter the bronzed doors, set down my pack, and proceed up the nave. Colossal columns and ornate archways tower overhead. Each sniffle or scuffle echoes off the cavernous walls. I find myself treading lightly, though no one else is present. Am I being quiet so as not to disturb or pester God? Such a question spawns a host of others: Does God get disturbed? Or pestered? How large are the ears of God? Dunno; it might help to know what is meant by the word "God."

Behind the silver altar hangs a painting of the Last Supper; Jesus and the apostles are set to dine on roast guinea pig, a traditional Andean entrée known as cuy. Positioned in the center of a table, the rodent lies on his back with scrawny forelegs aimed skyward. Is this painting a testament to the endless adaptability of the Christian narrative? Or a provincial depiction of a poor man's god? Or, is it just plain cheesy?

I leave the cathedral and pass the fountain where Juan the Baptist worked his magic. I think back on the day of my own aborted baptism; Pastor Pete came to visit two hours later. Lucky for him, Mom was not home; she'd have strangled the guy. Dad welcomed him in, though he didn't quite know how to act. Should he be embarrassed over my mom's actions, or indignant over my near drowning, or thankful I was still breathing?

Pete asked if he could speak with me. He and I sat on the couch, and when he leaned forward, I leaned back and looked to my father for reassurance. Dad gave me a he's-OK nod.

Pete said, "Theo, I am so sorry for my clumsiness today. Can you forgive me?"

I was six. Here was an adult, asking me for forgiveness. His eyes conveyed so much: sorrow, kindness, weariness. His pink skin made me think he had a fire going inside him – not so much a raging inferno as a campfire on a chilly night.

I said, "Okay."

Pete took hold of my hands and thanked me, then he took a Bible out of his coat pocket and handed it to me. "I want you to have this," he said solemnly. He asked what I'd learned that day.

I thought before answering. "Don't drown anybody. But if you do, say you're sorry and give 'em a book."

He laughed at that. Boy, did he ever! His laughter was full of joy and revelation, snorts and sneezy noises. At the time, I was not sure why he laughed, but it didn't matter. He was not making fun of me. Pastor Pete had a fire inside him and it warmed me.

Years later, Phil told me that Pete delivered a sermon based on my reply, which flattered me. But now, reflecting on the events of the day of my baptism – Mom rescuing me from drowning, and the visit from Pete – I find myself wondering how Gracie would weigh in. I bet she'd say something like: Each of us, even a six-year-old, has the power to forgive, and salvation can come from a worldly mother as readily as from a heavenly father.

I head for the train station, wheezing and wobbling down narrow streets, and I'm reminded that Cusco itself is a museum. Scattered throughout the city are dozens of sites where the Spaniards built on top of Incan stonework, the construction of which is invariably superior to that of the Europeans. Even while hell-bent on destroying or desecrating Incan temples, the invaders recognized the value of a rock solid foundation.

Fuckin' Spaniards.

By the time I arrive at the station, I'm on the verge of passing out. A mangy cat spots me and scurries away, taking shelter beneath a wooden bench, where it can keep me in its sights. How do you say, "Here, kitty," in Español?

To leave the valley in which Cusco lies, the train to Machu Picchu must first negotiate a series of switchbacks. We inch forward uphill for three hundred yards, then stop while the tracks behind us switch. We back up three hundred yards, stopping again as the tracks ahead of us switch. This back-and-forth goes on for the better part of an hour.

The sun is well up by the time we get rolling northward, following the muddy waters of Rio Urubamba, which in two thousand miles will empty into the Amazon River, which in turn will reach the Atlantic Ocean four thousand miles after that.

We are steadily descending, a change appreciated by my lungs. Machu Picchu is situated three thousand feet below Cusco.

Our train stops frequently in shanty towns, where crumbling stucco buildings haven't seen a paint brush in decades. Leathery-skinned women approach open windows, hawking rugs, popcorn and toys. Sales are rare. Twelve-year-old boys sell panpipes; there's one hauntingly familiar melody that every kid in every town plays. I ask the guy sitting across from me if he recognizes it.

He answers with an Irish accent. "'El Condor Pasa' – 'The Passing of the Condor.' It's an Andean folk song popularized by Paul Simon." He leans out the window and buys panpipes from a bright-eyed kid for three soles – just under three bucks.

A half hour later, he's figured out how to play "El Condor Pasa," though his delivery is breathy and uneven.

We are just coming out of the rainy season, and Rio Urubamba constricts in places, creating a swirling froth as it roars through sheer canyons. The Irishman says rains have been heavy up here the past few months; there's concern about flooding.

Flooding – that word calls to mind a sin I committed when I was thirteen or so. At least it was a sin in my dad's eyes. Mom thought my only mistake was leaving my Bible on the kitchen counter where anybody could see it.

Dad opened to a dog-eared page and demanded, "Who wrote this?"

Rowan saw that he'd opened the Bible near the beginning. "Genesis?" she asked in sign language. "Adam wrote it. Or was it Jesus?"

"No, I'm talking about this other stuff."

Uh-oh. I had made notations in the margins regarding the Great Flood. In my defense, Mom wrote in books all the time, and nobody told me you weren't supposed to write in the Bible. Dad began reading my comments, and he was horror-struck, just as he'd been when Phil's bulldog left us a little surprise on our brand new carpet.

My commentary ignored the more obvious reservations people have regarding The Flood, like where'd all that water come from. Shoot, Humphreys Peak in Arizona is 12,000 feet high; were we supposed to believe it was underwater in Biblical times? And where'd all that water go after The Flood? Did it evaporate? Were clouds way the heck bigger back then?

No, my notations addressed less obvious issues:

How'd Noah catch a T rex? OK, maybe they were babies.
Noah had forty days worth of bunnies to feed his T rexes?
God drowneded people cuz their wicked, why drown bunnies? Not fair.
If you HAD TO choose, would you rather drown or get

eaten by a T rex?

Noah was old! How bald would you be at 950? Eyebrows and pubes would fall out.

Dad made the mistake of showing my scribblings to Mom, who read them aloud. She managed to keep a straight face until she got to the part about the pubes falling out. She cracked up, slappin' her knee and stompin' her foot. Poor Dad.

He did not speak to her for the rest of the day. Poor Mom. At dinner he called his sister in Montana and asked her to pray for our family and my Bible. Being deaf, he didn't hear much of her response. Prior to that phone call, I hadn't known you could pray for inanimate objects.

Near the end of our four-hour journey, I peer up the mountainside, trying to catch a glimpse of the hidden city. The terrain is rugged and varied: One mountain is barren, the next a lush green. In places, the Andes rise almost vertically from Rio Urubamba. Our train passes beneath rocky overhangs where the cliff face had been blasted away to make room for the tracks.

Referring to Machu Picchu as a "hidden city" is something of a misnomer. The locals knew it was there all along, overgrown though it may have been. When Yale professor Hiram Bingham emerged from the Andean forest in 1911, people were growing crops and living at Machu Picchu. But not until the site was excavated was it identified as the lost city that had fed rumors for centuries. For the next four years, Bingham packed up Incan treasures – ceramic dishes, human remains, silver statues – and carted them back to Connecticut.

We reach the end of the line at Aguas Calientes – "Hot Waters" – and board a bus that climbs four miles of narrow, dusty, harrowing switchbacks up to the Incan city.

Many visitors arrive at Machu Picchu after hiking the Inca Trail for several days. Others camp out down by the train station and catch the bus up every day. To maximize my time here, I hope to stay at the Sanctuary Lodge, located a hundred yards from the ruins. It's a gamble, showing up without reservations.

The bus drops us by the lodge, an appealing fusion of stone, stucco and grand wooden beams. Everyone makes for the deserted city; I am the only one who enters the deserted lobby. The receptionist, an especially dark-skinned young man, shows me a layout of the hotel and asks which room I'd prefer.

"Which are available?"

"Only three are taken," he laments, then points out a corner room on the second floor. "This one has the best view."

"Why so few people here?" Suddenly wary, I wonder what others know that I don't.

"Sendero Luminoso, they blow up buildings. Americans stay home." He hands me a key and a map of the ruins.

The drop in altitude has breathed new life into me. I take the stairs two at a time, dump my gear, then hustle downstairs and trot up to the entrance. I pay the nominal entry fee and walk a narrow path with a ten-foot stone wall on my left. Turn a corner, and there it is:

Machu Picchu!

Photographs do not begin to capture its grandeur. The Incas situated the fabled city in such a way that renders it invisible from below. Tucked away on a saddle between two peaks, the Spaniards never found this place. Such audacity, to hide a city in the Andes!

Questions come at me in a flurry: Why build here, so far from Cusco? Was this a winter getaway? Or did the Incas use it for religious retreats? Was it a royal estate, or a military post? Archaeologists theorize that Machu Picchu had already been abandoned by the time of the European invasion. But why would they leave?

The Incas had no system of writing, and they left behind no carvings or record of their lives. What we know about their culture comes from speculation based on the writings of sixteenth century Spaniards, not the most unbiased of observers.

A solitary llama descends a stone staircase, acting like he owns the place. Ignoring my presence, he swings his head lazily from side to side. I climb a flight of stairs that empties onto a small plateau, and stop to catch my breath. The view is instantly recognizable. Here, right *here*, is the spot from which those classic pictures of Machu Picchu are taken. The grass roofs that covered the buildings below rotted away centuries ago, but the stone walls are still in place, making it easy to discern the city's layout. In some quarters, homes are arranged in tidy rows and narrow alleys. Other neighborhoods are laid out like a maze.

Machu Picchu was not imposed upon the mountain. Rather, it incorporates itself as *part of* the mountain, gracefully conforming to the contours of the Earth, thereby enhancing the site's natural allure. What a place to live! And yet, I am undoubtedly romanticizing a way of life that must have been arduous and austere.

The llama crosses an expansive field below, appearing as an ant on a carpet, and at this moment I get a true sense of the city's scale.

I descend to the quarry, where mammoth boulders lie partially carved, an indication that this city was a work in progress when it was abandoned. The stones themselves seem lonely. It's difficult to imagine a thriving city here, filled with farmers, priests and hydraulic engineers. I strain to picture the children who once played in that central field, or the women who climbed these stairs with infants swaddled in their arms.

I climb a staircase to the Intihuatana, the Hitching Post of the Sun. Whereas the masonry in the living quarters is simple and solid, this temple was constructed with artful precision. In the center of a stone patio stands a ceremonial sundial, harkening back to a place and time when astronomy, religion and agriculture were inextricably linked. With the approach of the winter solstice, the sun traced a progressively lower arc in the sky each day, and a priest would touch his forehead to the stone, thereby opening himself up to visions from the spirit world. He would then perform a ritual intended to tether the sun to the stone, thus preventing the sun from sinking lower and eventually disappearing. The sundial served as a calendar, marking the passage of seasons, cueing farmers when to plant and when to harvest. Unlike contemporary western culture, the Incas made no distinction between the realm of the divine, the theories of science, and the rhythms of everyday life.

Other intihuatanas were built throughout the Incan Empire, but all were destroyed by the Spaniards. The existence of this particular hitching post is taken as proof that Spanish invaders never found Machu Picchu.

In the early evening, I open to the first blank page of my journal and write "Machu Picchu, March 5, 1992." Then I wait, with pen poised.

And nothing happens. My hand does not move. Where could I possibly start?

Today I experienced the Lost City in myriad ways. I saw it through the eye of a photographer, searching for optimal vantage points from which to shoot. I imagined myself an archaeologist, poking amongst burial sites. I explored the intricate web of alleys as an adolescent boy. I was a tourist, poring over my map, trying to get a sense of what happened when, why, where and how, to whom.

How does one convey the sadness and splendor of Machu Picchu? An entire civilization, brutal though it may have been, no longer exists. A cataclysmic event must have occurred here; why else would the Incas leave? Why did you go? Where did you go?

Why, and where, did you go?

Through my open window, the sounds of a pan flute and a charango drift up from the lobby. The Andean music resonated with me in Cusco, but I am now overwhelmed by its power and melancholy. The minor chords and melodies chronicle the demise and decay of a lost world, the echoes of an empire. Yet underlying this sorrow is an exuberance that celebrates the survival and renewal of the Incas' descendants. It fills me with a euphoria that is wholly unfamiliar. I've had the good fortune to see a city that is still majestic, centuries after being abandoned.

The music burrows down inside me, sending pinpricks across my shoulders and shivers up my spine. It fires up an untapped faculty, able to simultaneously abide anguish and ecstasy. I rise and look out the window, past the road to the ruins, out to the craggy mountains and beyond. The sky is laced with gossamer clouds infused with purples and oranges, vestiges of the fading sun. My sense of self feels as though it's expanding, and it is no longer only Machu Picchu that strikes me as painfully beautiful. At this moment, it seems as if *existence* is reaching out to embrace and smother me. I am possessed.

Something snaps inside me; I collapse on the bed facedown and sob, shattered by equal parts joy, heartbreak and a flood of other emotions I'd be hard pressed to name.

My tears eventually subside, and I roll onto my back, washed out. What just happened? I have not cried in years. Even after my parents took a vacation in December and Mom didn't return, I bore my heartache stoically, stashing it behind a wall of outrage and irritability.

Downstairs, the flute and charango play a sad, upbeat song I've never heard, yet it seems perfectly familiar, leaving me with a visceral sense that some innermost part of me has been cleansed.

Chapter 4: Blue Muña

When my watch alarm goes off at six, I'm already dressed and ready to go. The prospect of experiencing a deserted Machu Picchu at sunrise left me unable to sleep. I eat a banana and a handful of Brazil nuts while rereading a capsule history of the city.

I don a second sweatshirt while making my way up to the ruins. The word "ruins" is misleading, however. Because of the superb Incan engineering, and because the Spaniards never found the mountain hideaway, it has survived nearly intact. Most of the city is in pristine condition, and any walls that collapsed over the centuries have been reconstructed.

At daybreak I enter the ghost town that is Machu Picchu. Sitting upon a roughly hewn stone wall, I bring my arms in close and wait for the sun to rise. Campers from Aquas Caliente will make their way up starting at nine or so, and day trippers from Cusco will arrive a couple hours after that. Incredible! One of our planet's premier archaeological sites, and I have it all to myself, thanks in part to the Shining Path guerillas, who have effectively pulled the plug on American tourism.

There is no consensus among scholars on why Machu Picchu was abandoned. Were they wiped out by malaria? Or, when the Incan empire began to come apart, maybe the city was not self-sufficient. Or did they run short on water? Fountains are scattered throughout the ruins, connected by an elaborate web of aqueducts. This being the dry season, they are not in use right now, as water from a spring further up the mountain is diverted to the lodge. So maybe the Incas left because the spring ran dry.

Floods in the valley, drought in the hills.

Hearing footsteps behind me, I turn to greet the newcomer. But it's only the llama I saw yesterday, seemingly in search of something – food or family, or a mate. He walks on past in the cemeterial stillness, paying me no attention. Does he belong to someone? Did he wander away from his herd? Yesterday he struck me as self-reliant, but he now seems lost, forlorn, out of place. He disappears up a flight of steps, leaving me alone with the stony silence.

Though I live by myself, and have done so for years, such moments of quietude have been a rare treat lately. After Mom departed, her eye-of-the-storm role got passed on to me, and my siblings always seem to be dealing with one trauma or another.

I wander, steeped in semi-sweet melancholy. But each time I turn a corner, or climb a set of stairs, or rotate ninety degrees, I am treated to a fresh vantage point from which to view the city, and every time a sense of awe wells up within me.

I head back to the lodge at dusk, and guards lock the gate behind me. Approaching the open air restaurant, a voice calls, "Hey! Blue Muña!"

I glance down at my jeans and blue sweatshirt, then peer into the shade of the restaurant.

Other voices sing out, "Blue Muña!"

Oh man, this is too good to be true! I have read about the so-called "Gringo Trail"; you can meet people on a beach in Rio, then run into them a week later in a Cusco museum, and meet up again rafting down the Amazon. There exist a small number of South American guide books that highlight a limited number of big draws, so travelers tend to take similar paths through this immense continent.

Gracie leaps up and dances over to me, greeting me with a squeal of delight and a neck-twister of a hug.

Cole slings his arm around my shoulder and presses a beer in my hand. "Just opened it, amigo. I'll get another." He's on his way to the bar before I can protest.

Fiona, still seated, flashes a smile that devours me. "Well, Machu Picchu – how is it?"

"Oh, you haven't been in yet? It's the most, uh.... you can't believe.... Let me put it this way.... Fine, go ahead and laugh."

To make room for another chair, Barry pushes his suitcase to one side. "The train was late, because a slide covered the tracks. We just got here."

Cole returns with beer in hand and takes a seat.

I ask, "How was the bridge at Squishtaco?"

"Qeswachaka," Gracie giggles. "It was cool, but we only stayed a couple hours."

Fiona waves her hand. "My fault. Thirteen thousand feet did me in."

Cole says, "Another hour and we'd have had to scrap her for parts." The women elbow him, then stand and high-five one another over his head.

After dinner, we order a round of Inca Kolas, and take them out to the patio. Cole holds up his bottle to a light – the contents are pale yellow with a green tinge. "Know what this looks like? I saw a llama takin' a—" Fiona clamps a hand over his mouth.

Gracie takes a swig and grimaces. "It's like…. Well, it's not *like* anything. You gotta try it." Reviews are mixed:

Barry: "Isn't like Pepsi."

Fiona: "Not much fizz to it. I taste bubblegum."

Me: "Mmmmm…. pineapple *and* bubblegum."

Cole: "Fruity, yet rancid. You know the llama we saw…."

Fiona elbows him, nearly upending her bottle of Inca Kola.

"Smooth move," says Barry, then tells Cole, "She's always doing that. I hope you don't share her klutz chromosome."

What a pissy thing to say. But Fiona laughs it off, and Gracie lets it slide. So, is this my problem? Has a lifetime of cuing into my siblings' pathological maneuverings made me overly sensitive to such trivialities?

But then I look at Cole; his lips narrow, his eyes narrow, and his forehead crinkles up like a wad of aluminum foil. It's now clear to me why he dislikes his future brother-in-law. Barry went out of his way – *way* out of his way – to belittle Fiona, and he did so in front of her family and a stranger. It reminds me of the way Claire treats my brother Phil. I'm half hoping Cole clobbers Barry.

To change the subject, I suspect, Gracie asks me where I got my charango.

"Didn't I tell you? I ran into Professor Plum again, and I asked him to show me a music store. So he leads me down a winding alley…." I lower my voice. "…. that gets narrower and narrower…." Barry folds his arms and leans back; bad move on his part – his stick-in-the-mud attitude spurs me on. "…. and the walls get taller and taller…."

Cole adds in a creepy voice, "And the muña bushes grow greener and greener…."

My voice is now a whisper. "The dingy alley fizzles out. Professor Plum points to a door and says, with a nasty little gleam in his eyes, 'After you.' So we enter a dimly lit room, and...." I drop the horror story bit: ".... and it's filled with these beautiful charangos. Get this, one was made from an armadillo body."

Fiona asks, "So it was a guitarmadillo?" Barry's laugh is louder than the rest of ours; it strikes me as proprietary in nature.

"Craziness!" says Cole.

"Crazy things happen on...." Gracie pauses dramatically and points at the moon, setting over the Andes. ".... on the night of the crescent muña!"

Cole turns to me. "She's just going through a phase; a phase of the muña."

"Hey, Theo," says Fiona, giggling. "Gracie and I went to the library in Cusco and researched muña. It's a bronchial dilator."

I say, "Let the record show that my crotch was not dilated at the moment of grope."

"It also serves as an insect repellent."

"We could market it as 'Wang-A-Way,'" says Cole. Like he's doing a voice-over on a commercial, he asks, "Are *you* concerned about Peter and The Twins? Try Wang-A-Way. It's a mosquito repellent *and* a stimulant."

"Peter and The Twins?" asks Barry.

"Don't ask." Gracie slugs her husband in the shoulder, then opts for a change of topic. "Do you play in a band, Theo?"

"Yeah, we've been together about a year; we play blues and rock."

Fiona says, "Cole's in a band, called Dread the Donkey. They play mostly grunge. He's a madman on drums. They have a killer guitarist and bass player, but then ya got Jake, our cousin...." Cole's forehead crumples up, and she continues, "He bangs on a piece of sheet metal with a hammer."

"How'd you come by that name?"

Fiona explains, "Jake's dad – our Uncle Dick – has a sorry old donkey that looks like he has bangs and dreadlocks. He named him Dread the Donkey."

Cole says, "I lobbied for 'Bang the Burro,' but Uncle Dick wasn't havin' it. We're on the lookout for a better band name."

Barry says, "Look what I have." He pulls out a coin and

drops in on the table. "Ten intis."

Cole gets the weirdness of that right away. "That can't be right!" He picks up the coin and inspects it. "Where'd you get it?"

"At lunch yesterday, as part of my change."

Gracie asks, "Why would they make a coin worth....?"

Cole finishes for her. "Nothing? Good question. Actually, it's worth...." He cocks his head. "....a thousandth of a penny."

Barry says, "Before inflation went wild, the inti had value." He pauses, then grins at Gracie. "By 'inti,' I'm talking about money, of course, not your sun god." She smiles back, whereas Cole and Fiona fold their arms. Barry adds, "Anyway, that's why Peruvians like American dollars; they hold their value." He asks me, "Hey, did you hear about the kidnapping? Yeah, an American was snatched off a bus, in Lima I think it was, taken into the hills, robbed, stripped, and left to find his own way back."

"Where did you hear that?"

"English guy we met on the train."

Gracie is skeptical. "I think maybe something like that happened once. Years ago."

Cole agrees. "Then the story makes the rounds, until it sounds like one guy in three is getting his nuts stolen, frozen and sold for transplant."

Barry gives them a resolute shake of his head. "You have to watch every step you take down here." He gets up and says, "Time to call it a night."

"Sleep well," says Cole, but he frowns when his sister also stands. "Already?"

"This altitude wears me down," says Fiona. "Night, all."

They head inside, and Gracie massages her husband's neck, saying, "Everything happens for a reason."

I ask, "Why do you believe that?"

She is clearly annoyed that someone would question her on this. "I just don't believe that things happen for.... no reason."

"Everything?" I ask. "Is there a reason for... uh, these bread crumbs? And if so, what would that reason be?"

"Those crumbs are there so that you'd notice them, and then we could discuss them." She smiles winsomely.

"That's my Slick," says Cole. "She don't win or lose the debate; she derails it."

She asks, "Theo, do you think it was coincidence that we met up again?"

"We met up partly because of coincidence, partly because this is popular with tourists. But don't get me wrong, it was a fabulous coincidence."

Her smile fades. "This was no coincidence. There are spiritual winds that blow here." She ignores Cole's roll-of-the-eyes. "I'm gonna do a little stargazing, away from the lights of the lodge. You guys wanna come? This is supposed to be one of the best places in the world to spot UFOs – some people believe this was built as a landing facility."

"Oh, c'mon! To think of Machu Picchu as a cosmic airport insults the genius of the Incas."

"I'll let you know if I see ET." She jumps off the three-foot terrace and saunters down the road, away from the ruins.

"UFOs!" scoffs Cole. "She reads this New Age bunk about Machu Picchu: the vortex theory, the built-by-aliens theory, and this business of 'spiritual winds.' God knows I love that woman, but she makes me crazy."

"How'd she ever get started with all that?"

"When we met, she was still feeling guilty about the abortion. But when we got engaged, she said it suddenly made sense. The abortion was necessary; it had to happen, in order for her to move to Seattle and meet me."

"Ah-ha! So it was your fault."

He chuckles. "Yeah, I guess. Here's my take: The idea that stuff happens randomly is terrifying, so we connect the dots and fill in missing bits with fiction, then we write it down as truth and slam the door. Humans get scared so easily. You're walking through a park at night and see a shadow or a branch out the corner of your eye, and your mind imagines it to be a snake or a thief or a demon, which is a good thing if a thief *is* there, but...."

A critter scurries past his feet.

"CHEEEE-ses!" He jumps up and knocks his chair over. "What was that?" He rotates slowly, eyes scanning the veranda's stone surface. "See what I mean?"

"Where'd you ever get that CHEE-ses bit?"

"I say that out of deference to my dear sister; she doesn't approve of me taking the Lord's name in vain. But most people think I'm saying 'Jesus.' You're the only one that's ever asked about it." His tone implies a question.

"I spend a lot of time learning guitar solos. I've developed a pretty good ear."

He nods and sits down, keeping an eye out for varmints.

I say, "How do people grow up in the same house, same parents, and end up with such different beliefs and personalities?"

He bobs his head up and down. "I know what you mean. Fi and me, we don't even look alike. One of us must be related to the mailman. How about you? Are you like your sibs?"

I unintentionally snort. "Oh God, I hope not."

"Why do you say that?"

"When I was ten, my sister Claire moved out, and I got her room. That was the happiest day of my life. My brother fancied himself a painter; he always had his brushes spread all over the place. I never cared if my clothes got paint on them, but I was protective of my guitar. And my sisters – they hate each other."

I am talking in a way that I never do at home. Maybe it's the distance from my day-to-day reality that makes it safe to disclose my inner life with a stranger – no, an acquaintance – who I may never see again. Or am I changing? Maybe Machu Picchu takes in unsuspecting travelers, hollows them out, and sends them away a few days later, filled with a new essence. Perhaps, I think wryly, there are "spiritual winds" that blow here, and they've torn me loose from my mooring, spurring me to explore new worlds. Or maybe Cole is bringing me out. We have music in common, and I instinctively trust him. Though he and his sister spar, they share affection and loyalty. And, like me, his mother is no longer a part of his life.

I say, "You and Fiona; how'd you end up so different?"

"I used to be a True Believer." Cole gives me a hard look; I get the sense he's gauging my trustworthiness, trying to decide what version of his life to tell me. "I lied the other night when I said my biggest test was my parents' break-up. Hell, I was glad Mom split – she was a fighter, and it annoyed her when Dad didn't retaliate. And she messed around. After she took off, I overheard Uncle Dick tell my dad: 'Good riddance, bro; that girl has a soft spot for a hard-on.' Yeah, sometimes I wonder if Fi isn't my half-sister."

He gives me that piercing look. "Still, I was a believer, until my grandpa got old. Ever know anybody with Alzheimer's? No? Consider yourself lucky. We didn't know how bad it was until my grandma died. She'd been covering for him. He'd forget stuff that happened an hour ago." Cole divides the last of the wine between us. "Crampy Q thought Dad was stealing from him, so he'd hide, oh, say, his keys, then he'd forget where he stashed them, which only confirmed his belief that Dad was swiping stuff." Cole stares out at the darkness. "Crampy would be running around like a madman, looking for something, and Uncle Dick would look at Becky and crack up, which made me wonder if he was hiding Crampy's stuff as a joke." He inhales deeply and shakes his head. "Naw, it was just the damn Alzheimer's." Cole's eyes water. "Crampy used to take me fishing, until his memory got bad, then Dad wouldn't let me go anymore; said it was unsafe. I prayed for Crampy Q to get well, but of course he didn't, and when he left, he took God with him. I saw God as an old man with a white beard, just like Crampy Q, Santa without the red suit. Yeah, yeah, I know, it's a naive approach to life and religion and all, but, hey, I was sixteen."

"What did he die of?"

"Don't know." Cole's bottom lip quivers. "He took a walk and didn't come back. We searched for a week; the cops did too. But we never found him. For all we know, he broke a leg, fell in a ditch and got eaten by coyotes." He takes a breath. "Sorry, that's disgusting. Anyway, that's when I got interested in science, so I could study the real world, and leave that Jesus mumbo jumbo to Christian witch doctors."

"So you made a conscious decision not to believe?"

"Hmmmm. I'd like to say it was, but, no, my faith trickled away over time. It was only afterward that I realized it had dried up completely."

"And your sister?"

"Fi changed too when Crampy Q died; that's when she started praying. Crazy, huh? We switched places. She believed he had moved on to a better place – her words. The saddest part is what happened between her and me. We used to be best friends, but she keeps her distance now."

"Sorry, but I have to disagree. You ought to see how she

looks at you.... Ah, I should shut up. I don't know you well, but, Cole, she adores you."

"Thanks, but.... Look, I adore her too. And sometimes I think: Okay, religion is silly, but it's not so bad; it doesn't hurt anyone. But here's what gets me – she thinks that anybody who doesn't believe what she believes is gonna roast in hell for a trillion years. And we'll deserve it. Theo, she believes that."

"Yeah, it seems harsh; an infinite amount of punishment for a finite amount of crime."

His head snaps up. "I hadn't thought of it like that." I get the sense he's storing this bit away for future debates, and I regret saying it.

He says, "Still, ya gotta admire their whole set-up. Heaven and hell – the sweetest carrot and the biggest stick." He drains his glass and continues in a dreamy voice, "I wish you could have known Fi when she was fourteen; she was so confident, so sassy and relaxed. She used to come out and play football with me and my buddies. We had these trick plays worked up." His voice trembles. "God, I miss her."

We sit in silence for a few minutes, then he stands up, steps down onto the road, and ambles up the hill toward the entrance to Machu Picchu.

Gracie bounds up the stairs from the other direction. "Hey! I saw two shooting stars at the same time! You know what that means?" She pointed at a spot over the ruins. "They started over there and.... Where's Cole?"

I point out at the night. "He's up there somewhere."

"What's he doing?"

"Not sure; he's pretty broken up. He told me about his grandfather."

"He did?" She looks at me wide-eyed. "He never tells anybody about that."

"Sad story, about him and his sister."

"He told you *that*?" She squints up the road. "Oh, Theo, you've got the gift."

"What gift would that be?"

"You get people to talk. About life, about things close to their hearts."

"Well, so do you. Matter of fact—"

"No, not like you. But what I notice is that you don't talk much about yourself. The other night in Cusco, you asked us all about our biggest test, but you never shared yours." Seeing my confusion, she says, "Oh my god. You weren't even aware you'd clammed up."

I try to conjure up that biggest-test exchange, but the sequence is fuzzy. Did they ignore me? Or did I hide? I honestly don't know. And what would be my biggest test? Something to do with my mother's disappearance from my life.

"Even now you've shut down," says Gracie, "and I have to wonder why that is."

"Goofy family," I say, shaking my head. "They're.... um, needy."

"And after everybody else says their piece – let me guess – there's no time left for you." There. In one sentence, she's nailed my role in the Duncan family in a way that I have never been able.

"It's as if my time gets.... no, my life gets eaten. *I* get eaten." I stare at her in bewilderment. "But how did you know?"

"I recognize the lost child in you. When a family goes to hell, one person rebels, another overachieves, and one of us...." She swallows heavily. ".... never asks for anything." Her next words are barely audible. "She disappears."

"I'm surprised to hear you say that; it's so easy for you to connect with people."

"Huh? What? Oh, well, thank you. Cole can take some credit for that; he brought me back out."

"And somehow you manage to stay connected without getting sucked into the.... what did you call it?"

"The Endless Debate."

"You don't seem to have a need to be right."

"Yeah, but maybe that's not such a good thing, considering how I was treated as a teenager. Trust is still an issue for me. Sometimes I'm afraid I'll wake up and Cole will be gone."

"Not a chance. He's no dummy." I stand and rub my eyes. "Look after him; he's a good man."

She presses her waif-like body against mine and wraps her arms around me fiercely. "You are a good man too, Theo."

From the direction to the ruins, we hear someone yelling in Spanish, followed by an unintelligible English response. Gracie and I take off up the road. I'm ready to back up Cole if he's gettin' mugged, whereas I imagine Gracie's intention involves peace-keeping.

Cole comes trotting down the hill, and waves us back. "The guard thought I was trying to sneak in," he says.

"Were you?" asks Gracie.

"Well, sure," he says with a guilty grin. "Slick, how do you say 'Please don't point the machine gun in my face' in Español?"

Chapter 5: Stalemate

We spend the morning exploring terraces, temples and communal grave sites. We are kids again, navigating precarious drop-offs with no guard rails. Terraced fields reach down the steepening hillside, far past the point where farming would seem possible.

Walking along a stone wall, I trip and fall, landing on the next terrace four feet below. I land on a relatively grassy patch and roll when I hit, but rocks cut into my hip and hand. Fiona shrieks. From her vantage point, I've disappeared; for all she knows, I am bouncing off granite outcroppings, reaching in vain for scraggly tree limbs, falling toward the river, twelve hundred feet below.

My companions are on me in seconds. I test out my sore wrist, then give them a phony chuckle and assure them only my pride is injured.

"Thank God," says Barry, relieved. "He is not done with you yet." It's not clear if he means that his deity considers me a work-in-progress, or if He has other pratfalls in store.

Fiona regards me sternly. She doesn't appreciate me making light of the situation.

Cole gets behind me, leans over and reaches his hands under my armpits. He lifts me to my feet, saying, "Almost gave me a coronary, pally."

Gracie palms my cheeks and scolds me. "Be careful, Theo. If you fall, I'm never speaking to you again." We guys crack up over that, and so does Gracie, once she realizes what she said. Fiona is not amused.

My five-second disappearing act gets us talking about fear, and Cole tells us about a recurring dream:

"An object or being of infinite destructive power is coming at me, moving so fast I won't be able to jump out of its way. I can't make out what it is, because there's a blinding light on the front, like a train. And it's loud. Approaching from my left is a wave, like a tsunami, only it's a force for good. The question is, will it arrive in time to deflect the train? The wave is coming, I feel it, I hear it, but I can't tear my eyes away from that light. They're both closing in, getting louder. And then I wake up, with the sense that these two.... uh, somethings are locked in mortal combat. Scares the holy hell out of me."

Fiona and I look to Barry, to hear his take on Cole's dream. He smirks but says nothing. The religious significance of the two forces is so obvious as to make commentary unnecessary.

We climb up to the Watchman's Hut and perch on the stone patio, our legs dangling over the edge. We are silent for several minutes, which is unusual for the Quinns. Machu Picchu tends to calm and quiet visitors, much as a cathedral does.

Finally Gracie proclaims, "This is a spiritual place."

I have no idea what she's talking about, but so what? I have not been able to offer up a more lucid description of The Hidden City. Still, I ask what she means.

Gracie gives me a sharp look, but she softens upon realizing that my question is posed out of curiosity rather than antagonism. "This is a sacred vortex," she says, "a focal point for the life energies of the people who lived here. It generates an energy field that resonates with my spiritual essence."

I scratch my head, striving to scale that wall of gobble-de-goop. But, shoot, where do you get a toehold? And yet, I believe Gracie feels a sense of awe here, as do I. "What do you mean by 'soul' and 'spirit?'"

"I can answer that," says Barry. "'Soul' means the part of us that doesn't belong to this physical world, this material reality."

Cole clasps his hands behind his head and leans back. "Too cryptic for me."

I say, "Barry, you can't define something by saying what it's not. If you ask me what a.... a.... bersnootch is, I wouldn't define it by saying what it isn't."

"What is a bersnootch?" he asks.

"It's not a turnip."

Barry gives me a "pox upon thee" look. "But you can define darkness as a lack of light."

Cole says, "Nice try. Light is the presence of photons. 'Darkness' as an entity doesn't exist. We could define the 'soul' as 'a lack of reality,' I guess, but it doesn't get us anywhere."

"Then let's define "God" by what He does. He created the

universe."

"Or we could define the Great Bersnootch as creator of the universe," says Cole. "Again, where does it get us?"

Barry turns away from him. "And you, Theo? You're an atheist, right?"

"No, an atheist denies the existence of god. I don't even know what that word means."

Surprisingly, Gracie seems to approve of my response, but only, I suspect, because it gets Cole and Barry thinking long enough to provide us a respite from The Endless Debate. Eventually she says, "By 'spiritual place,' I mean this is heaven."

Barry is adamant. "No, this is most certainly not. Heaven transcends all of this."

"I don't want to transcend life." Gracie hugs herself. "I trust it; I want it to envelop me."

"That's a pagan point of view."

"All right then, I'm a pagan. How could anyone need more than this, right here?" She raises his hands, palms up. "Look at the sky, look at Fiona. How could you need more?"

"It's not a matter of needing more. I'm saying there *is* more."

"But where is heaven?" asks Cole, earning him a scowl from his wife. "And what would a typical day look like, sitting beside The Almighty? Imagine Jesus' forecast: Sunny through the weekend, followed by a billion years of blue sky. It'd bore me to death."

"Your take on heaven is too literal. You twist Jesus' message and reduce it to nonsense."

"Look, Barry, Jesus no longer exists – not in my world, he doesn't. You can't communicate with somebody that's not *here*. Jesus is gone – capital G."

I say, "But, Cole, a hundred years ago, before radios were invented, the thought that we could talk with someone a thousand miles away would have seemed impossible – capital I."

He shoots me a look that accuses me of betrayal, as if to ask: Aren't we on the same team?

Then, without bothering to weigh my words, I drop this gem: "So maybe in a hundred years, we will figure out how to talk to God."

This notion satisfies no one: It waters down my agnostic stance; Cole acts like he's been double-crossed; Barry regards me as an infidel; and Gracie, who communes with her pantheon of gods on a regular basis, has no idea what I'm talking about.

Fiona also looks displeased. "Some of us already speak with God." She looks from Cole to Gracie to me, but she doesn't acknowledge Barry, though he's doing his damnedest to catch her eye.

"As for God," says Barry, trying to get back in the game, "the best minds in the world have acknowledged His existence for millennia. To write Him off is silly."

To which I respond, "But we write off, say, numerology, though it was widely believed for millennia."

Gracie says, "Not all of us write it off." This silences us, which I suspect may have been her intent. No, she's dead serious.

Cole waits for the breeze to dissipate her remark. "There are four reasons people believe in God. Some never question what their parents told them; others see order and beauty in the world, and they want to know how they fit in; some are afraid of death; and others are afraid of life."

Surprisingly, Fiona agrees. "Many Christians will tell you they walk hand in hand with the Lord, but most have never felt His Presence." Again Barry vies for her attention.

Cole picks up on their awkwardness. To stir the pot, he says, "You're a Christian, Barry. When, and where, do you sense this presence? Do you get that feeling in church?"

"Yes, in a way," he says, embarrassed. "But I feel it most strongly up in the mountains. His glory stretches to the horizon. Look through that pass there; I know there must be a God."

I'm about to move the conversation around the circle, but Gracie beats me to it. "How about you, Theo? Ever had a spiritual adventure?"

I recall my first evening here, and that eruption of euphoric bewilderment. I'm unable to conjure up that sensation with any degree of clarity, though it's still burbling away, right beneath the surface of my skin, or just beyond the reach of my consciousness. See my problem? I'm not even sure how to categorize it. Mental? Physical? Emotional? Spiritual? Whatever than means.

"I'm not sure what you're asking me, but I had something

happen two days ago." I hesitate, unsure of the nature of my meltdown, and how it will play. Was it a profound experience, a glimpse of glory, a realization that we are part of something larger? Or will they think I suffered a nervous breakdown? Worse, will they consider it an insignificant, cathartic splash of tears?

I've clammed up. Gracie winks and glares at me. So I dish up a faltering version of my whatever-it-was, after which my companions weigh in:

Cole: "CHEEE-ses, pally! That is freakin' awesome!"

Barry: "That's Jesus, knocking on your door."

Gracie: "Yes, yes, yes! You were visited by spirits, to keep you company."

On the face of it, that sounds plain silly. But, on second thought, my experience was so utterly alien that it's not a stretch to think of it as a visitation. Or invasion is more like it.

Fiona remains silent. She gives me a look that is disconcertingly familiar. Where have I seen it? Oh, right, it's the same look her brother gave me last night, while deciding how much of his guts to spill. The two of them do not look alike, so it's odd, seeing his expression grafted onto her face. Her gaze intensifies; she's crawling around inside me, searching for my core.

"Next," I say to Cole, glad for an excuse to turn away.

He says, "When I was, oh, nine or so, Christmas carols filled me with a sense of peace and warmth, and something I can only describe as reverence." Barry perks up at that, but he slumps as Cole continues: "Of course, we only sang the first verse or so; the later verses always talk about how vile humans are."

Fiona and Grace shoot each other an ohhh-no look, which the men don't catch.

Barry says, "Those songs were inspired by God, and the last verses lay out His Plan."

"And what a swell plan it is, if you're part of The Club. Let me ask you this: How old were you when you dedicated yourself to Christ?"

"I was twelve."

"Ooooh, double digits. So, at twelve, you decided what makes the universe tick?"

"Well, at age nine, you felt reverence. And you dedicated

yourself to music."

"Fair enough," says Cole, bringing sighs of relief from the women. "How about you, sis? Heaven?"

"I haven't had any one experience that stands out, in the way you're describing."

Gracie says, "Or maybe, for you, most days are like that."

Cole adds, "Which is why no single moment stands out."

Fiona regards them with warmth and gratitude. I try to imagine my siblings having this conversation, and find myself envious of the Quinns.

"OK, Slick, whattaya got for us?"

"One summer I worked for the Forestry Service, building trails. On a good day we'd make a hundred yards, but if we had to cut through a downed fir, we might only get thirty feet. After two weeks in the woods, I was all grubby, so I hiked out after work alone. I'm crossing a moonlit meadow, toting a forty-pound pack, eyes on the ground to keep from tripping, and I come face to face with an elk with a huge rack. He's staring down at me, not afraid, not aggressive, just curious, and he's trying to tell me something."

Fiona says, "Like...."

"I don't know. But right then, I was a creature, communing intimately with another creature. I belonged."

"All of God's creatures belong," says Barry.

"Yes," says Gracie. "That was how I felt. And that's how I feel here and now with all of you. We belong."

We wander the ruins, sometimes as a group, sometimes in pairs, other times alone. By mid-afternoon, my brain is bloated, my eyes are numb. My stupor reminds me of listening to hot music for too long. I'm able to invest myself for a couple hours, after which the sounds drift right on past.

So it is with Machu Picchu. I need to step back and digest, so I retreat to the open air restaurant and order orange spice tea. On the next table lies a copy of Jack Kerouac's <u>On the Road</u>. On the inside cover is written: If you read a lot, you're considered to be well-read. But just because you're well-known doesn't mean you know a lot.

Beneath Graham McHugh's signature, it reads: Save de whales. Save de bliss.

"Aha!" says a voice behind me. "I was wondering where I left that." Cole takes a seat across from me.

I hold up the book. "Graham McHugh."

"Yeah. Wanna hear something crazy? Whenever I travel, I wonder if I'm gonna bump into him. Silly, I know, but today I half expected him to emerge from the tomb beneath the Temple of the Sun, which is ridiculous – I have no idea what he looks like."

"What's this 'save de whales, save de bliss' business?"

"Got me. When he sends books, he always writes stuff like 'save de day, save de bliss.' " He shrugs. "That's supposed to be my Jamaican accent. Crampy Q took our family on a cruise when we were in junior high."

"Do you write him back?"

"He hardly ever writes his return address, but when he does, yeah, I write to say thanks and tell him what I'm up to. I stopped asking what he does, because he never answers."

"That's wild." I hand him the book. "Where's the rest of the gang?"

"Gracie invited Barry for a walk up the Inca Trail; she's trying to welcome him into the family. Fiona's taking a nap in Barry's room; says it's warmer in there."

For no good reason, this revelation cheers me. "They're not sharing a room?"

"No. He says it would be tempting."

"You mean he hasn't…. he's never …."

"Stormed the pearly gates with his purple-headed devil? Apparently not. They're savin' themselves for marriage."

"Why is that?"

"Don't know," says Cole. "Something to do with Jesus. But I've read the Bible cover to cover, and nowhere in the New Testament does it say, 'Don't have sex 'til you're married.' Six words, that's all it would take. Course, I'd still consider it rotten advice, but at least we could discuss it rationally."

"How about the Old Testament?"

"It's bizarre; no sane person would use it as an ethics guide. Example: A guy with his nuts crushed or his dick cut off shouldn't be allowed to attend church." In a protective gesture, Cole crosses his legs.

"Come on; it does not say that."

"You're right; they say 'privy member' and 'stones.' "

"Did the Hebrews lose their privates often?"

"Often enough to make a rule about it, evidently."

"Why couldn't they go to church?"

"Good question. And how would they know who had their marbles mashed?"

"Well, they would have heard the screams."

"Good point," he says. "Funny; we didn't cover this in Sunday school."

"Yeah, neither did we."

"The Bible does say we shouldn't sleep with hookers, and it says to get married in a way that's holy and honorable. Oh, and we're not supposed to have immoral sex."

"Immoral sex – now, that'd be.... what? Sex with a llama?

"Yep," he says, "that'd qualify; bestiality is punishable by death, for man and llama."

"How about sex with a married llama?"

"Sex with a married anything is adultery. Again, it's punishable by death, according to Leviticus."

"How about gay sex with an underage llama on a Sunday morning?"

"Better get yourself a good lawyer, pally."

A harrumph from my left catches our attention, and there stands Fiona, eyes aflame, regarding us like we're a couple of degenerate aliens. I hold back my laughter until Cole cracks up.

After dinner we retire to the veranda, where Cole holds up a travelling chess set and asks if anyone wants to play. I'm ready to volunteer, but Barry beats me to it. The rest of us get a game of Hearts going. We all talk about the ruins or books or our childhoods, while enjoying the low-key rhythm of playing games and drinking sodas. Fiona and I have developed a taste for Inca Kola. Cole winces and crosses himself whenever I open a new bottle.

Every now and then I check on the progress of the chess game. Cole is picking off Barry's pieces, winning a war of attrition, while Barry is backing Cole's king into a corner.

At one point Barry is taking a while to make his move, and Cole says, "Hey, pally, grab your charango, would you? I want Fi to see it."

I leave and return five minutes later. The pieces on the chessboard have thinned out considerably. Barry rises and says he's turning in. When Fiona remains seated, he gives her a peck on the cheek and heads inside.

I hand my charango to Fiona, who holds it gingerly, as though it's made of porcelain. "It's gorgeous," she says. "Why is it so small?"

"According to Professor Plum, natives used to be prohibited by the Spaniards from playing ancestral music. So they built an instrument that could be hidden under a poncho."

Cole asks, "How is it tuned?"

"It's very odd – the pairs of strings aren't arranged from low to high, like on a guitar or a violin. They're all tuned inside one octave, which makes for a powerful wall of sound, at least within that range."

Fiona passes it back with care. "Can you play us a tune, Señor Muña?"

"Nah, not yet." They all looked at me expectantly, so I add, "I only know a few chords."

Cole says, "C'mon, that's enough to play a million tunes."

"All right, let's try this." I fiddle around with a simple chord progression from "Blue Moon," an upbeat, corny old song.

I start singing, and am pleasantly surprised when Cole joins in with a higher harmony line. A moment later, Gracie adds the comical bom-buppa-boms and dip-duh-dip-duh-dips. For the last verse, we sing the lyrics as "Blue Muña." We crack up, and the song fizzles out.

Fiona says, "Play it again, but slow it down. And make it pretty."

I mess around with a slower tempo in 4/4, but we sing in 3/4 this time, giving the song a lazy syncopation. Cole adds a harmony, his voice managing to sound both smooth and gravelly. I'm taken with his ability to follow my phrasing, syllable for syllable. To harmonize well, a singer has to be willing to set aside his own timing, and give himself over to another's interpretation of a song. Many singers cannot, or will not, do that; they have their own sense of how the song should be sung, and by God, that's how they're gonna do it. So when I say Cole harmonizes well, it also speaks to his ability and willingness to connect with people.

Gracie and Fiona add their voices on the second verse, while Cole softly pounds out an offbeat rhythm on the arms of his chair. "Blue Moon" is a short song, so we play it through twice, giving Cole a chance to experiment with various harmony lines. When we sing the line about saying a prayer for a loved one, Fiona wears a grave expression, tinged with sorrow. Our eyes meet for a good four seconds, a long time to hold the gaze of a near stranger. When the song ends, no one says a word.

Eventually Fiona asks, "What is a blue moon?"

Cole answers first. "Krakatoa, an Indonesian volcano, erupted in the nineteenth century. You could hear it three thousand miles away. Ash was thrown up into the atmosphere across the world, making the moon appear to have a bluish tint."

"Or," says Gracie, "when there are two full moons in one month, the second is called a blue moon. It's a rare occurrence. Like love."

I say, "A pamphlet was put out in the 1500s, attacking the English clergy. One passage read: 'If you say the moon is blue, we must believe that it is true.' So 'blue moon' meant something absurd, like saying the moon is made of green cheese."

"I've never heard any of those explanations," says Fiona. "I read the song as 'blue' being a sad color, and 'moon' having to do with night. Sad night."

"I love that," says Gracie, "when something takes you in four directions at once. It's like the song confuses the brain, and sneaks past it….. Zhwooommm! Straight to the heart."

Cole reaches an arm around her. "Craziness, Slick. I like it."

Fiona looks back and forth between her brother and me. "You guys sound good together. Your voices mesh nicely."

I say, "Thanks, but Cole could make anybody sound good."

"Back at ya, pally."

Gracie says, "You two should start a band."

"But you have to get a better name than Dread the Donkey," says Fiona. "At least pick a more appealing animal."

I ask, "Did you guys see the lone llama wandering the ruins today? It seemed like he was looking for something."

Cole nods. "Looking for love, I imagine. In all the wrong

places."

Gracie says, "Love the Llama; now there's a band name for ya. Except the 'double l' sounds like a 'y,' so technically it's 'yama.'"

Cole says, "I probably shouldn't mention this, but the desk clerk told me locals ate the rest of the herd. So how about we call our band 'Yum the Yama?'"

I give him a two-thumbs-up, but Gracie protests, "No, no, no! As self-appointed manager, I'm making a unilateral decision: We're sticking with Love the Llama."

"Agreed," says Fiona. "Somebody's gotta love the llama; he looks lonely. But let's spell 'love' with two l's."

With finality, Gracie proclaims, "Llove the Llama it is."

Cole says, "Not sure how it happened, pally, but we been out-voted."

Fiona yawns. "Now that we've got that settled...."

"Already, sis? C'mon, we're just getting warmed up."

"I know, but Barry doesn't like it when I stay out late." She goes inside, and Cole's forehead folds up into that by-now-familiar bulldog face.

I say, "You don't care much for Barry."

"Christ, he treats her like an incompetent. And for all the issues Fi and I have, she's the most competent person I know."

"He's just being protective," says Gracie.

"Patronizing is more like it," he grouses. "Who does he think he is, for God's sake, her pastor?" If you ask me, he had to reach for that one.

Gracie leans over and kisses his forehead, dissolving the wrinkles. "Barry cares about her. When Fiona sprained her ankle coming off a diving board last fall, he made her stay off it so it would heal faster. She says he was a saint – cooking, cleaning, carrying her books." Cole nods, though it pains him to do so. Gracie continues, "Barry even gave her foot rubs; now that's dedication. Cole doesn't rub my feet." She gives him a playful smack. "And I wouldn't touch his yucky toenails if you paid me."

We decide to call it a night, and I check out the chessboard before heading inside. Barry, playing white, has only a king and a bishop left. Cole is down to a king and a knight. They've reached a standoff. Each side lacks the firepower to checkmate the other.

They could scoot their pieces across the board for all eternity and neither would win, regardless of the cleverness of their moves or the other side's ineptitude.

Stalemate.

Chapter 6: Moby's Trip

I wander the central field at dawn, soaking up the sadness and serenity. The stillness of Machu Picchu is infectious. My time, my life, are not getting eaten. Still, I am consumed by the idea that people inhabited this splendid city and then left.

Why, and where, did you go?

That line repeats itself in my head, but this time it blossoms with a slow, mournful melody. I sing it aloud, over and over. I am tempted to return to the lodge, to play it on my charango and write it down before it drifts away. But the tune is catchy, and by now it's firmly fixed in my mind. Besides, I don't want to miss the sunrise. The eastern sky flaunts an ever-brightening mix of blues, reds, and purples.

I hear footsteps behind me and turn to see Fiona approaching. She announces, "Here comes love."

"Wha.... what?"

"Here comes love." Her smile lights her up from the inside, a transformation that, oddly, brings to mind *Terminator II*, which came out last year. That's the one where Schwarzenegger, as the good cyborg, faces off against his more technically advanced evil counterpart who has the capability to morph his appearance from one person into another.

Her smile broadens, softening her severe facial angles into a nuanced beauty that kindles a warm ache in my chest. All I can do is gape at her.

"Llove, the Llama," she says, pointing over my shoulder. "Here comes Llove."

I turn to see the llama moseying towards us, his head pivoting from right to left and back again, in search of his herd, which, according the desk clerk, was eaten.

"Oh," I say, hiding my dejection. The beast takes no notice of us as he passes. "Catch ya later, Llove."

The llama, as if realizing he'd been spoken to, turns to face us. His ears shoot up and rotate toward us like a pair of fuzzy satellite dishes.

"His ears remind me of somebody," Fiona says coyly. "Now, who could that be?"

"Nope, mine aren't that furry."

She laughs pleasantly and asks what I am doing out here.

"I love being out here by myself." Realizing how that sounds, I pull an about-face. "But I'm glad you decided to join me." Llove the Llama saunters off.

"Almost a good recovery, Señor Muña." She laughs again. "But I know what you mean; it's so peaceful and sad and pretty, like that song you were just singing."

"What? Oh, yeah, it's not a song, not yet. It just popped into my head."

She gives me a how-can-that-be look. "So the song writes itself?"

"Yeah, kind of," I say. "Music moves in mysterious ways."

Fiona doesn't know quite what to make of this mutation of the "God moves" quote, and to be honest, neither do I, except to say it's a habit of mine to agnosticize issues whenever possible. As an aside, I'm not sure if "agnosticize" is even a word, and right now I have no means of determining whether it is or it isn't.

"How much longer are you staying here?"

"Leaving today at one."

"Oh. I'm disappointed."

My eyebrows shoot up, and I find myself wishing I hadn't booked a round trip ticket back to Cusco. Seeing my irrationally buoyant brows, Fiona back-pedals. "I mean, uh, I'm disappointed because you're leaving before you finish your song." My brows slump, and she asks, "What are the words? What's it about?"

"I'm not quite sure yet. Leaving, I guess." That's not much of an answer, and we lapse into an uneasy silence. "How about you? What are you doing out here? Where's your crew?"

"Asleep. I was looking out at the mountains, and saw you walk up toward the entrance. I thought you might like some company." There is not yet enough light for her to see me blush. She says, "You looked lonely."

"You've got that half right: I do enjoy your company, but I wasn't lonely. In fact, I don't know that I've ever felt lonely. Alone, maybe, but not lonely."

Her smile fades, and I see her again as I did upon first

meeting her. Her angular features strike me as being severe. But I would no longer characterize her as plain-looking, not at all. Projecting an inner strength, Fiona fixes me with The Look; those steel-grey eyes are seeing straight into me, which is unsettling but not unpleasant. Who is this creature?

"I don't believe you." Her soft voice, at such odds with her grave expression, unbalances me further. I try to swallow, but my throat constricts, like it does when you're caught dispensing a half-truth, even if unintentionally. It may be hard to believe, but until this moment, I have not been aware of my loneliness.

"Theo, I've been thinking about that experience you had a few nights ago. Now, this may or may not be medically accurate, but my physiology prof said that when you cry, it washes your brain. Here's how I think of it: The function of tears is to make fluid those parts of our minds and hearts that are able to enact change." She roils her hands around as she says this. "Change and growth require fluidity. Tears wash away the old, like a flood, to make room for the new."

This insight fills me with hope. We *can* evolve; change *is* possible. "Yes! Exactly! It felt as if my tears were washing away impurities; a baptism of the brain. Thank you!" My outburst embarrasses me, and she takes pleasure in my unease.

She asks, "Do you have a favorite spot here?"

"Yeah, I'll show you." It's a relief to have that high-powered gaze focused elsewhere. We climb winding paths, past The Watchman's Hut, arriving ten minutes later at a point high above the ruins. The oranges and pinks of the eastern sky are becoming more vivid, and the first rays of sun light up the tallest of the surrounding peaks, but as yet Machu Picchu is left in shade and cold silence.

"You have an eye for beauty, Theo."

Watching her out the corner of my eye, I think: Ya got that right.

She says, "I keep imagining what it was like to live here."

"Me too. Was life brutal or beautiful? Would you have wanted to grow up here?"

Her answer takes me by surprise, though it shouldn't have. "No, the Incas worshiped false gods. They didn't know Jesus."

I hesitate before saying, "But there was no way they could

have known Jesus."

I know how Gracie would respond: The Endless Debate, here we go again.

Now it's Fiona's turn to hesitate. "I don't know about the Incas, but how about you, Theo?" Yes, she is trying to change my beliefs, but her question carries a genuine sense of curiosity, and her tone is compassionate, rather than confrontational.

"I don't know what to think, and I don't know that anybody else knows either." See? I agnosticize whenever the opportunity presents itself. "Why do you believe?"

"Because nothing else makes sense. It's a better world with God in it."

"But just because it's desirable doesn't make it true. Why did you choose Christianity and not.... oh, say, Zoroastrianism?"

"What's that?"

"A Persian religion. Standard stuff – god and devil, good and evil, fire and water."

She laughs lightly. "Now you're making it complicated."

"Maybe it is complicated."

"That's something Cole would say. It's funny; he used to enjoy church – the music, the sense of security, the people. He comes across as all anti-religious, but believe me, he's conflicted." Given Cole's recurring train-and-tsunami dream, it would be hard to disagree.

My take on dreams: Most of them result from the erratic firing of restless brain cells, while others seem consequential, and they'll poke at us until we face unaddressed issues. I mention this because Cole's dream seems to point out a fundamental difference between the two of us: Whereas he does his best to discount any proclivity he may have regarding matters of spirituality, I would very much like to believe. In something.

Fiona says, "I had no use for Sunday school as a kid."

"What changed?"

"I prayed, and my prayers were answered."

"How did you know who to pray to? How did you know not to pray to, say, Allah?"

"I prayed to God, and Jesus answered. Don't look at me like I'm nuts. The Holy Ghost speaks in a code that only the soul understands."

"Fiona, I believe you experienced something profound." I pause to chart my course. "But if there is a universal truth, wouldn't God have made it available to everyone? Would a loving God place create some people and say, 'Okay, you can be happy,' and then tell others 'Forget about it?' Fiona, it wouldn't be fair."

"That's why we have missionaries, to spread the gospel."

"But what about the Incas who lived here? Missionaries never got to them." And I think but don't say: When you have a good enough product, it sells itself. "If they didn't know Jesus, they had no possibility of being Happy, with a capital H."

"Yeahhhh, but it's an amazing coincidence the Incas used the cross as a religious symbol. It's almost like they were intuitively drawn to the presence of Christ."

"That's a stretch. A cross is the simplest two-dimensional shape."

"I'm no good at debating this. I don't know the Mind of God. You're trying to figure it out with logic; accepting The Lord is a matter of faith. If the Incas never heard of Jesus, I'm sure He had a plan for them."

"Then missionaries open up the opportunity for more people to reject Jesus, which would then condemn them to hell." I give her a minute to mull that over, and then say, "See how convoluted it gets, thinking that way? It wears me out."

"Then don't think that way." She laughs and we stare out at the awe-inspiring landscape, as sunlight slowly makes its way down the western mountainside.

"Fiona, your starting point is a belief in Jesus. I don't understand that, but from what little I know of you, you live in accordance with your beliefs, and I respect you. My starting point is this: If there is a Truth – capital T – it would be made available to all. And I don't believe such a Truth exists."

"At some point, logic will fail you, Theo." She pats her heart. "I believe. In here."

Feathery clouds float by, partially obscuring the city.

She asks, "Would you mind if I pray for you?" Seeing my consternation, she correctly surmises that I am considering whether to be offended. She smiles disarmingly. "Don't worry; I won't pray for you to become a monk or a priest or anything."

"What, then?" Oh, I wish I could take that back. We will

be going our separate ways in a few hours, and the prospect of this woman holding me in her thoughts is warm and wonderful.

"I will pray that you find your way."

"Do you think I haven't? Found my way, I mean."

"Only you can answer that."

Her pitch is so low-pressure that there's nothing to push back against. "Fiona, I have felt lost lately.... No, I've felt lost for a very long time, and I would love it if you'd pray for me. But promise you won't worry. Worry demonstrates nothing so much as a lack of faith."

She reaches out her hand in a sisterly way. "I promise."

I take her hand, though my feelings for her are far beyond brotherly. We look out over the ruins, and I take comfort in her presence, though our inability to reach one another is frustrating. It's not until I recall my philosophy class from the U of A that the issue crystallizes. Two branches of philosophy are: metaphysics, dealing with the nature of reality; and epistemology, addressing the scope and nature of knowledge. In her quest as a naive teen, Fiona wanted to know, metaphysically, what is true? What is real? My interest in philosophy has long been epistemological in nature: How do we go about deciding what is true?

How do we bridge that gap? How do we connect the branches? Are they connectable?

Fiona squeezes my hand. "What are you thinking?"

"I envy you and your capacity to believe."

Again, her response surprises me. "I envy you and your sensitivity to this place. You get it, at a deeper level than I do. Where does that come from, Theo?"

"Like you said, this place is peaceful and sad and beautiful. Andean musicians somehow capture that feeling perfectly. They take something painful and forge something.... uh, divine. Their songs pick me up and carry me away." This time my exhilaration causes me no unease.

"That's how believing is," she says. "I am more interested in how Jesus lived than in his death and resurrection."

Maybe we are not as far apart as we seemed one minute ago. I ask if she has a nursing job lined up.

"I'm holding off, until Barry and I decide where we want to live. We're supposed to be getting married in the fall."

Supposed to – is there a less enthusiastic way to put that? And the way it came out was "sposta," as in: You're sposta floss. You're sposta eat your broccoli. She says, "Barry looks forward to becoming part of our family."

She did not say: *I* am looking forward to Barry becoming part of our family. Nor did she say: I can't wait for our wedding. It strikes me as odd that she could be so insightful as to the nature of crying, yet utterly clueless regarding her impending marriage.

"Cole told me your grandfather had Alzheimer's. That must've been hard."

She lets go of my hand and faces me. "What did he say?"

I relate his story from two nights ago, and she echoes Gracie's sentiments: "I'm amazed he told you that story. But for me, there's more to it."

"Yeah?"

She doesn't respond right away. "I know this will sound crazy, but for months after Crampy Q left, I thought he was alive. I expected to come home from school one day, and there he'd be, sitting in our kitchen."

"Why?"

"The day before he disappeared, I found a locket with a picture of him and my grandma on our dining room table, where I sat at the dinner table." From a chain around her neck, she lifts a silver locket from inside her sweatshirt, and opens it for me. "My grandparents."

I lean in to get a look at the tiny photo, then raise my head and tell her, "You have his eyes."

She holds my gaze briefly, then closes the locket and turns away. "I thought Crampy Q had moved on to a better place. His Alzheimer's wasn't as bad as Cole makes it out to be. Crampy got tired of everybody meddling. He felt like he'd lost control of his life."

"How do you mean?"

She gives me The Look. "I don't know why I'm telling you this, but after Grandma died, Dad did take things from Crampy, like the deed to his house, so he wouldn't hide it and forget where it was. Everybody knew. Dad had power of attorney because of the Alzheimer's, and it bugged the heck out of Crampy. There was talk of Uncle Dick and Aunt Becky moving in with him

– her idea. She told Dick they could expect to be compensated for giving up their freedom, but he refused. He's so selfish, and she's an angel of mercy. She helped Crampy keep his place clean. And she keeps Dick sober, well, mostly.... Boy, listen to me; yap, yap, yap. Anyway, Crampy never went anywhere without that locket. I took it as a signal he was leaving."

Pretty flimsy evidence, but a nice sentiment. We turn to face Machu Picchu, now becoming sunlit.

I say, "From up here, the city's layout is obvious, but down there I get disoriented. I get all twisted around, like I'm walking on a.... Do you know what a Mobius strip is? You take a strip of paper, give it a half twist, and tape the ends together."

Her eyes light up. "Oh, right! Crampy Q showed me when I was little. It seems like there are two surfaces, but it's really only one." She looks down at the city and says, "Mobius trails."

That would make an intriguing line for my song, and I'm about to say as much when she bursts out laughing. "Sorry," she says. "When Crampy Q showed me the Mobius strip, I asked, 'Who's Moby?' Because, see, I thought he'd said, 'Moby's trip.' I was picturing this little critter named Moby running along the surface. And then one day I was in a bad mood, and Crampy wrote: mope hiss drip."

"Oh! It sounds like 'Mobius strip.' Clever."

"I laughed so hard, it made me snort. He snorted back, and that got us going! Oh, that was my best day growing up! He invented this game where he'd spell things phonetically, more or less, then Cole and I would have to figure out what he meant. So he'd write 'Seattle' as 'see ant hill,' because he thought it had become too crowded. He called the game 'Funetics.' The world was a better place with Crampy Q in it. I thought, He can't have left. He left Cole a sign too, though he never recognized it as such. The day I found this locket, Cole found his fishing pole next to the front door – that's where he'd put it when he waited for Crampy to take him fishing."

Man, talk about fishing....

"After Crampy Q left, I imagined him out there on his own, sleeping who knows where.... I lost a little bit of him every day. He died so gradually, his death didn't seem real. Our pastor came to visit one day; he said his mission was to 'serve and save.' He told me to place my grandfather in God's care. We prayed, and the phrase 'moved on to a better place' came to mean Crampy had gone to heaven. I wanted God to take care of me too, so I asked forgiveness, and the Holy Spirit entered into me, leaving me with one thought: I know there's a God."

"Isn't that what Barry said yesterday?"

"Close. He said, 'I know there must be a God.' Not quite the same." She gives me a droopy smile. "Anyway, our pastor inspired me to become a nurse, to serve and save."

"When we were sharing spiritual experiences yesterday, why didn't you tell this story? It's powerful. It's beautiful."

"I'd be embarrassed. I used to think Crampy Q was still alive, and a tiny part of me still does. Cole doesn't know that. Keep it to yourself, will you?"

"Okay, but why not just tell him?"

"Oh, he'd say it's silly. He thinks of me as his little sister."

"Maybe so, but I happen to know he adores his sister. How could he not?"

Her bemused look rearranges itself into a half-smile, and I am again captivated by her ability to transform her being. I'm about to take her hand again when she looks past me and points. "There goes Llove!"

I force a grin. "Bye bye, Llove."

She checks her watch. "Time to meet the others."

Barry is waiting in the lobby with an overstuffed daypack. He shakes a few pills from a bottle into Fiona's hand. She thanks him and heads upstairs.

"The altitude still gets to her," he tells me. "Want some?"

"No thanks. I'm finally acclimated."

The chessboard is lying undisturbed from last night, and I say, "Stalemate."

"Not necessarily," Barry replies. "I've been trying out different endgames. Watch." He moves Cole's black king into a corner, and places the white king two squares away. He moves the black bishop next to the black king, cutting off its escape route, which allows the white bishop to move in for the kill.

"Checkmate," crows Barry. "I can't wait to show Cole."

"Yeah, but he'd have to make exactly the right sequence of

wrong moves. He'd have to back himself into a corner, which he would never do."

He smirks. "Oh, I don't know."

"Does it work the other way? Is it possible for him to checkmate you?"

"With just a king and a knight?" He eyes the chessboard and frowns. "Nope, no way."

But now that he's shown me how the white side can win, it's a simple matter to switch a few pieces around and make it so black prevails.

Barry regards me like I'm not playing fair. "Yeah, I guess it *could* happen, though it's not real likely."

I'm not sure how well he'll fit in with the Quinn family, but he'd blend in just fine with us Duncans.

Cole and Gracie exit the lobby. Barry doesn't mention the checkmate scenario he figured out.

Wearing a sloppy smile, Cole takes a shot at speaking Español. "No ponies la pistola de la machina in mi cara, por favor." Grace winces, and he says, "That's 'Please don't point the machine gun in my face.' Slick is giving me lessons."

"Try it again," she says. "You too, Theo. It may come in handy."

He and I repeat it several times. Gracie, acting the part of a crusty old school marm, slaps the back of our hands when we mess up. Cole and I hang our heads and whimper, "Sorry, ma'am."

In that classic shot of Machu Picchu, or "Old Mountain," there is a second wedge-shaped peak situated behind the ruins. Huayna Picchu, or "Young Mountain," towers a thousand feet above The Hidden City. Barry suggested last night that we climb it, and we agreed.

Entering Machu Picchu, Gracie says, "There goes Llove the Llama." We catch a glimpse of his mop-like tail disappearing behind a stone wall.

I repeat my line from earlier. "Bye-bye, Llove."

Cole picks it up right away, breaking into the old Everly Brothers song with that title. I add a harmony line, while Gracie snaps her finger on the off-beats.

Passing through the central field, we stop and gaze up at

Huayna Picchu. Fiona asks, "We're going to climb *that*?"

Good point; the mountain face appears to be nearly vertical, but thousands of others have climbed it, so we soldier on. We enter a stand of trees, and soon the path narrows down until we are traversing what Fiona refers to as "the edge of a knife." On either side, the ridge drops away to the valley floor.

We begin our ascent by way of a series of steep, narrow switchbacks without guardrails. We scramble up rockslides, using gnarled roots and the occasional tree limb to pull ourselves up. While the rest of us find it laborious, Gracie scampers up the trail like a mountain goat. Barry gives Fiona a boost up at critical junctures. The altitude is making her lightheaded, and though I feel a stab of jealousy, it's a relief to know he's looking after her.

I try to conjure up the melody I heard earlier, but it's gone. Why, and where, did you go? I repeat the phrase a dozen times, to no avail. Damn! When you get a freebie like this, you can't let it drift away. You have to nurture it.

Nearing the top of Huayna Picchu, we march up a grand Incan staircase, passing narrow terraces that had once been ornamental gardens. Any spot that could be cultivated, had been. Arriving at the peak, we marvel at the 360 degree view. The Andes stretch as far as we can see, forming a rich tapestry of verdant hillsides and parched ridges. Looking down on Machu Picchu, it's clear why the Incas chose this site to build. Lying inside and above a bend in Rio Urubamba, the nearly vertical drop on three sides renders the city inaccessible.

Two men with East European accents stand on the edge of an outcropping. With hands on hips, one of them asks, "Well, is this what there is to see?" What an ass cactus.

I whisper to Cole over Gracie's head, "If he leans forward a little.... bit.... further...."

"Don't even think about pushin' him off," he whispers back. "Cheee-ses, man, grab his camera first."

Gracie smacks us in our stomachs with the backs of her hands. "Savages."

Fiona points across the valley cut by the river. "The desk clerk told me archaeologists found ruins over there that might be as extensive as Machu Picchu." Squinting, we follow the line of her outstretched arm to the distant mountainside. Though we see no evidence of human presence, it's exciting to imagine another city hidden in the lush green.

Barry rummages through his pack and passes around ham sandwiches, saying he ordered them last night. He brings out a bottle of apple juice and paper cups, and we thank him as he pours. We sit and make small talk as we eat, until Gracie makes a crack about "Machu Picnic," prompting me to call out, "Safety blitz!"

Fiona, Cole and I jump her, though gently because of the rocky terrain. We get up giggling, and Gracie admits, "I had it comin'."

Barry seems annoyed. He asks where I'm headed next.

"Down to Puno on the Bolivian border, then on to Ecuador. You?"

"We're going to visit some other ruins and then fly to Ecuador. We're spending a few days in a jungle lodge."

"No fooling? Oh, that's sounds great!"

Gracie suggests we meet up again, so we compare itineraries and figure out we'll be in Lima this coming Thursday. I propose we meet outside the Inquisition Museum at three.

I check my watch. "That will be the 10th.... Oh, damn! I gotta get going! Train leaves at one. Bye, all. See you in four days!" I shake hands with each of them, except for Gracie, who slams her slender body against mine.

I take off down the path, as Cole and Gracie begin singing:

> Blue-oo Muña
> You left me standing alone
> On top of Huayna Picchu

Their voices fade as I start down the switchbacks. I miss them already.

Chapter 7: Anatomically Confused

The next morning I embark on an eleven-hour train ride to Puno, situated on the shore of Lake Titicaca, which straddles the border between Peru and Bolivia. The tracks lead south out of Cusco, following the murky waters of Rio Urubamba upstream. Adorning the dry hillsides are cactus plants, looking like oversized cucumbers.

The cacti call to mind my band, Cactus Smacked Us. I wonder how they're getting on without me. I imagine Slider, our bass player, saying, "No problem. The three of us'll just play louder."

The day before our first gig, we hadn't yet chosen a band name, and Slider called to suggest we "go to the desert, seek our vision, discover our essence, whatever. Hey, it worked for The Doors, at least in the movie."

Slider proposed we get some peyote, "to grease the celestial skids," but he didn't know how to get hold of it. I didn't mention that Rowan could probably dig some up – she deals in all sorts of "medicinal commodities" – but I didn't want to encourage her illicit business. Otherwise I might have given the peyote a shot.

Our other guitar player was working that day, but Donny, our drummer, considered it a most excellent plan. He showed up at Slider's with a bottle of tequila – no mixer, no limes, no food – and the three of us piled into Slider's Jeep, along with two guitars and a pair of bongos. Oh, and a machete, which Slider termed a "totemistic thing."

It was, all in all, a half-baked plan for half-wits, with Slider acting as self-appointed shaman, seeking a vision. Or at least a suitable band name.

We headed east on Highway 10, then pulled off onto a dirt road and parked in a dusty stream bed. We hiked a half mile and hunkered down in the shade of a gnarled, massive saguaro cactus. We sang and played for hours, while passing the hooch around. It was ninety-five degrees out, so we became dehydrated, which Slider insisted was part of the mystical experience.

When Donny passed out in mid-afternoon, Slider claimed he was opening himself up to "parties from the other side of the divide." Slider put the "sham" in "shaman."

I slapped Donny's cheeks back and forth, back and forth; he drooled in response.

"Not to worry," said a wobbly Slider, hefting his machete. "A saguaro holds thousands of gallons of water. Or is it dozens?"

"It's illegal to damage saguaro," I said, falling back on my elbows.

"Bigger issue at stake here," he replied, his eyes appearing to do loop-de-loops.

He took a mighty swing at a spiny arm of the cactus, which explains how Donny's neck and my arm came to resemble pin cushions. Hence the name, "Cactus Smacked Us." The toxic swill we got from that sliced-off cactus arm was undrinkable, even when mixed with the last of our tequila, though its bitter taste revived Donny.

The dry, rolling hills are dotted with sparsely placed evergreens, which remind me of the thousand-mile Duncan Annual Ford Trips we took when I was growing up. Claire proposed we call them DAFTs. We'd get up at four, pack up the trunk and car-top carrier on our Ford Fairlane, and set off for my grandparents' farm in the Bitterroot Valley of Montana. If we rolled in by midnight – and we usually did – Dad deemed our DAFT a success.

The sway of the train and the hypnotic rhythm of the metal wheels transport me back to 1973, the last time all four of us kids traveled together. Rowan had just turned seventeen, and she informed us this would be her last DAFT, because she'd begun working for a prominent herbalist. We were all impressed, until Claire found out two years later that he was twenty-nine, her lover, and a major supplier of high quality weed for Tucson.

My brother Phil sat up front with my parents, leaving me wedged between my sisters. Rowan was, in Mom's words, "big-boned." She took up a goodly share of the back seat, which nudged me over toward Claire, a thirteen-year-old nuisance who was always jockeying for a bit of extra space. Being six years old, I was constantly being squished, squashed, prodded, poked, and, the two times I was foolish enough to protest, sat upon.

I learned how to shrink down to nothin'.

My sisters would argue for hours about the color of our Ford. I didn't know the word "turquoise" back then, and apparently, neither did they. Rowan swore the car was blue; Claire saw it as green. Claire thought Ro was dopey, and Ro considered her sister to be ornery. Each of them, inflamed with the surety of a zealot, took her own observation to be self-evident, then attempted to shore up her position with insults and colorful language for the next hundred miles.

"Definitely blue."

"Nuh-uh, it's green."

"Any idiot can see it's blue!"

"Well, then you must be an idiot. It's as green as the inside of your nose."

At a pit stop in Provo, I sat down on the sidewalk to tie my sneaker and happened to look up at the Ford, framed against the electric blue of the Utah sky. Our car was green, no doubt about it. Claire was Right, with a capital R.

But when Mom leaned against the Ford and got Dad to take her picture, her lime green blouse instantly transformed the car to Blue, capital B. I was tempted to wave my hand and call out: Hey! I'm only six, but the car is green-blue – let's call it "grue." But to do so would have incurred the wrath of both sisters, each of whom held tightly to her own little piece of the truth and mistook it for the whole works.

Years later, I would look back on their asinine conflict and come to consider my impartiality a mark of sophistication, but at the time, their mulish talk drove me nuts.

Checking his watch, Dad told us to "Hustle up, let's get going."

The sun was now shining from the west, and Claire said, "Let's switch, Ro. It's your turn to sit on the sunny side." As usual, Rowan fell for it, and Phil, trying to get in good with Claire, snickered and gave her a thumbs up.

If things ran smoothly for too long, Claire would say something like: "Roll up your window, Rotunderella! You're ruining my hair."

If that made Ro whimper, I'd give her some M&Ms which, along with my Donald Duck imitation, would cheer her up. She was not a born fighter, but Claire would goad her, and the trip would invariably spiral down into a full-on squabble fest:

"When Ro goes to the zoo, the elephants feed *her* peanuts."

"Yeah? Well…. on Halloween, people dress up as *you*."

"These old songs are dorky. Mom, would you turn the radio on?"

"The Beatles are better than Black Sabbath, and you better get used to eight-track tapes. You are listenin' to the future."

Minor stuff, I know, but it went on and on. Dad worked construction, and twenty years riding a jack hammer had left him legally deaf. Our family doesn't have any of those stories where Dad says: Settle down back there! If I have to stop this car….

Dad did all the driving, rendering him blind to all that went on in the back seat. My sole memory of him on that DAFT is looking up at his brown, slicked back hair. My mom was just happy to have us all together, which left me stuck in the middle of my sisters' wrangling. Every now and then, Claire would reach over my head to smack her older sister, and I'd say something like: "Hey! Stop fighting over me!" Claire got a kick out of cracks like that, which would bring me as much as thirty miles of peace and quiet.

This being eight months after the '72 election, they jumped fearlessly into the political fray. While passing through Idaho – or it could have been Montana – Rowan made the mistake of quoting Nixon: "Sometimes you have to fight for peace."

Claire responded with a George Carlin line. "Isn't that like screwing for virginity?"

I had no idea what all of this meant, but I could tell by Claire's smug delivery and Ro's beaten look that Nixon had been neutered. Listening to such exchanges, I developed the ability to sniff out a sloppily formulated argument at an inappropriately young age. Cynicism does not wear well on a six-year-old.

When Mom got fed up with my sisters' bickering, she'd tell them to "Can it, damn it!" They would then switch to sign language, which we were all learning in order to communicate with Dad. So now I got to *watch* their cat fights:

Claire signed: "The shadow of your ass weighs a thousand pounds."

"Nuh *uh*."

"Uh *huh*!"

"I hear you can suck-start a Harley."

At the next pit stop, I asked my brother what he knew about virginity and suck-starting. Phil, being an anatomically confused eight-year-old, offered up a graphic explanation that served as my introduction to sex ed. Neither of us got laid in high school.

Phil tried sitting in the back one time, but Mom moved him up front again because, as she told me years later, "He doesn't have your constitution." That was Motherese for "Phil is scared shitless of Claire." She added, "It wasn't fair sitting him in back."

Fair? It wasn't *fair*? No, I'll tell you what wasn't fair – cramming me in between a pair of quarreling sisters-from-hell for a thousand miles.

Our DAFTs were not always hellish, however. Music was the one tool in Mom's bag that could soothe Claire's disquietude and smoldering anger. Mom would sing the first line to something from *Sound of Music*, and my sisters would add harmony lines. Claire in particular had a sweet alto. I had the croaky voice of a little kid, but I'd pick out one of their lines and quietly sing along. Rowan would wrap a warm, fleshy arm around me, and our little world was truly harmonious, except that Mom would look at Dad wistfully, wishing he could hear us sing. The upside of his impairment was that Mom could lead us in singing "Imagine," John Lennon's call for a religion-free world, without subjecting Dad to the "Imagine there's no heaven" line.

Our paradise, however, was usually short-lived. If Ro hit a sour note, Claire would say she sounded like a walrus in heat. The spell broken, my sisters would revert to squabbling. I learned not to take sides in their altercations.

I dreaded those interminable DAFTs. Grandpa Duncan, a Lutheran minister, used to say the journey is more important than the destination, but that was not true for me; the destination was all I lived for. Upon arriving in the Bitterroot, I spent my days exploring and building forts in the woods beyond the wheat fields.

On my ninth birthday, Grandpa taught me to fly fish. After that, I would take off at dawn and return in late afternoon with a half dozen rainbow trout. In Big Sky Country, I finally had some space to myself. Upon turning ten, I packed up Grandpa's tent and hiked a mile over to the Bitterroot River.

One time Dad made me take my brother camping with me, which struck me as odd, seeing as how Phil was two years my senior. "Be your brother's keeper," Dad told me. Phil was not unkindly, but it was always me who set up the tent, started a fire, and tended to business while he loaded film and wandered off with his camera. After that I went camping on my own. Eventually I figured out that if I just left a note, saying I'd be back in two days, it was easier on all concerned.

As Grandpa Duncan told me with a wink, "It's easier to ask forgiveness than permission."

One night there was enough breeze to keep mosquitoes away, and I slept under the stars, reading <u>Astronomy for Kids</u> by flashlight, intrigued by the term "heavenly bodies." I turned off the light, and lay in the darkness. I was a mile away from any house or highway, so the Milky Way lit up the sky as though comprised of a hundred billion suns, which it was, according to <u>Astronomy for Kids</u>. This was early August, and meteorites passed overhead every ten minutes or so, burning themselves up in a matter of seconds.

Snuggling down inside my sleeping bag, the question that nuked my noggin was this: Is this cold, wondrous universe finite or infinite? Both options seemed absurd. Because how could space go on forever? On the other hand, what would a boundary to the universe be made out of? Still, it had to be one way or the other. It *had to be*, though how could you determine which?

The moon rose, gradually washing out the Milky Way, leaving me with the notion that a heavenly body can eclipse its competition, if it's nearby and if it shines brightly enough.

<u>Astronomy for Kids</u> got me in trouble on more than one occasion. I used to bring it to Sunday school, to check it against the stuff Mr. Moss taught us. One morning he asked us to open to Psalms 104. A new kid asked what page that was on.

Mr. Moss regarded him with confusion. Apparently he had never been asked that question. He was an old, soft-spoken man with a huge Adam's apple, though at the time, I didn't know that term, so I had no idea what that lump was doing under the flappy skin of his neck. He gulped when he got baffled, and it looked like he had a mole squirming its way up and down his throat.

I was an easily distracted boy.

"Well, golly, what do mean, what page?" asked Mr. Moss. Gulp. "It's right after Job."

The new kid looked around. "Where's that?"

I was not one to cause trouble, but how could anyone resist a sweet set-up like this? "Right before Psalms," I said with a straight face.

Mr. Moss gulped at me, and told the boy, "Job is about halfway through."

The kid thumbed through his Bible, blinking in confusion.

Mr. Moss said, "Let's begin with Psalm 104 Verse 5: 'He set the Earth on its foundations, so that it should never be moved.'"

I flipped through my astronomy book until I came to the part about the solar system being formed from a giant cloud of gas. As the cloud collapsed from gravity, it had started spinning, like water spins as it goes down a drain, which explains why the planets orbit our sun.

Being a curious kid, I asked Mr. Moss to explain about orbits, while I held up my book to show my classmates the layout of our solar system.

"Well, now...." he gulped. "See, the Earth's foundation is its orbit around the sun." Gulp, gulp. In response to our blank faces, he clarified himself: "It's meant to be poetic."

What? Blink. Gulp. Wait a minute. Huhhhhh?

Poetry is absolutely the worst way to sell cosmological concepts to a bunch of befuddled eleven-year-olds. We all blinked like crazy, while poor old Mr. Moss ran that mole ragged.

The new kid was still thumbing through his Bible. "Where are we?" Blink blink.

I held up the solar system picture and pointed out our planet. "Right here." All right, so maybe I was a troublemaker.

I'm surrounded by Germans, and they attempt to strike up a conversation with me, but they speak even less English than I speak German. Phrases like "Macht schnell!" and "Achtung!" and other phrases excerpted from WWII movies will hopefully be of little use on a train ride through the Andes.

We pass rolling hills of farm and forest. Expansive fields of coffee plants are tended by broad-hipped women. Herds of llamas graze beside Rio Urubamba.

The tracks separate from the river and take us up to 14,000 feet. The higher we go, the more barren becomes the land. Still, the desolation holds a beauty of its own, with remnants of snow-capped volcanoes peeking through passes. The under-oxygenated air does not adversely affect me, giving me hope that the altitude will no longer be a problem.

Locals board the train, each wearing several layers of heavy clothing. They carry their belongings on their backs, rolled up in blankets of blue, red and black.

I chat up two teachers on sabbatical from Switzerland. Natalie and Christine have been traveling for six months, improvising as they go. They purchased open-ended round-the-world plane tickets, wherein they are allowed an unlimited number of flights for one year, provided they keep moving west to east. Like me, and like most backpackers I encounter, they wear rumpled, baggy clothing. But Natalie is appealing anyway, with her French accent and blonde ponytail flopping about.

Christine is interested in my stay at Machu Picchu. I tell her about the lodge and the view, and having the whole place to myself one morning, but I find myself being protective of my Ecstatic Meltdown, as I've come to call it.

We arrive in Puno at dusk, and I check into the hotel where Natalie and Christine are staying. The lobby is clean, though cold and echoey. That's okay; this is simply a place to sleep. I ask the women if they want to get some dinner, but they tell me they're turning in early.

I walk down to the waterfront and draw my jacket around my neck to ward off the chilly wind blowing in off Lake Titicaca. At 12,500 feet above sea level, it's the highest navigable lake in the world. According to Incan religion – or mythology, depending on your point of view – the lake is considered sacred. It was here that Manco Capac, the first Incan king, was born of the sun god Inti. Manco rose from the lake, and went on to found the Kingdom of Cusco, thus sowing the seeds of the Incan Empire.

Quechua, the Incas' language, is still the most widely spoken language among indigenous people in the Americas. I read that "Titicaca" in Quechua means "rock of the puma," but I don't believe it. No, I'm convinced the lake was named by an anatomically confused eight-year-old boy. Peruvians insist that they have the titi, and Bolivians got the caca.

The wind picks up, so I find a restaurant recommended in my guide book. I order Chicharrón de Trucha – trout rolled in flour, then fried and served with a baked potato and creole salad. The potato is hard as a rock, but the trout is moist, firm, scrumptious.

The quarter-mile walk back to the hotel leaves me panting.

My room opens onto the lobby, enabling me to hear everyone who comes and goes. A commotion arises outside my door at midnight. I don my jeans and go to investigate, only to find Natalie and Christine squabbling with the desk clerk.

"Room smell bad," Natalie is saying, "like old underwear." Christine backs her up with nods and harrumphs.

"Is only room," says the man behind the desk. "Lo siento." I'm sorry. For all three of them, English is their second language.

Natalie says, "We are liking to have the money back."

I ask what the problem is, and the women are plenty eager to tell me. "When you flush, it smell like llama give birth," says Christine, and Natalie tacks on, "Then llama die!" With hands on defiant hips, they stare down the manager, ready for battle, belying the fact that Switzerland is the only European country to never have gone to war.

"Ask to see the manager," I say.

Christine cries out, "He *is* manager!"

Doors open down the hall, and the harried man, not wishing to escalate the ruckus, begrudgingly refunds their money. Christine asks if he knows of other hotels close by. He says he does not.

Natalie tells me they are hesitant to walk the city at night. "We can sleep with you?"

Christine quickly adds, "On floor?"

"My room's a double," I say. "You're welcome to the other bed."

The manager opens his mouth to object, but a bowlegged, elderly American clad in boxers appears in the lobby. "What's all the danged hollerin' about?" The manager coaxes him back to his room, while glaring over his shoulder at Natalie and Christine.

The women drag their backpacks into my room, while I strip down to my briefs. I get in bed, and roll away from them, to allow them a measure of privacy. They turn off the lights soon afterwards, but they whisper back and forth, and one of them gets up a few minutes later, turns on the light and calls Aeroperu to confirm a flight. After apologizing to me, she climbs back in bed and they continue to whisper.

Eventually I drift off, but am awoken by Christine. "Theo, you are awake?"

"Am now."

"Sorry. Is cold. Extra blankets to be found?"

"Check the closet."

She turns on the light, and starts fussin' and cussin' at something. I roll over just in time to see her put a foot against the wall and give the door knob a yank. The closet door jerks open and crashes against the wall, knocking her on her bottom. There's an immediate knock on our door, which Natalie answers in panties and bra. The manager speaks in a quiet but agitated voice. Natalie responds in French, but Christine cuts her off by slamming the door in the man's face.

The act of adding blankets is a major production. To hell with their measure of privacy. If they're gonna keep me awake, I want the pleasure of watching Natalie's shapely Swiss tush peeking out from her skimpy Swiss panties as she bends over to straighten the blankets. Each of them walks around the bed a dozen times to make sure everything's even. When Natalie realizes I'm following her every move, she smiles good-naturedly and apologizes.

They turn out the light, but one of them gets up to take a leak while leaving the bathroom door open. She sounds like a llama whizzing in Rio Urubamba.

CHEEE-sus!

Chapter 8: Our Native Tongue

I awaken with a category five headache, which, based on my labored breathing, is likely due to a lack of oxygen. And I'm sleep-deprived, having shared my room with a pair of chatty Swiss women with petit' bladders. While the three of us get dressed, Christine asks about my plans for the day. I tell them I'm taking a boat out to Uros, a floating island community, which was my primary reason for visiting Puno. They ask to come along.

We all order scrambled eggs at the restaurant next door, but I don't feel much like eating. Or talking or moving, or even breathing, for that matter. I'm content to have the women tell me about their travels. Natalie has a little ski jump nose that twitches when she laughs.

What would Fiona think of me ogling this woman? Then again, why would I care? She and I held hands for all of two minutes. Against all reason, however, I find myself being regretful of my quiescent infidelity. I do not possess Fiona, though she surely possesses me. A heavenly body can eclipse all competition, even though she's far away, if she shines brightly enough.

The three of us walk down to the pier just before ten, and pay six bucks each to Daniel, who will be our pilot. He's a chunky man who appears even chunkier by wearing more clothes than you could fit in a suitcase. We hop into his battered motorboat and take off right away. Now it's clear why he's dressed so heavily. Though it's a sunny day, the wind chills us to the bone.

Natalie, in her lilting French accent, asks, "This is sweet water?"

My addled brain cannot make sense of that. "Huh?"

"Sweet water, not ...." she hunts around for the English word. "Not.... salt water?" It takes me a moment to see that her dichotomy is not salt vs. fresh, but rather salt vs. sweet.

"That's right," I say. "This is sweet water."

I picture Manco Capac rising from these waters to become leader of the Incas. Did people believe that story? Literally? Do they still? Or do they understand it as myth, meant to imbue their first emperor with superhuman powers, thus enhancing his legacy?

And Fiona: Does she believe the story of the Great Flood, which tells of the entire Earth being submerged? Even the Andes, four miles high? Sorry, there's not enough water, a contradiction I could see way back in Sunday school.

And yet, having experienced the terror of a four-second baptismal submersion in three feet of water at age six, it's easy to understand why the author of Genesis, whoever that was, would have been tempted to exaggerate the magnitude of the deluge. If a flash flood caught you by surprise, and suddenly you and your family and your boat full of cattle and vermin were being tossed about on the tempestuous waters of a newly formed lake that's, oh, say, a thousand feet deep, or even a hundred, it would certainly seem as if the entire Earth was drowning.

So what say we cut the Biblical story tellers a bit of slack.

The Incas had their own myth about a great flood, foretold by a crystal-ball-gazing llama. All I can say is: Wow, who writes this stuff? Following torrential rains – courtesy of the creator god Viracocha, with an assist from the rain god Pariaqaqa – rivers overflowed their banks, the Andes were submerged, and everyone drowned, except for two people in a box. Sound familiar? Shoot, a lot of cultures have a story like that.

Floods happen.

Many deluges are, or were, widely believed to be caused by some sort of deity, who often provided a warning to humans, which would go something like this: Clean up your act or else.

Here's an interesting twist on the flood narrative from the Pima tribe in Arizona:

Members of the tribe were told repeatedly by Earth-Maker to be less quarrelsome or else suffer the consequences. The Pimas ignored these warnings, so South Wind informed Suha that he and his wife were the only people worth saving. They were instructed to fashion a giant ball made of gum from a spruce tree. They did so, and stocked it with jerky – which, as an aside, is a Quechua word – and nuts. When the rains started, Suha and his wife climbed inside the gumball, sealed it up, and rolled around on the waves for months before coming to rest on Superstition Mountain, outside of present-day Phoenix.

As another aside, Phoenix was so named because it rose

from the ruins of the Pueblo Grande, whose builders had attempted to irrigate their valley with a hundred miles of canals. It is believed the Pueblo people were done in by drought.

While we're at it, the word "Pima" is thought to derive from the tribe's words "Pi mac", meaning "I don't know", which would have been their response to most questions posed to them during first contact with Europeans.

I went to Pima Community College my freshman year. I got a kick out of attending an institute of higher learning whose name derives from "I don't know." Had PCC's founders been aiming for irony or humility? Or did they not know the word's meaning? I made a habit of asking professors about the etymology of "Pima," and every single one of them answered, "I don't know," which pleased me immensely. My classmates and I referred to PCC as "I don't know U."

As for validating Incan mythology, there'd been centuries-old rumors of the existence of a temple at the bottom of Lake Titicaca, and the presence of ancient roads leading into the water lent credence to such tales. In 1967 the Bolivian government allowed divers to explore the lake bottom, and sure enough, they discovered slime-covered temple walls a hundred feet down, as well as a 2600-foot stone wall, indicating that a flood occurred here. Now, let's not assume it was a Great Flood, but it must have been a Real Big One.

Back to Fiona – what does she think about the Biblical story of Lot, a "righteous man?" Let's hear from him as he addresses the predacious, oversexed townsmen of Sodom: "I will not allow you to rape the angels staying at my home, but hey, my virginal teenage daughters are up for grabs. Have at 'em." Then Lot knocks back a few drinks, and knocks up his own daughters. The story isn't just goofy; it's downright nauseating. And what could possibly be the moral of such a tale? None, I would hope.

It's not difficult to guess what Fiona's response would be: Yeah, well, that's the Old Testament; the heart and soul of The Bible are in the New.

But, but, but God allegedly oversaw the writing and editing of that story. And two billion people are convinced He holds the publishing rights.

I know these Bible tales from Sunday school and church,

though I didn't pay them much mind as a young adult. At sixteen, I got a job at Saguaro Music, and being the new guy meant working Sunday mornings. My father was displeased that I stopped attending church. He had named me after Grandpa Duncan, the minister, in hopes I might follow in his footsteps.

Still, church-related matters have long intrigued me. In college I took Intro to Philosophy, Bible as Lit, and a Comparative Religions class taught by a self-described "ex-Catholic-cum-Hindu." An elderly, liver-spotted man, he used to joke, "In case of emergency, call me an ex-priest." He was a big believer in karma, which he defined as "cosmic payback," a model of ethics and responsibility that appealed to my sense of fairness.

Until recently, religion has been simply an intellectual exercise for me, though I've always sort of assumed that I would buy in at some point. I'd like to. Pastor Pete's warmth looms larger in my mind than do the nonsensical teachings of ol' Mr. Moss. And Fiona has ignited a new fire within me, a desire to understand the deeper workings of life.

So then, what to make of Jesus? Did he die on the cross to provide salvation for those who believe? Or is that just one more myth? Does Fiona believe that a long dead carpenter from Nazareth might one day show up at Ace Hardware in Walla Walla, Washington? Would a guy who resembles Groucho Marx or who sings like Bob Dylan be recognized as the Messiah? Or, the next time around, maybe Jesus will be a rich man from Richmond or a masseuse from Marseilles.

Three miles out from Puno, the floating islands are home to a couple thousand Uros, a tribe which pre-dates the Incan civilization. Though the Peruvian government has offered them land on shore, they opt to remain where they are. Our boat docks at one of forty-some islands, and we step out onto a spongy surface.

Daniel begins our tour by saying, "For us, totora is the source of everything. Ev-er-y-thing. This island itself is made of totora reeds that grow in the shallows." He shows us canoes made from tightly woven reeds. The largest canoe has a mast made out of totora, as is its sail. He points out a twenty-foot lookout tower erected from reeds.

"Totora is edible," Daniel says, passing around greenish-beige samples that taste something like celery. "It's also used for medicinal purposes. And we Uros grow potatoes and other crops out here, in soil created by decaying reeds."

Christine asks, "Can we hear Uros language?"

"Our language died out five hundred years ago," he says. "We Uros interbred with another tribe on the mainland, and eventually we abandoned the Uro language."

We set out walking, and Daniel explains how the islands came to be. "The dense roots of the reed naturally interweave, and the Uros built a foundation of totora five feet thick – that's what we are standing on. The reeds on the bottom of the island rot away every few months, so new reeds are constantly added on top. The islands were originally built for defensive purposes. They're anchored with ropes attached to huge stakes driven into the lake bottom, and if a threat arises, this island could be moved."

It occurs to me that these islands would not be imperiled by a Great Flood. Cut the ropes and rise with the tide; you've got forty-some arks, sitting high and dry.

Daniel leads us into a one-room schoolhouse built out of, naturally, totora reeds, and we are introduced to a dozen students of various ages sitting attentively in antique desks. Up to this point, this has been a pretty neat tour; we are observing first-hand a way of life that is unlike any I've ever seen or even imagined. But interrupting a lesson so a bunch of foreigners can gawk at a classroom of cute, snotty-nosed, blank faces strikes me as tourism at its very worst.

Stepping back outside, I marvel at the world these people have built. Their lives have remained fundamentally unchanged by the passage of centuries or the arrival of new thoughts and customs from overseas.

Traversing the island, we are shown into homes constructed from reeds. A family of six lives in a meticulously woven teepee measuring a dozen feet in diameter. Their neighbors live in a wobbly shed standing seven feet high at its peak. Entering these homes seems horribly invasive, but then, tourism has become an integral part of the Uros' twentieth century lives. Maybe it's not as bad as I make it sound.

But then school lets out, and we're mobbed by five-year-olds, half of them begging, the other half hawking souvenirs. I buy a shoddy toy boat for one sol, thinking these little hucksters will then leave me alone. Yeah, right.

By the time we arrive back at our hotel, I ache all over. It's all I can do to take the next breath. Is this altitude sickness? Where's Professor Plum with a fistful of muña when you need him? Or did I get bad trout last night?
Christine and Natalie collect their gear and hoist their packs onto their backs. They thank me for sharing my room, and before I get a chance to ask if they want to have lunch, they're out the door, waving bye-bye, catching a flight to.... oh, they told me, but I don't remember. It must be obvious I'm not firing on all cylinders. In Peruvian parlance, you might say I'm a few llamas short of a herd. I'm not up to socializing anyway. Even so, it's disappointing to see them go. I ruefully watch Natalie's blonde ponytail sway back and forth, brushing the top of her pack on each pass.

I'm tempted to go to bed, but it's only noon, and how often do you make it to Puno? I leave and wander up to Plaza de Armas, dominated by a massive cathedral. God, guns and guilt.

I walk on, oblivious to my surroundings. I come to an intersection and choose the steep road to my right, in search of the city's high point, hoping it might offer a view and a place to veg out. A hundred grueling yards later, the road curls to the right, dead-ending in a small park overlooking the brown city and sparkling blue of Lake Titicaca, surrounded by hilly desert. Just what the doctor ordered. In the middle of the park stands a majestic, 150-foot statue of Manco Capac, sculpted from white stone. Decked out in headdress, cloak, robe, leggings, and sandals, he's pointing toward the lake with one hand, holding a spear in the other.

Panting, I lie down on the three-foot-high, sun-warmed stone wall that makes up the park's perimeter. My sluggishness calls to mind the lizards native to the Arizona desert. Being cold-blooded, they bask in the sun, in order to speed up their metabolism. In my case, I'm hoping the sun will melt away whatever is ailing me. My headache reminds me of an old aspirin commercial, which presented a cross-sectional view of a human skull with a pudgy man inside, hammering away on an anvil.

Mister Pudge has set up shop behind my left eyeball.

I sit up, and make my inhales deeper and quicker. It doesn't help. The sun reflects off the rippling surface of Titicaca, generating a diamond-studded scintillation. I am miserable, but that does not keep me from discerning beauty in the lake. Is there design in this phantasmagoric splendor? Some would say no; life is meaningless and chaotic, a position which renders beauty nothing more than an overlay of human perception and physiology.

A clamor arises in the distance, at Plaza de Armas. A parade is leaving the plaza, headed in my direction, following the route I took earlier. Children, clad in brightly colored costumes, zip in and out of the marchers, many of whom sing with gusto. When they are directly below me, they take a right turn up the hill.

A few minutes later, the parade turns the corner and enters the park. What have I stumbled upon? What has stumbled upon me? The scene buoys my spirits. Four men set up a PA system. A hundred families flood into the park, kids jumping for joy as barrel-chested Indian women and men unload boxes of flowers and food from a flatbed truck.

This scene gets me thinking about my own family. What drama or feud is playing out at this moment? Are they helping out Dad? This is the first time he's lived alone. Poor man – somehow he's got to see that he's not responsible for what happened with Mom. It would help if he knew I don't blame him. But what else would he think? I've been combative the past few months. I have felt lost, bedeviled by her memory. My resentment, however, is aimed at the situation, not at him, and I have told him as much, but my offers of absolution fall on deaf ears. He misses Mom horribly, as do I. But my siblings? No, I do not miss them.

There – I said it. Yet here I am, alone, three thousand miles from home, rotting from the inside.

A band is getting ready to play, featuring the standard Andean line-up – drum, guitar, charango, panpipes, flute. Next to them, a mother is helping her toddler stand, and as the music starts, he begins bobbing up and down. Being no more than a year old, his moves are limited, but he is definitely dancing – there's no other word for it. This smiley boy will be unable to form sentences for another year, but his brain and body already recognize rhythm, and he goo-goos along with the beat, making me wonder if music isn't our first language, our native tongue, which later gets shunted aside for clunky vocabulary and constrictive grammar.

My thoughts return to my new-found acquaintances.... no, that's not right; they are now my friends, and I miss them. Other than my parents, when was the last time I missed someone? During college, my girlfriend dropped out to join the Peace Corps, and I was sad to see her go, but superimposed on top of my sorrow was the same invigoration I used to feel when I'd go camping by myself. I like being on my own. Right now, however, I would not use the word "invigorated" to describe my state of mind.

A microphone squeals; announcements are made. An officious man prays, and then congratulates the kids, who perform a skit that's incomprehensible to me. I take out my journal and describe what seems to be a children's religious festival. All is well, until someone cranks up a boom box and places the mic in front of it, treating us to musica folkloric played through The World's Worst Sound System. My journal entry:

<u>How to Get That Peruvian Sound</u>

> Buy a ghetto blaster that sounds like crap. Bash in
> one speaker, douse the other with Inca Kola. Set the
> tone control on "tinny." Dial in your favorite station,
> but turn the dial a bit, so you pick up a ton of static.
> Crank it to eleven, and hey, you are ready to party.

Mister Pudge, my evil spirit, is banging away on that anvil. I leave the park and roam the winding streets of Puno, past homes, shops and churches, ending up back down at the lakefront, where an icy wind blows in off the water, driving me back into town.

I stop at a store and ask the clerk, "Como se dice 'aspirin' in Español?"

The man shakes his head and says, "Lo siento."

He's sorry. About what? That he doesn't have aspirin? Or that he doesn't understand my Spanish? Does he not know the word "aspirin?" Or is he was sorry that Mister Pudge has set aside his anvil and is now hammering away on my eyeball? Maybe the clerk is apologizing for being an unhelpful jerk.

I'm aggravated, and try to work up a nasty response, but I

don't, for several reasons: I don't know how to say "ass cactus" in Spanish; the effort makes my headache worse; and my aggravation brings to mind The Ugly American, a book we read in high school. I leave.

The sun is sinking, and the temperature drops accordingly. I return to my hotel and ask the woman behind the desk for drinking water.

She shakes her head. "No comprendo."

"Agua, beber." Water, to drink. She says something I do not understand.

I enter my room, put on another sweater, and haul out my guide book. There's a quiet knock on my door, and I open it to find a shy teenage girl, who hands me a plastic bag of liquid with a red twist tie. I hold up the bag to the light. It's filled with weak tea or hearty water. The girl makes a drinking motion, accompanied by glug-glug-glug sounds. I gracias her and close the door. So this is agua, beber. In a bag. Is this standard practice? Where did this water come from?

I set the bag in the shower stall, and begin reading a capsule history of Puno, which means "bleak upland." It fits. Two paragraphs in, I have not absorbed anything, so I re-read it, taking in nothing of substance on the second pass. Or the third pass, or the fourth. Stupidly and stubbornly, I do this for a long time. Moby's trip. I thumb through the book and find a blurb on altitude sickness: headache, malaise, no appetite, fuzzy head, stay hydrated, hard to predict who'll get it and who won't. I define altitude sickness as the desire to curl up and cease to exist.

I rummage through my pack and pull out Another Roadside Attraction, a Tom Robbins novel. I lie down and open to the dog-eared page. Jesus is telling Tarzan that he must choose between thinking carnally and thinking spiritually. Tarzan rides his goat into the desert, asking Jesus if there's a law against thinking both ways. Jesus yells, "You're either with me or against me."

It's a fun read, but I keep nodding off, and it becomes difficult to tell where the book ends and a dream or hallucination begins. Robbins' non-linear style only adds to my disorientation.

It's getting darker outside and colder inside. I haven't showered in two days. Maybe a blast of hot water will revive me. Attached to the showerhead is a contraption with bare wires sticking out every which way. Como se dice 'electrocution' in Español? Maybe I'm not so cold and grubby after all. I turn on the hot water in the sink and wait for it to heat up. It doesn't.

I go see the woman at the front desk. "No agua caliente in mi quarto." No hot water in my room.

She nods her head in agreement and says, "No."

I re-enter my room, splash cold water on my face and call it good. Having not drunk anything in ten hours, my mouth tastes like Llove the Llama came tromping through it, searching for a warm spot to bed down. I'm thirsty, but that bag of water makes me nervous, as does the water coming out of that tap. I eat some toothpaste.

I consider going out for dinner, but my stomach threatens to revolt at the mere thought of eating. I take two blankets from the other bed and throw them on top of mine, then take off my jeans and one sweater, and crawl beneath the covers. With the blankets up around my neck, I stick a hand out to hold the paperback.

At some point I realize the book is not making sense. I turn out the light, pull the covers up over my head and poke out my nose. I lie this way for what seems like hours, not moving, so as to avoid contact with new territory in those icy sheets. Would a complaint to the management about the heat, or lack thereof, be helpful? The prospect of stepping onto the frosty floor dissuades me.

Machu Picchu is a distant memory. Was that only two days ago? If I were granted one wish, I'd return to the City in the Clouds, and be blessed with the good fortune to run into the Quinns again. My last thought before falling into a fitful sleep is of Fiona, hoping she's lying in a warm bed. Is she praying for me? I hope so.

God knows I need it.

Chapter 9: Return to Earth

Head hurts. Cold shoulder. Pull up covers. Need sleep.

Daybreak. Day is broken. Don't wanna move.

I'm thirsty. Out of bed. Clothes. Feet, move. Open door. What now? Go back to bed; or stand here; sit, speak, roll over.... Where am I? Lobby.

The guy behind the desk asks me a question in Spanish. It does not register.

The guy behind the desk asks me a question in English. It does not register.

He leads me to a chair and disappears. He returns with a steaming cup of something that smells like lawn clippings. Sip it. Take anything anyone offers me and swallow it.

Before me lie the mummified remains of children. Is this a dream? Don't remember falling sleep. Kids are sacrifices to Incan mountain gods. Will this happen to me? Gods? So this is heaven? Huh? Don't wanna be in heaven. Don't wanna be sacrificed. Return to Earth.

My cup is empty. How do I get more? Where did it come from? Neck is cold. Reach back, lift hood on sweatshirt. Tug on it. It will not move.

The man behind the desk comes over. He's nice. He takes my cup and leaves. Why did you go? Where did you go?

Why, and where, did you go? Softly I sing that over and over. Where did this song come from? It's peaceful, sad, pretty. Why, and where, did you go?

The nice man brings my cup. It's full again. Drink.

A while later, I look around and get my bearings: Oh yeah, Puno. A kid must have left her dolls on the floor; they were not mummies after all. I take my empty cup to the guy at the desk and say, "Es muy bueno." It's very good.

He smiles. "Muña tea."

"Muchas, muchas, muchas gracias."

I return to my room and brush my teeth without water. Catching a glimpse of myself in the mirror, I see that my hooded sweatshirt is on backwards. I gotta get out of here. And by "here," I don't mean this room, or this hotel or Puno. I gotta get out of the Andes and return to Earth, where there is breathable air.

I turn my sweatshirt around and grab my guide book. Wheezing, I thank the clerk again on my way out and enter a cafe. Waiting for my scrambled eggs, I grab a newspaper off the next table and stare at it. It makes no sense. Oh yeah, Spanish.

The eggs come, served with rice and tamales. I wolf it all down, then guzzle my orange juice and order another. I check the map of Puno in my guide book and locate the Aeroperu office, only a five-minute walk away. I need to confirm my flight to Lima tomorrow.

At the Aeroperu office, I take my place in line behind a Peruvian man and his two kids. His teenage daughter is telling him how she wants to cut and style her little brother's hair. The dad wants it cut a different way, so he and the daughter debate this matter. The boy is about ten, and he tells them not to cut his hair. The girl clamps a hand over his mouth, so she and her dad can converse without unnecessary interruption. They are now third in line, and the boy takes to watching the TV sitting on a shelf behind the agent. His eyes are glued to the screen, while the future shape of his head is discussed.

That could have been me fifteen years ago.

Or, shoot, that could have been me up until three months ago, at which point our family dynamic was permanently altered when my parents went to California and Mom didn't return. So my sibs looked around for someone to play her part, to mediate and attend to legal issues....

Well, heck, Theo's done all right for himself. Let's give him a shot.

Actually, that's not quite how it happened. My siblings weren't "looking around," and they certainly didn't look to me. They were looking at each other, and when they didn't see anyone who would, or could, come anywhere close to filling Mom's shoes, their eyes landed on me, the none-of-the-above option. Which bugs the holy hell out of me, because, once I turned eighteen, my unarticulated deal with them was simple: I leave you alone, you leave me alone.

That's all an oversimplification, of course, because we get together for birthdays, and I like them well enough, in small doses. Phil is a sensitive sort, Rowan is kind, if confused, and Claire has a sense of humor that, when she tones it down, livens up a party. And nothing brightens up the holidays like singing Christmas carols in four-part harmony. But prior to last December, I had never asked much of them, and they'd been pretty good about returning the favor.

The boy in front of me fingers a cross hung around his neck. I imagine he's praying for his dad and sister to leave him the hell alone. That cross gets me thinking about religion, which of course leads me back to Fiona.

She is here to serve and save. Have I ever met a kinder soul? And is not her Christian belief the foundation of her kindness? I thirst for her surety. I want that. Given her certainty, I find it surprising that she seemed perfectly relaxed that last day at Machu Picchu when we argued.... no, that's not right, when we debated.... no.... when she and I explored one another's beliefs. She was not frustrated by our differences, because she, unlike Cole and Barry, does not seem to take them personally. She even enjoyed our give-and-take, as did I. This was new ground for me; had my sisters been present, they would have turned our exchange into a philosophical food fight.

And how about Cole? After his grandpa died, he jettisoned religion. Would he then classify himself as an atheist? Or maybe he's taken up agnosticism, of which there exist multiple strains, the weakest of which is to say you don't know if God exists. A stronger version is to maintain that no one knows. Or, stronger still, maybe Cole believes it's Impossible – capital I – to know, in which case he wouldn't just be saying that *he* hasn't figured it out, or that he hasn't figured it out *yet*, or that he will *never* figure it out. No, he'd be saying nobody will ever determine whether God exists, and any understanding of His essence lies beyond the impressive, though finite, reach of human faculties.

I adopted that third strain of agnosticism long ago, the Nobody Can Ever Know version, paired with utter bewilderment as to the meaning of the word "God." Rowan contends, however, that my perplexity regarding religious vocabulary is rooted in a question Claire asked our dad years ago: "What the hell do you mean by 'heaven,' and who gives a shit anyhow?"

Events of the past few days have made me question my Nobody Can Ever Know stance. First off, I was surprised and shaken by the words that slipped from my mouth when I was not paying attention: "So maybe in a hundred years, we will figure out a way to talk to God." Maybe it's time to downgrade my position, to a more humble Nobody Knows.

Secondly, I'm not sure what to make of my Ecstatic Meltdown, but whatever it was, it did not seem like a meaningless experience. It echoed Fiona's sentiments that knowing God is a matter of the heart, rather than a mental exercise.

Boy, listen to me: yap, yap, yap. This is all very confusing, and fussing with philosophy requires more oxygen to the brain than the rarified air of Puno can provide.

Regardless of which version of non-God we're talking about, Cole's charm and sass flow directly from his irreverence. He defused that potentially troublesome run-in with that gang of boys in Cusco by engaging them in a manner that was self-deprecating, fearless and a bit raunchy.

And Gracie: What should I make of her oddball, new-agey, No Accidents outlook? With her love of life and her disinterest in The Endless Debate, she will be the one who holds the Quinn family together. As muddled as her thinking seems to me, she is gracious, even when dealing with Barry, that toad.

And what about Barry? Well, you can't accuse him of being wishy-washy.

I reach the agent's counter a few minutes later, but a commercial is blaring, making it impossible to hear the woman, so I ask her to turn down the TV.

She cups her ear and shrieks at me in Spanish. I think she's saying: I can't hear you 'cause of the TV!

I twist my fingers on an imaginary dial. "The volume! Bajo, por favor!" Down, please!

She brings her thumb and index finger together, leaving a half-inch gap. "Inglés, poco!" English, little bit!

I step around the counter and search for the volume knob,

but the TV doesn't seem to have one. Nor can I find the on/off button. The agent is scolding me, but I ignore her and yank the cord out of the wall socket. Silence falls. The agent looks as though she might slap me, but who gives a damn? I am the ugly, thoroughly pissed-off American. I show her my reservation to fly out tomorrow.

She motions for me to return to the other side of the desk, and then thumbs through a stack of papers. "Not confirmed."

I hold my reservation up to her face. "Nine thirty mañana."

"Lo siento." She does not sound sorry. "Waiting list."

"Por que?" I ask. Why?

"Full."

"Por que?"

We go back and forth like this while the people behind me get crankier with each por que. Eventually I wear her down, and she grumps, "Empty seat today."

"Que hora?" What hour?

"Once y cuarto." 11:15.

I check my watch. 9:50. Let's see, five minutes to the hotel, five minutes to pack, five minutes to check out, twenty miles to the airport.... "Si."

Staring at a boxy monitor, she begins banging away on her coffee-stained keyboard, while people behind me grumble about their precious televisión being turned off.

Precious minutes pass. I ask, "Is okay?"

She nods slowly and keeps on typing.

More minutes pass. I'm getting fidgety. "Problemo?"

She shakes her head slowly and keeps on typing.

Another five minutes pass. "What the hell're you doing?"

Her English turns out to be quite good: "When a change is made, Aeroperu requires me to enter every flight you have taken in the past month or have reserved in the future."

"Por que?"

"Company policy."

She hands me my ticket five minutes later and wishes me a safe trip, her tone indicating that she hopes my flight terminates in a fiery, piss-your-pants plummet from 30,000 feet.

I stumble back to my hotel and ask the clerk to call a cab. Gasping for air, I pack in three minutes flat, dumping my books, toothpaste and razor in with my socks and undies. Now, strap on the pack, grab my charango, wobble over to the desk. I pay in cash, leaving the clerk a tip of ten million intis. My watch reads 10:24.

By the time the cab arrives five minutes later, I'm frantic. If I don't get out today, there's no telling when, or if, I might escape. These mountains will eat me up. I cram myself into the back seat of the vintage Volvo, holding my pack on my lap.

"Aeropuerto, por favor!"

He takes off at a leisurely pace, and I order him, "Rapido, por favor!" He floors it, which has no effect on the ancient engine.

I dig out my map and discover, to my horror, that Inca Manco Capac Aeropuerto is a good 30 miles away. We're doing 70 kilometers per hour, and, let's see, 8 kilometers equals 5 miles, so that's.... Damn, I'm in no mood for story problems.

"Mas rapido, por favor!"

We arrive at the tiny airport at 11:17. I toss the driver a wad of bills, then drag my pack over to the check-in counter. Not unexpectedly, there's no line; other passengers would have arrived an hour ago. I picture myself hoofing it down the tarmac while a baggage handler hurls my pack onto the plane as it taxies down the runway.

I check in and hurry to the gate, just in time to....

Sit down and wait. Over the crackly airport intercom comes an announcement, only three words of which I understand: Aeroperu, problemo, mecanico.

After checking into my hotel in the Miraflores district of Lima, I chug two liters of water and take my first shower in three days. In retrospect, it's clear that my altitude sickness was exacerbated, if not caused, by dehydration. Thirty-six hours without liquids is dangerous in a dry clime, two and a half miles high. But the four-hour delay at the Juliaca airport is behind me, and water has resurrected my body.

I set out on foot to explore the Miraflores, which means something like "Look, flowers." Though smog-laden, the sea-level air fills my lungs in a delicious way. The traffic crawls by, and most cars, even newer models, are dented or scraped up. Some are missing bumpers, headlights or windows.

The din becomes deafening as I near the retail area. Each shop owner has fired up a gas-powered generator on the sidewalk and run a cord inside. This was all explained in my guide book, but I hadn't quite believed it: Lima suffers power shortages, so electricity gets turned off for several hours a day at different times for various neighborhoods, leaving it up to individual businesses and homes to provide for themselves. Each generator, besides causing a head-numbing racket, belches clouds of smoke. Cars tiptoe through intersections; even traffic lights are deprived of power, which explains why most vehicles look as if hooligans took sledgehammers to them.

I wander down a side street, where upscale, multi-story homes are fronted by well-tended gardens, and bougainvilleas spill over ten-foot-high stucco walls in cascades of red and purple. Look, flowers. Intimate courtyards are tucked away behind arbors and wrought iron gates. This neighborhood strikes me as idyllic, until I notice the iron bars on windows and the walls topped with shards of glass. And this is the nice part of Lima.

The road dead-ends at a bluff overlooking the ocean. At the bottom of the cliff lay heaps of trash and rusted-out shells of automobiles and washing machines. Perched on what could be, and should be, a gorgeous lookout onto the Pacific, I feast my eyes on a garbage dump. Waves crash against the shore as they cleanse and crunch the sand. Given time, the ocean will pulverize the piles of debris, but for now the trash lies beyond the water's purifying reach.

Heading back toward the busy part of Mira Flores, I pass a man hawking AAA batteries, and I steer clear of a guy holding a thick wad of cash, trading currencies on the black market.

Having not eaten in eight hours, I duck into a cafe off Parque Kennedy, named after JFK. The chorizo sausage and onion omeletta arrives quickly, disconcertingly so. It's greasy, but hot and tasty. Looking out the window, I witness a collision between two VW vans, one of which t-bones the other. The drivers are apparently uninjured, and they assess the damage. There are no apologies, no recriminations, no yelling. Matter of fact, neither man exhibits animosity or even stress. And why would they?

This is a typical day.

Chapter 10: The Devil's Harlot

After sleeping until noon, I ask the woman at the desk to order me a cab with an English-speaking driver who can give me a tour of Lima.

Twenty minutes later, I'm sitting in the front seat of a late model Toyota, as the cabbie delivers a capsule history of his city: "The Spanish Crown named Pizarro as governor of all lands he conquered. In 1535, he founded Lima as The City of Kings. He ruled his empire from here."

Once downtown, he chronicles the woes of Lima: One in three Peruvians lives here. Three million out of eight are out of work. The population has doubled in twenty years, as people flood in from poor rural areas. He points out a collapsed building. "El coche bomba – car bomb, compliments of Sendero Luminoso."

We stop at an intersection, then sit motionless through three cycles of the light. My driver mutters, "Hijo de puta!" When I ask what that means, he answers reluctantly, "Son of a whore. I shouldn't talk like that, but this traffic! It doesn't move!"

I show him my map and ask, "Donde es aqui?" Where is here? He points out a spot three miles from the Inquisition Museum. I pay my fare, plus a guide fee, plus a million intis for teaching me how to say "hijo de puta."

Exiting the cab, my senses are assaulted. A poorly tuned bus spews black smoke, momentarily cloaking the feverish stench of fungus-ridden feet, rust-eaten sewage pipes and deceased, diseased, belly-bloated rodents. Nope, it's worse than that. Is there a llama carcass decomposing nearby? I've seen photos of Lima, but you can't smell an eight-by-ten glossy.

A man sputters past on an over-revved Honda 90, with two kids sitting behind him and a puppy on his lap. A disheveled old woman shuffles towards me, offering to shine my shoes. I shake my head; my sandals are fine as they are.

Is this a typical third world city? Is this how most humans live? The air is gritty, almost chewable. Every bus, building and road is covered with layers of grime, leading me to believe that this city needs nothing so much as a good long shower, and I'm not speaking figuratively. Forsaken by the rain god Pariaqaqa, Lima has gone years without appreciable rainfall. The ongoing drought is leaving behind an urban desert.

Shoot, even in Tucson we have our summer storms, followed by the occasional flash flood. That being said, water is a precious resource in Arizona. A hundred years ago, you'd have hit an aquifer if you dug down twenty feet; now you have to go two hundred. And the Santa Cruz River that once flowed through Tucson is dry most of the year.

We inhabit a thirsty world.

I set off in the general direction of the Inquisition Museum. Jostled by shoulders, elbows and knees, I stop to consult my map, making me a target for a man selling fingernail clippers. I back up against a wall, holding up my map as a fortress. I get my bearings and check my wallet, which is a mistake, having just telegraphed its location to would-be pickpockets. Wearing an eyes-wide, jaws-clenched glower, I set out with an aggressive stride, daring passersby to accost me.

I enter a cafe twenty minutes later, not because it looks appealing or sanitary. Just get me off the street for thirty minutes. Lima has the feel of a city under siege.

At three o'clock I'm treated to a most welcome sight. My friends are huddled outside the Inquisition Museum, and I yell, "Muña! Getch yer red hot muña!"

They turn at once and come running. Gracie launches herself at me, Cole wraps us up in his long arms, Barry follows with a handshake, and Fiona lavishes upon me a bewitching smile. It's a joyous reunion – at any given moment, three of us are joking or swapping adventures. Fiona asks if I've finished writing my song.

"Not yet." I don't want to admit the tune has deserted me.

Barry breaks in. "Here, Theo; I got you a ticket."

The museum, which housed the tribunal for the Peruvian Inquisition from 1570 to 1820, sobers us up instantly. I don't understand all of what our Spanish-speaking guide says, but the instruments of torture speak with horrifying clarity. These tools and machines were engineered by devout men to burn, break, slice, flay, twist, stretch, choke, puncture and crush. Each exhibit is accompanied by a short explanation of its intended use.

Imported from Spain, the Inquisition was established in Lima with the aim of eliminating heresy. In the interest of maintaining political and social stability, inquisitors were given license to make "inquiries" of whomever they suspected of not following Catholic orthodoxy. Their list of transgressors included Protestants, Jews and natives who refused to convert, as well as those who had converted but then exhibited signs of backsliding, thereby forfeiting their right to exist.

Using a mannequin, one display shows how to simulate drowning by pinching a heretic's nose shut, then stuffing a strip of cloth down his throat and forcing him to drink as much as two gallons of water, inducing a prolonged sensation of drowning. The bloated sinner would then be beaten severely on his belly to intensify the pain.

In Europe, interrogators weaponized water in other ways: Heretics were boiled or frozen to death. Or, if there was a backlog of suspects, they might simply be drowned; even the inquisitors' most expeditious means of killing conjures up a memory of the most terrifying four seconds of my life.

One "instrument of repentance" that I'm unable to chase from my mind is merely a rope, pulley and a pair of twenty-pound weights. A heretic, or someone suspected of being a heretic, or someone named by a suspected heretic while in the hands of an inquisitor, would have the rope tied to his wrists and the weights attached to his ankles. Using the pulley, two burly men in black masks would hoist him up to the twenty-foot-high ceiling. The prisoner was dropped ten feet, whereupon the masked men would catch the rope. The jarring stop dislocated wrists, shoulders, knees and ankles. The inquisitor was attempting to pull the truth from the heretic's body.

The prisoner might be dropped and caught after a fall of two feet, thereby dispensing less pain, but inflicting profound psychological agony. Or the prisoner might be dropped and caught just short of the floor. Sometimes the prisoner's hands were tied behind his back, and he'd be lifted by his wrists, then dropped and caught, thereby ripping his shoulder blades away from the connective tissue in his back.

After several of these sessions, the victim's ligaments and muscles would be irreparably stretched or torn. A heretic who had not yet repented would then be relajado – "relaxed" – at the stake. As the prisoner had permanently lost all ability to walk or raise an arm, death by burning was a welcome reprieve.

We stand mutely outside the museum, attempting to process the methodical malevolence with which the Inquisition operated. Fiona is especially staggered by its horrors; the muscles in her face have gone slack, her lifeless grey eyes are half covered by drooping lids.

An old woman shuffles up to us with a handful of combs. "Special deal."

The crush of people on the sidewalk brings us to, and Barry suggests we get a bite. He picks out a nearby restaurant from his guide book and points diagonally across the street. We follow his finger, dodging cars and pedestrians. We arrive at a nondescript cafe five harried minutes later.

As soon as we've ordered, Cole starts in: "Has there ever been an uglier chapter in human history? And all in God's name. But Christians are brilliant; you place yourselves number two in God's world order, Jesus' faves, so you have all the benefits and power, but no matter how barbaric things get, you can claim you were 'Just following orders. Hey, I was only the hired help.' "

Barry is ready for him. "The Inquisition was perpetrated in the name of God, I'll grant you that, but certainly not our Christian God. It was carried out by Catholics."

"Oh, come on! Catholics read your Bible, pray to your god, and they hung people up by their nuts."

"Catholics don't understand the Bible's message."

"And let me guess: You do."

Fiona is about to say something, but Barry cuts her off. "Yes, I do. The Word is there for all to understand."

Gracie is more conciliatory. "You can't blame all that savagery on the Bible, husband. Torture has been around forever. The world was more savage back then. Christianity has evolved."

"Yes, it has, because of advances in science."

Barry replies, "But if you worship science as your god...."

"I don't *worship* anything. Science and secular values keep religious fanatics in check."

"Secular humanists are destroying our country. They have an agenda."

"Oh? And what agenda would that be?"

"To suppress freedom. Freedom to worship Christ. Our founding fathers—"

"Believed in separation of church and state—"

"Believed in freedom *of* religion, not *from* religion. There is a war going on—"

"It's not a war. It's a debate.... a one-sided debate, because we atheists have no need to proselytize—"

"Sure, you do. You're proselytizing right now."

Gracie taps her fork against her glass, making a single "ting." It isn't loud, but it cuts through the clamor of the cafe, silencing both men. "You each have well-practiced arguments, but you don't listen to each other. It.... is.... tiresome, listening to deaf men bicker." Cole starts to speak, and Gracie threatens to ting her glass again.

I ask, "Do any of you have doubts?"

Fiona speaks for the first time. "I do. That's why I pray, for strength and understanding."

"I have doubts too," says Cole. "I'm an atheist, but if there was reason to change, I like to think I would."

"I don't have doubts," says Barry. "I know I'm right."

"So you're infallible?" I ask.

"Certainly not, but the Bible is. Fiona, now, her faith is still in its infancy—"

"Shut up, Barry." Cole's voice is ominously quiet. "You are ignorant and arrogant."

Dinner comes, we eat in silence. I ordered a butifarra, a sandwich made with pork, onions and peppers. Imagine chewing salty cardboard. Or perhaps the Inquisition has pulled the appetite from my body. I eat a few bites and set it aside.

"For anyone who doubts the existence of the devil," says Fiona, "we saw irrefutable evidence of his presence today."

Cole responds in an ultra-calm voice. "*His* presence? The devil is a *guy*? Fi, understand where these beliefs come from. A thousand years ago, if you had seen an epileptic, or a psychotic or even a sleepwalker, you'd have thought they were possessed. Why do you believe in the existence of a devil? Do you see her? Talk to her?"

"No, but I see evidence of his works.... okay, *its* works, when people turn away from God."

Barry sniffs, expressing contempt. "It's unfashionable to speak of evil these days, but that doesn't mean it doesn't exist."

Cole's eyes shuttle back and forth between Fiona and Barry. "When you die, and you're up in heaven, dining with Jesus on bacon-wrapped Bon Bons, will it bother you, knowing I'm downstairs roasting my heinie? 'Cause If I were to die today, you believe I'd go to hell."

Barry folds his arms. "I don't make the rules." The icy rigidity with which he delivers this irks Fiona, but she does not repudiate her brother's allegation.

Cole responds quietly, his voice taut, like an over-wound guitar string. "Yeah, but I'm asking if it would bother you."

"It would bother me," says Fiona. "That's why I want you to hear the Word."

"I did hear it. And I believed it, until I grew up, said good-bye to my imaginary friends, and left the church."

Barry says, "Those who left were never right with Jesus in the first place."

Cole echoes him: "Those who left were never right...." Logically, how can you argue with that?

Barry says, "I accept that people hold opinions that differ from mine, but non-Christians have an almost visceral repulsion to God's Word. Why is that?"

Cole ticks off reasons on his fingers. "Let's see, holy wars, witch-burning, impeding science; Galileo was—"

"Ancient history; what has *you* so worked up?"

"Telling five-year-olds they'll burn in hell if they don't toe the line; that's child abuse."

Barry shakes his head. "There was a reason our founding fathers included the words 'under God' in the Pledge."

All right, he's gone too far. "Actually they didn't," I say, offended. "The Pledge of Allegiance is celebrating its hundredth birthday this year. Congress didn't adopt it until fifty years ago, and 'Under God' was added in '54."

Barry snorts, "Whatever. The US is a Christian nation, but

it's turning away from not just my truth, but the Truth of the Bible."

I say, "But it's just your opinion that the Bible is true. And Nobody Knows if it is."

Cole says, "We aren't wired the same, Barry; you're able to accept things on faith." He sounds both envious and disdainful.

Though it's now Barry against the both of us, he remains undeterred. Still, he considers Cole to be his chief adversary. "But you have faith too. Atheism is your religion."

"Calling atheism a religion is like saying not collecting butterflies is a hobby." Cole smirks. "We can thank men of reason for lifting us out of the Dark Ages."

"As Martin Luther put it, 'Reason is the devil's harlot.'"

Stalemate. They can scoot their arguments around, here and there, forward and back, parry and thrust, over and over for all eternity without reaching resolution. Of course, one of them could hope the other backs himself into a corner, but that's wishful thinking.

As an engineer, Cole demands tangible evidence before committing himself to a belief. He needs to be able to stand outside and look in, and say: See? There it is.

As for Barry, those who disagree with him, or who even question him, have fallen victim to wickedness. Opposing lines of reasoning are, by their very nature, profane. Barry's theological fortress is impregnable. Sacsayhuaman is flimsy by comparison; its 400-yard-long walls might just as well have been made of cellophane. And like a latter day version of Jericho, those colossal Incan walls were revealed to be anything but impenetrable by invading Spaniards.

Though stalemated, Barry is not finished. "There are two kinds of people in the world – those who believe and those who don't." I nod.

"Close," says Cole. "There are two kinds of people – those who can believe and those who can't." I nod again.

Barry says, "Actually, there are three kinds; let's not forget those who won't believe." I'm undecided about whether to nod.

Fiona looks back and forth between Cole and me. "There are also those who want to believe." I nod.

"There's only one kind of people," insists Gracie. "Those

who want to belong."

I nod one last time, whereas Cole, Fiona and Barry hang their heads and stare at their untouched plates. It seems odd that Gracie's comment, meant to unite us, is the most divisive of all. The others don't want to come together; they don't want to budge.

Barry and Fiona walk out without saying good-bye.

"Here's what I think," says Gracie. "Religion is necessary for some – it allows us to turn off the never-ending questions: Why are we here, what am I supposed to be doing, where do we go after we die, who what where when why?"

"Well then," Cole replies peevishly, "maybe we should lobotomize everyone who shows a hint of restlessness or curiosity."

"I'm saying there needs to be a balance, hubby, between being settled and being curious. For some, having faith is like turning off a fire alarm that stabs at us constantly, and distracts us from appreciating what's right in front of us. Maybe the purpose of knowing Jesus is not to seek truth so much as it is to find peace, to quiet the restless human mind, so you can get on with living and loving and playing music and working and raising kids."

Cole says, "Maybe so. But still, I wish I'd have said, 'Look how Christians acted when they had the law on their side,' and—"

She places a finger on his lips. "Nobody gets converted, or unconverted, because they lose an argument. You Scorpios are so stubborn."

Until that last sentence, she had Cole's attention, but now he scoots his chair back, hangs his head and shakes it.

Gracie sizes me up. "What sign are you, Theo?"

"What would you guess?"

"Definitely a water sign. You adapt well to new situations, so I'd say you're a Pisces."

"When is that?"

"Late February to the third week in April."

"Sorry, my birthday is—"

"Lemme try again. You're a water sign, for sure, so that means either Aries or Scorpio."

"October 21st," I say. "So that makes me a what?"

"Gemini, an earth sign." She frowns. "Ohhhhh, I see! That's only two days away from Scorpio, which is close enough to influence you. You're on the cusp."

"Why do you believe in astrology?"

"I had my chart done five years ago, and it nailed me. Why do you not believe?"

"I don't know much about it, but I've got two concerns. First, forecasts are often vague enough to describe anybody, like: You're outgoing, but you value your privacy. And second, people use astrology to excuse bad behavior, like—"

"Lemme guess; when I said we were late because I'm a Pisces."

"I wasn't going to say that, but, yeah, that's the idea."

"We're not in control as much as we'd like to think."

"Are you saying that you couldn't decide to be on time?"

She doesn't answer right away. "I get what you're saying. I use astrology as a crutch sometimes. But astrology works. It fits. I didn't nail your sign, exactly, but I was close."

Close? You call that close? That's like saying the US and Peru are close because the US borders Mexico, and Mexicans and Peruvians speak Spanish.

Cole lifts his head. "I wish I'd have said—"

Gracie throws up her hands. "Turn it off! Your sparring partner leaves, so you bring the fight inside your head and start it up again. You put up walls too." She takes his hand. "Hubba-hubby, we're all in this together, doing the best we can. Life is scary, and if a god offers comfort, then let us be." She sings, "When you wanna win, you lose your love again."

"That's beautiful," I say. "What song is that?"

She blushes. "Oh, it's just something I made up."

Cole takes her hand. "See why I married her, pally?" They kiss and she gives him a lascivious leer.

He responds with an almost imperceptible nod and says, "Theo, we're heading back to the hotel."

"Right-o."

"But drop by later on – it's only a few blocks away. We can get dinner, stir up some trouble."

"Not tonight. I need to sleep another forty hours. How about tomorrow?"

Cole defers to Gracie, who says, "Sounds good."

"C'mon, pally. We'll show you where we're staying."

On the way to their hotel, Cole asks me, "You know what a palindrome is? Like 'radar' or 'Madam, I'm Adam.' They read the same forward or backward. Crampy Q showed Fi and me a few palindromes when we were young, and challenged us to come up with our own. The best one I ever came up with was: Live not on evil. And Fiona invented: Devil never even lived." Cole gives me a weary smile. "Funny, huh?"

We round a corner, and Cole nearly smacks foreheads with a soldier. I've gotten used to seeing Peruvian military personnel with machine guns, but this guy has his finger on the trigger. He's immediately joined by a fellow soldier, who raises his rifle and barks at us in Spanish.

Raising his hands, Cole stutters, "Pony la pistol in me car!"

Gracie, her face a chalky hue, elbows her way in front of him. "Por favor, no ponies la pistola machina in mi cara!"

I toss in another "por favor" for good measure.

It's at this moment we notice the yellow tape around a bank building that has an entire wall blown away. Compliments of the Shining Path guerillas, no doubt.

The first soldier yells, "Vamanos!"

Stepping over the rubble, we hustle away, but as soon as we're out of the soldiers' earshot, I can't resist: "There's a pony with a gun in my car?"

Gracie cracks up and pounds her husband on his chest. "Last time I'm gonna teach *you* anything!"

Cole regards her imperiously. "A student is no better or worse than his teacher."

Chapter 11: Band o' Leer

At eight o'clock the next evening, I find Cole reading a book in the lobby of his hotel. "Don't tell me," I say. "A gift from Graham McHugh?"

"Yep." He holds up <u>The Metamorphosis</u> by Kafka. "What a bizarro story. This guy wakes up one morning as a giant insect. And so far it's not clear if it happened randomly, or if he chose to become a bug, or if he's been a bug all along and is just now realizing it, or if he's a bug in the eyes of his family."

"Wow! That's wild. Hey, where is everybody?"

"Waiting in the bar."

"Is Fiona speaking to you?"

"Huh? Ohhhh, you thought she was upset with *me*? Okay, she was, but mostly she was bothered by Barry's whole 'I don't make the rules' bit. They have different visions of Christianity – Love versus The Law." Cole stands and leads me into the hotel lounge, where a band is playing "Hotel California." The audience is a roughly equal mix of Peruvians and, judging by their height and pale skin, Americans or Europeans. Ogling the twenty-foot mirror behind the dark wood of the bar, I think: Nicer than the places Cactus Smacked Us plays.

Cole leads me to a table just off the dance floor and announces to his family, "Look what I found."

It's a relief to see Fiona. After the contentious exchange of the previous day, I've been worried she wouldn't show. Gracie suggests we catch a cab and go hear some tunes in a club, away from all these tourists, but the pace and decay of downtown Lima has sucked the life out of Fiona and Barry. There's talk around the table of turning in early, but when Band o' Leer lights into a smoky, hard-driving version of Stevie Ray Vaughn's "Cold Shot," Cole and I convince everybody into parking ourselves.

The barmaid comes by to take our orders. Barry orders a virgin piña colada, and Cole mutters, "Fitting."

"From a drummer's point of view," Fiona asks Cole, "what makes this band so good?"

He cocks his head and closes an eye. "It's that bass player. The drummer's okay, he's holdin' down the fort, but that bass is a freakin' freight train."

The last chord of "Cold Shot" fades, and the guitarist immediately plays a skanky intro to an up-tempo R & B number. People flood the dance floor. Fiona asks Barry to dance, but he declines, so she grabs Cole's wrist and says, "C'mon, brother." They're instantly swallowed in the crush of dancers.

I zero in on the bass player. He hits a few offbeat staccato notes, rest for a beat and half, then lay down an arpeggio I didn't see coming. He's a riot; he stands motionless while singing, but when the guitarist or keyboard player takes a solo, he bobs his head like a chicken at feeding time.

Cole and Fiona return, laughing. She says, "Gracie, you been teachin' this boy how to dance!"

Gracie takes his arm and drapes it across her shoulders. Affecting a snobbish air, she says, "I do what I can."

Barry asks where I'm going next. I'm pleased that Fiona leans forward to hear my answer.

"I'm flying to Quito tomorrow, then going up to Otavalo."

"Where's that?" asks Gracie. "What's the draw?"

"It's a town in northern Ecuador, with lakes and volcanoes. The outdoor market pre-dates the Incas; it pulls in farmers, artists, and craftsmen from all over. The music scene is supposed to be the best. And you guys are going to the Amazon?"

"Correct," says Barry. "We're flying to Quito in the morning. On Tuesday we're off to the jungle."

"Oh man, I'm jealous."

"We'd invite you along," says Barry, "but the lodge is booked up." He does not sound displeased.

Gracie says, "They had travel brochures in the lobby. I found one from the company we're using." She digs through her purse and pulls out a folded-up leaflet featuring a jungle scene, over which is printed: You Won't Come Back....

The others have apparently not seen the brochure. Their reactions are varied:

Barry: "Sounds ominous."

Cole: "No, I read it as: We won't come back from the jungle; we'll want to stay there."

Fiona: "I take it to mean you'll never go back there; this is a once-in-a-lifetime trip."

Gracie clasps her hands and cries, "Bravo! They mean it in a different way, but your interpretations are just as good." She opens the brochure, where it reads: ....the same.

"See?" she says. "You won't come back the same." She reaches over and taps me on the arm. "Hey, there's a place outside Quito called Mitad Del Mundo, which means...." We finish in unison, "....the Middle of the World."

"Yeah," I say. "They've got a planetarium and museum on the equator. Let's meet up."

"How about noon, day after tomorrow?" says Cole.

Gracie says, "Better make it 11:30. We want to make sure we're on the equator at noon."

When Band o' Leer takes a break, she approaches the stage and returns with the band in tow. We shift our chairs to make room, and Cole buys a pitcher of beer. The drummer, a jovial Peruvian, makes a point of shaking everyone's hand. The keyboard player is a rail-thin Englishman who keeps to himself. Reed, the guitarist, sits across from me. An American with shades and a long dark mane, he does most of the talking.

The bass player plops down next to me. Also an American, he sports a patch of pubic fuzz on his chin. I tell him I like his playing, but he's pretty stand-offish until I say, "You know, the bass line on 'Hotel California' sounds like reggae."

He perks up, as if noticing me for the first time. "Yeah, ya don't often say 'reggae' and 'The Eagles' in the same breath, but.... yeah."

"Not much of a melody, but great lyrics, killer guitar."

"Parker," he says, extending a hand. "What was your name again?"

"Theo."

"You play in a band?"

"Yeah, guitar. We play skuzzy bars."

The waitress brings our drinks, and as she's offloading the last mai tai, she gets jostled by a passerby, causing her to dump the drink. The glass shatters on the corner of the table.

"Ow! Dammit!" Reed clenches his hand. When he opens it, a globule of blood balloons up at the tip of his ring finger.

The waitress hands him a napkin. "Lo siento!"

Reed wraps the cloth around his finger. He pulls it away, and the blood wells up again. He wiggles the finger, then winces. "Ow! Sorry, Parker, it's my left hand. I'm done for the night."

"It's okay. You need stitches?"

"Nah."

"You sure?" says Barry. "I'd be happy to call a cab."

"I'm a nurse," says Fiona. "Well, I just graduated. Let me see." She pries Reed's right hand off the wound. "No, you won't need stitches, but there's a sliver of glass in there. Hold still...." Reed grimaces while she squeezes his finger. "Got it. We need to put a bandage on it." She digs around in her purse and pulls out a band-aid.

Cole reaches for her purse. "Anything to eat in here?"

She slaps his hand away. "Stay outta there, you gorilla." While applying the band-aid, she tells Reed, "If this soaks through, I'll take you to the front desk and ask for something heavy duty."

Reed thanks her and looks around the bar. "Our contract tonight is for a four-piece. You guys could pull it off as a trio, no prob, but you know Two Cent Jacinto – he'd do anything to get out of payin' us."

"Ah, bloody 'ell," grouses the keyboard player, no pun apparently intended.

I lean toward Fiona and say, "Bloody 'ell, this is no time for one of your safety blitzes!"

She cracks up, spraying mai tai out of her nose. "I'm gonna safety blitz *you*!"

"What are we gonna do?" asks Reed.

Parker scans the bar; his eyes come to rest on me. "Theo here plays guitar." His bandmates look me up and down.

"Ya any good?" asks the Englishman.

"Not as good as Reed, but I know how to fit in. I wouldn't get in your way, and I learn quick." All true. I have a solid grasp of music theory, but my playing often sounds mechanical.

"Back in a sec." Parker walks away.

"Will Two Cent go for it?" asks the Englishman. "Theo doesn't look like Reed."

Reed gives me a sheepish grin. "Don't tell anybody, but I'm, uh, wearing a rug. You can borrow it if you want."

Parker returns and slides a song list across the table at me. "You know any of these?"

"Let's see, 'Losing my Religion', that's in A minor, right? And I know some of these Beatles tunes." We come up with a list of a dozen songs, more than enough to get us through the next set.

Reed says, "I need a diversion."

Without hesitation, Gracie grabs Cole and hauls him out to the middle of the dance floor, where they begin swing dancing. For good measure she starts singing "Blue Moon." The bar goes nuts; people clap and shout along.

Reed tells me, "Down we go." He and I slide our chairs back and duck under the table, where he removes his wig and presses it onto my head. Snickering, we swap shirts, then crawl past one another. I squirm up into Reed's chair, while smoothing out his black silk shirt.

Fiona straightens my wig. "Nice. Axl Rose meets Llove the Llama."

Reed, now sporting a military do and a receding hairline, slides his sunglasses across the table at me. "Better wear these, dude. You got some serious brows."

Parker says, "I don't know, Theo. You're not as ugly as Reed." He checks his watch. "Time to play."

Fiona frowns at me. "This won't do; I can't see your llama ears. How will I know which songs you like?"

"Hopefully you'll love 'em all." I cross the dance floor, hop up on stage, turn on Reed's amp and strap on his black Les Paul. With the volume turned down, I play a blues lick. The strings are a lighter gauge than I'm used to, but my fingers will adjust. I test out his foot pedals – the distortion box and delay will come in handy.

We open with Bob Seger's "Old Time Rock 'n' Roll," a three-chord ditty with no surprises. I suspect they chose it to see if I can play at all. Or maybe they wanted to give me a chance to get used to Reed's gear. In any case, we all start and end together.

"Okay, this'll fly," says Parker, relieved. "Let's do a blues shuffle in A. I'll sing two verses, Theo, take a solo, then.... Aw, we'll figure it out." The Englishman bangs out a standard intro and the rest of us jump in. Parker sings:

> I was born in Lima
> Lord, I never had it soft
> Born in Lima
> No, I never had it soft
> Baby brought my Mai Tai
> Damn near cut my finger off

I look over at my friends' table, where Reed is about to bust a gut. Parker sings the next verse with some grit in his voice.

> I woke up dis mornin'
> I was feelin' just fine
> Woke up dis mornin'
> You know I's feelin' jis fine
> Count to ten on m'fingers
> Now I only get ta nine

Without cracking a smile, he nods at me. I stomp on the distortion box to give me some volume, sustain and a touch of nasty. Still feeling my way with Reed's guitar and amp, I stick to pretty basic riffs. These guys are good enough that I don't need to do anything flashy. I am simply the icing on a very tasty cake. Being their sideman suits me fine.

The Englishman takes a solo, twice around, then Parker sings a third verse:

> Ya took yo' ring off my finger
> I ain't jis talkin' smack
> Took yo' ring off my finger
> No, I ain't jis talkin' smack
> Dropped yo' ring in yo' pocket
> And ya gave my finger back

Grinning broadly, he signals me to take another solo, after which he sings the first verse over and the Englishman brings the song to a close. Cole and Gracie yell their approval over the crowd's applause.

Six songs later, Parker gives me a nod, and I play the

opening to "Losing My Religion." I like REM's version, but Band o' Leer gives it a kick in the ass. The drummer's snare has a nice sharp attack, and Parker leans into his bass line. At the end of the second chorus, he signals me to take a solo as he steps away from his mic.

Cactus Smacked Us didn't always play in sync, whether tempo-wise, groove-wise, or whatever-wise. It often felt as if we were "pushing the river," whereas Band o' Leer moves as one. They've opened a door for me, and I shoot through it, swept away by the exhilaration that comes with soloing. And I'll be damned! Under Reed's wig, my ears extend up and out and back! We're getting on just fine, until Cole and Fiona get up to dance, which brings to mind something Slider once told me: Women can't dance well until they've had sex. Good sex.

Well, either my cousin's adage about sex and dancing is all wrong, or Fiona has been faking her virginity. Good God, she can move! She apparently has joints in her hips that I lack, and she's got more rhythm in her neck than I do in my entire body.

Parker shoots me a where-the-hell-are-you look.

Focus, Theo.

As the song ends, Gracie bounds up to the stage. "Can you guys do 'Blue Moon?' "

We all look at each other and shrug. "Sure" seems to be the consensus.

Parker says, "Let's do it as a ballad, in E."

The drummer lays down his sticks and plays congas, giving our band a lighter, airy sound. Parker croons the melody, and I surprise him by adding a harmony on the second verse. He has apparently forgiven me for spacing out on the last song.

We take a break, the band joins us at our table, and Cole orders two pitchers of beer. Gracie and Fiona are effusive in their praise of my playing, which I deflect by asking about Reed.

Gracie replies, "His girlfriend came by and pointed out a splotch of blood on his pants. She took him somewhere to wash up. They were pretty lovey-dovey; I wouldn't count on them coming back any time soon."

Looking over the band's song list, I pick out another ten tunes to play, making note of the key for each.

Gracie peers over my shoulder, saying stuff like: "That's

my favorite!" and "Oooh, play that one!" and " 'Can't Help Falling in Love' – is that the UB40 song?"

Parker says, "Well, Elvis did it originally, but, yeah, we do a reggae version."

"You hafta do it! Hafta hafta hafta."

"Sorry, that was Reed's song."

"Cole sings it," says Fiona. "He's got an awesome voice."

The Englishman regards him skeptically. "You in a band?"

"Yeah, I play drums and sing."

"Look," I say, "he sings better than I play guitar."

Parker says, "Sorry, Band o' Leer has a rule: We never let anyone sit in unless we know 'em...." He looks at me. "Or unless we need 'em.... Ah, what the hell, Cole bought us beer."

Between songs, a man brings four shots of tequila up to the stage, proclaiming, "Cuervo gold!" We thank him and down the shots. An agreeable burn spreads through my chest.

Cole and Gracie approach my side of the stage, bowing and chanting, "We're not worthy!"

Parker invites Cole up to sing "Can't Help Falling in Love." The keyboard player begins with a loping rhythm, hitting the offbeats, creating an impression the song is twice as fast as it actually is. The drummer joins in, his snare playing the third beat of the measure – unlike most rock music where the emphasis is on the second and fourth beats – making the song sound half as fast as it is. I add a chicka-chicka rhythm, completing an overlay of tempos that creates a lazy but up-tempo feel.

Cole jumps in, exhibiting a good deal of restraint. I spot Gracie dragging Barry onto the dance floor. Like a llama being led to a slaughterhouse, he is openly appalled at this debauchery.

For the second verse Cole adds some bite to his voice, but it's still a measured performance.

We get to the second refrain, and there's Fiona, sitting alone, her eyes on me, laser-focused. She mouths, "I can't help falling in love with you."

What! Is this happening? No, no, she's just singing along.

We then come to the middle break: "Like a river flows, surely to the sea...." Cole sings it with a bluesy tinge, but his delivery is still smooth and low-key. When I add a harmony to the last line of the break, "Some things are meant to be," Cole looks at me wild-eyed and his forehead crumples up like an old t-shirt. We charge into the third verse, and he comes out a'swingin.' I realize that I've only heard him sing when he's goofing around.

Fiona and I sing the refrain to one another across the room.

Cole signals me to take a solo. Charged with a shot of adrenalin, a shot of tequila, and the intimate gaze of a luscious woman, I play a riff I've practiced a thousand times, but tonight I make Reed's guitar howl like a wounded coyote. My trills come out sweet, my vibrato frenzied. Parker grins appreciatively and adds some growl to his bass line. We're all feeding one another. The spirit has moved us; all is well with the world. When Cole repeats the first verse, I'm finally able to grasp how much he's been holding back. Man oh man!

Revelers in the crowd have been drinking steadily for hours now, and they bellow their fevered approval at song's end.

I wrap an arm roughly around Cole's neck and say, "You fucker! I didn't know you could sing like that!" He's all smiles, especially when Parker invites him to stick around to play congas.

An attractive young lady hovers off to the side of the stage, her dark eyes zeroed in on the drummer. He winks at her and asks Cole, "You want to sit in for a song or two?"

"Thanks, but I'm a lefty. It'd take too long to rearrange your kit."

I scan the room, just in time to see Fiona and Barry heading for the exit. She's looking over her shoulder as she disappears. My body sags. Well, dummy, what did you expect? A wave? A wink? An invitation up to her room? Dumb ass.

My playing now has an edge to it, raging and ragged, matching the mood in the room.

Cole, Gracie and I help the guys break down the PA system and haul it out to their van. I slip off the wig and ask Parker to return it for me.

"I'll pass it along. Thanks for bailin' us out, Theo." He takes a roll of bills out of his shirt pocket and hands it over.

"What's this?"

"Your share."

"Oh no, you don't. This was my pleasure."

"Tell ya what," says Gracie. She takes the money and puts it back in Parker's pocket. She holds up the sleeve of Reed's shirt. "Theo looks hot in silk. As his agent, I propose that he keep this shirt as payment for services rendered."

Parker nods. "Look us up next time you're in Lima." He and his bandmates pile into the van.

"Buy ya a drink, pally?" asks Cole, draping an arm across my shoulder.

"Yeah," says Gracie, "we don't have to be at the airport for another...." She twists Cole's right wrist around to look at his watch. "....three hours."

Chapter 12: One Too Many Zeroes

I lie in bed, fuzzy-headed from three "just one mores," reliving last night's adventure. That was a guitar player's dream: no rehearsal, no setting up, no hauling the damn equipment home. Just play. Play with guys who are good. Play with Cole – man, I wanna do that again. Expanding on the music-as-river metaphor, playing with Band o' Leer and Cole is not a matter of swimming with or against the current; no, it's more like shooting the rapids, holding on for dear life. There's nothing like playing to a butt-rockin' audience with Fiona in it, singing "I Can't Help Falling in Love with You." Yes, she was just singing along, and I was lip-reading across a loud, lusty barroom – I know all that – but still....

Her x-ray eyes make me feel naked.

My flight doesn't leave until two, so I wander Miraflores. It's a Saturday morning, the sidewalks are clear of generators, traffic lights are operational. The atmosphere is cleaner and quieter than it was two days ago.

A bus approaches, heading for downtown. On a lark, I jump aboard, and get off twenty minutes later at Plaza de Armas. Dominating one corner of the brick square is a statue of a well-armored Pizarro, sitting astride a horse and brandishing a sword. With technology and God on his side, he projects an air of invincibility. There is, however, a growing consensus that the statue is offensive, and should thus be moved to a less conspicuous site.

Across from the statue stands the majestic Catedral de Lima, built on the remains of an Incan temple. In 1977, workers discovered a skull in a lead box, sealed in a niche beneath the church. The box bears the inscription: Here lies the head of Francisco Pizarro.

By examining the skull and its multiple sword wounds, and by referencing portraits of the conquistador, forensic experts have determined the inscription to be accurate.

On an adjacent side of the plaza lies the imposing

Presidential Palace, referred to as The House of Pizarro. Built on Incan burial grounds, it spans the full four hundred feet of one side of the square. Pizarro chose this site in the mid-1500s for his headquarters, from which he would rule Peru. This is also where he was assassinated by supporters of Daniel de Almagro, a one-eyed conquistador and one-time associate of Pizarro. Almagro is credited with quashing the last attempt by the Incas to retake Cusco. He claimed the city as his spoils of war, thereby incurring the wrath of Pizarro, who had him summarily decapitated.

Two years after the execution of Almagro, as Pizarro lay dying from sword wounds, he cried out for Jesus, using his own blood to paint a cross on the palace floor.

After a quick lunch, I drop the bill and a pile of soles on the counter. As I'm heading out the door, the cashier calls out, "Señor!" I turn back to hear her complaint, but the only words I pick out are "No correcto." She points back and forth between my bill and the stack of money I gave her.

I recount the pile of intis. CHEEE-ses! I added one too many zeroes to the bill, giving her ten times what I owe. "Gracias, gracias, gracias...." I must have said it ten times. She laughs and shouts back to the cook. The kitchen erupts in laughter and rapid fire Spanish. I quadruple her tip and scurry out the door.

A nearby street is blocked off for the weekend market. Several stalls display well-crafted textiles and rugs. The entire inventory of one booth consists of three lamps, a casket and two guitars, one of which is well made, while the other has a warped body, which reminds me of my first guitar, a birthday present from my dad.

And it wasn't just any old off-brand. No sir, he bequeathed to me his Martin, the gold standard when it comes to acoustic guitars. It had been given to him by his father, and while Dad never played it much, he kept it on prominent display in the living room, as though it were an artfully crafted piece of furniture. When it was new, I imagine, it had been a fine instrument, sweet-toned and a joy to play, but by the time I got hold of it, the neglected Martin was sixty years old, and the arid Tucson air had not treated it kindly. The bridge had begun to pull away from the face, warping the body, which in turn increased the action, that is, the strings were too far from the fretboard to play easily. Dad could see how much difficulty I had pushing the strings down, but he was unable to hear how awful the guitar sounded, so he couldn't understand why I was not enamored of this family heirloom.

He'd tell me, "You need to practice more."

Which I did, until Mom said, "You can't make good music on a bad instrument." So for my next birthday, she agreed to get me an electric guitar of my own choosing. Before picking out an instrument, I did some research first, reading articles and pestering the salesmen at Saguaro Music, which, incidentally, is how I ended up getting a job there. I tried out Fenders, Gibsons and Epiphones, as well as a few lesser known makes. After playing dozens of instruments, I chose a Fender Stratocaster, white, with a maple neck and whammy bar. My first love.

I've moved eight times since high school, and the Martin always comes with me, but it stays in the closet. Last year I asked Slider if he could fix it. He works with me at Saguaro Music, as a guitar repairman. He picked up my guitar, turned it this way and that. Sighting down its neck, he said, "A Martin? With expired warranty? I wouldn't touch it. We'd have to cut off the bridge by melting the glue, press the top back into shape using clamps, and then apply heat to.... Nope. Sorry, dude."

I buy an Inca Kola, and pay with a ten sol bill. The vendor eyes me warily, as if I might be heading up a counterfeiting ring. I've gotten this look before; paying with anything bigger than a five sol bill is a major production. He excuses himself and bustles next door, returning two minutes later with a wad of bills and a handful of coins. He counts out my change: 9,840,000 intis.

An old man whose right knee bends backwards approaches me, cackling and mumbling through a mouthful of rotten teeth. He wobbles past on spindly legs in a side-to-side, back-and-forth corkscrew oscillation that has to be excruciating.

One stall features a photo of a redhead blessed with snow white teeth and substantial knockers. Next to her hangs a painting of Jesus, a profile shot of his haloed head, bowed, his eyes zeroed in on Red's cleavage. With his blonde ringlets and weak chin, this Son of God is a weenie. He wouldn't stand a chance with her.

I'm at the airport, waiting for my flight – my delayed flight, that is – and my thoughts drift back to Cole and Fiona. The geneses of their differing world views can be traced directly back to the death of their grandfather. Abandoned by God, Cole has become a hard-headed, good-hearted freethinker. Of course, in Fiona's eyes, he's a full-blown cynic, viewing all things religious with a jaundiced eye.

She, from that same traumatic experience, took a different road. Out of need – or desire or revelation or faith, it's difficult to say which – she came to believe that her grandfather had moved on to a better place, and she now embraces the whole of Christianity. When Fiona proclaimed, "I know there's a God," she was suggesting a more intimate rapport with The Almighty than Barry indicated with his "I know there must be a God."

At least, that's my take on their journeys. For me, the origins of belief generally hold more interest than the belief itself.

So, what about me? Why am I where I am? For that matter, where am I? If anywhere? Why, and where, am I? As Gracie pointed out that first evening at Machu Picchu, I'm good at drawing others out, but I don't show much of myself. What's there to show? If people were countries, I have been Switzerland for most of my life, eschewing battle, refusing to take sides. And that's a good thing. Isn't it? Perhaps, except that lately I've begun to understand the origins of my fence-sitting agnosticism – during those Duncan Annual Ford Trips, picking a side meant getting pummeled by a sister or two.

As for not showing much of myself....

My mother passed away in December, but I keep it to myself. Sure, some people found out through my siblings, but I didn't even tell Slider for weeks. Why? Hard to say. Was it because I was afraid I'd erupt in anger, or that I'd start crying and not stop? Or maybe I didn't want people coming up and saying, "I know how hard it is. When my mom died...."

Why did I keep quiet? Force of habit, maybe. I'm used to looking after myself.

Actually, come to think of it, I never did tell Slider. Phil came into the store one day to borrow five bucks, and he made mention of her passing. Slider is goofy, with his quasi-mystical leanings, but he's a decent soul, and when he expressed heartfelt condolences, I found myself wishing I'd told him. My cheeks had gotten sore and twitchy from acting cheerful forty hours a week.

Aeroperu announces that my flight is cancelled, no reason given. Travelers mill about, moaning and groaning, while a well-coiffed British woman leans across the check-in counter, brandishing a rigid index finger. "I demand to see your manager! And if you don't contact him now, *now*, young man, you shan't be employed here tomorrow."

A patient woman makes the rounds, telling us we can fly out tomorrow morning at seven. She hands out vouchers, saying that Aeroperu will put us up at a hotel tonight, dinner provided.

Hmmm.... seven o'clock tomorrow – that should give me time to get to my hotel in Quito and catch a bus out to Mitad del Mundo by 11:30. I take the voucher and go hail a cab.

A decrepit VW bug sputters up to the curb, and the cabbie shoves my pack into the tiny trunk. Without asking for a destination, he takes off, zigzagging through the turbulent airport traffic. The floorboard is rusted through on my side, allowing me to see the pavement zoom by beneath my feet. Fred Flintstone would feel right at home. I stretch my legs and find a little ledge under the dash to set the toes of my sneakers. We merge onto a four-lane highway that presently carries six lanes of traffic.... no, hold on, make that seven.

"Downtown, por favor," I say.

It hasn't rained here in years, but today there is enough mist to warrant use of the cab's wipers, which are apparently outfitted with the original blades. They smear years of grime across the windshield, which requires my driver to crane his neck high and low, left and right, until he finds a relatively clear spot in the glass, enabling him to dodge the cars and buses zooming by at fifty miles an hour, four feet away.

After botching the pronunciation of the hotel, I hand him my voucher and point out the hotel's address. He glances at the voucher, then at me, out the windshield, back to the voucher, and back to me again. He points at his eyes and shakes his head.

Oh, great. He's blind. We're gonna die.

"Uno momento," he says, pulling a grubby lens out of his shirt pocket. Steering with his knees, he holds the lens in one hand and my voucher in the other. Using a guess-and-check approach, he jerks his torso forward and back, while moving his lens or the voucher closer or further away, attempting to draw a bead on the address.

By this time, we're nearing downtown. I take out my map and locate my hotel, but I'm unable to read street signs through the filthy windshield. I roll down my window and stick my head out, calling directions to the cabbie: "Derecha!" Right! "Isquierda!" Left! But I have no idea how to say: Watch out for the fuckin' dump truck!

The dark wood lends elegance and heft to the hotel's foyer, lit by a grand chandelier. Is it standard practice for Aeroperu to cancel flights and then put their passengers up in swanky hotels? How do they afford it?

By the time I eat, buy postcards and return to my room, it's after eight, the end of a wasted day. I write postcards to my family, chronicling my adventures.

The card to Dad is filled with numbers: temperature in Fahrenheit and Celsius, the cost of a dinner in dollars and soles, the height of cathedrals. It's a quantitative account, exactly what he'd want.

I write Rowan, telling her of my burgeoning friendships with the Quinns and sitting in with Band o' Leer.

I tell Phil he should come to Peru, ride the trains, and "bring your camera, for sure." After signing my name, I read through his postcard and throw it away. I can't imagine him ever getting together the money or gumption to travel.

The cards to Rowan and Dad look safe enough, although I hope Ro doesn't show hers around. I can just hear Claire: "Oh right, like you can form a friendship in a week and a half. No, I take it back – Ro, how long did you know ol' what's-his-face before tyin' the knot?"

To Claire, my most adventuresome sibling, I take a shot at describing the mystery and magic of Machu Picchu. But then I read through her postcard and find myself grimacing by the end of it. Fearing she'd rip my entire adventure to shreds, I beat her to it; I tear up the card and toss it.

Machu Picchu. I'm still not sure what to make of my Ecstatic Meltdown. I'd been staring out at the ruins, lit by the kaleidoscopic sunset. Alone but not afraid, I felt happy and heartbroken and whole, even as I dissolved into a useless puddle.

Alone. I wonder how Llove the Llama is doing. I imagine him climbing a flight of stairs in late afternoon, arriving at the Watchman's Hut. He surveys the deserted ruins, hoping to spot a loved one. When the sun goes down, he realizes he's alone; his clan is gone for good. Llove considers ending it all by hurling himself off a cliff.

And now, unbidden, that elusive melody returns to me: Why, and where, did you go? To welcome it back, I sing it again and again. I allowed it to drift away when it first came to me at Machu Picchu, but it has apparently chosen to give me another chance. But now that I think about it, I vaguely remember hearing this tune on my last morning in Puno, before the muña tea brought me out of my stupor. This song has been pursuing me.

I plunk out the melody on my charango and put chords to it. I look through my journal and pick out phrases from my time at Machu Picchu. Twenty minutes later, I have a verse and chorus, complete with chords and melody.

> Hidden well, our citadel
> Where mist and mountain meet
> No sound, in a ghost town
> A single llama roams the street
>
> Silence etched in stone
> Strength I've never known
> Why and where did you go?

I play through the partial song a dozen times, messing around with alternative fingerings for the predominantly minor chords. I fill a page with phrases I'd like to work in, my favorite of which is "Mobius trails." Finally, I try out various harmony lines – I can't wait to try them out with Cole tomorrow in Quito.

It has not been a wasted day after all.

Chapter 13: Sidestep Death

It's 6:53, we're not boarding yet, and I'm getting squirmy. The area around Gate Four is filled with grumpy passengers, a few of whom I recognize from yesterday. Slouched on gray plastic seats, we share commiserative glances.

At 7:15, the woman at check-in announces that our 7:00 flight is delayed. She will let us know when she knows more. The skepticism in the air is palpable. CHEE-ses! How does Aeroperu stay in business?

At 8:11, the woman informs us that our flight will be delayed further. She remains maddeningly calm. Tempers flare. Citing the gospel of somebody, there is much "wailing and gnashing of teeth." I schedule my day: two-hour flight, twenty minutes at baggage claim, thirty minutes to a hotel, hop on a bus to Mitad del Mundo. I won't make it by 11:30, but my friends will surely stick around a while.

At 9:02, the woman thanks us for our patience, and asks us to remain seated. She doesn't appear the least bit bothered when every traveler at Gate Four leaps up and lays siege to her check-in counter. Dealing with rabid travelers is evidently an integral part of her job. An elderly man trips and gets swallowed in the crush. He is unable to rise until two soldiers with machine guns show up. Brandishing rifles and yelling, they disperse the crowd and help the feeble man to his feet. His face is not bleeding badly.

How long will the Quinns stick around? "Hijo de puta," I whisper. Son of a whore.

At 9:43, the woman announces that boarding will begin soon. She asks passengers sitting in rows forty through fifty-six to form a single line. Everyone rushes the boarding gate.

Hmm, I'll catch a cab at the airport in Quito and head directly out to Mitad del Mundo. Yeah, that'll work, as long as I have Ecuadorian money in hand. I find a currency exchange and swap soles for Ecuadorian sucres.

"Sucre," by the way, is derived from the same word as "sugar." I imagine the conversation my friends would be having:

Fiona: Money is sweet.

Barry: Yes, but with 50% inflation, not as sweet as it was last year.

Cole: But sweeter than it will be next week.

Gracie: Better spend it while we've got it.

I castigate myself for leaving Lima without a backup plan. My friends are walking the streets of Quito, and unless we lift off soon, I will have no way of contacting them. Why did I not get their addresses, or the name of their hotel? How careless.

What was it Cole said at Machu Picchu? Look, Barry, Jesus no longer exists – not in my world, he doesn't. You can't communicate with somebody that's not *here*. Jesus is gone.

And now so are Cole, Fiona, and Gracie. They no longer exist – not in my world, they don't. They are Gone – capital G – leaving me no way of tracking them down.

. Although....

When Mom passed away, she went quickly, or so we were told. Still, it's been a devastating time for my family. Mom was here one day, gone the next. How do we possibly make sense of that? I have no idea, which is why The Endless Debate is of interest to me; the matter of what happens after we're gone is no longer merely an intellectual exercise. If anybody has a fresh perspective on this, I am dyin' to hear it.

Because Mom's body was never found, we held a memorial for her, at which Pastor Pete referred to her *passing*, a term that bewilders me. Webster's dictionary offers 38 distinct definitions for the word "pass" – it can mean damn near anything you want.

The only good to come from Mom's passing is that Ro and Claire were finally able to resolve a longstanding dispute regarding our parents. My sisters and I went out drinking four years ago, on my twenty-first birthday, and they began comparing childhood memories. Claire claimed that Dad used to come home late after drunken binges: "Don't you remember all those tearful Friday nights with Mom, wondering where the old boozer was, and who he was with?" Ro insisted that was nonsense: "Dad would never do that! They don't make 'em like him anymore." Being much younger than my sisters, I had nothing to add. As far back as I could remember, Dad was home at night. Claire maintained that by the time I came along, his midlife crisis had run its pathetic course. Their dispute was ongoing, with zero chance of being resolved. Claire's sordid memories could be neither verified nor dispelled. I mean, how would we go about broaching this issue?

Dad, question: Did you used to whore around on Mom?

And remember, we would have been asking this in sign language. Mom was Gone – capital G – leaving us no way to track down the truth regarding Dad's alleged infidelity.

Yet there we were, a month after Mom's memorial, going through her stuff, and we came across her diary from when I was a toddler. None of us knew about it, not even Dad. Most of her entries were mind-numbingly boring, but sandwiched between a trip to Safeway and a late night thunderstorm, there it was: an account of being holed up in her room one tearful Friday evening. Dad had gone to a lip-reading class and, being a prideful man, he asked Mom not to tell us kids. So Claire was correct in saying that Dad went out Friday evenings, but dead wrong about where he'd gone. According to the diary, my mother was grieving for her husband's disability, not for herself.

As for the prospect of tracking down my friends in Quito, however, there would be no stumbled-upon diary. Maybe I could call information when I get home.

Home. Tucson. Are those places still one and the same?

At 10:10, people begin boarding. Goddammit! Would you hurry it up? "Hijo de puta!" The soldiers with rifles notice that I'm no longer whispering.

By 10:53, everyone is aboard, and the pilot comes on to assure us we'll be leaving soon. I recalculate every few minutes, coming to the same bitter conclusion each time: My friends are on the bus right *now*, and they will leave Mitad del Mundo after a few hours, thinking I blew them off. I search my guide book, again, hoping to find an obvious tourist destination that would draw my friends. But Quito is full of cathedrals, monuments, museums and parks; I could search for weeks and not find them.

At a quarter to noon, we back out from the gate and get in line to take off.

Quito, the capitol of Ecuador, lies in a valley surrounded by Andean volcanoes. My hotel window boasts a stunning view of Cotopaxi, its nearly symmetrical cone covered by one of the world's few equatorial glaciers. Birthed by fire, buried in ice.

By the time I settle in, it's late afternoon, leaving me time for a quick hike around town. Still furious at Aeroperu for screwing up my rendezvous, I take off on foot, stomping toward the historic district, where the city's main attractions are located. It's a long shot that I'll get lucky and run into the Quinns, but, hey, it happened at Machu Picchu. I find myself wishing I shared Gracie's no-accidents outlook.

I reach for my camera to get a picture of the street sign over Avenida John F. Kennedy, but then remember I'm out of film, courtesy of sticky-fingered baggage handlers at Aeroperu. Hijo de puta! I pass a video rental store that features action movies starring the likes of Steven Seagal and Chuck Norris – there's not an Oscar winner in the bunch. In the expansive Parque El Ejido, I watch a group of men play bocce ball. Incorporating elements of bowling and marbles, the game involves tossing grapefruit-sized steel balls down a narrow dirt court. The rules are beyond me.

This being Sunday, all government buildings, most museums and many stores are closed. I stop at a sidewalk cafe where entrees range in price from 3000 to 5000 sucres. I order a steak, medium well, which, at 1400 sucres to the dollar, will cost about three bucks.

Four soldiers with rifles march by. I avoid their eyes.

Two leggy brunettes sashay past, wearing long dark skirts that sway back and forth hypnotically. They are followed by a young man playing a pan flute, a Pied Piper scenario in reverse.

My dinner arrives, a lamb-and-tomato dish that looks nasty and raw. Apparently I don't read Spanish as well as I thought. I manage to hack off a bite of meat – or maybe a ligament – then I tenderize it with my molars and swallow it whole. The waiter goes inside, and I slip the gelatinous lamb to a teenage beggar hovering nearby. When the waiter returns, he's confused by my empty plate, but pleased when I order a different dinner.

"Bueno, si?" he asks proudly.

"Yum."

The waiter spots the beggar and flaps his apron at him. The boy taunts him with a goopy grin, and the man responds by clapping his hands at the boy, while chiding him for harassing his customer. The kid chuckles and ambles away, gnawing off a hunk of gristle.

A self-assured señorita with wavy black hair stops and asks me for the time. I fumble with "a quarter to five" in Spanish, and hold up my watch. She grabs my hand to get a look at the digital display and turns her dark, perky eyes on me. We try to get a conversation going, but neither of us speaks enough of the other's language to make it fly.

The waiter brings my second dinner, beef and banana soup, which is twice as unsavory as it sounds. Stick to the trout from now on. While I slurp my dinner, an old woman in a tattered dress shuffles by, scraping along the rutted sidewalk like a receding glacier, stopping every few seconds to hock a loogie in a pothole.

CHEEE-ses!

That word calls to mind Cole's half-assed attempt to honor Fiona's wish that he refrain from speaking Jesus' name in vain. Her request would have seemed downright indulgent to the ancient Hebrews, who issued an injunction against speaking God's name at all. Saying His name demeaned His existence and bastardized His nature. They believed that the reality of God – as opposed to humans' feeble understanding of such – transcends language, and thus Moses, speaking as God's emissary, decreed that blasphemers be stoned to death. Because ancient Hebrew was written with vowels omitted, we're not exactly sure how they would have pronounced YHWH, the name of their god, but we know Its spelling has evolved, or devolved, to "Yahweh," nicknamed "Yah," and later translated as "Jehovah."

The King James Version of the Bible, by the way, translates "Jehovah" as "I am that I am," a tautology, thought to mean that, unlike the rest of us, there is a reason for God to exist, that is, He is a necessary being. How would that line of reasoning sit with Cole? I can just imagine his reply:

Necessary? As in *needed*? No, what we need is music. Hot music. And love. Yeah, All You Need is Love, pally.

A backpacker trudges up the sidewalk, rousing me from my reverie. He's American; the Nikes and Grateful Dead t-shirt give him away. He notices me, I suspect, but he doesn't acknowledge my presence. I've noticed this before; we travelers didn't come all this way to hang out with compatriots, so we often ignore one another, even as we're advertising American brands. Then again, maybe he's ignoring me because of my sour vibe.

His Dead t-shirt sports a skeleton adorned with a crown of blood red roses. The hollow eyes look past me, as if I don't exist. That smirking skull elicits a vision of Death, as personified in low budget movies:

The Grim Reaper lurks in a dark corner, brandishing a scythe, cowl pulled forward over his eyes. Wearing a malevolent grin, he singles you out with a long, bony finger, to let you know your time's up; the party's over. But hold on; that's not how He operates in real life, or in real death, I should say. No, the Reaper drags you out the door, kicking and screaming, and He allows the party to go on without you. Of course, if you're a Hindu, you get to go to another party; you'll even do a bit of party-hopping. Heck, you might do a lot of it. And if you're a Christian, you get invited to a way better party, with harps and Jesus and glory and stuff. But God must hold a special fondness for Muslims, because He throws them the most excellent party imaginable, set in an idyllic garden, through which flow rivers of milk and wine and honey – these are three separate rivers, mind you – while men are provided their fair share of servants and frisky virgins.

Cole dismisses these rosy visions of an afterlife. He theorizes four reasons why people believe in God: fear of death; fear of life; blind acceptance of parents' beliefs; and seeing beauty and order in the world. To this list I'd add loneliness, by which I don't mean the neglected feeling you get from sitting home Friday night, or even the disconcerting realization that I'm four thousand miles from Tucson, unmoored, with no desire to go home.

No, I am talking about the desolation that descends upon us following the loss of a loved one. Sure, families pull together in times of despair; even my sibs treated one another in a civil manner, offering consolation, sharing memories. But their good will dried up in a matter of days, as their darker natures insisted on having their say:

Claire: I'm taking bets on which Duncan is next to go.

Me: You're not really helping.

Rowan: We never found Mom's body. Maybe she's still alive.

Claire: Yeah, and maybe you're an ass cactus.

Phil: Can somebody borrow me ten bucks?

In sign language, Dad said, "I can't believe she's gone," a cliché if ever I've heard one. But seeing it signed, rather than hearing it, provided me a fresh look at it. Dad was literally unable to accept the fact that he would never see his wife again. Oh, he'd get glimpses of a future without her, but two weeks after her memorial, he was still beginning sentences with things like: "When Helen gets home...." Then he'd catch himself, and the poor man would bury his face in his hands and weep.

To which Claire responded on one occasion, "He says he believes Mom's waiting for him in heaven, but he sure as hell don't act like it." She said this aloud, in front of my deaf dad.

It must be a comfort to believe – I mean really believe – in a god who is given to neither fault nor frailty, who has the capability to sidestep Death, who offers love for all eternity and beyond. The desire to fall for such a divine being is seductive. I mean, who wants to be an atheist, if it means you must buy into the idea that dead people are.... well, Dead? How do we wrap our minds around the possibility – or the likelihood – that this big, wondrous, awful world is devoid of meaning, lacking in design, with no end game worked up?

Does there exist a God of Loneliness? Maybe it's more apt to think of Loneliness as a demon, a duplicitous character who prefers to conduct his pitiable business out of the mind's spotlight, skulking around backstage, keeping to the shadows so as to remain unnoticed. Loneliness burrows into the marrow of our bones, and most of us refuse to acknowledge His presence until disaster strikes; in my case, until my mother passed away. Otherwise we're pretty good – aw hell, we're masters – at keeping the demon at bay. We treat our musings about death as fodder for jokes, and philosophy gets relegated to the interesting-but-pointless file.

Nothing to fear but fear itself, my ass. What about the fear – my fear – that the forces of nature are indifferent to human desires? I'm no expert when it comes to the laws of physics, but who would dispute their icy impartiality? Gravity dispenses no exemptions; if you hurl yourself off a cliff, you're a goner. End of story. Equations don't give a rip about our need to be.... to be.... to belong, is how Gracie would put it.

We long to belong.

Wellll, listen to me. How'd I get started on all this? That's easy – a backpacker with a Grateful Dead t-shirt happened to walk by, which got me thinking about the Grim Reaper and Loneliness and Mom's passing. Of course, Gracie would say the backpacker didn't just *happen* to walk by. He did so for a purpose, to make me pay attention to spiritual matters. She'd say the t-shirt was a catalyst for my growth. Really? Funny, I don't seem any bigger.

Had Gracie been here, she might have safety blitzed me.

The old woman turns around, and totters back down the sidewalk, her clogged windpipe sounding like a rusty cement mixer. Let's hope she doesn't drown in her own bodily fluids.

The woman, the backpacker, the skeleton, me – we're all out of place, though not out of time. Not yet anyway. Okay, maybe the skeleton is, but for the rest of us, it's our awareness that our time here is limited that lies at the root of our loneliness. And few of us – not me, certainly – have the guts to face it straight on.

Not so, Barry might say. Most of us do face our loneliness, by reading the Bible. And Christian ministers address these issues every Sunday morning, with clarity and compassion, for those brave enough to listen.

Not so fast, Cole might reply. A minister offers up answers for his compliant flock, sure, but they tend to be easy answers, profound in tone, childish in content, verbal sedatives administered in hopes of quelling our curiosity and restlessness.

Barry and Cole would then go back and forth like that, slingin' custard pies at one another, without a prayer of resolving their differences. Do they feel lonely around each other?

Lonely. I'm lonely. Sitting at this cafe, I have to wonder if I'm reading too much into all of this. It's simpler – and perhaps more fitting – to believe my loneliness stems from being out of place, a stranger in a strange country, lost.

Aw, quit yer bitchin', Theo. This has been a great trip – meeting the Quinns and Professor Plum, sitting in with Band 'o Leer, and Machu Picchu was beautiful and powerful and....

The congested old woman is beside me now. She stops to discharge a particularly viscous mass, bending over as she does so, to increase the odds of clearing her belly. She does not succeed.

I drop my spoon and push myself back from the table.

CHEEEEE-ses!

Chapter 14: The Source of All

I awaken, feeling like I've been gutted with the jawbone of a llama. I miss my friends. I miss Fiona. Her last words were mouthed to me: "I can't help falling in love with you." Will I ever meet someone like her again? She's one in a million. No, not true; I've seen the population stats for Quito – Fiona is one in 1.1 million. It's not fair. Then again, life isn't fair. Death, on the other hand, is. Or at least it's equally unfair to all.

Aw, save your breath, Theo, it serves you right. Save and Serve – it sounds like the name of a thrift store.

During breakfast at a nearby cafe, I pick up an abandoned newspaper off the next table. I'm able to decipher roughly two out of every three words, which allows me to flesh out the rest of a story by context. On the front page are photos of a mudslide in a nearby village, in a region known to be seismically active. According to the accompanying story, rainfall has been particularly heavy around Quito, and a hillside collapsed, burying houses, cars and people.

Also on the front page is an article about the US democratic primaries. As was expected, Arkansas Governor Bill Clinton won nearly all of the Super Tuesday primaries last week.

Page two features a story about an international oil consortium's plan to hightail it out of Ecuador. After drilling in the Amazon for thirty years, a multi-billion-dollar class action lawsuit was filed against the company for not cleaning up their lakes of sludge and toxic waste. A spokesman for the oil giant not only claims that they did clean up their drilling sites, but he says they have documentation from federal regulators who signed off on their efforts. As for reports of unusually high rates of cancer in communities located downstream from their sites, the spokesman blames the increasingly common practice of dumping raw sewage into waterways.

I open to the business section and fumble through an article about inflation. Here's the basic gist: Ecuador's rate of inflation is holding steady at fifty percent, so the sucre will likely be devalued, again, at the end of the week. Today is Lunes, Monday. So by Friday, the exchange rate will probably be....

Hold on. Today is Monday. I planned to meet my friends yesterday, on Sunday, when many places are closed. Irrationally hopeful, I rifle through my beat-up guide book. And there it is: Mitad Del Mundo is closed Sundays! So, what would my buddies do then? Wouldn't they go back out there on Monday at 11:30? Of course they would. That makes sense. Well, doesn't it?

It's now a quarter past ten – plenty of time. I gobble up the rest of my omeletta and toast, while reading directions on how to get to the Middle of the World. I leave 4,000 sucres on the table and dash out.

I run the half mile to the bus station, stopping once to buy film. I arrive out of breath, and two minutes later, I board an already packed bus and stand in the aisle. There's a hand on my wallet and I whip around to nab the little thief who's pawing my butt. Everyone stares straight ahead, poker-faced.

Did I imagine the hand on my pocket? There's a lot of jostling going on, and it's a tottery old bus. Maybe there's nothing to it. But I untuck my shirt anyway, letting it fall over my jeans.

Not surprisingly, Ecuador straddles the equator. Thus, over the course of a year, there is never more than a two-minute variation in the length of daylight. The sun traces a tidy east-to-west arc across the sky.

I arrive at Mitad del Mundo just after eleven. Equal parts museum, monument, geographical marker and tourist attraction, the Middle of the World features a bright yellow line painted across a brick plaza, purporting to be the equator.

My friends are nowhere in sight, but it's early yet. I check the outdoor tables of the restaurant, to no avail, then head over to the museum, which features exhibitions of the various tribes of Ecuador. The displays are well done, but my heart isn't in it. I exit the museum and give the grounds a once-over. My watch says 11:32. Oh well, it was worth a shot.

Did they leave me a message? Where would they have put it? On this obelisk? I walk around the monolith, looking for cracks where a note might be slipped in. No such luck. Would they have left it with someone who works here? No, this whole place was closed yesterday.

My friends are Gone – capital G.

I straddle the yellow line, a position of neutrality, abiding neither hemisphere. I take out my camera and look around for someone to take my picture. Five Americans are speaking with an Ecuadorean woman who's filling an oblong metal basin with a hose. They're occupied, so I place my camera on the ground, propping up the front with a wad of intis. I hit the six-second timer and scurry back to my impartial spot on the equator. One second before the camera clicks, a riotous chorus of voices calls out, "Blue muña!"

My shoulders slump; I sigh in relief. Gracie skips across the plaza and flings herself at me. I catch her in my arms and spin her around. Cole smothers me in a comradely hug. Fiona greets me with an awkward, one-armed embrace-from-the-side and a smile that's both comforting and discombobulating.

Barry picks up my camera and hands it to me. "We came out here yesterday, not knowing it was closed."

"We were afraid you ditched us, pally." Gracie whacks him on his shoulder. "Ooooh," says Cole, "do that again."

"My flight got cancelled."

Fiona says, "We know. When you didn't show yesterday, I called Aeroperu, but they wouldn't tell us your new flight number. Cole even took a cab out to the airport to look for you."

"I thought...." My voice catches in my throat. ".... I was never going to see you again." It takes every bit of will power not to look at Fiona when I say that.

The Ecuadorian woman breaks in, announcing that she's about to demonstrate the Coriolis Effect, and everyone is welcome to watch for a thousand sucres, about seventy cents. I hand her five thousand sucres.

Her basin of water sits on a four-legged metal stand. The half-full basin has a rubber plug in the bottom. She sets a ten-gallon plastic bucket on the ground, beneath the drain hole.

She explains, "Hurricanes blow counter-clockwise in the northern hemisphere and clockwise in the south. This is due to the Coriolis Effect, which involves centrifugal force and angular momentum. The same thing holds true for sinks and toilets. Now, what should happen on the equator?"

Gracie answers, "The water should go straight down, especially since we're close to the equinox. It's all about balance."

The woman nods, and advises us to get our cameras ready. She reaches into the water and pulls the plug, taking care to lift it straight up. Sure enough, the water drains straight down, no swirl at all. It looks stranger than I'd have thought.

Calling out, "Follow me!" the Coriolis woman hauls the basin thirty yards north.

Cole maintains that thirty yards could not possibly make a difference. Barry, carrying the woman's water bucket, agrees.

The woman plugs the drain and empties the bucket into the basin. She pulls the plug straight up, just as she did the first time, and voila! The water begins swirling counter-clockwise. Cole and I frown and scratch our heads.

Fiona pokes him in the side. "Not possible, huh?"

Calling out, "Follow me!" the Coriolis woman hauls the basin thirty yards south of the yellow line. Barry carries the bucket again. Cole shakes his head in consternation.

The woman fills the basin and pulls the plug, just as she did before. And now the water swirls clockwise. The woman thanks us and takes her leave, after which my friends and I offer up opinions about the demonstration:

Barry: "Somethin's fishy here...."

Me: "Agreed."

Fiona: "But you saw it with your own eyes. How can you argue with science?"

Gracie: "That was dudical!"

Cole stands silently, arms folded, eyes closed, nose turned up in distaste. Eventually he says, "Let's run the experiment ourselves." He leads us to a men's room fifty yards north. He enters and announces, "All clear."

He plugs the sink and fills it with water, then takes great care to pull the plug straight up. Sure enough, the water doesn't swirl at all; it drains straight down. But when the sink has emptied halfway, the water begins to swirl clockwise.

Fiona furrows her brow. "It should spin the other way."

I say, "The drain is not in the center of the basin. It's cock-eyed. Maybe that affects it."

"Or maybe the whole theory is cock-eyed," says Barry.

"Do it again," insists Fiona. This time the whirlpool rotates clockwise.

"Maybe we need to place the sink in a wind tunnel," says Barry, referring to Cole's job at Boeing. He's rewarded with hearty laughter. Though it's good to see them getting along, I am envious of Barry's assimilation into the Quinn family.

The third time, when the water begins to swirl counterclockwise, Cole dips three fingers in and rotates them clockwise, thereby changing the direction of the swirl. The fourth time, I dip a single finger in and push against the water. The swirling halts, then starts up again in the same direction.

Two bugs are caught in the vortex. One of them is too close to the eye of the storm, and though it's fighting for all it's worth, it's a goner. The other is further out, and still has a chance to break free. With each passing second, though, it's drawn toward the center, swirling ever faster. Without giving it a thought, Fiona flicks the tiny beast out of the water, onto the floor. But she's too late; it's not moving. But then it shudders, shakes and flutters away on soggy wings.

"Let me give it a whirl," says Barry.

"Safety blitz!" All four of us pick him up and hold his butt over the sink until he cries, "Uncle! Uncle!"

Still chuckling, Barry takes a shot at counteracting the vortex, but, after a momentary pause, the water starts spinning again. Draining liquids crave a vortex. They suck. They want to swirl, one way or the other. After running the test ten times with inconclusive results, we leave the men's room, with each of us offering up theories and counter-theories.

We return to the yellow line to get pictures of us straddling the equator. We begin with individual shots, followed by a series of group pics: Fiona and Barry, Gracie sitting on Cole's shoulders, Fiona and Cole cheek to cheek, the women, we guys acting serious, we guys acting like idiots, and so on.

As we complete our photo shoot, the Coriolis woman is straddling the equator, running through her demonstration again to a group of four, who ooh and aah at the non-swirling water. Her experiment still seems dubious, but the possibility that whirlpools don't necessarily happen, that drains don't have to suck, holds a certain appeal to me. On the other hand, even when water doesn't swirl, it goes straight down the drain, taking with it everything in its clutches.

"It's all about balance," Gracie says again. "Especially with the spring equinox being only five days away."

Fiona asks what "equinox" means.

Gracie answers, "Literally, it means, 'equal night,' the first day of spring, when the length of day and night are the same. And here we are...." Gracie leaps, landing with one foot on each side of the line. ".... half the planet to the north, half to the south." She grabs Cole's right wrist and twists it to see his watch. "Noon in three minutes." She chants:

> Noon on the equator
> Soon, the equinox
> Sky, sun, creator
> Never so near, our gods

Ignoring her, Barry says, "Look down. We aren't casting shadows." He extends his arms and rotates his body. "Unless you do this."

"Oh, that is rad!" Gracie makes a hand shadow, a credible image of birds kissing.

I create a shadow of a head with two ungainly ears flopping about. "Anybody recognize this guy?"

"Llove the Llama!" Fiona cries out.

She makes one too, and Gracie says, "It is our karmic duty to llove the llama."

Cole reaches an arm around my shoulder. "Hey, pally, I was clowning around earlier. It's really good to see you."

"Oh man, you too. Hey, here's a bit of a song I'm writing: Why, and where, did you go? All right, you sing that, and I've got another part to go with it."

We sing the line, but I mess it up. "Again." I almost get it right the second time. "Again." The parts mesh nicely this time, with my part moving independently of his.

Gracie applauds. "You should quit your day jobs and go on the road." She hoists a bottle of water, and says, "A toast, to Llove the Llama." She takes one last look at Cole's watch. "Okay, it's noon, right.... riiiiight now! We're two miles high. The sun has never appeared bigger or brighter than it does right here." With her face upturned, she lifts her arms, offering up a solar embrace. "In a few days, we will be closer to the sun that we've ever been."

Fiona looks up and squints. "This sun is unforgiving." She pulls a pair of sunglasses out of her purse. When Cole suggests we head over to the planetarium, she walks away, saying, "I need to stop by the ladies' room. I'll meet you there."

"No, we'll wait," says Barry.

Gracie resumes her love fest with the sun. "The ancient Egyptians recognized Ra, the sun god, as the source of all."

"How quaint," Barry snipes.

"But they were right," says Cole. "The sun is literally the source of all. Two hydrogen atoms fuse to form an atom of helium. Hydrogen and helium fuse to form lithium, and so on. The sun *is* the Creator."

"As is every star," adds Gracie. "So we have billions of creators."

"Whatever." Barry removes his money belt and loosens the band. "This thing is killing me. And while I'm at it.... Boy, it's getting hot." He hands the belt to Gracie. "Here, hold this, would you?"

As he begins to pull his sweater over his head, we're approached by an elderly woman wearing a dress that may have once been white. She holds an empanada and napkin in one hand, a ketchup packet in the other. She bites the corner of the packet and accidentally squirts ketchup on my shoulder.

"Lo siento, señor!" She drops the empanada, grabs my shirt, and tries to wipe off the ketchup with her napkin, smearing it all over my arm. "Lo siento!" She won't let go, so my friends encircle me and try to pry her bony fingers off my shirt.

That's when it happens: A skinny kid of ten or so snatches Barry's money belt out of Gracie's hand and takes off. He's gone before Cole or Barry realizes what's happening. The woman has my shirt in a death grip, and she artfully bumps Gracie, delaying her pursuit of the kid. The boy tosses the belt to an accomplice, then the two separate, causing Gracie to hesitate – who should she chase? She decides to pursue the kid with the belt, but by now he has a head start and he knows the terrain.

The woman is still fussing over me, and I yell, "Stop it, you hag! Stop it!"

She continues to wail "Lo siento!" until Gracie returns empty-handed. The woman abruptly lets go and walks off.

Gracie has the look of a four-year-old whose wicked sister showed her a photo of their parents wrapping presents from Santa. She says, "That lady and the boys – they're working together?"

"Yeah," Cole says, "but you'd never be able to prove it."

"Hijo de puta," I whisper to Cole. "Son of a whore."

Gracie apologizes to Barry, over and over. Her default emotional state of joyful serenity has been stripped away.

He lays a hand on her forearm. "It wasn't your fault. It could have happened to anyone. I can always get another passport. And traveler's cheques are replaceable." In his shoes, would I be as magnanimous? Doubtful. I am begrudgingly impressed.

Barry then proclaims, "And you can be quite sure the Lord will deal harshly with those boys."

I say, "The Gospel according to Barry." He glares at me, leaving no doubt he believes the Lord will deal harshly with me.

When Fiona returns, Gracie explains what happened. Fiona removes her sunglasses, exposing reddened eyes and a drippy nose.

Back in Quito, we accompany Barry to the American consulate. A woman with an autocratic air listens to his story, then checks her schedule. "Come back tomorrow at ten. Bring ID, your birth certificate, if you have it, and four photos."

Barry's entire body sags. "How long will it take to get my passport replaced?"

"Could be a day, could be a week…." She shrugs.

"What does it depend on?"

"Where you entered the country, police reports, whether you have a current driver's license, that sort of thing."

We exit the building and huddle on the sidewalk. Fiona is especially glum. "Well, there goes our trip to the Amazon." She looks back and forth between Cole and Gracie. "But you guys will have a great time."

"No, Fiona, you can still go." Barry is making a concerted effort to be cheerful. "I'll take care of getting a new passport."

"But, I don't want you to…. No! I'm not going to leave

you here on your own."

"I'll be fine. Besides, you've already paid for the trip and it's non-refundable."

Gracie says, "It was my fault. I will reimburse you for—"

"No, no, no. In no way was it your fault."

Cole waits a judicious ten seconds before asking Barry, "If Theo was interested in coming with us, would you be willing to sell your trip to the jungle?"

"If you want it.... yeah, I guess it's for sale. Four hundred bucks."

Looking around the circle of faces, I ask, "Is that okay with you?" The women nod somberly, whereas it's all Cole can do to keep from doing backflips. "Thanks, I'd like to go. I'm just sorry it had to happen like this." I take four one-hundred-dollar travelers cheques out of my money belt and sign them over to Barry.

He says, "Hopefully I'll get a new passport tomorrow, and join you at the lodge, if they get a cancellation." That's a long shot, but we all nod in agreement. He holds up the cheques. "I need to find an American Express office. Can we get together for dinner?" Again, we nod. "Fiona, I'll see you back at...."

"No, I will come with you."

Gracie apologizes one more time, but Barry waves her off. He takes Fiona's hand, and they set out.

On our walk back to the hotel, Gracie is subdued. Is she feeling guilty about Barry's predicament? Or have I overstepped some unseen family boundary?

I say, "Look, is it okay that I'm coming along? Because I don't want to horn in on your—"

"Theo, everything happens for a reason." Gracie's doleful manner belies the surety of her words. "We'd love to have you join us." She hugs me, and her dangly earring nearly perforates my cheek.

She untangles herself from me, and Cole wraps an arm around my shoulder. "Pally, there ain't nobody we'd rather get lost in the jungle with."

Chapter 15: Those Few Who are Blessed

The air in the Amazon is so thick, you could slice it up, toast and butter it, and serve it for lunch. The rainforest smells of moisture and mushrooms, hot and rot, green and growth. Being from Tucson, where visitors grouse about the bone-dry air sucking at your eyes and lips, this tropical sauna will take some getting used to. But when you contrast it with Puno's meager atmosphere or the befouled air of Lima, this is respiratory heaven.

On our first afternoon at the jungle lodge, the guests offer up rave reviews of the soup, sandwiches and fruit served by the kitchen staff. The lodge's hub, this dining room, is located on the shore of Lake Sachacocha, with boardwalks emanating like spokes from a half wheel, leading to grass-thatched huts.

An American guide wearing a headband and tie-dyed shirt introduces himself as Logan. When asked about the day's forecast, he replies with a straight-face, "Chance of rain."

After lunch, Logan leads ten of us on a hike through the rainforest. "We animals take in oxygen and exhale carbon dioxide. Plants do the exact opposite. Twenty percent of our planet's oxygen is produced here. Welcome to the lungs of the Earth."

We flew over the Andes this morning in a rickety biplane. Cresting the mountains, we caught a downdraft, leaving us airborne inside the plane. Upon landing, we took a bus to a small town on Rio Napo, then navigated a maze of waterways in a motorboat, ending up at Sachacocha, or "Little Lake."

From the air, the Amazon basin appeared as an impenetrable green shag carpet, carved up by meandering brown rivers. Below the canopy, however, the jungle is fairly wide open, though dusky in hue. Giant ferns and broad-leaved swamp plants adorn the landscape. Vines swoop down out of the gloom, a hundred feet overhead. A bee or turquoise fly will occasionally buzz around my ears, but few actually land.

Cole points out a tree that measures thirty feet wide at ground level and quickly narrows to maybe six. "Why is it shaped like that?"

Logan says, "Most of these trees either have a wide base or extensive roots, because the Amazon has poor soil, making it difficult to soak up nutrients. So it's doubly sad that the jungle is being bulldozed and burned for farmland. Crops don't grow here very well."

I ask who made the path we're hiking.

"It's an animal trail, used mostly by tapirs. Look here, you can see tracks, and if we're lucky—"

He's interrupted by Dixon, who wears a t-shirt reading:

Virginia
born & bred

"Y'all ever seen a hogwar?" he asks, mangling the Spanish pronunciation of "jaguar." A carpenter, Dixon introduced himself at lunch, saying he's here specifically to photograph a hogwar.

Logan says, "I've lived here two years; never seen a cat."

Dixon hitches up his khakis over a capacious belly. "All right then, have y'all ever seen hogwar tracks?"

Logan is congenial. "Later today, we'll visit a place I saw them last week."

"Ah would surely 'preciate that."

We come across a tree that fell recently, and Logan directs our attention to the jagged skylight. "Come back in two years, that opening will have closed up."

Fiona asks where he studied biology.

"Here," he says. "I take correspondence courses. But I got my degree in philosophy from UC Berkeley." He points out a tree from which hang long, droopy sacks. "Anybody want to guess what those are?"

"Bee hives?"

"Ants?"

"Piñatas?"

This earns Cole a smack in the arm from Fiona. She was subdued on the plane ride, but the luxuriance of the Amazon has revived her.

"Homes for a bird called the oropendula," says Logan. "They raise cowbirds that pick parasites off baby oropendulas."

"Why would they do that?" I ask.

"Symbiosis. During the last ice age, many species on Earth

were wiped out, along with their symbiotic relationships. But the ice didn't touch the Amazon, so relationships here tend to be more complex; they've had more time to develop." Somebody asks what symbiosis means. Logan says, "Example: The domestication of dogs was symbiotic; they got a free meal, and in return, they warned villagers of impending danger. Man and dog also kept one another warm at night. It's been a fabulous partnership."

I say, "But it's odd that one species drops off its young with another. Like birdy day care."

"Isn't it amazing? But that's how natural selection works. Over millions of generations, bizarre alliances occur randomly. As long as they're mutually beneficial, they get retained, either genetically or through educating their young."

We walk on, and Fiona became increasingly perplexed until Cole takes notice and asks what's up.

She says, "It seems absurd that symbiosis just *happens*. It's more reasonable to think these relationships were designed."

"But why explain this admittedly unlikely world by positing the existence of an even more unlikely being that doesn't exist in our three-dimensional world? Where'd God come from?"

Gracie, still in a funk from the money belt debacle, rolls her eyes. "Borrrring."

Fiona says, "God was always there.... I mean, here."

Cole says, "Sittin' around in empty space – oops, nobody had chairs back then. So God was just hangin' out, for gazillions of years, pondering the meaning of his dreams, no drums, no tacos, wishing somebody'd pop over with a six pack."

"The Bible says the universe was created eight thousand years ago."

"That's silly, Fi. Sorry, there's no other word for it. Why put such trust in a translation of an edited collection of folk tales handed down from a cult of superstitious, militant nomads wandering a Middle Eastern wasteland thousands of years ago?" It's good line, but the way he rattles it off makes it sound rehearsed.

Gracie notices that others have tuned into the debate. "Be civil, husband."

Cole ignores her. "Right now we're being hit by photons emitted from stars that blew up a billion years ago. As for natural selection, we share most of our DNA with chimps."

"About 98%," says Fiona. "Don't look shocked; I took biology. It makes sense that God would use the same building blocks to create different species."

"Good point," he says.

"And evolution; that's only a theory."

He sighs. "C'mon, Fi. You're mixing up theory with guess or hypothesis."

"But theories change."

"Granted. Newton's theory of gravitation was discredited by Einstein's theory of relativity. But we still use Newton's theory to fly planes, because it's simpler, with negligible error."

"Too cryptic for me," says Fiona.

"To understand relativity, you have to think in four dimensions."

"And you can do that?"

"Yes.... well.... Okay, not very well."

"We're three-dimensional beings; you just said so. Do you know anyone who understands relativity? No? Tell me, what *is* gravity? Why believe in something you can't conceptualize?"

"Because Einstein's theories work; they're measurable. He theorized that space must be curved, and that was borne out by experiment."

"Christianity works too. I've seen lives transformed. And if Newton's theory was discredited, why use it?"

"It's a more usable model of gravitation."

Fiona smiles. "I don't want a usable model. I want, in Theo's words, Truth, with a capital T."

Cole's smile mirrors hers. "But you assume the Bible to be true."

"Just like you assume quarks, whatever they are, to be real, even though you've never seen one. You take it on faith. You trust the word of strangers who claim to see quarks."

"Well, no, it doesn't work like that. Nobody *sees* them. But we see evidence of their existence in particle accelerators, when they smash into atoms at a billion kilometers per hour. They're never observed directly or found in isolation."

"Because our equipment isn't sophisticated enough?"

"No. Even with perfect gear, you couldn't detect them. By

measuring a particle's location, you change its velocity. And vice versa."

That comment perks up my agnostic ears. "So there's a physical limit to how much we can know?"

Cole nods. "That's the gist of Heisenberg's Uncertainty Principle. Quarks are too small and fast to measure precisely."

Fiona says, "God is too big and too, um, *patient* to measure at all. He's never observed directly or found in isolation. But what *is* a quark?"

"They come in flavors: top, bottom, up, down, charm, strange. Physicists have a quirky sense of humor."

"A quarky sense of humor," giggles Fiona.

"You're lucky the ground's muddy; otherwise we'd safety blitz you."

"You could try," she says with a sassy grin. "But tell me; who dreamt up this stuff about quarks?"

Gracie looks pleased, which makes me realize Cole and Fiona are conversing, rather than debating. Is the change due to Barry's absence?

"The model was proposed in the 60s."

"Proposed?"

"That's right. We're talking science here, not revelation."

"Getting back to that four dimensions business; I'll need that explained."

"Actually, some physicists hypothesize the existence of ten dimensions."

"Ten? You need ten to make sense of our three? As you'd say: That is craziness! Couldn't one of the ten be a spiritual dimension? Look around; are you telling me this grand, orderly world came into existence by accident? Just the right amount of oxygen, just the right amount of.... everything. That would be like a monkey sitting down and typing the Bible. It wouldn't happen."

"Probably not, unless you had a million generations of a million monkeys, and every time a correct letter got typed, it got saved – that's how natural selection works. Our lungs evolved to fit the atmosphere, not the other way around. The world appears grand and orderly because of our anatomy."

"But the universe *is* orderly," I say. "The pull of gravity is the same everywhere."

"True," Cole concedes. "And every hydrogen atom weighs the same."

"And reducing life and love...." I glance at Fiona for one second. ".... to chemical reactions and biological urges is a clumsy way to define who we are. That's like defining music as ink spots on a treble clef, or sound waves, or electrical impulses in the brain."

"Right," says Fiona, "music is designed."

Gracie says, "Yes. Designed by angels who plant melodies in our heads." Our dialog grinds to a screeching halt. "There's no way Kurt Cobain could have written that stuff alone."

Eventually I say, "What amazes me is that *anything* exists. Design, accident – both explanations seems absurd."

Cole says, "Interesting. The design-or-accident dichotomy reminds me of an age-old physics debate: Does light consist of waves or particles? Well, sometimes light acts like a wave, other times like a particle, depending on what experiment you run."

Fiona frowns. "But particles and waves are.... What's the phrase I'm looking for?"

"Mutually exclusive. Crazy, huh? Physicists talk about the dual nature of light. They live with the contradiction. Light is a wave *and* a particle."

"Or could it be neither?" I ask.

Cole nods vigorously. "Maybe humans have not evolved enough to comprehend the nature of light. Just like a spaniel couldn't understand, say, the number pi. Wave or particle: maybe that's not even the right dichotomy."

I say, "Like if you ask: What's the opposite of 'right'? You can say 'wrong' or 'left;' more than one dichotomy applies. Maybe a new model will render the wave/particle division obsolete. As for the issue of God-or-no-God, shoot, maybe that's not even the right question. In a hundred years, maybe we'll recognize it as a false dilemma."

"Maybe we aren't evolved...." Fiona turns up her nose. "....enough to comprehend God intellectually, but spiritually, we are. We *are*. As for living with paradoxes, that's how it is with Jesus and me. Some paradoxes bother me, but I live with them. Here's one: We have free will *and* God is all-knowing, just like light is a wave *and* a particle."

It's this insight that wins over Cole. He puts his arm around her waist and we walk on.

We are joined by a short man wearing only green shorts and a machete hanging off his belt. His black hair frames a wide face devoid of tension. Logan introduces him as Yachay, and says he speaks Quechua.

Gracie whispers, "No shirt, no shoes, no nervous."

Yachay points to a tree behind us.

Logan turns, and says, "Ah, the grey potoo." He directs our attention to a broken-off limb.

Squinting, we ask, "Where?" Then we squint some more.

"You're looking in the right place," says Logan. "You're just not seeing."

Cole is getting frustrated. "Okay, where is it in relation to that gnarly branch?"

Grinning, Logan approaches the tree. The branch twists its head toward us.

Everyone jerks backward. The branch – actually it's a bird – is ugly as sin. Its huge eyes, colored a sickly shade of yellow, sit way down on its face, above the corners of an oversized grin. Scraggly whiskers adorn the end of its beak. Mottled feathers blend in perfectly with the tree bark. The potoo could star in a horror movie.

"Craziness," says Cole. "How'd Yachay see that?"

"Simple," Gracie snipes. "He shuts his mouth and opens his eyes."

Dixon adjusts his black plastic bifocals and drawls, "Butter my butt 'n' call me a biscuit."

We follow Yachay, and a few minutes later he kneels. We crowd around as he lays his hand on the ground and coaxes a four-inch scorpion forward with a delicate fern frond. It slides its bronze, translucent pincers onto his palm. Everyone leans back; if it attacks Yachay, will he fling it into the air?

"Why doesn't it sting him?" Gracie asks.

Logan says, "He hasn't given it reason to. Who wants to hold it?"

"Theo would love to," says Cole. He shoves me forward, and I reluctantly hold out my hand.

With prodding from Yachay, the scorpion inches forward,

its tail curving ominously over its body. Every cell in my body screams, Noooo! But I do it; I cradle the little body in my palm.

Cole asks, "What would be a reason for it to sting someone?"

Logan, aware of my distress, deadpans his reply: "If Theo was, say, jittery, it might sense that and become aggressive."

Everyone except Fiona has a good laugh at that. I give her a wink, but it probably looks more like a facial tic. Yachay steps forward to reclaim the beast.

I shiver and grumble, "Gee, it's nice to have friends."

"Admit it, pally, you were enjoying yourself."

I wipe my palm on the shoulder of his orange and green Hawaiian shirt. "Just so you know, that little fella took a whiz on my hand."

We come to a stream crowded by ferns and shrubs. Yachay pushes through the foliage and wades in to mid-thigh. He bends his knees and leans forward, arms dangling in front of him. He freezes in place, as do we all. A minute later, he suddenly dips at the knees and comes up with a twenty-inch fish. He steps out of the water like it's no big deal.

"Dinner," says Logan.

Oddly, we applaud. Yachay grins and holds up the squirmy yellowish gray prize. And just like that, he walks away, following a faint trail into the forest.

"Well, Ah'll be dipped in doodoo," says Dixon. "Sure ain't how we fish back home."

Cole whispers, "I'd give my left nut to see what Yachay sees."

"Agreed," I say. "I'd gladly give your left nut."

Gracie hisses, "Shush! You two are a bad influence on each other."

Logan becomes somber. "Okay, listen up. Never do what Yachay just did. Do not.... leave.... the trail. And do not.... split.... up. It's a jungle out there."

We turn to look at Yachay, but he has disappeared.

Watching the cockatoos and parakeets navigate the tangle of vines overhead, Gracie says, "Now that's what I call a usable model of gravitation."

Many birds are emblazoned in outlandish greens, reds and yellows that scream: Here I am! Hey! Over here!

"Logan," asks Fiona, "why is it that some birds do whatever they can to stand out, and others try to be invisible?"

"Anybody want to take a shot at that?"

Dixon drawls, "That brown 'n' green bird keeps hisself invisible so he don't get eaten."

Someone else says, "It's easy for him to sneak up on prey."

"Good answers," says Logan. "How about that parrot?"

"Mating," says Cole. "The louder and brighter he is, the more likely he is to get some action."

Fiona holds up the sleeve of his Hawaiian shirt. "Better keep an eye on this boy, Gracie."

Logan says, "Most of these birds don't migrate. This is paradise, so why leave, right? But the ones that do fly north use the sun, maybe even the stars and the Earth's magnetic field, to navigate. Their little bird brains *know* where to go."

We walk on, and Gracie says, "If birds know what path to take, it makes sense that humans would have that faculty too, but more developed. We're born with a guidance system that always points us in the right direction." Fiona nods, and Gracie continues. "And just as not all birds fly the same route, we each have our own path." This time it's Cole who nods.

Fiona says, "Some of us wander off our path and get lost."

Cole stops nodding. "Some prefer to get a machete and make our own path."

Fiona pokes him in the ribs. "Some venture far, far away, and return home later."

He pokes her back. "But most of us never leave home."

Giggling, she shoves him in the general direction of the river. "Sadly, some people trip and fall into gator-infested waters."

We approach a steeply canted wooden staircase built against a tree trunk. It rises twenty feet to a small platform, then turns ninety degrees around the trunk and rises to another landing, then turns again, eventually disappearing into the canopy.

"How far up does it go?" asks Fiona.

Logan gestures toward the stairs. "One way to find out."

Gracie's exuberance has returned, and she takes the stairs two at a time. Logan tenses and begins to protest, but when she stops at the first platform and cries out, "Come on!" he motions for us to follow her.

We are soon engulfed in the canopy. After a final flight of stairs, we burst out onto a thirty-foot-square platform. Though the sky is clouded over, we shield our eyes from the light.

Logan comes up behind us wearing sunglasses. "Welcome to our treehouse."

Up here is where all the action takes place. Scarlet dragonflies play tag and spiders weave elaborate webs, while butterflies of iridescent blue and yellow flutter by. Flamboyant in flight, they virtually disappear upon landing. Flowers, ferns and moss cover every inch of every limb. We gaze out on the endless garden, squeezing our eyes shut when the sun breaks through. Logan talks more about symbiosis, and Fiona nods in a barely perceptible way.

An hour later, we descend and re-enter the gloom.

"That treehouse was awesome," says Gracie, "but I prefer it down here. Humans always want to transcend life, to get above it, to feel safe. Me, I'll take the jungle any day."

That evening I head down to the bar, a hexagonal gazebo lit by kerosene lanterns. From beyond the protective spray of light comes the yowling and singing of jungle beasts. Cole, Gracie and a dozen guests listen in as guides teach one another bird calls. Fiona is sitting on a bench with legs extended, a book in one hand, Inca Kola in the other. I ask what she's reading.

"<u>The Mysterious Stranger</u>, a gift from Graham McHugh. I like every book he sends me."

Cole says, "Ditto that. I like his taste better than my own."

"You two need to track him down," says Gracie. "You've got a ghost sending you gifts."

Fiona says, "She's right, Cole."

"Amen, sister. Soon as we get back." He picks up a chess board off the bar and waves it in the air. "Hey, pally, let's play for the championship of the three-dimensional universe."

We start a game, and Cole catches me staring at Fiona. He says, "Somethin' special, ain't she?" I pretend not to know what he's talking about. "Don't sweat it," he says.

Gracie also caught me staring; she inhales deeply and gives me a head shake.

Cole sees this and says again, "Don't sweat it."

A cocky, middle-aged guide enters. Wearing a white shirt unbuttoned to his navel, he has an eight-inch snake coiled around his thumb. Everyone gathers round.

He says, "Check out this baby boa. Right now he's trying to kill me." He uncoils the snake and holds it out to Fiona, who tentatively accepts it in her cupped hands.

"It looks slimy," she says, her face bathed in delight. "But it isn't. Where's her mama?"

The guide opens a bag and hauls out a fifteen-foot snake skin. "Haven't seen her, but don't leave your door open tonight." Every eyeball within earshot snaps open. He laughs and drapes the skin over the bamboo railing. I ask why snakes shed their skin.

He says, "As we grow, our skin grows with us. But snake skin doesn't expand much, so when a boa grows, it sloughs off its outer layer." He checks his watch and frowns. "I have business to attend to, but I hope you're all still here when I'm done." He says this to Fiona, then leaves.

Cole smirks. "Sister, you got more than a snake wrapped around your finger."

"Pig. Not everyone's as easy as you are."

"Better watch it, Theo. Adam was tossed from the garden because of a woman and her serpent."

She sighs. "You don't even know that story."

"I know it better than you do. As I recall, you were a hell-raiser in Sunday school. Remember when you smooshed pudding in that kid's Bible?"

When he returns to our game, she drops the boa down his neck. He leaps up and spins around, writhing until the snake drops to the bamboo floor. All present laugh and applaud. Fiona takes a bow.

"CHEEEE-ses, Fi!" He picks up the snake and shakes it at her. "Theo, if she offers you an apple, you better run for it."

For all their sparring, it strikes me how solid and intimate is their bond. I'm envious. In ten days, I will fly home and re-insert myself into the constrictive fabric of my family, and watch as my siblings fling themselves headlong and heedlessly into the Duncan emotional maelstrom.

Cole keeps looking over his shoulder. "Warn me if Psycho Sis is about to drop a scorpion down my shorts." He makes a series of blunders, allowing me to beat him easily.

"Congrats, pally, you are champ of the 3-D universe." He orders martinis from Felipe, a cheerful Ecuadorian with a scar cutting diagonally across his forehead.

The clouds open up, and within seconds, the rain is deafening. Without warning, Gracie whips off her blouse and shorts, and dashes outside in her undies. Turning her face skyward and extending her arms, she cries, "I am baptized!" Half-crazed, half-drowned, she places a finger on top of her head and twirls herself, then dashes off down the boardwalk, calling, "The Mother of All Baptisms!"

I am pleased to see Fiona join in our laughter.

Cole shakes his head in bemusement and pride. "I married a wild woman."

We listen to the downpour, and he says, "I think music was invented by drummers, trying to copy the sound of rain."

"Could be. Or I heard a bird today that sounds like this." I whistle a descending arpeggio. "Maybe birds invented music."

"The grey potoo," says Felipe. He whistles the same notes, bending notes and adding trills. Cole and I are wowed.

Fiona says, "Such a beautiful song, such an ugly bird."

I ask to borrow the charango hanging behind the bar. Felipe hands it to me, and I pick out the potoo's melody: G – E – D – B – G. Together, they form an E minor seventh chord, or you could think of it as a G major sixth. Whereas major chords tend to sound upbeat, minor chords often generate a feeling of desolation or sadness. So which is it, major or minor? Both? Neither? I don't know.

The rain stops, as if a spigot is turned off. Logan enters and asks if anyone wants to go canoeing. Cole volunteers immediately and says, "C'mon, pally."

I hesitate. My aborted baptism instilled in me a fear of water. I didn't learn to swim until college, and boats unnerve me. But travelling is all about trying new things, so I volunteer too.

"Anybody else?" asks Logan. "We have two canoes." He

gets no more takers, so the three of us walk out onto the dock and turn a dugout right-side-up. We lower it into the water, and Logan hands us flashlights. When I ask why, he smiles mischievously.

"You'll see. Hey, if you want to go canoeing tomorrow, Sachacocha is fed by three streams. Going counterclockwise, take the second one. The bird life up there is unbelievable."

He gives us a push, and we glide out onto the perfectly calm surface. We paddle to the middle of the lake in two minutes. At least we guess it's the middle – except for the lanterns from the lodge, all is black. We marvel at the volume and variety of animal sounds, the singing and squawking of birds, the growl of howler monkeys.

"What Logan wants us to see?" I aim my light up into the trees surrounding the lake. "Nothin'. You see anything?"

"Nada." His light plays over the surface of the water. "Now what the hell is this?" A pair of red eyes watches us from the shrubs at lake's edge. "Whatever it is, there's another one."

The combination of water, darkness and demonic red eyes is enough to paralyze me.

Cole rotates in his seat. "CHEEEE-ses, Theo! Over there! There's four more!"

"Let's hope they're friendlies." Let's also hope my voice isn't shaking.

"Well, I'll be a.... How did you say 'son of a whore'?"

"Hijo de puta."

"I'll be a hijo de puta. I'm glad we're not sleepin' out there tonight, pally."

We find Logan chatting with Fiona and Gracie in the bar. He anticipates my question, saying, "Caiman, they're relatives of gators. They can get to be fifteen or twenty feet long."

"You ever have problems with 'em?" I ask.

"Nah, they keep to themselves."

"There's a diving board out on the dock," says Fiona. "Does anybody use it? Is it safe?"

"Oh yeah. Caiman keep to themselves." Ask me, it's one of those things you repeat in an effort to make it believable.

Dressed in dry clothes, Gracie has a towel wrapped around her head. "Speaking of keeping to themselves, where's Yachay?

Where's he live?"

Logan shrugs. "Don't know. Sometimes he stays here."

She leans forward. "What's he do? What's he believe?"

"He lives the way his clan has lived for a thousand years. He hunts with bow and arrow, or blowgun, or as you saw today, with his hands. Felipe calls them the Unseen. It doesn't translate very well, but Yachay calls us 'shavers.' "

"Because white men have beards?"

"No, because when we drill for oil, or build suburbs, or become farmers, we shave the land, that is, we clear-cut forests."

"What about.... I'm not sure what to ask."

"Their history is common: They worship animal spirits, so missionaries come, and they're killed, so more missionaries come, and natives convert to Christianity, sort of. Natives are told to wear clothes, but without washing machines, their clothes are fungus-ridden. Oil companies come, natives get pushed aside, their population is decimated." He slows down his narrative. "They believe they're descended from animals, and—"

Fiona has been sitting quietly. "Like evolution?"

"Yeah. Uh, no, not really. As I understand it, they believe they're the offspring of a jaguar and an eagle."

"Which was male and which was female?" asks Cole. "Because how...?"

Gracie goes to punch him, but Fiona beats him to it.

"What's your story, Logan?" asks Gracie. "How did you end up here?"

"I was bumming around Ecuador and fell in love with the land, the people. I went home, sold my car, gave away my TV, quit my job. Sometimes I wonder if I've sold out, showing rich Americans around the jungle – no offense – but if tourism helps save the rainforest, heck, I'm all for it. We may be too late, but let's go down fighting. That's my philosophy."

"Speaking of philosophy," says Gracie, "you were listening in on our conversation today. Any observations?" Logan blushes. "Not to worry; that's how we met Theo. He was eavesdropping on what I refer to as the Endless Debate."

"We talk too loud," says Cole.

"Some of us do," says Gracie, and asks Logan again, "Any observations?"

"I enjoy the dialogue between science and religion. From what I've read, there have historically been three ways of thinking about God and truth."

Fiona and I ask simultaneously, "With a capital T?"

Logan chuckles. "I guess so, but that's a tall order." He pauses, gauging our level of interest. "Christianity cycles through three approaches: proof, faith, and mysticism. So, for a century, theologians take a whack at proving God's existence."

"But when you get right down to it," says Fiona, "logic doesn't satisfy."

"Exactly. And people are inclined to try proving whatever it is they already assume to be true. So then faith will get top billing for a few generations, which tends to foster certitude in believers."

Fiona adds, "And faith binds a community together. That's why we're on Earth, to look after one another. To save and serve."

"Yes, but faith pits religions against one another, leaving no way to reconcile. And faith is unverifiable, which brings us to a third approach: mysticism, a direct communion with some ultimate reality, which tends to be a nonverbal encounter." He says, "I have no idea what I'm talking about, but if you ever have such an experience, good luck trying to put it into words."

This gets me thinking about my Ecstatic Meltdown, which was neither faith-based nor any sort of proof. So was it a mystical experience, or something else? A nothing, maybe.

We call it a night, and make our way down the lantern-lit boardwalk to our huts. I open my door and shine my light around, just as a gecko slithers under the bamboo wall.

I strip down, lift the mosquito net, climb into bed, turn off the light and listen to the noises that seem to come from inside my hut. Hum, slither, click, buzz, drip. Tiny legs skitter up the wall and burrow into the straw ceiling. I tell myself not to picture that beast.

I turn on the light to make sure the mosquito net is tucked in under the mattress all the way around. It is. I switch off the light. Are there rips in the netting?

I turn on the light and inspect the net. No rips. The only beings that could get through the net are bacteria or a caiman with a stepladder. I kill the light, lie down, and focus on sounds coming from outside. The animal choir is well-balanced, yet one voice rises above all others; I am whistled to sleep by the sweetly hypnotic, five-toned lullaby of the grey potoo.

A downpour awakens me. It sounds as if the Amazon's two hundred inches of annual rainfall will fall before dawn. The rain god Pariaqaqa must be working overtime. The din is constant, the darkness absolute. The air feels neither hot nor cold on my skin. Though this environment is alien to me, immersion in the supersaturated atmosphere seems familiar and comforting, as if a primal part of my brain recalls sloshing about in the amniotic ocean a quarter century ago, six years before my baptismal fiasco.

I wonder where Yachay is. He and his tribesmen believe themselves to be the offspring of jaguars and eagles, which serves to strengthen my conviction that Nobody Knows. Given Yachay's reproductive model, it's tempting to dismiss his beliefs as being too far out to even consider. But are his beliefs any more bizarre than those of Christianity, with its Flood and resurrection? Or how about Hinduism's reincarnation-based caste system, or modern physics, accessible to those few blessed with the intellectual horsepower to conceptualize ten dimensions, and who imagine time as pliant, and quarks that are.... well, who'd like to tackle that one? Belief systems are outlandish; they all are. Physics provides us with a usable model, sure, but it seems fanciful, so who's to say that traditional religion, or Yachay, does not have something valuable to say about the workings of this world?

Nobody Knows – that statement is too strongly worded. Maybe it's time for another downgrade: Nobody I know Knows.

Now, rather than picking out individual voices from the jungle chorus, I allow it to come at me as a single wash of sound, an amalgamation of a thousand creatures.

Though I would not have thought it possible, the rain grows more thunderous, as if a dam has broken. At this moment it's conceivable that the Great Flood happened precisely as chronicled in the Bible. Half asleep, I submit to unseen currents that sweep me up and carry me forward, leaving behind my arid, sterile world, crossing an ill-defined boundary into untamed territory.

I lie motionless, swaddled in the warm, wet, welcoming arms of the Amazonian blackness.

Chapter 16: Dry as a Bone

"Slept like a baby; feel like I've been reborn."

That's my response to Fiona's "How are ya?" on the way to breakfast. She looks at me askance, but lets it slide.

The buffet offers a sumptuous array of quiche, chorizo sausage, fruit and coffee, during which Fiona, Cole and I finalize our plans to canoe up one of the streams feeding Sachacocha. Gracie bows out, opting instead for a hike to a butterfly farm.

Logan makes us promise to be back by four. "Trust me, you do not want to be out there after dark." He hands us box lunches prepared by the kitchen staff.

Cole and Fiona launch their dugout, and as I'm boarding, Dixon waddles onto the dock. "Mind if Ah tag 'long?" Without waiting for reply, he drops his day pack into the front of my canoe and grabs a paddle. He climbs in, adjusts his Virginia Tech cap and calls out, "Tally ho!"

We shove off, and his butt cheeks spill over the seat like a pair of jumbo muffins. Our canoe rides low, and every time he squirms to get comfortable, water sloshes over the side, forming a puddle in the bow. With the image of those demonic red eyes fresh in my mind, I have no desire to take a dip.

I find myself hissing: "Sit stillll!"

The first time I say it, he replies, "My 'pologies, Ah'm as fidgety as a hooker in church." But after that he says, "Don't git yerself riled up now," or "Don't git yer testes in a twist."

We plan to paddle upstream for three hours, then float back down in the afternoon. But in actuality, the Amazon basin is so flat that "upstream" and "downstream" have little meaning. The Amazon River, after its precipitous plunge from the Andes, loses an average of two inches in elevation per mile as it oozes toward the Atlantic. The water in this lake will not reach the ocean for months. The Amazon is more of a swamp than a river.

Paddling around the lake counterclockwise, we pass a stream about sixty feet across. It's enticing, but we continue to the next stream, which, according to Logan, boasts a wider variety of wildlife. But low-hanging branches make the channel appear tunnel-like, so we decide to return to the first stream.

Entering the waterway, our canoes scrape over submerged tree trunks. Ferns and chest-high grass obscure the shoreline, while trees, hungry for light, lean precariously over the water.

Dixon eventually settles in, except for when the occasional spider drops in unannounced. Whenever anything, live or dead, lands on Dixon, he slaps at his head and wiggles frantically.

"Sit stillll!"

At one point he gestures toward a tributary entering from our right. "Don't lack much a'bein' a river."

We consider heading back at noon, but Cole is keen on going further. Fiona, reclining with bare feet and elbows perched on the sides of the dugout, points out a six-foot caiman lazing on the left bank.

Dixon lets loose a raspy snort. "Christ, he fell out of an ugly tree and hit every branch on the way down."

The caiman slides into the water, gliding toward us with only his eyes, bony snout and the hump of his scaly back visible. Dixon leans to our right, allowing water to pour into our canoe.

"Sit stillll!"

Cole says calmly, "Dixon, hold still. It's too small to...."

The caiman chooses this instant to dive, and Dixon stands up, brandishing his paddle like a club.

"Heyyyyy!" I yell. "Siddowwwwn!"

Instead, Dixon picks up his pack and says, "Got mah camera in hay-er." He heaves it into the bushes along the shore. The motion sends him off-balance, and I grab the sides of our canoe to steady us, but it's no use; he windmills his arms and tumbles backward into the stream. I reach out to give him a hand, but he goes for my friends' canoe instead. Attempting to climb aboard, he overturns it.

Fiona goes under, and I dive in after her, my aquaphobia be damned. A submerged limb rakes the back of my left shoulder, and I surface. The muddy stream bottom is clogged with branches, and Fiona, barefoot, has a hard time getting traction. I sling her over my shoulder and wade awkwardly toward the shore.

Cole helps me lift her out of the water, then he and I turn

back in time to watch Dixon clamber atop the overturned canoe. In doing so, he rams his knee through its hull, lodging his chunky thigh in its splintered side. He looks over his shoulder as the reptile surfaces, ten feet behind him. Dixon kicks wildly with his free leg, but he's unable to break free, and the caiman zeroes in on him, ignoring the churning water, or maybe he's drawn to it. Though the beast is only six feet long, those jaws fly open and clamp down on that flailing foot. Dixon emits a quavery howl that seems to last for minutes. The caiman doesn't let go.

Cole grabs the oar out of my canoe and starts bashing away at the beast's head, while spouting obscenities I've never heard. Fiona re-enters the water, and Cole cusses at her to keep the hell back, damn it Fi! But she's here to serve and save; in this case she intends to serve Dixon by saving his life. Thrashing madly, he manages to extricate himself, from both the canoe and the caiman, which then dives again. Fiona and I grab Dixon's wrists, and drag him across the canoe. With his doughy arms draped around our shoulders, we guide him out of the water. Cole follows, walking backward, slapping at the water with the oar.

Spitting up river water, Dixon limps fifteen feet inland and collapses on a giant fern. Fiona inspects his right leg, and thanks God it's still attached. She removes his sneaker and sock. His foot is not bleeding, but he winces when she touches his ankle.

"Let's hope you don't have any broken bones," she says, her voice oozing compassion.

While she tends to Dixon, Cole and I return to the stream, where the caiman lounges on the far side. The fatally wounded canoe drifts around a bend, and my canoe has come to rest in a cluster of reeds. We haul it onto solid ground. Fiona's Air Jordans, with socks stuffed inside, have popped to the surface; Cole retrieves them and brings them to his sister.

"Whar mah glasses?" Dixon rises to his knees, and we hear a sickening crunch. He stands and picks his glasses out of the mud. One grubby bifocal falls from the mangled frame, the other is crisscrossed with cracks. He wipes off the intact lens and squints through it. "Ah, Christ in a Chrysler!"

"CHEEEEE-ses, sis!" Cole points at Fiona's blood-stained blouse. "You got bitten?"

"I.... I don't think so." She lifts her blouse, revealing a

tanned, toned, unbitten stomach.

"That's not her blood." I pull back the left shoulder of my sleeveless shirt and crane my neck, but I can't get a look at my wound. Reaching back, I come away with a streak of red.

"Theo!" Fiona is all over me. "The caiman got you?"

"Nah, just caught a snag."

"We need to get that cleaned out." She takes my hand and leads me back to the stream. The caiman is nowhere in sight.

Dixon calls, "They kin smay-ell blood! I reckon they kin!"

Cole turns on him. "Since when do you give a donkey's dick, Pillsbury?"

Standing in knee-deep water, Fiona washes my wound, paying no attention to the reptile that may or may not be gunning for us. She says, "We need to bandage this." She tries to rip off a strip from the bottom of her blouse, then turns her eyes up to me. "Would you?"

I grab her blouse with both hands and pull, but it won't tear, so I kneel and bite the fabric with my eye teeth, doing my best to ignore that marvelously arched tummy. I rip off a wider strip than intended. "Sorry."

"It's okay." She winds the cloth around the right side of my neck and under my left armpit. "Too tight?"

I flex my arm. "No, that's fine. Thank you."

Fiona purses her lips and swallows. "No, thank *you*." She gives me The Look, which is more intense now, stern even. Having her probe around inside me is both uncomfortable and pleasurable.

She says, "We're alike, you and I. We were put here to serve and save."

I don't know how to respond to that, so I nod and say, "Let's go make sure Cole doesn't kill that bozo."

I start to leave, but Fiona wraps her arms around me. She pillows her head on my shoulder and whispers my name. My head is swimming; my chest is caving in.

"We were lucky, Theo. That wound is close to your heart." She's overdoing it, but her concern for my well-being thrills me. She places a hand on my chest, saying, "And I have grown quite fond of your heart." She takes my hand and leads me back to Cole and Dixon.

Still flustered, it's all I can do to pose the question, "Can we all fit in one canoe?"

Dixon vomits in response, right down the front of his Virginia-born-and-bred t-shirt, obscuring some of the lettering. It now reads: Virgin born. Wiping his mouth on his sleeve, he moans, "Four of us in one boat? Oh, *hay-ell* no! Be s'crowded, you couldn't swing a cat!"

Cole says, "Then how 'bout the three of us tow Pillsbury along behind us, as gator bait."

"Call me that one more time, boy, and Ah'm gonna—"

Cole smirks and points at Dixon's t-shirt. "OK, we'll call you 'Virgin Born' from now on."

"Git uppity with me, Ah'll whup ya like a rented mule."

Fiona yells, "Stop it! Both of you!" She pauses to make sure the ceasefire holds. "Options?"

Her clothes are soaked, in effect shrink-wrapping her body, showing off how fabulously curvy she is. Firm thighs taper down to sleek, nicely-rounded knees. This isn't the time to be drooling over a woman – another guy's woman – but I am rapt.

"Two of us could paddle back," I manage to say, "and return with the motorboat."

"Knucklehead," says Dixon. "Stream's too shallow."

Ever the faithful one, Fiona says, "We should wait. When Logan sees we're not back, he'll come looking for us."

Cole shakes his head. "We don't wanna be sitting around in the dark, hoping he'll show."

"He'll bring flashlights," she says.

"That'd be cool," Cole admits, "paddling back at night."

"Be okay by me," says Dixon, "s'long as he comes back with a shotgun." He aims an imaginary gun toward the stream. "Ka-BOOOM! Have us a mess of gator steaks."

"Two streams feed into the lake," says Fiona. "Does Logan know which one we took?"

The fear in her voice gives me a sinking feeling. "There are three streams," I say. "Logan thinks we took the second one."

Cole says, "I say we hike out."

"The jungle is too thick," says Fiona.

Dixon holds his grubby lens over one eye by scrunching up his cheek. He surprises us by agreeing with Cole. "You go inland a piece, the jungle opens right up. Better chance of seein' a hogwar in there anyways."

Fiona furrows her brow. "What if we get lost?"

"We just follow the stream," I say.

"Beg to differ," says Dixon. "River's been curvin' to the right for a good part of the morn'. We head perp'ndic'lar to the riverbank, ah'll have y'all home in no time."

Fiona points out that hiking out is the most idiotic idea she's ever heard.

Cole says, "Two of us can paddle back in the one canoe we have left...." He pauses to glare at Dixon. ".... and return with two canoes."

I say, "There were only two canoes on the dock."

"Then how about this? Two people go back, one returns, three of us paddle home."

I shake my head. "It'd be dark by the time we paddled home and back."

Cole says, "Not if we leave now. And we can pick up flashlights at the lodge."

"All right. Fiona goes, along with one of us."

Dixon sets his hands on his hips. "Ah'm not gettin' back in the river without a rifle. Whar there's a baby gator, there's bound to be a mama close by."

I say, "Okay, Dixon and I will stay. Cole and Fiona can paddle back, she stays there, he picks up a flashlight and gun, if they have one, or a machete." This is sounding nutty, but that doesn't stop me: "Cole returns for us, we all paddle back."

"No offense, Virgin Born," says Cole, "but we'd sink with you, me and Theo in a canoe."

Dixon glowers at him but refuses to engage. "Ah'll stay hay-er, and the three of you kin paddle on back. Then one of you kin return for me. With rifle and flashlights."

"We are not leaving you out here alone!" insists Fiona. "Forget it!" We are silent, looking up at the wall of green.

Cole folds his arms. "That settles it. We hike out."

Fiona asks Dixon if he can walk.

He shifts from side to side, testing his ankle. "It'll serve. And like Ah said, we need to go perp'ndic'lar to the river."

"I agree with Theo," says Fiona. "We follow the stream."

"Might jis' as well be herdin' cats here." Casting his eyes skyward, Dixon intones, "Oh Lord, why've y'awl forsaken me?" He asks us, "What about that incomin' stream we passed? What then? We gonna walk on water?"

"We'll have to wade across."

"Oh, now hold on! Don't want no gator sneakin' up and chewin' my tail."

"Wouldn't worry about it," says Cole. "I'm sure gators have standards."

Dixon ignores him. "Two of us could paddle back; two of us could hike out."

While I'm working through the pairings, Fiona says, "You heard Logan: We don't split up."

Cole says, "That's it then; we hike out. But I'm starving. We got anything to eat?"

I get my box lunch out of the canoe and take inventory: ham sandwich, mango, liter of apple juice, six cookies. Dixon finds his pack and carves up the mango with a Swiss Army knife, while I divvy up the rest. We each take a swig of juice, then stash the trash in the canoe.

Cole says with finality, "Let's get movin'."

So we set off. The jungle thins out immediately, and our plan seems manageable: Turn right, follow the water downstream. Dixon is limping, but he doesn't slow us down.

Cole sings, "Like a river flows, surely to the sea."

The stream is concealed by foliage, but we parallel it as best we can. We soon come to a thicket, and we have to make a decision. Going left means leaving the stream, going right means entering the stream, and going through will be a bitch. We plunge into the brush, and two minutes later we back out with torn-up arms and legs. We look left and right, undecided as to which way to go.

Dixon picks thorns out of his scalp. "The lodge is still a consid'rable piece off to our *lay*-eft."

Cole starts right, seemingly out of spite, but Virgin Born has already detoured left. Fiona and I follow him, and we pick up a trail emerging from the thicket.

We come upon the tributary Dixon pointed out earlier, and he finds a place to cross via a combination of two downed trees.

"Lemme go first. If these trunks will hold ol' Dixon, they'll sure as shootin' hold you skinny folk." We reach the other side without incident, and Dixon kneels to inspect a set of tracks. "Might jis' be a hogwar."

We soon come upon a swamp forest, a seasonal wetland submerging the bases of trees. "Right or left?" asks Fiona.

Ignoring her, Cole yanks a yam-sized plant out of the ground. "Guys, check this out. Isn't this what Logan showed us? Remember? It tasted like a sweet potato."

Fiona sniffs the gnarly tuber. "He said if you aren't sure to rub it on your skin or lips."

I set the tuber on a log and crush it under my heel, then I rub a bit of mush on my forearm and wait. "No problem there."

Cole smears a wad on his lips. "No prob…. uh…. CHEEses, that smarts!" He leans over and washes his face. "CHEEEEses!" he shrieks again, and the rest of us jump back, even before we see the four-foot mucus-hued snake slither past the spot his face had been.

We're nuts to think we can bushwhack out of the Amazon. But Cole is undaunted. He veers around the swamp to the right.

For the next hour or so, we make pretty good time. But then we come upon another stream.

"Guys," says Fiona. "Uh, guys?"

I say, "Must be a second tributary we didn't notice."

"No way," Fiona replies. "One or two of us might have missed it, but not all of us. Is this the stream we canoed in on?"

"Nope, can't be," says Cole. "This stream flows from left to right. The stream we came in on will always be moving right to left, unless we cross it."

Dixon says, "What kinda mess you geniuses got us into?"

"Shut up, Virgin Born!" I clench my fists and advance.

Fiona wedges herself between Dixon and me. Cole makes no move to help separate us.

Instead he finds a stick and starts drawing in the dirt. "Bad news; when we detoured around that thicket, we left the stream and never got back to it. See, here's the lake, here's the stream, and here's where Dixon…. uh, here's where we lost the canoe."

x

"Then here's the tributary."

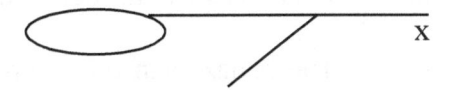

"The tributary has streams coming off of it, like so. We must have come this way."

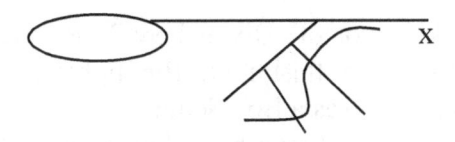

I motion for the stick. "Or maybe this way."

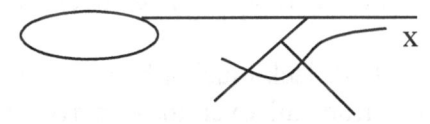

Fiona says, "Either way, we just have to head back toward the lake."

I say, "Maybe. But Cole drew the streams as straight lines. In real life, they wander all over. So that means we're—"

Dixon butts in. "Lost. It means you got us good 'n' lost. Anythin' else you collitch boys wanna tell us?"

Cole delivers a swift left cross to his jaw.

"Son a *bay*-itch!" Dixon wails, sinking to knees.

Fiona shoves her brother in the chest, and bellows, "Cole!"

"This son a *bay*-itch damn near got you killed today!"

Dixon gets one foot planted squarely beneath him and makes like he's going to stand. But having watched my share of football, I recognize the crouch of a defensive tackle, listening for the snap count. Evidently Cole sees it too. Sidestepping the big man's charge, he yells, "Safety blitz!" and winces as Dixon executes a wicked five-point landing – knees, knuckles, nose.

The Virginian rolls onto his back, holding his injured ankle. "Son a *bay*-itch."

Fiona picks Dixon's lens out of the mud and wipes it on her blouse. "Here you go."

He jams the monocle into his eye socket and looks around.

Squinting for all he's worth, he says, "Ah, Jesus in a Jeep! It's all scratched up!"

Cole offers him a hand. Dixon considers it, then struggles to his feet on his own.

"Night's coming," I say. The Amazonian din is growing louder.

Massaging his left wrist, Cole looks up into the gathering darkness. "We'll have to spend the night out here. I wish we could get a fire going."

"Good thing you kids got ol' Dixon here." Revived, he opens his pack and pulls out a flashlight, Bic lighter, box of granola bars and a camera. "Ah was a Boy Scout."

Cole starts to respond, but Fiona beats him to it. "Well, I for one am glad you're here. Let's find a place to camp."

We scatter, and a minute later, she calls us over from fifty yards away.

Dixon arrives first. "Don't lack much a'bein' a gully. If it rains t'night, water'll collect from all over these parts. Girl, if brains was leather, you couldn't saddle a sparrow!"

My turn; I ball my fists and lunge at him.

Cole leaps in front of me and grabs my shoulders. "Whoa," he says, "easy."

Fiona says, "It's okay. Dixon's got all the charm of a dung beetle, but he's right." She peers into the forest. "Anybody see a lady's room?"

"Whole dang jungle's a lady's room," mutters Dixon. She leaves, and he approaches Cole with outstretched hand. "Ah'm sorry 'bout puttin' your sister in harm's way. Ah truly am."

Cole regards him coldly, but takes the proffered hand. "I accept that. But you need to set things right with her."

"Ah will do just that."

Cole turns to me. "And you. You dove into a river with a caiman in it to help Fi." He gives me that same hard look his sister did. "I'm not gonna forget that any time soon." Leaving me no chance to respond, he heads into the woods, saying, "Let's find some firewood."

Most of the wood we find is too wet, but Cole comes across a downed tree, under which we find a trove of dry branches.

"Gracie must be going nuts," he says. "She comes across

as all goodness and sunshine, but when we don't return.... She's always been afraid I'm gonna leave her."

"What? I don't get it."

"Me neither. But being disowned by her dad messed with her. She's not as secure as she comes across." He pauses. "Damn Dixon. Don't lack much a'bein' a clusterfuck."

We rejoin Dixon, who has set up camp beside an odd-looking tree. Ten feet over our heads, it sends out ridged roots at a forty-five degree angle, protecting us on two sides from.... well, I have no idea.

Fiona returns with an armload of surfboard-sized leaves, saying, "This will make good bedding. Feel." The waxy leaves are softer than they looks.

Dixon passes around granola bars, then kneels and covers the empty box with twigs. "M' Bic's on her last legs."

Fiona closes her eyes, and I realize that she's praying; petitioning for The Creator of All to intervene on her behalf.... actually, on our behalf. Regardless of the validity of her beliefs, I cannot deny the purity of her heart.

Dixon, squinting through his dirty monocle, flicks his Bic and holds it under the box, which is damp, like everything in the Amazon. He pleads, "C'mon, darlin'." The cardboard blackens but doesn't catch. A handful of leaves flare up, then dies, and we hold our breath. But a twig catches and then another, while Dixon adds larger pieces of kindling. Cole and I blow on the flame until our lungs fill with smoke and we succumb to coughing.

When it's clear the fire is here to stay, we whoop it up, and Dixon proclaims, "Don't lack much a'bein' a campfire."

The rest of us scatter and return with enough wood to hopefully last until dawn. The fire smokes and spits, but our clothes are soggy, so we stand as close to the flames as is tolerable.

"Look what I found." Cole holds up a crusty old boot and a candle. "Fi, remember when Crampy Q used to play that game with us?" He explains to me, "He had us name three random things and then we'd invent a story around them. Let's try it."

Fiona picks up a y-shaped stick. "Here's our third object. Okay, here goes: A one-legged man walks through the jungle...."

I go next: ".... by candlelight, searching for...."

Cole holds the stick by its stems. ".... for water, using a

divining rod...."

"Hold it," says Dixon. "Hold it right *thay-er*! How's a one-laigged man s'posta walk? An' where'd he rassle hisself up a candle? And why'd he go lookin' for water in the firs' place? He's smack dab inna middle of a rain for'st."

Cole says, "Chill, Virgin Born. This is a kids' game."

"Yer game's 'bout as useful as a trapdoor in a canoe."

Fearing that Cole will belt him again, I say, "Let's figure out who's sleeping where."

Fiona divvies up the huge leaves into four piles. Cole and I arrange our leaves on either side of hers.

Dixon situates himself against the tree trunk, ten feet away. "If y'awl need to take a leak, Ah'm puttin' my flashlight under this here log. Feel free to avail yerselves of it."

We thank him, then discuss the prospects of hiking out tomorrow, but no new ideas are forthcoming. Eventually Fiona says she's turning in, and Cole stokes the fire one last time. Our wood has been drying for the past hour, and it catches right away.

"Hotter'n a goat's butt in a pepper patch." The flames illuminate Dixon, sitting against the tree with his camera up to his eye. "Ah come down here to get me a pitcher of a hogwar. Jis' wanna be ready." Cole snorts disdainfully.

We lie down on our makeshift beds, and though I'm exhausted, sleep eludes me.

Drinking in the jungle's uproar, I pick out the descending arpeggio of the grey potoo and hum along: G – E – D – B – G. How wondrous, and unlikely, for evolution to naturally select a birdbrain that would be conversant with music theory, with the chops to create a melody that's both appealing and emotionally ambiguous to a human.

As much as I appreciate the potoo's musical ability, I wish I'd never seen one up close. I imagine the bird swooping down on us, putrid yellow eyes glowing in the dark, its Halloween mask grin drooling in anticipation of gorging on the delectable pink flesh of well-fed tourists. Though the night is warm, I shiver.

We hear the rain before we feel it. The canopy holds it off for fifteen minutes, the leaves overhead serving as tiny reservoirs, the moss acting as sponges. But the rain eventually overwhelms our roof, making the fire hiss and pop. My companions and I each cover ourselves with a giant leaf.

Fiona whispers, "Theo? How's your shoulder?"

"Sore, but it's okay. Thank you for taking care of me."

"I was scared when I saw that blood."

"It looks worse than it is."

"Theo, you are…. special to me." She reaches over and takes my hand.

My chest is caving in again, and I've got a woody coming on. "You're special to me too." CHEE-ses, Theo, you moron, is that the best you've got? In a voice that hopefully sounds brave, I whisper, "We'll get out of here tomorrow. Have faith."

The fire is fighting a losing battle against the rain and darkness. Something skitters past our feet, and Fiona asks, "What was that?"

"I don't know, but if it's anything dangerous, Virgin Born will take a picture and blind it with his flash." She starts giggling, but then yelps. "What! Fiona, are you OK?"

"A trickle of water just ran down my backside."

"Bad trickle," I scold. "Bad."

She laughs again. "Are you dry?"

"As a bone." Considering the lump in my shorts, this is a wince-worthy pun, and a safety blitz from Fiona would be most welcome. I would even consider thanking God for it.

Then, as if a prayer has been answered, she crawls in beside me, laying her head on my uninjured shoulder. Now what is *this*? Is she afraid we're gonna die? Did someone slip her a muña mickey? Or is the oxygen-saturated air affecting her? Does she think Cole is asleep? *Is* he asleep? If not, will he punch me in the jaw? By now he considers me a friend, but this is his sister after all.

"We'll get out of this," I repeat. "But if we don't, I will die a happy man."

She lifts her head, but the dying fire is too weak to illuminate her grey eyes. She slides her thigh over mine, making me gasp. She kisses me, tentatively at first. I'm trying to keep silent, but not succeeding. Can Cole hear my panting? Fiona rises up and straddles me. She kisses me again, and we grind our hips together. The leaves beneath us make a crunching sound.

"Jungle boogie," comes the whispered singing from Cole.

"Jungle boogie." Fiona and I crack up, and Cole intermingles his singing with bouts of laughing.

"The *hay-ell*'s goin' on over there?"

Cole starts singing "The Lion Sleeps Tonight," and Dixon joins in with uncommonly good background vocals: "Weema weh, a weema weh, a weema weh—"

Cole interrupts him. "A weema weh? That's not right. It goes: Weenie whack, a weenie whack."

Fiona joins in too, and I add a harmony. Once we have the background vocals going, Cole sings the falsetto part as: "The hogwar sleeps tonight." Any cat in earshot would have headed for the hills by now, had there been any hills.

The song dissolves in howling and hilarity. Fiona rolls off me and lays her head on my shoulder. Water courses down my back. Our amorous moment has passed.

"Theo," she whispers.

"Fio," I rhyme.

She snickers and caresses my ear. "I'm sorry for kidding you about your llama ears. They're your best feature."

"You are not yet qualified to say what my best feature is." She runs a hand across my chest, and I say, "I got altitude sickness in Puno, and I hoped you were praying for me. At my lowest point, I wasn't thinking about my family.... well, that's not true – I miss my mom." I consider explaining myself, but this is not the time. "I found myself thinking about you. It was freezing there, and I hoped you were warm."

She brings her body in close. "I did pray for you. And I missed you. When you didn't show up at Mitad del Mundo, I was afraid I'd never see you again." She sniffles. "But all of a sudden, there you were, making Llove the Llama hand shadows and singing with Cole. And I...." She's crying now. "I put on sunglasses and went to the ladies' room so nobody could see me bawling." She buries her face against my chest and convulses.

"I thought I'd lost you too."

We're silent for while, then Fiona asks, "Have you finished writing your song?"

"Working on it," I say, and nestle her in closer.

"Theo, there's no place I'd rather be." Her breathing slows and deepens.

Dixon is rustling around behind us. I picture him leaning against the tree, his camera hopefully keeping dry beneath the bill of his Virginia Tech cap, his finger on the button, waiting for a hogwar to stroll by. What a goof.

Every so often a bug dive-bombs me, and I swat it away, doing my best not to awaken Fiona. Fiona.... I like the sound of her name. Fiona, Fiona. Or maybe I'll call her Fio.

I dream about zoo animals getting loose. A jaguar rips off my left arm, while a llama stands on my right. It leans down and grins.

I awaken, staring up into the claustrophobic blackness. Something is pressing on my shoulder, and a panic takes hold of me. I gotta get outta here!

But then I feel Fio's hand on my chest, under my shirt, and I exhale in relief. My breathing and heartbeat return to normal, and her presence warms me. Though my arm has gone to sleep, I keep still, out of a desire not to wake this woman that.... that I.... love. Yes, that is the right word. I love her. I'm twenty-five years old; this is a first for me.

My clothes smell of smoke and sweat, trees roots are poking me in the back, my shoulder throbs, my heels are blistered from hiking in wet shoes, and my ankles itch from bug bites. And, oh, we're lost in the Amazon. God knows what sort of animals are closing in on us. Boas? Scorpions? A potoo? A hogwar or two?

All in all, I have never been happier.

Chapter 17: He Sacrificed Himself

My eyes pop open. Did I hear something? Well, of course I did; the nocturnal jungle party is still in full swing. But this sound is different; it's nearby. Easing Fio's head off my shoulder, I lift my head, and search for the source of the noise.

Dawn is coming, but this bears no resemblance to an Arizona dawn. In the desert around Tucson, the coming sunrise announces itself with no modesty whatsoever; the sky offers up a dazzling panoply of reds and blues, gold and fuchsia. Against that backdrop stand the dark outlines of saguaro cacti, some graceful, some monolithic, others twisted, and all beautiful. By contrast, dawn in the jungle progresses from blackness, to almost blackness, to can't-see-squat, and so on as you work your way up to the dusky hues of midday.

I sit up and squint, but can't quite make out.... There! Something is moving. I'm blinded by a flash, and then two more.

Dixon howls triumphantly. "Ah got choo, you son a *bay*-itch!" He turns on his flashlight and swings it back and forth. "Oh baby, got me a hogwar!"

Fio sits up. "Dixon? Are you all right?"

"Right *hay*-er, lil' lady. And they said ol' Dixon couldn't do it! Ha!"

"You saw a jaguar? Where'd he go?"

"Flash scared 'im off, I reckon!" He flicks off his light.

"Virgin Born," Cole grumbles. "Go to sleep."

"Got me a pitcher of a cat! A big 'un!" By the sound of it, he's up and dancing around.

Cole says, "Don't lack much a'bein' a fuckin' asshole."

With undisguised glee, Dixon says, "Ah reckon he smelt yer blood, Theo!"

What! Is that how he sees me? As bait? As a sacrificial llama? His remark reminds me of something Claire would tell Phil, half-jokingly.

I lie back down, and reach out for Fio. She crawls on top of me and kisses me, long and deeply, while I massage her hips.

She rolls onto her back, pulling me on top of her. Leaves crunch and crackle beneath us.

"CHEEE-ses, you two," grouses Cole. "Get a room."

Fio and I kiss and caress until she informs me that my shoulder is bleeding. It's getting light out now, and she leads me to the stream to wash and dress my arm. She rips off another strip of her blouse, exposing three more glorious inches of midriff. While tying off the makeshift bandage, she eyes me with tenderness and confusion. "Theo, you are special to me, but I cannot be with a man who doesn't share my spiritual convictions."

My stomach gurgles in response. At some point she will have to choose between Barry and me. Still, I take her concern as a promising sign that I'm in contention.

"Our beliefs can't be that different," I tell her. "Try to be open-minded."

She mulls that over, then says, "I will, but I will ask the same of you. Your belief is more fixed, more absolute than mine." In response to my dropped jaw, she explains, "When I say I know Jesus, that statement applies to me, only me. But when you say stuff like 'Nobody Knows,' you're speaking for billions. Your stance dismisses pretty much everyone's beliefs, even atheists. It treats everyone equally, but not justly."

Oh my. Believe it or not, this had not occurred to me. On the face of it, Nobody Knows sounds so temperate, so humble. It sounds fair. But she's right; even Nobody I know Knows reeks of arrogance. It makes me sound, ironically, like a know-it-all. Are there any downgrades left? Perhaps: Who Knows?

Fio takes my astonishment as an encouraging sign. I take her hand and lead her back to camp, where Dixon is packed and ready to go. His jaw sports a nasty bruise.

Cole lips are red and swollen, from, I assume, that tuber he tasted yesterday. He stares up longingly at a cluster of bananas, hanging four feet out of his reach. The tree trunk is too smooth to climb, so he throws a piece of firewood at the cluster, mashing three bananas into baby food.

Fio grimaces. "The bananas are kind of green anyway."

"Nonsense," says Cole. It comes out "Donthenth." "Here, sis, we'll give you a boost." He and I lean against the tree and make our hands into stirrups. She grabs our shoulders and places a muddy shoe in my hands, then bounces a few times and hoists herself up. She places her other shoe in Cole's hands, and we lift. Standing on our shoulders, she gives Cole a playful smack in the head.

"Hey! What'd I ever do to *you*?"

"You mean besides telling me Timmy the Turtle died when I was six? Besides—"

"Okay, okay, I apologize for a lifetime of emotional abuse. Now grab us some nanners."

She pulls off a clump of bananas and tosses them to Dixon, then Cole and I lower her to the ground. He grimaces and holds his left wrist. It's been bothering him ever since he slugged Dixon.

The bananas are not quite ripe, but they're edible.

"Don't lack much a'bein' breakfast," says Cole, after eating two. Rinsing his hands in the swamp, he asks, "What now?"

"Ah'll tell ya what now." Dixon pushes his monocle into his eye socket. "Y'all kin talk about tribbletares 'til yer blue in the face, but the river curved 'round to the right all morn'. I'm cuttin' straight through the jungle there. You kin come or not."

"Let's discuss our options," I say.

"No, Ah didn't get a lotta sleep last night, what with all the racket and festivities." He leers at Fio, who blushes and looks away. "And the one time Ah did nod off, Ah dreamt there was a hogwar chasin' me, and Ah's a'wearin' pork chop panties."

Cole grins. "Gotta remember that one."

"Anyhoo, Ah've weighed m'options. Ah'm headin' back." He hoists his pack over his shoulder and hobbles off.

Fio blocks his path. "Please. Your glasses are broken, and your limp is worse today."

"Ah 'preciate yer concern, lil' lady, but my foot'll be fine. Mah glasses are mostly fer readin', and Ah didn't bring 'long any lit'rature."

She places a hand on his arm. "Please, Dixon. I'd hate for someone to find your lighter, hat and camera, and make up stories about you."

"Jis' to make sure that don't happen...." He digs around in his pocket and tosses me his Bic. "Now if y'all will kindly remove your hand.... Ah'll have 'em send a rescue party."

"Dixon, we need you," she says.

He shambles off, calling back over his shoulder, "Don't piss down my back and tell me it's rainin'. You kids got no need'a me. Y'all been to collitch."

Cole says, "No use, Fi; he is one stubborn son a *bay*-itch. Let me drain my radiator, then let's figure out a plan."

He steps behind a tree, and Fio says, "Theo, I haven't been fair to you. Or to Barry. I.... like him, and respect him."

A rabble of butterflies takes flight in my stomach. "Fio, I love you, and I trust that you will take the right path."

"But what if Barry gets to the lodge and I'm not there?"

I have no answer for that.

When Cole returns, I find a stick and draw on the ground. "All the streams around here end up in Lake Sachacocha. So when we come to a stream flowing left to right, we cross it and head downstream."

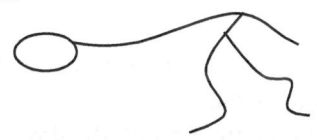

Fio asks, "Why cross it?"

Cole says, "The further upstream we cross, the narrower it will be." He frowns. "Which is fine, as long as there's not another river system we don't know about."

"Doesn't matter," I say. "Look. It will still lead us back to the lodge. All streams take us home."

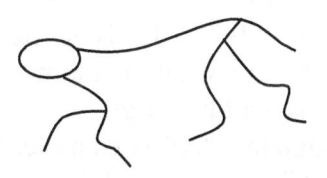

Fio motions for the stick. "But three streams enter the lake and one leaves. Like this."

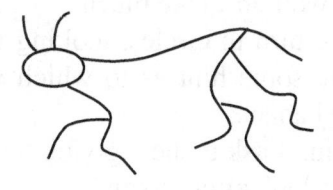

This is irresistible. I take the stick and sing as I draw. "In the jungle, the mighty jungle, the llama sleeps tonight."

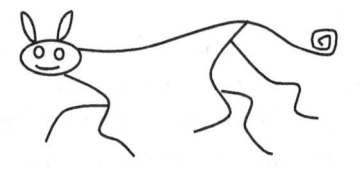

Cole scratches his head, and Fio asks, "That's a llama?"

I sing, "Hush, my Fio, don't fear, my Fio, the llama sleeps today."

Fio calls out, "Safety blitz!" and tackles me by driving her shoulder into my belly. She slides forward until she's sitting on my chest, and says, "You were warned: Anybody makes a truly horrible joke in the Quinn family, we tackle 'em."

Bewitched by her bare tummy, I ask, "Does this mean I'm family now?"

"Gettin' there." She pins my wrists and kisses me. "Theo, you are a better guitar player than artist."

"Well, you're a better kisser than football player. I let you tackle me."

"I can take you down whenever I want."

"Promises, promises." She rises and gives me a hand up.

It may seem strange that we're engaging in horseplay – or foreplay – in such dire circumstances, but that's just it: Our situation is so grim that it doesn't quite seem real. Yes, we all have to go sometime, but this isn't how I die, lost in the Amazon, eaten by hogwars or swallowed by a boa. This is not how my story ends. On the other hand, I'll bet that's what my mom was thinking as she drew her final breath. This isn't how I go....

Cole is studying my diagram. "All streams lead us home, unless there's another watershed."

I say, "But that could only happen if there's a ridge to separate the two systems."

"This land is so flat, it wouldn't take much."

That sobers us up. We turn in circles, looking up into the trees, as if they might provide some hint as to which way to go. Cole tosses each of us another banana.

Fio bows her head again. I ask if she's giving thanks.

"No, I'm asking God to look after Dixon."

Cole scowls. "So you're trying to get God to do something he wasn't already gonna do? You're lobbying God to change his righteous mind? Look, Fi, Dixon will either get lucky or he won't. God's got nothin' to do with it."

At this point, he's just trying to pick a fight, which dashes my hopes that the Quinns' dialog would become less contentious with Barry out of the picture.

"It's all about faith," she says patiently. "Praying is simply putting faith into words."

"Prayer doesn't work. Miracles don't happen now like they supposedly did in Biblical times."

"Sure they do. Cancer patients get healed all the time."

"Yes, sometimes they do. By science. But if you lose a leg, God's not gonna grow you a new one."

"Okay, then," says Fio, "how do you explain the return of the Jews to Israel? That was prophesized two thousand years ago."

My History of the Middle East course comes drifting back. "Jews began a mass immigration to Palestine in the 1800s. They were backed by Christian Restorationists, who coined the slogan 'A land without people for a people without land,' which was nuts, because Palestinians were already living there."

Cole asks, "Why were Christians so hot on having Jews settle in the Middle East?"

"Partly because Jewish people had been persecuted and slaughtered in Europe for centuries, so—"

Cole asks, "Wasn't Martin Luther part of that?"

"In his later years, yes. 'Burn their synagogues, and drive them out like mad dogs,' is how he put it. Anyway, in the mid-1800s, Christian leaders lobbied for Jewish people to have their own country. But many of them pushed for Israel's restoration in order to fulfill prophecies from the Book of Revelations."

Cole says, "That's like prophesizing someone is gonna die, then you stab him. That's not prophecy; it's murder in the first."

A rant is coming. Oh well, it will keep the hogwars away.

"See?" he says, arms flyin'. "This is what I'm talking about. Once people commit to a faith, they stop questioning, stop thinking even. Next thing you know, otherwise reasonable people are talking about virgins having kids. Crazy stuff. And what about that Methuselah guy who lived nine hundred years? Did he have

Alzheimer's for his last eight hundred? Let me ask you, Fi: When was the last time you altered your beliefs?"

This may have been a fair question, were we not floundering around in the jungle, and I'm about to say as much when she answers, "Last night, thinking about evolution. Maybe the world was not created in six days. I can live with the idea that the world is way older."

"I'm impressed," says Cole. "But if Genesis isn't meant to be taken literally, how do you know about the rest of the Bible?"

"Good question." Fio ponders that. "I'm not sure. By the way, I don't believe you're evil.... you're feisty, maybe...." She gives him a sly smile. "And goofed up, definitely—"

"But what about your belief in the devil and—?"

"Don't ask me to solve your pathetic little puzzles! I'm no good at them. Jesus' message is all about love, and how we live. That's all that matters." She gives him an appraising look. "What about you? When was the last time you altered your beliefs?"

He palms his forehead, mulling that over. "Been a while."

"You believe in.... quarks and ten dimensions. Crazy stuff. But do you believe in anything that gives your life meaning?"

"Enough," I say. "We need to get a move on."

Fio smiles sheepishly; Cole exhales loudly. He finds The Endless Debate frustrating, whereas she's here to serve and save. In this case she is serving God by attempting to save Cole from eternal disconsolation, if not out-and-out damnation.

I say, "Let's follow the river downstream."

Fio shakes her head. "We should follow Dixon."

Cole is aghast. "Sis! He couldn't find water in a bucket! Let him go."

"He's out there on his own." Again, this is an opportunity to serve and save.

I say, "Cole, there's a chance he's right."

"That, as they say, is a fat chance."

Fio hurls a banana peel at him and turns away. "I'm going after him."

Cole shouts, "Fi! He's got a ten-minute head start! We'll never find him."

There's no way I'm letting Fio take off alone. "The ground is soaked, Cole, and he's a big guy. Check out these footprints.

C'mon. We can retrace our steps if need be."

"CHEEEE-ses!"

I'm not sure what direction we're walking. All I know is we're putting distance between ourselves and the stream, which is our one sure way home. I'm surprised Fio would be so willing to walk away from it. Then I remember something she said: But what if Barry gets to the lodge and I'm not there?

So, is this why she so readily followed Dixon? Because she's afraid Dixon will get back to the lodge before? In which case, he would tell Barry about the "racket and festivities."

We catch up with Dixon an hour later and follow him, despite protestations from Cole about the blind leading the blind. Virgin Born trudges on silently, crossing two streams, the first of which he walks across on the surface of the water, evoking a fantastical vision of Jesus walking upon the Sea of Galilee. Fiona's jaw drops. When we reach the water's edge, however, we can see he's balancing on a submerged tree trunk, an inch beneath the surface.

Coming to a second stream, Dixon walks straight in and promptly falls on his face. He comes up sputterin' and cussin', looking and sounding decidedly un-Jesus-like. He crawls out the other side, and the rest of us wade across.

We soon come upon another waterway, and without hesitation, Dixon turns right, following the water upstream, eyes on the ground. "Got somethin' Ah want y'all to see."

Fio locks elbows with her brother. "Give him ten minutes."

Cole is fuming. "The dumb shall lead the really dumb!"

In order to skirt a thicket, we have to leave the stream. We pick it up again right away, but I've had my fill of being lost.

"Why the hell are we heading upstream?"

Dixon ignores me, but a minute later, he says, "Here's why," and points out our canoe, sitting by the shoreline.

Cole glares at Fio. "Oh great! We just wasted half the day! What were you thinking, following Virgin Born into the jungle? CHEEE-ses! We're right back where we were yesterday!"

"Except fer t'day it's two hours earlier." Dixon collapses on a fern, without bothering to take off his pack. "And three will fit in that canoe. Yessir, they will."

"Oh?" says Cole. "And which three would that be?"

But Fio is way ahead of her brother. "No, Dixon, we've discussed this. We are not leaving you here."

"Don't you worry yer purdy head 'bout me, lil' lady. Ah got y'all into this fix, and this here's my chance to set things right. If the good Lord's willin' and this here creek don't rise, you'll be back at the lodge in time fer lunch. Ol' Dixon kin take care a'hisself, leastways 'til one of you comes back fer me. Ah'm gonna curl up and take me a little nap, soon's I see the ass end of yer canoe disappear 'round that bend."

Cole asks, "How did you know we'd follow you?"

"Ah didn't, not fer sure. But Ah figgered yer sister wouldn't leave ol' Dixon traipsin' through the boonies on his own. Ah figgered she'd convince y'all to follow. If not, Ah would'a canoed back by m'self, gators or not."

I'm incredulous. "Why didn't you tell us you were coming back here?"

He eyes me like I'm feeble-minded. "Because, if Ah'd a'told you, boy, you wouldn't never a'followed me. You'd'a let me paddle myself down the river."

Fio folds her arms defiantly. "Doesn't matter. We're not leaving you here."

Dixon gives her a raspy laugh. "Tell ya what. Ah'm gonna take a leak and a look around, then we kin discuss it all ya like." He struggles to his feet and makes off through the bushes.

We debate our options for several minutes, then Cole says, "Wasting time. Let's cast off."

Fio isn't having it. "We're not leaving Dixon."

I ask, "Where is he anyway? And why'd he take his pack? He got TP in there?"

It apparently hadn't registered with Cole that Dixon's pack was gone. He exhales and shakes his head in admiration. "That sly son a *bay*-itch; he ditched us."

Fio says, "We can follow his tracks, just like this morning."

Cole shakes his head again, this time in resignation. "Nope. Look, the ground has dried up some. This morning he left tracks intentionally."

Fio screams Dixon's name, but gets no response.

"Let him go, Fi." Standing behind her, Cole sets his hands on her shoulders. "And say a prayer for him."

I wait ten seconds before saying, "The sooner we get going, the sooner they'll send out a search party. Who knows? Maybe he'll make it back ahead of us."

Only after that last line has left my mouth am I aware that I'm fishing for a response. Will my words give Fio hope? Or will she be distressed by the possibility that Dixon might inform Barry of our "racket and festivities?"

Scanning the shadowy forest, Fio seems disheartened, but is that because she's afraid Dixon will get back first before us, or that he won't get back at all? Either way, she's got disappointment waiting.

I retrieve the orange juice bottle and stick it on a limb overhanging the river, for searchers to use as a marker. Cole and I tip the canoe on its side to dump out the rainwater, then slide the dugout into the stream. We climb in and shove off. We only have one paddle, and Cole takes the first shift paddling. Fifty yards downstream, we find the other canoe, resting amongst a cluster of reeds.

"Let's see how bad she's banged up," says Cole. He and I step into the knee-deep stream and lift the dugout. Water pours from the jagged hole, three feet from the bow. We set the boat back in the stream, and I steady it while Cole climbs in. Water surges back in through the hole, and he finds himself sitting in a deepening puddle. When he scoots back, the water follows.

"It's a goner," says Fio. "Even using the OJ bottle to bail, you'd sink in two minutes."

An hour later, Fio tenses and points out a caiman lazing on the right shore. This is no cuddly six-footer. I drag the paddle in the water to slow us, and we coast to a stop on the left shore.

Fio points downstream. "And there's a bigger one!"

"Where?" says Cole. "By that log?"

"That's no log!"

"CHEEEE-ses!" The reptile slides into the water, and Cole orders us out. We step into the water and lift our canoe onto land. He says, "Let's carry it downstream fifty yards and shove off."

"No way!" says Fio. "Did you see how well camouflaged

that big one was?"

"Let's hike out," I say. "We've gotta be halfway back." My friends agree.

A half hour later, the clouds unload on us, but it's a warm rain, and a sense of well-being washes over me. We will not die of thirst, and I'm hiking through the jungle with Fio, my newfound love, and Cole, my newfound friend, whose devil-may-care attitude is rubbing off on me. We are not out of the woods, so to speak, but we are headed in the right direction, and we have the paddle with us to whack through thickets. I stop and look up, allowing the rain to run down my face.

When Fio gives me a bemused smile, I pick her up and swing her around, saying, "Gonna be fine." We continue in buoyant silence, as if the rain is carrying us on invisible currents.

We stay closer to the stream today, which means thicker brush, which slows us down. The sky is beginning to darken, so we decide to set up camp. The rain stops, but everything is soaked, so it takes a while to find firewood. Eventually Fio finds a trove of tinder beneath a downed tree.

The Bic is running on fumes; we'll only get one shot at this. The lighter emits a feeble flame, but the tinder catches right away, and we add larger twigs. The fire is soon going strong, though the moist wood sends up thick plumes of smoke. We huddle around the flames to dry out.

Cole says, out of the blue, "Fi, I'm sorry for acting like a horse's ass this morning."

Fiona is about to respond, but instead she looks past him and yelps. I whip around, expecting to see a charging jaguar. But there is Yachay, machete in hand, grinning like crazy. We crowd around and pelt him with questions, none of which he understands. He knocks the wood off the fire with his machete and scatters the ashes. He then walks into the jungle, and we follow, asking the same questions over and over:

"How'd he find us?"

"How far from the lodge do you think we are?"

"Why are we leaving the stream?"

The trail is not well-defined, so Yachay whacks away vines with his machete. Daylight is waning, but he shows no signs of stopping. My friends and I have to stare at the ground to keep from tripping, so we have no idea what direction we're going. For all we know, we're walking in circles, keeping to the contours of the Mother of all Mobius Strips. We've placed our lives in the care of a man whose language we don't speak.

We've been hiking for half an hour when Fio says, "Guys. Uh, guys?" A faint glow lights up the forest. "Is that what I think it is?"

Cole drawls, "Don't lack much a'bein' a jungle lodge."

Fio throws herself at me and squeals with joy, while Cole thanks Yachay repeatedly. The trail widens, and Fio places herself between Cole and me, arm in arm in arm. We step up onto the kerosene-lit boardwalk, just as an older woman leaves her hut; she eyes us like we've returned from the dead.

By the time we arrive at the bar, most everyone has heard the news, and we're mobbed: "Good to see you where were you your shoulder is bleeding...."

We hear Gracie shrieks from forty yards away. The crowd parts to let her through, and she assaults Cole, yelling, "Creep! I hate you!" She beats on his chest with her tiny fists, then wraps herself around his neck, as everyone laughs and claps and cheers.

Logan elbows his way through the crush of guests. He's less ecstatic than the rest of us.

Fio asks, "Did Dixon make it back?"

Logan spins around. "He's not here?" Silence, instantly. "You *split up*?"

"I.... we tried to get him to come with us, but he insisted on finding his own way back."

"First rule of survival: Don't split up!" He glares at me. "What were you thinking? We had people out looking for you."

"Dixon took a shortcut, and he—"

"Back up. Yesterday you paddled up the second stream—"

"No, we took the first one."

"Which is why searchers didn't find you. Why didn't you return yesterday?"

"One of the canoes got damaged," Cole explains. That last word comes out as "dammitch." It's hard to take him seriously. "We couldn't all fit in one boat, so we hiked back." He sounds like a kid who got caught messing around on a school outing.

Logan asks, "How did the canoe get damaged?"

Cringing, I say, "Dixon rammed his knee through the bow, because the canoe overturned when—"

"So Dixon is injured?" Logan focuses drill sergeant eyes on me. The amiable tour guide we met two days ago is nowhere in sight. The guests are horror-struck.

"No, he's okay, well, except he's limping, and his glasses broke when—"

Logan cuts me off with a raised palm. "So he's blind?" Surveying Fio's disheveled hair, scratched-up stomach and filthy clothes, he says, "Your shirt is ripped." He eyes me accusingly, then asks Cole, "What happened to your hand?"

"Huh?"

"Your *hand*. You're holding it like it's gonna fall off."

"I'm okay. But Theo's shoulder is bleeding." He takes a deep breath. "See, when the caiman—"

"Enough! Cole, follow me!" Logan then aims two rigid fingers at Fio and me. "First door on the right. The nurse will be in to patch you up."

We follow orders. Our elation at making it back lasted all of one minute.

Fio says, "If we had paddled back right away, like Dixon asked us to, he would have waited for us to return."

"Maybe he would have hiked back anyway."

She shakes her head dazedly. "He wouldn't set us up like that. Dixon was a bozo, but he wasn't malicious. I bet he hid in the forest and watched until we left before he took off." It's unnerving to hear her refer to Dixon in past tense.

"At least they'll know where to look for him," I say. "He's a survivor."

Fio looks washed out. I kneel and guide her head onto my shoulder. She doesn't resist, nor does she respond when I stroke her neck.

A teenage boy brings us each a bowl of vegetable soup and a hunk of bread. I devour mine. Fio swallows a few spoonfuls and sets it aside, saying, "I'm done."

An Ecuadorian woman enters to tend our wounds. She has a friendly demeanor, but wisely makes no effort to cheer us up. She bandages Fio's stomach, and cleans out my wound with something that stings and stinks. She gives me a tetanus shot, then tapes on a coaster-sized bandage and tells me to get my shoulder checked in Quito.

We thank her and head out to Fiona's hut. I turn my back while she removes her damp clothes and dons a nightshirt. She climbs into bed, but does not invite me to join her. I kiss her cheek and tuck in the mosquito netting, making sure it has no rips.

"Theo," she says weakly. "I trust you."

"That's just about the nicest thing you could say to me."

She still has not responded a minute later, so I tiptoe out, and stop by my hut for a shower. The lukewarm water washes away a multitude of indiscretions.

I return to the bar and find Cole, beer in hand, looking chastened. His greasy blonde hair is slicked back, his shirt is torn.

I slump into a wicker chair. "Did you survive Logan's Inquisition?"

"Fuck fuckety fuck," he moans. "We messed up, pally."

"Yeah, we could'a done better. Where's Gracie?"

"Calming Logan down. She'll be along."

"Do we have any idea how Yachay found us?"

Felipe overhears my question. "He could smell you."

Cole sniffs his own armpit. "Smells like roses." His Daffy Duck lips make it come out as: Spelth lie rozhuth.

"Yachay smelled your fire." Felipe sets a fruity drink in front of me. "Specialty of the house. Selva saliva."

"What's that mean?"

"Jungle spit, my own concoction." He watches expectantly as I take a sip.

A pleasing heat slides down my throat. Felipe nods and retreats to his post at the bar.

I tell Cole, "I hope Dixon is someplace dry."

"Well, he is a resourceful son a *bay*-itch." He scans the bar furtively. "Yeah, we could'a done better, but...." He leans in. "I don't know about you, pally, but these last two days, I had the time of my freakin' life. This'll make a hell of a tale."

I stifle a guilty smile. "As you would say, ditto that."

He calls out, "Felipe, could Theo borrow your charango?"

The bartender lifts the timeworn instrument off a hook and hands it across the bar. I strum a simple progression and sing: "In the jungle, the quiet jungle, the llama sleeps tonight."

Cole picks it up right away, as do several others. We crack up during the "weenie whack" chorus, and the song falls apart. People applaud, we take a bow.

Gracie enters, plops down on a bamboo chair and promptly dozes off. She apparently got less sleep than we did last night.

Felipe holds out his hands for the charango. Playing the same chords, he inserts a flurry of sixteenth notes. His right hand moves fluidly, like it's unattached to his arm. The song settles into a new groove, and everyone sings along. At song's end, everyone claps and woo-hoos. Cole asks Felipe to play another one.

"Sorry, I don't know American music." Felipe hands me the charango.

I fiddle with some chords and begin a halting version of "You Are My Sunshine." After two times through the progression, I give him back his instrument. "Can you do that?"

He starts through the changes, adding tones to spice up the chords, as a jazz player would do. He finds a zippy little rhythm and everyone sings along. More people enter, and Cole gets us clapping on the off-beats.

Fio is standing by the entrance, looking used up, and I serenade her across the boisterous bar. Cole adds a harmony on the verse, which tells of a smitten man's dream of holding his beloved. Strange, I've always considered this song to be a children's ditty, but tonight it sounds sweet and soulful.

Just as Gracie awakens, Logan enters, looking grumpy. She grabs his hand and coaxes him into the center of the gazebo. With a smile that is groggy yet irresistible, she sets her other hand on his shoulder and begins swaying to the music. With an ah-what-the-hell look, he places his hand on her waist and glides her across the floor. He grins broadly and twirls her.

In a later verse, the smitten man warns that if his beloved doesn't return his adoration, she'll regret it. He ends up in tears. She wasn't his sunshine after all. Fio gives me a feeble wave and leaves. The tune fizzles.

Felipe hands me the charango, and says, "Mas." More. He digs up a pair of bongos and hands them to Cole.

"Okay," I say, "this one's called 'Blue Moon.'"

People begin leaving at midnight, and we pull the plug on the sing-along. Cole, Gracie and Logan are swapping stories. All is apparently forgiven. I get my charango out of my hut and ask Felipe for a charango lesson.

"The trick is loosening up your right wrist," he says. "Like so." He begins playing a simple strumming pattern, then adds the stuttering in-between beats characteristic of Andean music.

"Wait a sec. Are those dotted sixteenth notes?"

"I don't understand all that. I just listen and play."

Just listen and play. Yeah, right. A half hour later I can imitate some of his rhythmic phrases, though my playing lacks finesse.

Eventually Felipe closes up shop and leaves with Logan. Gracie has fallen asleep again, chin on her chest, leaving Cole and me to soak up the sounds of the Amazon.

"Can you believe what Felipe did with those songs?" I ask. "I get the feeling he could do that with pretty much any tune."

"And did you see how people respond to that rhythm? Drives 'em crazy. We should put together a fusion band."

"Llove the Llama; let's do it." We clink glasses and drink.

A few drops of rain hit the leaves of a banana plant, and seconds later we're looking out at a deluge.

"Cole, I hope Dixon's okay."

"Yeah, when I told Logan where we went, I thought he was gonna pass a stone. He used the word 'serpentine' to describe the waterways." Cole and I sing, "Why, and where, did you go?"

"Dixon, you sly son a *bay*-itch." Cole gives me a troubled look. "Can you believe he.... well, he *sacrificed* himself for us."

This had not occurred to me. I tell Cole about Fio's guilt over not paddling back right away, as Dixon wanted us to.

"But it wasn't her fault." He pinches the bridge of his nose. "She's right though; we should have just left."

As it was happening, our jungle trek seemed like a grand adventure. But now, ensconced within the safety of the lodge, our caper seems reckless. I fear for the loud-mouthed, well-intended Virginian carpenter.

I stand up, groaning and massaging the small of my back.

Cole stands also and wraps his arms around me. "Wanna go canoeing tomorrow, pally? Me neither."

Chapter 18: Better than Hell

I awaken to birds singing, monkeys chattering and unseen critters buzzing about. But from inside the protective netting, it's a comforting wash of sound. I don shorts and t-shirt, and when I'm about to put on my sneaker, a beetle tumbles out.

Stepping onto the boardwalk, I'm pleased to see clear skies, which should make it easier to find Dixon. Unfortunately, we're shipping out soon; we'll be gone before the search party returns.

I look out at the lake, where a shapely female form flies off the diving board and enters the water with scarcely a ripple. She surfaces and swims effortlessly back to the dock, slicing through the water like a mermaid. She climbs the ladder, her silver one-piece showing off a creamy complexion. The tendons on the back of her knees stand out like steel bands. When she pushes the blonde hair from her face, I inhale sharply.

"You thinking impure thoughts about my sis?" Cole steps up beside me, grinning. "She's somethin', ain't she?"

"She's got great.... form." My face heats up.

"And her divin' ain't so bad either. Come on."

Gracie and other guests join us on the dock to watch her dive. Fio steps lithely onto the springboard and stills herself. She bounds forward and then, riding the bend of the board, she points her right arm forward while pulling her left arm above and behind her head, twisting her body in mid-air. We applaud the second she surfaces.

Cole helps her out of the water and hands her a towel. "Theo was just admiring your form."

Water has revitalized her. She takes noticeable pleasure in my unease. It's tempting to kiss her, but I'd feel awkward doing so in front of Gracie. How much has Cole told her?

"I'm starved," says Fio, and leads us into the dining room.

As waiters deliver quiche and fruit, she prays, "Thank you, Father, for returning us safely to this bountiful lodge."

Cole looks like he bit into a rotten kiwi. "Fi, we got back because we paddled and hiked back."

I say, "Yes, and because Dixon sacrificed himself for us."

"Yeah," says Cole, "but only after he caused that calamity."

"All of you are right," Gracie chirps.

Logan is listening in. His good humor apparently did not survive the night. "You're a bunch of crackpots. You got back, *kids*, because of Yachay."

Fio has heard enough. "Let's make it a quick breakfast, so we can join the search party."

"Not gonna happen," says Logan. "Our guides are on it. We don't want you getting lost again."

Appalled, Fio stands and grabs his arm. "What do you mean? We have to find Dixon."

Logan shakes his head. "Sorry. Your boat leaves at nine."

"What? No, we can't just *go*!" Her mission is to serve and save. The idea that we would leave before Dixon is found runs counter to all she believes, all she stands for, all she is.

"Sorry. New guests arrive at noon. We're booked up."

"But.... but we can't.... So we're giving up?" Fio wilts.

At the Quito airport, all four of us crowd into a taxi for the ride to Barry's hotel. Fio is anxious to see if he's gotten a new passport. I sit in the front, stewing about the two of them meeting up, but there's nothing to be done about it.

Hotel La Mirage is basic lodging in a seedy neighborhood. While Cole, Gracie and I check in, Fio starts up the stairs to Barry's room. On the fourth step, she turns and speaks with downcast eyes. "Let's get together for dinner."

"Theo," says Gracie, "you're bleeding again."

"Yeah, pally. You gotta see a doctor."

We're approaching La Plaza de la Independencia, Quito's social center since the 1500s, when the Spanish, afraid of the Incas poisoning their water supply, set up a protected well here. Water is survival. Water is life.

For the hundredth time, I twist my neck, but am unable to see my wound. I reach back my hand and come away with a smear of red. "Nothin' to worry about."

Gracie says, "You loon! You care more about others than you do about yourself. If Fiona's shoulder looked like that...."

She gives me a knowing look. "Go.... see.... a doctor."

I answer noncommittally. "Okay."

She grabs Cole's right wrist, to see his watch. "It's almost noon, and the equinox is tomorrow, so day and night are equal in length." I don't say it, but, because of Ecuador's latitude, day and night are always twelve hours long.

She says, "Life is in perfect balance, right here, right now."

"Easy for you to say," I grump. "Fiona is spending the afternoon with a man who wants to marry her."

"Theo, life will unfold exactly as it's meant to; the union of opposites and the symmetry of the world are in perfect alignment."

"Yeah, yeah." The confluence of equator, equinox and midday is pretty cool, I guess, but I'm in no mood to appreciate it. As much as I like Gracie, her everything-happens-for-a-reason outlook can be heartless.

In the center of the plaza stands a Statue of Liberty, torch in one hand, battle ax in the other. Cole asks why this is called Plaza de la Independencia.

I say, "Simon Bolivar signed Ecuador's Declaration of Independence two blocks south, in the San Agustin Monastery."

He nods at Quito Cathedral. "So there are two Catholic churches in one neighborhood?"

"Actually, Quito Cathedral is two separate churches."

Gracie says, "And don't forget the cathedral we passed three blocks ago."

Cole is confounded. "So there are *four* churches here? Can I see your map, Theo?" He unfolds it, grumbling, "That can't be right. Can't be."

Gracie points out map icons, each one indicating the location of a cathedral. Cole counts aloud, "One, two, three, four, five.... CHEEE-sus! Six, seven.... No, there are eight.... *nine* cathedrals in a.... let's see, five block radius!"

Gracie says, "Ten, counting Carmen Bajo Convent. But I bet they're not all this grand."

After navigating a labyrinth of cobblestone streets, we stand before the tenth gargantuan cathedrals. The granddaddy of them all, La Compania, towers overhead. Stone carvings of saints are nestled in niches of the façade. The Baroque columns are either majestic or tyrannical, depending on whom you ask. As with the previous cathedrals, Gracie, Cole and I slip into our roles as, respectively, art appreciator, cynic and historian.

I read from my guide book: "The façade is made from volcanic rock. The gilding required seven tons of gold. 'La Compania' translates to 'The Company' in English."

"Fitting." Cole turns his bulldog face up to the ornate stonework. "And lemme guess: This one, like the last nine, was built during the Spanish Inquisition."

"Bingo. Building began in 1605, finished 163 years later."

"I'll be a hijo de puta."

As usual, Gracie gushes, "You have to admit, though, it's gorgeous. I haven't attended Mass in years, but if we're here on Sunday, will you come with me, Cole? Please?"

Cole responds with a beleaguered nod, and mumbles something about "a gruesome din of obligatory zeal."

Upon entering, we are silenced by the opulence of La Compania. Every surface is awash in a golden glow. Gracie takes a seat in the back row; Cole and I wander up to the altar, where a quartet of robed men sings a Gregorian chant. Though the lyrics are incomprehensible to me, the simple harmonies echo and re-echo off the stone walls, instilling in me a sense of reverence.

I whisper to Cole, "The way the music bounces around, it seems like it's coming from everywhere."

"You could even trick yourself into believing it comes from within you." He's in a surly mood, and when he spots Gracie kneeling with head bowed, he stomps toward her.

She hears him coming and lifts her head. "I love how this place smells – candles and stone and old lady perfume."

Cole demands to know why in holy hell she's on her knees.

"Praying for Dixon," she says, "until I got interrupted."

Cole snorts and sneers and storms out. Gracie and I follow in his wake, passing through a disintegrating neighborhood. The plaster is crumbling, sidewalks are buckling, families live in hovels made of cardboard and tin.

"Seven tons, is that what you said?" asks Cole. "And gold is worth.... how much?"

"Three hundred bucks an ounce," I say, egging him on.

"All right, sixteen ounces in a pound, two thousand pounds

in a ton, seven tons.... so that's, let's see.... seventy million bucks. And that's one church, in one neighborhood of one city, in one country, on one continent. All that gold, and all this squalor." He surveys the shacks, then squints up at the sun. "There should be no shadows cast, but these people are buried in The Company's shadow. And their birth control ban ensures that each successive generation will be larger and poorer than the last."

"Maybe these people would be living in squalor anyway," says Gracie. "The church is the one place they can go to transcend their lives, to see something beautiful."

"I don't believe that, and I don't think you do either. The Company doesn't give a damn about its flock." He adds, "Mother flockers."

We're all irritated: Cole at Catholicism; Gracie at Cole and me for what she considers our unnecessarily hostile attitude toward the magic of deities; and I'm miffed at Fio for ditching me. Would she really settle for Barry, a guy she's sposta marry, who believes there must be a God, who speaks without moving his lips? On the other hand, when Barry had his money belt stolen, he handled it more graciously than I would have. But that's because he believed God was gonna smite those little punks.

We revert to silence until we get back to our hotel, where Gracie grabs my wrists and implores me to go to the hospital.

Cole says, "Yeah, pally, I'd hate to see your arm fall off."

They're turning into nags about this, but to be honest, it's nice to have someone looking out for me.

Cole asks, "You heading up to Otavalo tomorrow? If so, you want some company?"

This cheers me considerably. "I sure do."

"Tell you what," says Gracie, "if you promise to see a doctor, today, Cole and I will visit the bus station and check out the schedule. Deal?"

"Deal."

"But first, I have to go shopping for tonight. We're celebrating the arrival of spring. Will you come, Theo?"

"Sure. I'm always up for a party."

She shakes her head. "This is a sacred ceremony. Will you bring some red wine? And your charango, bring that too. Can you learn a song that speaks of hope and rebirth? One verse is all we'll need. This won't be the raucous affair it should be, but we'll make do. If we were going to celebrate properly, we'd find a clearing in a forest and have a bonfire."

"Cole and I know a little place, just across the Andes—"

"Our hotel room will suffice. Now, shopping will go faster if I do it by myself. Can you boys stay out of trouble for an hour?"

Cole and I give her looks that say: Who, me?

She says, "I'd tell you to get lost, but I'm afraid you would."

She leaves, and Cole asks, "Where to, pally?"

"There." I point to a winged statue standing atop a hill, a mile away. The huge sculpture dominates the landscape.

A well-dressed Ecuadorian sees me pointing, and he says in flawless English, "That hill is called El Panecillo, which translates as 'little loaf of bread.' And the statue.... Well, you have to see it to believe it." He walks off, shaking his head in puzzlement.

We're halfway up El Panecillo before we realize we're approaching a statue of the Virgin Mary. The winged Madonna is dancing upon a chained serpent that squats atop a globe, the South Pole of which is embedded in an observation deck, sitting upon a cylindrical base, situated in a park atop a loaf of bread.

Opening the door in Mary's base, Cole asks in a lewd tone, "Ready to enter the Virgin?"

We climb the stairs to the observation deck, which offers a panoramic view of Quito: the closely packed houses with tiled roofs, spacious parks, a multitude of cathedrals, and snow-capped volcanoes.

I read bits from my ragged guidebook: "Standing 125 feet tall, Mary was constructed from 7,000 pieces of aluminum. She's meant to be crushing a crocodile...."

Staring upward, Cole says, "A crocodile with horns."

I continue, "....which symbolizes the Virgin's ability to triumph over evil, and thereby ascend to heaven."

Cole says, "Personally, I'd like to see a caiman up there, chompin' on a canoe. Speaking of which, we screwed up, pally. Again. Remember when we found the damaged canoe – I got in, and water poured in faster than I could have bailed. But picture Dixon, sitting in the stern."

"Yeahhh?"

"He's a big boy, and the bow, where the hole is, would have popped up out of the water. We could have gotten a vine and towed him home."

My shoulders slump. "Oh man, how'd we miss that?"

I picture Dixon limping through the forest, hungry, lost, squinting into the trees through his grubby monocle. But maybe he's made it out by now. Is Fio praying for him? No, she's with Barry, and they are.... talking? Talking about what? Are they smooching? Are they...? Theo! Knock it off!

"There was no need for Dixon to sacrifice himself for us," says Cole. "I hope to God he makes it out; otherwise he will have died for nothin'."

I return my attention to the stunning vista, but it now appears flat, two-dimensional, a postcard of something pretty. Why, and where, did you go, Dixon? Neither Cole nor I speak as we circle the observation deck. I point out our hotel, and tell him we'd better leave if we're going to meet Gracie on time.

"No rush," he says. "She's never on time, on account of her being a Pisces."

We exit the Virgin and make our way downhill through a dodgy neighborhood, inhabited by shabbily dressed people who eye us with distrust, if not hostility.

Gracie is waiting for us in the lobby, holding a shopping bag with a bouquet of flowers sticking out the top. "You're late," she says cheerily. Her smile withers when she checks out my shoulder. "Theo. Doctor. Go."

"Yes, ma'am."

Cole rummages through her bag. "Got anything to eat?"

She slaps his hand away. "Stay out of there, you beast! This is for tonight."

A nurse treats me immediately upon my arrival at Hospital Metropolitano. She removes my bandage and backs me up to a mirror, then holds up a hand mirror, enabling me to see a thick flap of skin that opens on three sides. The gash bleeds a bit and oozes yellow around the edge. She cleans it out and asks me to wait.

After she leaves, an image of La Compania appears in my mind, and I hear my Machu Picchu song. I find a pen and paper towel, and a second verse takes form:

> The Sun God meets the Son of God
> No room for compromise
> How brutal, how beautiful
> Here the vanquished lie

A doctor enters as I finish writing. Twenty minutes later, a horseshoe of stitches adorns my shoulder. He holds up a mirror, and I say, "Bueno como nuevo." Good as new. He winces. I understand Español pretty well by now, but my ability to speak it has stalled at an infantile level.

I pay a small fee for the procedure, then return to the hotel to practice my charango.

"Fiona and Barry won't be joining us for dinner," says Cole as he and Gracie descend the hotel stairs. He slings an arm across my shoulder. "But get this; she's coming up to Otavalo with us. Barry, unfortunately, has to stick around Quito."

"Truly sorry to hear that."

"Yeah, apparently there's an 'irregularity' with his visa."

Gracie scolds us. "You two are incorrigible."

Cole says, "Fi's meeting us at the station tomorrow at ten."

Tomorrow, huh? Damn, that means she and Barry will…. Theo, think about something else. They'd have gotten separate rooms. Wouldn't they? Because Barry has never, in Cole's words, "parted the pink sea." But Fio is a passionate woman and….

She won't leave my mind. I feel those grey eyes boring into me, and the warming touch of her fingers on my arm, and those muscled calves tapering down to slim, elegant ankles. I am possessed.

As requested, I knock on my friends' room at midnight. Gracie, wearing a headband of white flowers, beckons me into the candle-lit room. A dark blanket is draped across her shoulders, and she's uncharacteristically wearing eye shadow and dark lip gloss. In the center of the room sits a coffee table covered with a flowery shawl, on top of which lay a plate and two bowls, one full of dirt, the other with colored eggs. The air is thick with incense, flavored with cinnamon, lemon and something exotic.

Cole sits cross-legged on one of three pillows arranged around the coffee table. He indicates for me to sit across from him, and then fills three ceramic cups with white wine.

I am skeptical about New Age spirituality, and Wiccan cults strike me as trendy, but Gracie has invited me to their spring celebration, so I tell myself not to treat it dismissively.

She takes my charango and kisses it lightly, then solemnly returns it to me. Kneeling, she says, "The first day of spring. Day equals night, light equals dark, north equals south. May our lives be forever in balance as they are here and now." She picks up her cup of wine, as do Cole and I. "May this wine fill your belly and feed your spirit." We drink.

Cole presses seeds into the dirt-filled bowl. Dowsing the soil with equal parts wine and water, he says:

> May the seed we plant tonight
> Become the plant we see tomorrow

Cole is even more of a skeptic than I, but he's being a good sport about this. He nods at my charango, and I finger-pick the opening riff to The Beatles' "Here Comes the Sun." We sing the first verse softly.

"Blessed be," says Gracie. "Now, bring to mind something you would like to exorcise from your life – an object, a situation, an ailment." She passes around slips of paper and pencils, or "wands," as she calls them. "Write down whatever you would like to be rid of."

As a private joke, I write "my family," but that's mean-spirited, and it's not what I want, not really. I add two words at the top, making it "time with my family." Hmmm.... that's closer. I squeeze in three more words, making it "so much damn time with my family." There.

Gracie folds her paper, then drops it on the plate and motions for us to do likewise. She places twigs on the papers, and sprinkles dried flower petals on top. Cole reads from a booklet:

> Tonight we bid these ghosts depart
> Embrace new morn with sacred heart

Using a thin candle, Gracie lights the pile of paper, twigs and pedals. Raising her hands in supplication, she intones:

> God of wine, vine and grape
> From holy water rain
> Spring at last, fill thy glass, and
> Consecrate this fane

Cole and Gracie call out, "Blessed be!"

She spoons a bit of powder from a cup onto the fire, causing it to send out a spray of tiny sparks. She continues in a higher pitch:

> God of sky, let fly the breeze, that
> Kisses lute and lyre
> Goddess green, in glade serene
> Sing all you desire

This is too cryptic for me, but I join in: "Blessed be!"

She places more sticks on the miniature bonfire and spoons out more powder. She chants, louder this time:

> God of fire, sire of sun
> Deliver leaf and light
> Goddess Moon, eclipse at noon
> May opposites unite

"Blessed be!"

Gracie pours powder on the fire and calls out with fervor:

> Goddess Earth, rebirth is nigh
> Send us son or daughter
> Fill thy womb, with bud and bloom
> Born of holy water

She dumps the remaining powder on the fire as we chant, "Blessed be! Blessed be! Blessed be!"

On the second "blessed be," the door flies open and Barry charges in. "What is going *on*?" He sniffs at the air. "Is this a séance?" He looks in horror at the candles and the geyser of sparks. His eyes land on Gracie. "Are you...? Are you a *witch*?"

"Well, what do you mean by 'witch?'"

"Witch! Witch! Wiiitch! Everybody knows what a witch is!"

With intentional calm, Cole asks, "How would you define that?"

"No, no, nooooo! It doesn't matter how you define it! You either are or you aren't!"

Cole lays his palm on Gracie's jaw and inspects her face. "No warts, no pointy chin. No pointy black hat." He looks around the room. "No broomstick. Nope, no witches here."

"You mock me! You'll see, though, mister, you cannot mock the Lord!" With fury etched on his shadowed face, and his accusatory finger threatening to smite us, Barry appears as an Old Testament emissary of The Lord. He stalks out, slamming the door behind him.

After a pause, I aim a crooked finger at Cole. "Warlock! You, mister, are a *warlock*!"

He scrunches up one side of his face and hunches a shoulder. Through cartoonishly swollen lips, he squawks back. "No, no, nooooo! You thmell like a warlog!"

"You smell like two warlocks.... no, like *nine* warlocks!"

"Oh, yeah? Well.... There are three kinds of turds in the world: mustard, custard, and you, poopy pie!"

Okay, that is easily the most idiotic thing I've ever heard, but I roll onto my back and convulse in laughter.

Gracie sighs and unhooks the clasp holding the blanket around her shoulders. "To hell with it. Let's party. Cole, pour the wine. Theo, play a song." I'm still writhing on the floor. "When you are able."

An hour later, we're still singing away. Sitting on a pillow, I play simple songs on my charango, while Cole sits cross-legged, drumming softly on Gideon's Bible. Gracie dances like a forest nymph. We're making an effort not to awaken our neighbors. I can just imagine Barry reporting us to the manager, or la policia: There's a witch in the next room, and.... Excuse me! Could you speak *English*?

We sing "Here Comes the Sun," all the way through. For the last verse, I set down my charango and do the lyrics in sign language while we sing a cappella. Gracie asks how I know how to sign.

"My dad is deaf."

"Boy, that's gotta be hard on your mom."

"She got used to it. We got used to it. And it's been hard on Dad too; especially after Mom.... um.... see...." My face gets hot, but it doesn't last. My friends' kindness has peeled away my simmering anger, exposing a deep-rooted agony. I pause one last time before taking the plunge. "Mom drowned in December."

This is the first time I have spoken these words. Matter of fact, prior to this instant, they had not yet taken shape in my mind. I've been afraid they would wash me away.

"Oh, Theo." Gracie kneels behind me, and encircles my neck with her slender arms.

"Sorry to hear that, pally," says Cole. "What happened?"

"My parents were celebrating their fortieth anniversary in San Diego. They were at the beach, Mom went swimming, and a rip current got hold of her, sucked her out to sea."

For the first time, I imagine Death: Cold, briny water forces its way down Mom's throat, violating her lungs as she gags and screams in silence. I recall the panic of my own botched baptism and multiply it by a hundred, a thousand, millions. And now, finally, I have arrived at the source of the fury that has so pervaded my being these past three months. The bitterness I've felt toward my siblings has been secondary, a by-product of indignation, borne of the knowledge that someone as good and kind as my mother could spend her last moments on this wondrous, rudderless world alone, in torment and horror.

It's not fair.

"Dad didn't hear her screaming," I say through clenched teeth. "People saw her dragged out to sea, and when they ran up to tell Dad, he was reading <u>Church Humor Digest</u>, by Billy Graham. Yeah, I know, doesn't that sound like a kick? Anyway, once they figured out Dad was deaf, they pointed out to sea. He went berserk. He dove into the surf, and *he* almost drowned. Some boaters pulled him out, but he pushed them overboard and dove back in. Dad's a wreck; he thinks it's his fault."

Gracie rocks me, side to side. "Why didn't you tell us?"

"I'm not.... I don't...." My hands shake and I stare at the wall, unblinking. "Look, I don't have a lot of friends."

"Ya got us, pally."

I blink once, and a flood of tears rushes down my cheeks.

Gracie says, "I'm sorry for being snippy with you today." She massages my shoulders. "I hate to ask, but did they find your mom's body?"

"No. Which made her passing even harder to take, maybe like how it was with your grandpa, Cole." He nods and gets teary-eyed. I say, "My sister Rowan thinks Mom swam ashore in Haiti and got a job tending bar, or teaching scuba diving. She's got this whole fantasy worked up."

"Hold on," says Cole. "Haiti? But that's in—"

"Yeah, I know. Ro is confused. She's well-intentioned, trusting and flirts with suicide."

"And your other sibs?" he asks.

"Phil fancies himself a starving artist. Sad thing is, he's getting to be pretty good, but he has no clue how to sell his stuff. And get this: Claire researched ocean currents, and figures Mom's body will wash up on Oahu sometime in June. Claire considers it her job to torment Phil and Ro, and she is very, very good at it. She told them, 'Hey, Mom always wanted to lie on the beach at Waikiki.' What a buncha losers."

My mother could never understand the lunacy swirling around her. She was the eye of the tornado, the calm spot, the Duncan family's island of sanity. But here's the thing about tornadoes – they form *because* of that calm spot. Air swirls around an area of low pressure because it wants *in*. That's what causes the twister and intensifies it. It sucks everything in. It just plain sucks.

Everyone wanted a piece of Mom. She kept Dad's books, she kept Rowan alive, she kept Phil in rent, she kept me in the loop, she kept Claire in line, and she kept the peace; at least she did her damnedest. As Dad used to say, "She's a keeper."

Taking stock of my life from the vantage point of another continent, my family's folly is brought into focus with a clarity that is at once profound and disturbing. "The Duncan clan is a vortex," I say, wiping my eyes and nose on my sleeve. "We can change the direction it swirls, but we can never stop it. My family sucks."

Gracie circles around in front of me and takes my hands. "Theo, you are a healthy person in an unhealthy situation." She kisses me on the forehead. "Remember that. It's hard watching families implode. Believe me, I know." She guides my head onto her shoulder, and the three of us fall silent.

My mother is gone. She drowned. I have not had the strength to face that hideous vision. My siblings have fared no better than I, though Ro claims that "Jesus is my staff," and Phil refers to Buddha as his anchor. Claire, a self-proclaimed cynic, rags on them about religion being a crutch instead of a staff, and by God, an anchor will take you straight to the bottom if a storm comes up and your chain is too short.

Which isn't true, but it makes for a nifty rant.

Mom's passing has sharpened my interest in religious matters. Until recently, God was an abstraction, an artificial construct, having little to do with the everyday business of paying rent and eating and getting to work on time. But now that she's Gone – capital G – the idea that there's nothing left of her is.... It's not simply nauseating, not just offensive. It's wrong. It's....

It's unfair.

Before I can stop myself, I ask, "Where do you think my mom is now? Heaven? Seems unlikely; she was not a believer. Hell? No way; she was good, right to the core of her being. Nowhere?" No commentary comes to mind for this prospect.

Why, and where, did you go?

Cole shrugs and says, "Nowhere is better than hell." Then, realizing you can take that two ways, he back-pedals furiously, "No, sorry, I didn't mean—"

Gracie cuts him off. "Your mother's led a busy life, Theo. She gets to rest now." This is a sweet thought, and I'm processing it when she adds, "Until she's ready to come back."

"You mean as another person?"

"That, or maybe as, say, a llama." This idea also has some appeal, until I picture Mom as a woolly pack animal with big ears.

Gracie then says, "Or a tree, or the rocks, maybe clouds or a dream."

This is moving too fast. We've gone from getting some rest, to rebirth as a human or an animal, or a plant or water vapor, finally coming to rest as a fantasy. A half-minute progression from death to hope to intangibility. I ask Cole what he thinks happens when we die.

He doesn't answer right away, because, I'm guessing, he doesn't want to say: Hell if I know. Which would make for a clever response, if not a particularly helpful one.

He says, "No idea. But as I'm dying, I hope I'm thankful."

I nod my head three times. On the third dip, my head stays down.

Cole adds, "But that's easy for me to say; here I am, young and healthy, hangin' with two of the best people I know." He shrugs. "Not much of answer, I know."

Actually, it's the perfect answer – authentic, modest, full of good will.

Cole asks, "You ever consider ditchin' your fam? Maybe move, far away? I mean, if I were you...." I lift my head in time to see Gracie shoot him a sharp look.

"Sorry, pally, I'll shut up. I come from a long line of meddlers."

"How so?" I'm happy to hand the ball off to someone else.

"Lemme know if you've had your fill of Crampy Q stories, but we Quinns have a history of buttin' in where we don't belong."

Many families have that one seminal event around which their emotional energies are crudely but constantly focused. For the Duncan clan, that event occurred when I was five. Mom registered us all for sign language class. From then on, Dad was no longer considered hard-of-hearing; no, he was deaf. Claire stopped inviting friends over, because she was embarrassed by Dad's "condition" and his need to communicate through those freaky hand signals. Stomping around our house, her pasted-on sneer asked of all she encountered: Could we be any less cool? That question was directed at my folks, us kids, even the furniture. At some point I too stopped having friends over.

For the Quinns, all roads lead straight back to the disappearance of their grandfather.

Cole says, "The last words I heard from Crampy Q were: 'Your Aunt Becky is finally gettin' her way; she and Dick are moving in at the end of the month. Busybodies! What, do they think I need diapers?' Hey, I was just a kid; what do you say to something like that? He left a few days later, and that's when the madness began. Dad thought Crampy left because Dick and Becky were moving in. Becky claimed that if they'd moved in earlier, he wouldn't have left." With weary finality, he says, "Families."

"Yeah." I'm depleted, in my head, my heart, my stomach. "You got anything to eat?"

Cole surveys the room. "Yeah, Slick, I'm starving." He spies the bowl filled with colored eggs.

"Oh, no, you don't," says Gracie. "We're having an Ostara egg hunt tomorrow."

"Where'd you get Ostrich eggs?" I ask.

"Ostara," she giggles, "an old pagan celebration; it's where we get the word Easter."

"Easter's in April, though, isn't it?"

"Most years, yes. It's the first Sunday after the first full moon following the equinox."

"What? Let me get this straight: The cycle of the moon determines the date for the most important Christian holiday?"

"Holiday, or holy day, however you want to say it, yes."

"And why is that? I can't believe I don't know this stuff."

"When early Christian missionaries came in contact with northern Europeans, their attempts to convert pagans weren't very successful. So they shanghaied Eastre, the Goddess of Fertility, and overlaid a veneer of Christian theology. Eastre, or Ostara as she's known by modern day pagans, was symbolized as a rabbit, hence the Easter bunny."

Cole has had his fill of religious history. He licks his chops and says, "Come on, Slick, let's eat. Celebration's over."

She replies, "Actually, this was the best Equinox Bash ever. From now on, let's eat the eggs at midnight on Equinox Eve."

"Excellent idea," says Cole, cracking an egg on the edge of the table. "New rule: Let's say we have to eat 'em in one bite."

"Let's not! I'm a pagan, not a barbarian."

Chapter 19: Your Daddy Ain't Your Daddy

My friends and I didn't turn in until dawn, so we begin our two-hour ride up to Otavalo at one-thirty. Fio and I sit across from each other near the back of the bus; Cole and Gracie take a seat behind her. Fio makes it clear through silence and body language that we are not to be considered a couple. Even Gracie is unable to engage her. It doesn't help that every time we see a volcano or a horse, or pass around a bag of peanuts, Cole and I call out, "Blessed Be!"

An hour into the trip, Fio turns to confront Gracie. "Barry said you were having a.... um.... What were you doing last night?"

"Celebrating the first day of spring. We say goodbye to old habits and embrace the new. Think of it as an emotional, spiritual spring cleaning. And we give thanks."

Fio looks back and forth between them, finally settling on Cole. "To who?"

"Well, for me, uh, to nobody. I express gratitude for this life we're given. I've done it for years. Before I go to sleep every night..... well, I used to say, 'I am thankful for....' And then I'd name three things."

"You *used* to say that?"

"Yeah, but it was awkward. I needed something to aim my gratitude at...." Cole begins to fidget. "So now I'll say: 'Thank you for Gracie, and my drums, and burritos.'"

"Who are you thanking?"

"Nothing, nobody. I just feel grateful." Fio fixes him with The Look. "I know," he says, flustered. "It doesn't make sense."

"You do believe in God. You *do*. Why not admit it?"

Cole doesn't respond, so Gracie goes to bat for him. "But it does make sense. My name is short for 'Graziella.' My aunt calls me Grazie, meaning 'Thank you' in Italian. Giving thanks and feeling grateful puts us in a state of Grace." Cole is relieved to be bailed out, but he is not thrilled when Gracie adds, "Which means we're sanctified by God."

Fio is intrigued, but not sold. "Who do you thank, Gracie?"

"I give thanks to earth gods and goddesses."

"Gods? Plural?"

"Yes, for me the dichotomy isn't 'god or no god.' It's a matter of deciding which ones to honor. Look around at this rich, diverse world; why would you assume there's only one god? I sense the presence of many deities at work and play. Maybe we put our trust in a god outside of ourselves because it's hard to believe there is something so glorious inside us. Fiona, if you choose to believe in one god and worship it, I accept that."

"It?"

"Or him, or her. Pick your pronoun. 'Them,' in my case."

Perplexed by such a foreign notion, Fiona resorts to quoting the Bible. "The first of the Ten Commandments says, 'Thou shalt have no other gods before me.'"

Cole gripes, "Sounds like a jealous, pissy little god to me."

"Jesus said, 'I am the way, the truth and the light.'"

"What does that mean?"

"The Bible makes it clear—"

"JEEEEEE-sus, Fi! To hell with the Bible! How dare you tell my wife who to worship!" Gracie puts a hand on his arm to calm him, but it's too late. "When Crampy Q died, you bought into this simple-minded bullshit."

"No, Cole, when he died, you closed your heart."

"No, I opened my mind. But remember how awful it was, listening to Crampy Q accuse our family of stealing."

"But they did steal!" This is the first time I've heard Fio raise her voice. Passengers turn and regard us disapprovingly. She clearly regrets saying it.

"Who is 'they'?" Getting no reply, Cole demands, "Fiona, who.... is.... 'they?'"

She answers in a frail voice. "Dad took documents, like deeds and bonds, so Crampy Q wouldn't hide them and then forget where they were."

"I know that. But he wasn't stealing."

She looks heartsick. "But Uncle Dick was. Becky would take Crampy Q out to lunch, then Dick would sneak in and take jewelry and money. And he'd steal random stuff like novels so it wouldn't look like burglary." Her head sags. "Crampy said things were missing, but no one believed him. Everybody thought he was hiding his stuff. He thought Dad was the thief."

"How do you know all this?"

"I went to see Becky, right after Grandma died. The door was open, so I walked in." Fio shuts her eyes tightly. When she opens them, tears tumble down her face. "Becky was sitting on a couch, sifting through Grandma's jewelry that Dick had stolen, trying to decide how to return them. Grandma's banjo was there, and I asked if Dick stole that too. She said no, that Grandma had always wanted her to have it."

Cole's confusion is evident. Should he be angry or hurt, or both? "How come I'm just hearing about this now?"

"Dick is a recovering alcoholic. I was afraid that if our family knew, it would push him over the edge again. Becky said Dick wouldn't survive. She told me, 'Trust me, dear, you do not want something like that on your conscience.' So I cut her a deal. If she could get Uncle Dick to quit stealing, I promised not to tell."

Gracie asks, "Did he quit?"

"No," she says, with bottomless fatigue.

Cole slumps. "But how come you didn't tell meee?" He sounds like a wounded animal when he squeezes out that last word.

"Becky was afraid – and I was, too – that you'd go after Dick. You were so angry."

With his face buried in his hands, he nods.

"Cole." Fio waits for him to respond. "Cole." She reaches over the seat and lifts his chin. He's devastated. "I should have told you. I hope you have it in your heart to forgive me."

As night falls, I don the black silk shirt I received as payment from playing with Band o' Leer. The Quinns are waiting in the lobby. Cole has recovered from his anguish over his sister's revelation, and Gracie is her usual cheery self, but Fio is distracted and glum.

I ask the man at the desk, "Donde esta la musica caliente?" Where is the hot music? Spreading out a map on the counter, he circles a restaurant down the street, and a tavern a half mile away.

On the way to dinner, Cole spots a shop that displays a rack of the black bowler-like hats favored by the men in town. "Hold on, guys; been wantin' to get me one of these." He tries on a hat that's way too small, causing his thick blonde hair to poof out from beneath the brim.

Gracie says, "Looks like you're hidin' a bale of hay."

Cole poses in front of a mirror. "Nonsense. It makes me look.... dashing."

That brings the first smile I've seen from Fio since we left the jungle. She says, "I never realized what a big head you have."

Gracie replaces the hat with a larger one, but it's still too small. He preens before the mirror, and she says, "Nice, a skullcap with a brim. You'd fit right in at an Andean Bar Mitzvah." She finds a larger hat, but it's still not even close to being a fit. "Ah, Charlie Chaplain does Ecuador."

With the hat balanced precariously on my head, he approaches a clerk and turns his eyes upward. "Mas grande, por favor." Larger, please. The man removes the hat and checks its size. He frowns and ducks into a back room.

Pointing at Cole's head, Gracie and I circle him, speaking in hushed tones:

"Is it sposta be that big?"

"I feel sorry for his neck."

"Whattaya s'pose he keeps in there?"

"How would you get something that big through customs?"

The man returns with another hat. He places it on Cole's head and pulls it down, but it's still comically small. His eyes bulge in disbelief. "Señor, su cabeza es enorme!"

Our maxim for dining out: You can't go wrong with the trout. We all have Trucha a la Naranja – grilled trout served with a sauce of white wine and orange. Consensus is that this is the best meal of the trip.

"Well, *so far* it's the best," Cole adds.

We discuss our plan for tomorrow, to hike out to Imbabura Volcano, have lunch along the way, and catch a bus back.

Gracie turns to Fio. "Let me say it again: I am so sorry for losing Barry's passport."

"You didn't lose it, that little.... kid stole it."

"I know, but if I hadn't been so careless...."

"It's okay, really." But her voice is suffused with sadness, and she's unable to assuage Gracie's guilt.

Cole says, "Hey, I called the jungle lodge company; they're

based here in Quito, and—"

Fio blurts out, "Did they find Dixon?"

"Not yet. But Yachay found his camera, a granola wrapper and a Virginia Tech cap. Logan has a dark room set up at the lodge, and he developed the film. Dixon only took three pictures, of a dark, gnarly log or something. It was blurry, even lit up by flash. They'll keep looking for him."

This is distressing news, especially to Fio. I place my hand on her shoulder to comfort her. She takes hold of my wrist for two seconds, then releases it and turns away.

As we're finishing dinner, Cole calls out, "Jahn!" I look across the room and see a muscular blonde making his way over. He must stand six foot six.

"Don't lack much a'bein' a Viking." I want to take these words back, even before Fiona shoots me a sour look. I add lamely, "Let's hope Dixon is all right."

Gracie introduces Jahn and asks him to join us for dessert. She and Cole met him last week in the Lima airport. A serious fellow, he's been wandering the world for five years. When he runs out of money, he heads home to Norway or up to Alaska to work on fishing boats for a month, then he hits the road again.

He sums up his life this way: "I won a dog sled race in the Yukon, studied in a Tibetan monastery, and hung with Rwandan revolutionaries. And I still—"

Cole breaks in, singing the refrain from the U2 song. "And I still…. haven't found…. what I'm looking for."

Jahn smiles for the first time. "Yeah, that's about it. Buy you a drink?"

We are finishing our dessert pastries when the band begins playing. I'm being generous with the word "band." Two guys shuffle onto stage, one with a trombone, the other with a clarinet. I'm being even more generous with the word "playing." The sign outside advertised the night's entertainment as "an evening of improv." After two minutes of squawks and squeals that might indicate profound gastro-intestinal distress, Cole growls, "Improv, my ass. An evening of 'improve' is what they need."

I say, "Yeah, there's a fine line between improv and makin' shit up."

"We don't have to listen to this musical snobbery," says

Gracie. Grabbing Fio, she dances her way up to the area in front of the stage, where the two of them lurch and clap along to an ill-defined tempo. A table of locals yowl their approval.

Mercifully, the "band" only "plays" three "songs," after which point Cole collects his wife and sister, and Jahn and I follow them out into the cool evening. I attempt to engage Fio, but she responds with matter-of-fact answers, and she refuses to meet my eye. Knowing that Barry is sixty miles away offers me little consolation.

We take our time getting to the bar. Jahn the Viking, as Cole is calling him, loosens up, and he sings a tune he learned while chumming for salmon in the Bering Sea. He begins with the chorus: "Yourrrr daddy ain't your daddy but your daddy don't know...." All of us except Fio crack up at the bawdy lyrics, and by the time we arrive at the bar, Cole and I have worked out harmony parts.

La taberna smells of sweat and spilled beer, but locals are dancing with unabashed revelry to a smokin' hot band. We snag the last open table, and Jahn spots an acquaintance of his, a dark-eyed, tawny-skinned woman from Tahiti. He calls her over and introduces us. She pours us each a half shot of something called guayusaso. Fio declines.

Cole toasts to "Musica caliente!" and we down our drinks.

His face flushes and he wheezes a long exhale. "What's in this?"

I say, "Lemon juice and lighter fluid is my guess. Mmm mmm *mmmmm*."

"It's good for snake bites," says Tahiti. She pours us each a full shot.

Gracie holds up her glass. "Gracias."

I down my shot and say, "Gracious."

Cole stretches his arm across my shoulders. "Hey pally, let's go check out the band."

I tell his wife, "Be right back, Gracious."

Cole and I stand off to the side of the stage, located in a back corner. Compared with other bands we've heard the past few weeks, these guys are more polished, more in sync. They cut a deeper groove. They're fronted by a guitarist and bass player who sing sweet, simple harmonies, but it's the drummer who powers the band. His playing is offbeat yet solid; you could use him as a metronome. The music is hard to categorize. It's too harmonically simple to be jazz, too rhythmically complex to be folk music, and it's not rock or reggae.

"Where's the *one*?" yells Cole, meaning he can't find the beginning of a measure. I try counting beats and watching chord changes, but it's beyond me. Cole shakes his head and laughs. "Can't find it!" We allow the infectious polyrhythm to wash over us. "But it sure as hell found me!"

A local approaches Cole and tenders a salacious smile. His teeth, all five of them, are stained the color of Grey Poupon. His voice is drowned out by the band. He lifts his arms and sways back and forth, trying to entice my friend to dance. Cole shakes his head.

I pat my heart. "Looks like true love!"

Cole pokes me in the chest, hard. "Mal hombre!" Bad man!

We turn back to the band, but the Ecuadorian is not easily deterred. He energetically shoves his middle finger in and out of his Grey Poupon smile. For all the razzing I've taken about Professor Plum and his muña, I am enjoying this spectacle immensely. "You and Colonel Mustard make a cute couple!" He doesn't get that, so I shout, "Look at his teeth!"

Cole grabs my arm and drags me back to our table. My recounting of the Colonel Mustard incident earns a variety of responses: Tahiti laughs and Cole hangs his head, while Jahn the Viking and Fio make no effort to hide their disgust.

Gracie giggles, "You're never gonna hear the end of this, hubba hubby."

Colonel Mustard flounces across the room and puckers his lips at Cole, who picks up Gracie and sits her on his lap. "My wife!" he shouts, then proceeds to lick her nose.

She responds with a slap to the back of his head.

The colonel looks around the table for fresh game. His eyes land on me.

"No! No gracias!"

Tahiti taunts me: "What's the matter? Don't you want to be his consolation prize?"

"Would you do me a favor?" I ask her. "Will you pretend

to be my girl?"

She sits on my lap and fingers the collar of my silk shirt, while we rub foreheads. It's not a convincing act, though, as neither of us can keep a straight face.

Colonel Mustard won't leave. He prances over to Jahn the Viking, who stands and pounds the wooden table with a fist the size of a smoked ham. Had he lived a thousand years ago, he and his fellow marauders might have made their livelihood sweeping down from the north on unsuspecting English villages.

Gracie leaves to look for a bouncer.

Tahiti runs her hands through my hair and yells, "Te quiero!"

"What does that mean?"

The song ends one second before she shouts, "I love you!" People turn to look and, upon seeing her embarrassment, they crack up. She adds, "But I'm not gonna marry you!"

"Fair enough!" Looking around, I see Colonel Mustard hustle out the door, watching over his shoulder for the agitated Viking.

Fio folds her arms and glares at me. It's tempting to say: Hey, you could have had me. Hell, you still can. But you cut me loose, and now you think you possess me?

On the other hand, does her jealousy indicate I have a shot with her? Feeling that ache in my chest, I regret causing her grief. Tahiti, seeing the depth of Fio's anger, regards me like I'm a cheater. She gets up and wanders off.

Fio gives me a defiant stare. "I can't trust you!" This is not the hard look she gave me in the jungle two days ago. No, this is fury, pure and cold. "If you act like this when I am around, how will you act when I'm not?"

My empathy burns away quickly. "What the hell's your problem? You've been moping around, acting like I don't exist. Besides, Tahiti and I were just foolin' around, and for you to—"

"I broke up with Barry." She gives me a laser-focused look, full of warmth and worry.

It takes me a moment to realize I'm holding my breath. "Why didn't you tell me?" I turn my chair to face hers.

"I've been confused, and I didn't think it fair to you—"

"Fio, I love you, let's start from there."

"And I...." She looks at the floor. "I care about you, Theo, in a way I have never cared for anyone." She brings her eyes up to mine. "But you aren't the reason I broke up with Barry.... well, not the main reason. He hasn't.... oh, maybe I shouldn't say this, but he hasn't been born again."

"How do you know?"

She folds her hands reverently. "He understands the laws, the mechanics, of Jesus' word, but he isn't.... he won't.... he doesn't...."

I finish for her. "He doesn't love." Fiona neither agrees nor corrects me. I ask, "Do you consider him a Christian?" This unsettles her, as so many of her questions have unsettled me.

"Yes.... no...." Fiona throws her hands up in frustration. "See? I don't know. But you can't define yourself by what you say you're not. You can't live by shall-nots." She calms herself and says, "But it's not for me to judge. I don't connect with him like I do with you." She takes my hand. "But tell me – what was going on last night?"

I opt not to mention Cole and Fiona's blessed-be fertility rite. "Well, we planned to have an Easter egg hunt, but your brother got hungry, so—"

"Figures! What an ape!" She gives me a half-smile. "We had a Quinn family Easter egg coloring contest when I was about twelve, and Crampy proclaimed me the winner. Later on I wrote: Fi own egg win. I'm pleased to say it stumped him." She eyes me expectantly.

"Fi, own, egg, win – Fiona Quinn."

"Yes! You are funetically gifted."

"Uh, guys?" Cole is tapping my shoulder. "Guys, those are some bad hombres." We follow his line of sight: Three men in their twenties swagger in, and though they're dressed more or less the same as everyone else, the locals clear a path. They are known.

I reach for Fio's hand, while asking, "Cole, you wanna find another bar?"

"Not just yet...." For him, this is just another adventure.

The band starts up again, playing a slow song with a sensuous rhythm. The tension eases, and Fio and I get up to dance, but ten seconds later, a fog sifts through the bar. My throat burns and my eyes water.

Cole yells, "Tear gas!"

Fio and I reach the entrance ahead of the crowd. We stand coughing and blinking in the middle of the narrow, deserted street.

Gracie exits behind us, tears streaming down her face. "Cole!" she shouts, spinning around frantically. "Where are you?"

He stumbles out of the bar, carrying three beers and Fio's Inca Kola. He moseys over, grinning and weeping like he'd just won the lottery. "Here, grab your drink." We do, leaving him a free hand to rub his watery eyes.

Gracie is incredulous. "You went back in for beer?"

"Hey! I'd have gone back for you too."

She hands me her beer and pounds him on the chest. "Fiona, your brother is a few clowns short of a circus."

"My brother?" says Fio. "Nah, this guy was left by trolls."

The bad hombres are the last ones out, and they evidently caught the worst of the gas. Two of them trip on the uneven sidewalk, one lands on his face. He gets up cussin' and bleedin' and chokin' and cryin', and they all stagger off.

Fio surprises me by saying: "Don't lack much a'bein' buttheads."

His eyes gushing, Cole says, "Bad hombres are muy stupido, gassing the joint while they were inside."

My ear for Spanish is improving by the day. "No, somebody said it was the owner who threw the gas, to get rid of those buttheads."

"He gassed his own bar? Craziness!"

The band has also exited the bar; one of them straps on a guitar and strums chords that hint at "The Hokey Pokey." I sing, "You put your left foot in...." My friends join in, as do several locals who know the song in Spanish. Having recovered from her earlier funk, Fio takes to leading the sing-along. She drags Cole into the middle of the circle and bellows, "Put your cabeza in, put your cabeza out, if it's enormo, then you shake it all about...." We sing that verse twice, and a dozen of us are now dancing in the street, head-banging and whooping it up. Tahiti appears with shot glasses and her carafe of guayusaso, which she refers to as holy water. Cole calls it "holy cow water."

The song eventually runs its course, and the tear gas dissipates. The band returns to the stage, the crowd re-enters the bar, and the dancing starts up as if nothing happened.

Stumbling back to the hotel at three, we stop to reprise "The Hokey Pokey:" "You put your sweet cheeks in; you put your sweet cheeks out..." Fio, hesitant about stickin' her ass into the Hokey Pokey circle, eventually shakes it all about in a most pleasing manner.

When our hotel comes into sight, Fio slows her pace, allowing Cole and Gracie to go on ahead. She takes my hand and says, "Theo, I am not ready to make love, but I want to wake up next to you. Would that be all right?" Amazingly, she asks this as if she doesn't know what my answer will be.

I kiss her cheek. "I would like nothing better."

She points at a spot above our hotel. "A sliver of a silver moon."

"That's good. Can I use it in a song?"

She leans her head on my shoulder. "Theo, you can have whatever you want."

Gracie calls back to us, saying the hotel is locked. She pounds on the thick wooden door, while Cole motions Fio and me over to a spot beneath a window. "Maybe thish opens in on the 'otel offiz," he slurs. He and I crouch down and make stirrups.

"Like huntin' for nanners," says Fio, and boosts herself up. "Higher," she whispers. We lift until she's standing on our shoulders. She starts to lose her balance and kicks me in the head.

"CHEE-ses! I thought you like my ears!"

"Sorry," she giggles. "I'm hangin' by my fingertips."

She's still tapping on the window when the front door opens. Cole tells me, "Maybe we shou' leave 'er up dere."

Once inside, we tiptoe down the hall. We come to my room first, and Gracie gives me a rib-cracker of a hug. "G'night, Theo. That was great fun." She continues down the hall.

I call out, "G'night, Gracious."

Though hammered, Cole has figured out what's going on with Fio and me. He gives her a bear hug and says, "Take care, sis." Leaning against the wall to stay upright, he follows his wife.

Gracie turns and sees that Fio has stopped outside my room. "What are you doing?"

Cole lays a paw on her shoulder. "Leh 'er be, Shlick."

Gracie, usually an easy-going, whatever-happens-happens sort of woman, says in an agitated whisper, "Fi, you are not spending the night with him!"

Cole sobers up, well enough to slobber, "Oh, yesh, she is!"

It's great to have him back me up, but I wonder if his real intent is to undermine Barry.

Gracie inches back down the hall. "No, she's not!"

Cole asks, "Wha' 'bout yer b'lief tha' ever'thin' 'appens fer a reason?"

"Bumpin' fuzzies with someone other than your fiancé doesn't happen for a reason. It happens when—"

"Oh, yeah?" says Fio. "You're just feeling guilty about the stolen passport."

"It happens when an otherwise bright girl falls in love with a guy's boom stick. Fiona, we have talked about this—"

Ohhh! Now it's clear – well, somewhat clear – why Gracie was snippy with me yesterday. For whatever reason, she's been trying to steer Fiona away from me.

With hands on hips, the hissing women swap whispered insults. Cole jumps into the fray as well, keeping the women from smacking each other, while they slap at his long arms. I play a pitifully flawed character in an all-too-familiar drama: As others debate and decide the future – *my* future – I stand by inertly, focused on the word "familiar", the root of which is, of course, "family." It occurs to me that these people feel like family, closer to me than my own.

Fio eventually disengages and asks what I'm smiling about. I shrug and slip my arm around her waist.

Gracie has not given up: "Look, Cole, I like Theo as much as you do…. Heck, I love Theo, but this…. this is—"

Cole finishes for her: "This is none yer bizness, doll." He spins her around and guides her up the hall.

I drop my key twice before managing to get the door open. I turn on a lamp, and Fio drenches me in a radiant smile, rendering all worries powerless. We kiss, slowly and warmly. This is unlike the mashing we did in the jungle: our embrace is less urgent, more pleasurable. I pull back and she bestows upon me The Look, which no longer causes me the slightest unease.

She undoes the top button of my silk shirt, and says, "Let's go to bed."

"Let me brush my teeth first. I have gator breath."

I return a minute later and kiss her again.

She says, "My turn. Can I use your toothbrush?"

I knock my pack off the bed, strip down and slip beneath the covers. My head is spinning from too much alcohol, and my eyes sting from tear gas, but I feel terrific. I shut my eyes and begin replaying the evening's events.

My eyes don't open until morning.

Chapter 20: Juan Dunbar

I awaken at dawn, my head and mouth full of cotton balls. But I'm not hung over. No, a hangover is something you get *after* you've sobered up. The room is slowly spinning, but I don't mind. Fio is rubbing my chest and nuzzling her cheek against my shoulder. A faint light filters through the window, and it feels like we're back in the jungle, except that we're warm and dry, with no critters gnawing on our ankles. And we're alone. I run my hand over her naked shoulder and back, and up the curve of her hip.

Touching my cheek with immense tenderness, she whispers, "Make love with me."

"Uh.... birth control?"

"It's a safe time." She rises up, and I sense her steely eyes bearing down on me. "And like Cole pointed out, it doesn't say anything in the New Testament about not making love."

"Are you sure? Because last night you said—"

"This is the first time I've ever been sure of anything."

Good enough for me. "You are my true north."

Fio kisses me with newfound urgency, and presses her heavenly body against me. She relinquishes her virginity with abandon and a good deal of pleasure.

The next time I awaken, the sun is streaming through our window. Okay, now I'm hung over. Fio, lying face to face with me, massages my uninjured shoulder. Through a tangle of blonde hair, she purrs, "Ready for some racket and festivities?" She slips her hand beneath the sheets and sings, "A weenie whack, a weenie whack...."

Laughing, I nonetheless respond to her ministrations, and she stops singing long enough to whisper in mock horror, "Senor Muña, su chorizo es enormo!" She starts up the "weenie whacks" again, and I toss in a harmony line.

Cole adds his falsetto through the paper-thin walls, singing: "The llama sleeps tonight."

Gracie joins in: "Hush, my hubby, don't sing, my hubby,

your wife would like to sleep."

I roll onto my back and Fio hops aboard, still singin' away.

After breakfast, the four of us hike out of town on a dusty road. Fio and Gracie, after apologizing for insulting one another last night, walk arm in arm. We hold out hope of reaching Imbabura Volcano, located ten miles east. It's an ambitious goal, yes, after a night of beer, tear gas, dancing, guayusaso, more beer and twenty-seven verses of "The Hokey Pokey." But a morning of love, laughter and black coffee has driven all but the most tenacious demons from my head.

"A weenie whack?" says Gracie. "Is there anything you guys need to tell me? What did I miss out there in the jungle?"

Big mistake on her part; we break into "The Llama Sleeps Tonight." She cheerfully adds the high-pitched trills at the end. I wrap an arm around her shoulder and sing, "Hush, My Gracious, don't fear, My Gracious, we promise not to sing."

We pass through a village, largely deserted except for a dozen pigs wandering the pot-holed dirt street. A dog growls off to our left and behind us. Pivoting to face our attacker, we meet the gaze of a stout, elderly woman, crouched on the porch of a run-down store. Did we misread the direction of the growl? All four of us? We rotate in unison, in case a dog is about to charge.

Fio whispers, "Did she just snarl at us?"

Cole says, "Think so. Let's hope she doesn't have rabies."

We walk backward until we reach the town's last building, a modest church with a padlocked door, which seems odd, seeing as how this is Sunday morning. Next to the church, a woman tends a small herd of llamas. Fio snaps a photo of a handsome six-footer with a reddish-brown coat. The woman picks up a stone and hurls it at us. She misses by a good twenty feet, but the message is clear: We are not welcome here. Gracie points out that people of some cultures don't like having their picture taken; the camera steals a part of their soul.

"Do llamas have souls?" I ask.

"If we do, I can't imagine why a llama wouldn't." Gracie looks back at the regal-looking fellow whose spirit she may have just snatched. "I think maybe I was a llama in a past life."

"I'm not sure about this reincarnation business," says Cole.

"People talk about past lives too casually, like they're telling you what they had for lunch. And most believers, apparently, led grand lives: 'Yes, I taught Mozart to play piano,' or 'I was a princess in Paris and invented the combo pizza.' But nobody claims to be the guy who emptied port-a-potties in Central Park."

Gracie says, "I think you were my concubine in a past life. One of many."

Clouds move in as the road meanders through a valley of small farms and marshes. We enter a village, and a mutt sidles up to us, wagging its tail and cowering. Gracie scratches behind its ears and strikes up a conversation with a woman sitting out front of a ramshackle house. Her clothes appear to be new; the brilliant red, blue and green of her blouse stand out nicely against her crisp white skirt. She speaks rapidly, even for an Ecuadorian, but I'm able to glean that she makes clothes for a living. Gracie introduces her as Daniela.

A light rain begins to fall. Daniela enters her house, and motions for us to follow. Cole, at six foot one, has to duck to get through the door. Daniela's living room is taken up by a weaving loom, a contraption the size of a grand piano. While Gracie and Fio gush over the clothing she's made, Cole and I inspect the machine, prodding it like a pair of chimps. I ask Daniela to show us how it works. She sits on a stool and performs an intricate series of operations, turning a hand crank, stepping on pedals, pulling and pushing levers, which feed brightly colored yarn from three spools into the loom. Slowly, a tightly woven surface of red, white and black materializes.

"Like watching grass grow," says Cole. Gracie and Fio glower at him. He says, "What? I like watching grass grow."

Gracie asks Daniela what she has for sale. The woman sweeps her hand proudly around the room. Fio picks out a white cotton skirt, embroidered with a blue and red hem. She slips it on over her shorts, then pirouettes and asks me, "Whattaya think?"

I respond with a word I've never used: "Lovely."

Protocol requires us to haggle, a process Fio has no use for, but she gets a kick out of watching Gracie go at it. We get great deals on the skirt for Fio, a shawl for Gracie, a shirt for Cole, a guitar strap for me, and belts for all. We tip Daniela generously, negating the effects of all that bargaining.

Daniela waves as we walk away. The skies have cleared somewhat. Just enough rain fell to clear the air and settle the dust. If I believed in Pariaqaqa, I would thank him.

Cole breaks into the chorus of that salacious song we learned from Jahn the Viking: "Yourrr daddy ain't your daddy but your daddy don't know." I add a harmony. Fio acted offended by this song last night, but now she claps along with Gracie.

We stop singing when we spot three disheveled men wobbling toward us. One is playing panpipes, another strums a charango, and the third guy has on a gorilla mask. He waves a half-full bottle of hooch, and calls out, "Buenos noches!" Good night! All three of them cackle as if that was the funniest thing ever said.

Cole waves back. "They're still on the way home from yesterday. Craziness!"

The men stop to yap at us, but their banter is impossible to follow. The gorilla holds out the bottle of murky liquid and shakes it.

Cole gamely takes a drink; his eyes glaze over. "Take a shwig, pally."

I do. "How do you say 'llama piss' in Español?"

"Yama piso!" the three men howl and slap me on the back.

I hand the bottle to the gorilla, who thrusts it at Fio. She declines.

Gracie points at the mask. "Por que?" Why?

They say something decipherable only to themselves, then crack up and amble on down the road. The four of us look at one another in bemusement and crack up. We continue on our way, and I slip my arm around Fio's waist.

She says, "According to Gracie, you and I make a great couple; something to do with Virgos and Libras – earth and sky."

"Who am I to argue with astrology?" I put no credence in this, but it's nice to have Gracie's support.

Fio leans her head on my shoulder and reaches her arms around my torso. "This morning you said I was your true north. What did you mean?"

"Ever since I've been here, I keep getting disoriented, because the sun is right overhead most of the time. But I don't feel lost around you. You are my true north."

She whispers something that stops me in my tracks. "What was that?" I ask, cupping my hand around my ear. "Not sure if I heard you right."

"I love you." Her smile dazzles me.

I've been waiting to hear those three words, and not just for the past few weeks. Nobody has spoken those words to me since I was little. That wonderful ache in my chest wells up, multiplied many times over. An unfamiliar contentment washes over me.

"Fio, I'd like to hear that again."

She places her hands on my shoulders and caresses my ears. "I love you, Theo Duncan, and I always will."

Imbabura Volcano rises gradually at its base and then steepens, so that near its peak, it inclines at a good fifty degrees. Its upper slopes are marbled with snow, and a cloud halo hovers above its crater. It's well past noon, and by now it's clear that we're not going to make it all the way to the volcano.

"Behold!" says Cole, holding out an upturned palm toward Imbabura. "The birthplace of religion." He still has a bit of a lisp, so it comes out: Zhe birzhplaith of relichun."

Fio regards him warily. "What do you mean?"

"Humans have buried their dead for thousands of years. Lava comes from underground, and judging by its destructive power, it was obviously produced by an evil being, which we will call.... oh, let's call it 'the devil.' And let's call her home 'hell.' That's the lava lake where we go after death. Humans were distressed by this, so we invented an alternative, heaven. And if there's a devil, it'd be nice to believe in a god, who gives us signs, like when you see a rainbow: Hey, happy days are here again. And the way refraction works, a rainbow always centers itself directly in front of you, the viewer; you never see one from the side. It was reasonable for Noah to believe God made a rainbow specifically for him."

Fio is appalled. "Where did you get *that*?"

Cole taps his head. "Thunk it up. In Exodus, before Moses picked up the Ten Commandments, he spoke to Mt. Sinai. It's burning and smoking, while the sky fills with lightning and thunder, trumpets are.... never mind; I don't get that business about the trumpets. Fi, Moses was talking to a *volcano*, thinking it was God! What a whacko! Whoever wrote Exodus wanted to portray God as the most powerful thing imaginable, so he chose a volcano."

"Where did you get this?"

"The Bible; you should read it sometime."

She does not challenge him on this point. It's ironic that Cole has read the Bible in its entirety, and she, evidently, has not. Of course, his aim in reading a Bible would be to poke holes in it, or poke fun at it. For him, it's an exercise in poking, whereas Fio considers reading and understanding the Bible a lifelong pursuit.

"Imagine that volcano blowing its top," says Cole. "The ground ruptures; lava and ash rain down on your head. It'd be hell on Earth."

Fio grimaces, Gracie rolls her eyes.

Cole says, "A thousand years ago, if you'd seen a tornado heading your way, you'd have thought somebody, some god, had it in for you. And if you saw an eclipse? My god, we're done for! Churches never would have been built had we not been terrified by twisters and comets and floods, oh my! All stuff that's easily explained by science."

I fear that if Cole pushes this matter any further, he and his sister's relationship will rupture, and I'll be caught in their scriptural blast zone.

He continues, "When people refer to heaven or hell, they're talking about a spiritual place, whatever that means, where the soul, whatever that means, resides after death. But people used to think hell was down *there*, literally, and heaven was up *there*. It wasn't until recently that we had any understanding of those lights in the sky." He shrugs. "Still, there's a nice symmetry to this whole heaven-and-hell setup, except that hell is always described in more vivid detail."

Fio turns to Gracie. "Is that what you believe too?"

"No, I believe there are gods – spirits, or energies – that place the planets in motion and breathe life into plants, and we are part of a web, a network that permeates the Universe."

"I still have a tough time with the idea of multiple gods."

"Why only one? You two argue about whether there's one god or none, but look around – life is complicated. Hmmmm, zeroes and ones; there's a word for that."

"Binary," says Cole. "Programmers sometimes use binary code because it's the simplest."

"But in this case, arguing ones and zeroes isn't just simple; it's simple-minded."

Cole and Fio both take umbrage at that. "Well, how many gods do you believe in?" asks Fio. "How many gods are there?"

"No idea, because the number changes. Sometimes gods go away, when they think they're no longer needed. Like Pele, when a volcano goes extinct."

Fio's eyes beseech me. "What do you think about that?"

"Oh, I'd have to think about it." Truth is, now that she and I are involved, I'm chicken to address this issue with her.

"Compared with the Biblical creation story," says Cole, "geology provides a richer, more beautiful account of how the world formed, and is still forming. Imagine the patience it took for that volcano to form, inches per year for millions of years. Contrast that to Genesis. Boom! Six days, done! It's too easy. It's lazy, thinking that way."

"But geology is your god," says Fio.

"No, it's not, because geology, unlike religion, can be edited. If somebody comes up with better ideas, heck, bring 'em on. Science looks forward, religion looks back."

"But geology doesn't say how things got started in the first place."

"You're right. We have a lot to learn."

Gracie skips ahead, singing "Baba O'Riley," written by Pete Townsend of the Who. The lyrics talk about not needing to be right or forgiven. The verse ends with: Yeah, yeah, yeah, yeah. It's not clear whether Gracie is sending a message to Cole and Fio, or if she just has her own soundtrack going. If it is a message, they don't hear it.

My brother Phil dabbles in Eastern religions, and he told me Townsend wrote that song as a tribute to his Indian spiritual teacher, Meher Baba. Whereas the ancient Hebrews considered it a heresy to speak God's name, Baba deemed it pointless to talk at all. Born to Zoroastrian parents, he took a vow of silence at age thirty and supposedly did not speak for the next forty years. He claimed that humans' inability to live by the word of God renders an avatar's teaching pointless.

When I floated the idea that maybe this Meher dude had not yet figured out how to say what it was he wanted to say, Phil became incensed. He informed me that I was not *aware*.

Fio asks, "How could this world come from nothing? What, or who, lit the fuse on the Big Bang?"

"Great question," says Cole. "Geology doesn't answer it, nor does it make any pretense of doing so. That's the realm of astrophysics and quantum mechanics; at the sub-atomic level, events happen spontaneously, without cause."

"Talk about lazy thinking. How could they just happen?"

"Think of it like this: You know how 1 + -1 = 0. Well, you can turn it around and say that 0 = 1 + -1. In other words, a nothing can be broken down into two somethings."

"So we can solve the mystery of existence with arithmetic? Cole, that's silly; it's mathematical trickery. *Who* broke zero into pieces? Why not call whatever created the universe 'God'?"

"It's impossible to know what happened before the Big Bang."

Uncharacteristically, Gracie joins in. "It's not the creation stories that bother me. I'm appalled at how eagerly religious people embrace the destruction of this gorgeous world. End times have been predicted for millennia, and who knows? Maybe the world will end tonight, but it's a sickness, wanting to watch the world burned and broken to bits."

Cole agrees, and he wants the world to know it. "The Book of Revelations was written by a sociopath with nightmares, for cowards who hope to survive death. Christians don't just predict The End; they ache for it. James Watt, Reagan's Secretary of the Interior, told Congress that protecting natural resources was unimportant in light of Jesus' imminent return."

Fiona doesn't seem to take his harangue personally. "I don't ache for The End, but if it's part of God's plan, I accept it."

"Fi, it bugs me when you say your way is best for all."

I say, "But Cole, you'd say your way is best."

"No, I don't!" He shoots me a look of betrayal. "How can you say that?"

"You're convinced it's impossible to know what happened before the Big Bang, and you think believers are deluding themselves. Shoot, if there's anything to it, I'd like to believe."

Growing up, I accepted all that Jesus stuff, to the same degree my Sunday school classmates did. We read the Bible when asked, and we prayed along with old Mr. Moss, though much of what he fed us didn't make sense, so the ideas never settled in; the Big Picture never took root. When I was about six, a girl asked Mr. Moss why we take offering. He told her the money gets sent to baby Jesus. I made the mistake of telling my parents that Pastor Pete loaded up rocket ships with bags of money and launched them into space.

Mom glared at Dad. "Maybe we should put Mr. Moss on that rocket ship; send the old space cadet back where he belongs."

"Huh?" asked my deaf dad. He and I had no idea what was bugging Mom.

Mr. Moss taught our Sunday school class for six years, and the older I got, the less sense he made. But Pastor Pete – now he was a different story. He had a fire inside him, and I always assumed that when I got older, my insides would catch fire too. But the flame never came to me, and I never went to get it. It goes without saying that my abortive baptism had left a bad, chlorinated taste in my mouth.

Cole acts as if I'm sucking up to his sister. "Theo, you consider yourself open-minded, and you bend over backward to accept people. But if you bend over far enough, you're gonna fall on your ass. You have to stand for something." He's getting worked up. "If you get to the point where you stop questioning yourself...." He stops to rub his forehead. "Okay, maybe I need to rethink this. Sorry, pally. But Fi, what sort of God would—?"

"I'm hungry," says Gracie, yawning. "For meatloaf."

Cole ignores her. "Fi, what do you get out your faith?"

"Well, humility, for one thing," says Fiona. Cole's eyes bug out in disbelief, and she says, "It's humbling to realize there's a power and goodness larger than yourself."

"That's how I've always thought of science," says Cole, and now it's his turn to respond to his sister's widened eyes. "It's humbling to discover how powerful and orderly and beautiful the universe is, and we only understand a small part of it."

Fiona bobs her head. The four of us link arms and walk on in contented silence. Gracie wears a see-how-easy-that-is look.

Later that afternoon, after catching a bus back, Fio and I take a stroll around Otavalo. Some buildings are falling apart, and some roads approximate the texture of cottage cheese, but overall people seem healthy and well-dressed, except for a few old women begging on street corners. Boys strut down narrow side streets, trying to look tough. Women carry corn stalks in bundles larger than themselves. Three teenage girls walk hand-in-hand down the middle of the street, swinging their arms and singing one of those old car crash songs: "Where, oh where, could my baby be? The Lord took her away from me." How odd. How cool.

From a backyard comes the sound of music and festive voices. "Señor Hokey!" a voice calls to us. "Señorita Pokey!" We look over the four-foot fence, wondering who these people are.

Seeing our confusion, a woman sings, "You do the hokey-pokey, and you turn yourself around…." Her fellow partiers join in: "That what it's all about!"

Oh, right! It's Tahiti! She opens a gate and motions us in. Fio hesitates; I imagine she's recalling my charade to get rid of Colonel Mustard. So I hesitate too, but a smiley man takes Fio by the elbow and leads her in. Drinks find their way into our hands.

Eying my drink, I ask, "Que es esta?" What is this?

"Agua loca," says Tahiti. Crazy water.

A guitarist begins playing a rollicking tune. Some guests sing along, everyone claps. The guitarist catches me watching his fingers, and when the song ends, he holds out the guitar. When I don't take it, he extends it further and makes a strumming motion. He asks, "Si?"

"Si." I set down my agua loca and take the guitar. The party grinds to a halt, as partiers wait expectantly. I ease into "Blue Moon," the slow version. I sing it as soulfully as I can, but it needs Cole's harmony to make it fly.

The song ends and people clap. I smile and hand the guitar back to its owner, who shakes his head. "Uno mas."

I ask Fio, "What should I play?"

"I can't help falling in love with you."

"Back at ya. But what should I play?"

Fio takes the guitar and hands it and her drink to Tahiti. She shouts, "Safety blitz!" and tackles me.

Lying flat on my back, I look up at the ring of concerned

faces and laugh. "Mi chica es loco! Muy loco!"

Relieved, two men help me up. Our drinks are refilled.

The smiley woman asks me, "Juan Dunbar?"

"Repeata?"

"Juan Dunbar." She takes the guitar from Tahiti and hands it to me.

Fio tugs at my sleeve. "John Denver! Do you know any of his songs?"

Having sung "Annie's Song" at two of Ro's three weddings, I strum the opening chords and right away the smiley woman sings along, which surprises me. She's unable to converse in English, but she knows the lyrics to a sweet, sappy Juan Dunbar song. As we sing the line "Let me always be with you," Fio watches me through glistening eyes.

The song ends, people clap, I relinquish the guitar. Women are setting up for dinner, so we say gracias for the drinks and bow out. As we walk away, Tahiti calls out, "Adios, Señor Hokey y Señorita Pokey." Fio blows her a kiss.

We wander into Parque Central, and check out a statue of Rumiñahui. I open my guide book and read bits aloud:

"Pizarro captured Atahualpa, the last Incan emperor, and demanded a roomful of gold for his release. The ransom was delivered, after which Pizarro ordered Atahualpa to be burned at the stake. The emperor protested, saying that dying in this manner would prevent his resurrection."

Fiona asks, "Why in the world would he think he'd be resurrected?"

"Strange, huh?" is how I answer that. I continue reading: "Pizarro acquiesced, and then sentenced Atahualpa to death by strangulation. Rumiñahui, the emperor's brother, learned of this treachery, and he vowed that invaders would not take Quito. So when Spanish forces laid siege on his city, Rumiñahui burned it to the ground and killed the temple virgins in order to preserve their purity. He was captured, tortured and killed by the Spanish." I close the book, and say, "Sucks to be a temple virgin."

"Or an Incan emperor."

"Or just about anybody who lived here in the 1500s."

She puts her arms around me and says, "I am thankful we live now."

"I am thankful for you." It's a cornball thing to say, sure, but it's true.

I buy us dinner at a sidewalk cafe. Fio raves about the Trucha a la Navarra – fried, with rice, peppers and almonds – substantiating the adage: You can't go wrong with the trout.

Fiona picks up an almond and says, "When I was twelve, I asked Crampy Q if you pronounce it '*ah*mond' or '*al*mond.' He said, 'Halfway between. You can *ah*most hear the 'l'. He was always playing around with words and how they sound."

"I wish I could have met him."

"Crampy was a toy-maker. Boy, you should have seen Christmas at our house! Oh, Theo, he would have loved our story about getting lost in the jungle." She turns serious. "Do you think Dixon made it out?"

"Don't bet against him, but I'm worried." Then I surprise myself by asking, "Fio, would you pray for him?"

"I do, everyday."

After dinner we head back to the hotel, holding hands. Now that the subject of Dixon has come up, I can't get him out of my head. There he is, sitting on his pile of leaves in the jungle, in a downpour, in the dead of night, finger on the button of his camera, waiting for a hogwar to walk by, like a model on a catwalk. Then it hits me:

That is how I've lived, waiting in the dark for Life to walk up and introduce itself. I waited for Fio to make the first move, because she was involved with Barry, and I wanted to respect that. But even after he showed himself to be a jerk, and even after she mauled me in the jungle, I was reluctant to push. She has been calling the shots.

Mom told me on my tenth birthday that I was the easiest of her kids to raise. I took it as a compliment until Claire, who had overheard Mom's remark, told me I'd misunderstood it. She said, "Mom's had a tough life, what with Dad being deaf and all. She's saying she wants you to be easy, to not pester her." Looking back, it was a rotten thing for her to say. Sadly, I believed her. Maybe she was right, but I suspect that Claire, as usual, was maneuvering for an ever larger slice of the Duncan pie. Regardless, I learned not to ask much of those around me, or even from myself. I've been drifting on a slow-moving current.

I have drifted long enough. "Fio, I could move to Seattle."

She doesn't answer right away. I'm guessing she doesn't want me and Barry living anywhere near one another. She says, "Or I could come to Tucson."

Now it's my turn to balk. Before she has time to misread my hesitation, I tell her, "I'd be proud to introduce you to anyone. But I'm not proud of the Duncan clan – drugs, suicide attempts.... It's a caustic situation."

Fio takes my arm. "It's okay, Theo. I could have gone down that path myself."

I stop walking and take hold of her hands. "I fly out this Thursday. You?"

"Next week."

"Okay, we have four days to come up with a plan. Deal?"

"Deal." After a quick handshake, we kiss and grope each other, right there on the street. Walking back to the hotel with my arm around her waist, I think: This has been the happiest day of my life.

Chapter 21: Buddha Would Agree

I'm awoken by a shriek. "Fio! Are you all right?"

She stumbles out of the bathroom, naked, howling in laughter, and I realize she's found the message I wrote in toothpaste on the floor of the shower stall: Isle of he – yo!

I say, "It's true, funetically speaking. I love Fio."

She hauls me into the shower and turns on the faucet. She scoops up the word "he" and rubs it on my torso. I press my goopy tummy against hers and kiss her.

"Fio, our bodies are a Mobius strip. Two surfaces are one." I am no longer concerned about sounding schmaltzy.

She caresses my ears and says, "You are my Isle of He."

"Yo." We say it together, and then make love standing up, complete with racket and festivities. The stall is tiny, so we keep banging the wall and shower door with our elbows, knees and heads, but we manage pretty well, all the while snickering and snorting and vowing to never do this again.

From next door Gracie yells, "We've got a herd of horny llamas living next door!"

"CHEEE-ses! Don't they ever sleep?"

The four of us are standing on the sidewalk after breakfast, and Cole asks if we want to rent horses and head for the hills. Fio declines immediately. She suggests that we meet up for dinner. As they walk away, Fio is antsy.

"What's wrong?"

Fio points at Imbabura. "I keep thinking about Cole and his lava-devil-god theory."

"Oh, right. I've never heard anybody lay it out like that."

"What do you think about it?"

The butterflies in my stomach take to the air, performing a discomfiting series of back flips and death-defying barrel rolls. I find myself feeling relieved that Barry is miles and hours away – out of sight, out of mind, out of heart. Still, an unsettling possibility crosses my mind: If she could dump him so easily, what's in store for me?

"It's interesting," I say, wishing Cole would keep his damn theories to himself.

She stops walking and turns to face me. "I want to share my relationship with Christ with you. It's important to me."

"I want to share everything with you."

"Will you pray with me?"

"I will." She's noticeably more relaxed as we head back to the hotel.

Back in my room, we sit cross-legged on the bed. She eyes me expectantly, so I close my eyes and pray silently: God, if you exist, I ask for guidance. I will gladly go in whichever direction you take me. I sit silently for a while before opening my eyes.

Fio purses her lips. "Will you pray to Jesus? Aloud?"

I close my eyes again. "Jesus, I pray for guidance. Please show me which path I should take."

"Why can't you let go? Have faith."

"I can't.... you can't.... people don't.... we don't *choose* what to believe. You couldn't choose not to believe in Jesus. You can't tell yourself all of a sudden to put your faith in.... say, Haile Selassie."

"Who's he?"

"An Ethiopian emperor; he died in the seventies. Many Africans consider him to be God Incarnate." She's dumbfounded. I say, "See what I mean? From the outside, it's weird. We don't even bother to ask if it's true. But if you'd been born in East Africa forty years ago, there's a good chance you'd have been a Rastafarian and thought nothin' of it. Is that any more outrageous than worshiping a dead carpenter from Bethlehem?"

Fio furrows her brow. Suddenly, she seems to be taking our differences personally. "Theo, you make this out to be a game or a puzzle. Of course we have free will. You chose to order trout for breakfast."

"Maybe. Or maybe my taste buds imagined a variety of dishes, and trout won out."

"By that reasoning, we aren't responsible for our actions."

"That's the purpose of education, to increase our chances of making good decisions."

"So you're saying we can *choose* to educate ourselves?"

That's a head-scratcher. "I like to think so, but maybe not. Because, see, if you're curious about something, of course you'll educate yourself. It's not really a choice." My response satisfies neither of us.

She takes my hands. "You won't be able to think your way through this, Theo. It's a matter of faith. And nothing compares to walking with Christ. Nothing is better."

I can guess how Cole would respond: I agree, *nothing* would be better – way better.

Fio continues, "You had a deep and meaningful.... uh, episode at Machu Picchu, but it's not the same as knowing Jesus."

Her words anger me. "You haven't walked in my shoes! You don't hear through my ears! You can't compare your.... uh, *episodes* with mine. And to say that nothing compares with Jesus is like saying Gibsons are the only guitars worth playing, which is silly if you've never played a Fender." She softens, and I respond in kind. "Fio, I'm not disagreeing with you. When you talk about God, I'm intrigued, but I don't get the concept, the vocabulary. Yet."

Had Cole been there, he might have added: And I don't believe you get it either, Fi.

"Maybe that's why we met, so you would understand."

I am not fond of the notion that she and I were introduced by an otherworldly being with ulterior motives. Does our love require a reason for being? Still, I'm willing to consider the possibility that God has set his sights on me. In which case, that *is* why Fio and I met, which leads me to think: Maybe Fiona Knows, even if I don't understand exactly what it is she knows.

"Fio, I'd love to have your certainty. It's imaginable that you know a fundamental truth about life that I don't."

"Well, then?"

"How did you come to believe? What happened before you accepted Jesus?" She looks pained. "Fio, I want to know you. When you bonded with God, was it a willful act?" Now she's confused. "Because you didn't reason it out, right?" She shakes her head. "Then did you decide?"

"It didn't happen all at once," she begins uncertainly. "After Crampy Q left, I found myself moving toward God.... no, that's not right – he drew me in. You could say he pursued me."

I nod. Having been pursued by my Machu Picchu song, I'm willing to take her statement at face value.

Her face blossoms into that enveloping warmth I've come to cherish. "I could feel Him," she says. "I was ready."

"So you know The Truth, with capital T's?" I ask this in jest, but she answers seriously.

"It's not like that, Theo. You're talking about a concept, an abstraction, whereas I know.... I know Jesus. I know God." This is a step up from her "I know there's a God," and light years beyond Barry's "I know there must be a God."

I know God – taken in isolation, these words can either sound profound or profane, simple or simple-minded. They may be submitted with grace or grandiosity. Fio delivers them matter-of-factly, with humility.

"Theo, you have to feel."

"I do. My love of music goes right to the core of who I am. Maybe it's the same thing as your love of God. Music, God – maybe they're just different names for the same thing, two sides of a Mobius strip."

I expect that one to connect. It doesn't.

"Theo, Jesus transformed me."

"In what way?"

"Remember how Cole said I raised hell in Sunday school? I hate to admit it, but it's true. I stole from the collection plate, I'd skip out to grab a smoke. Yeah, I know, I wasn't a very nice girl. Oh, and I'd ask Mrs. Fleeney questions like: What did God make stuff out of? Could God change the value of pi?"

"So? Those are great questions."

"Maybe, but I did it to make her crazy. She'd try to answer them and kids would laugh at her. Anyway, I changed, gladly, and every day I look forward to fostering a deeper relationship with Christ." She takes my hand. "What if you choose not to believe and you're wrong?"

"Is that why you believe? No? Then why expect me to think that way?" I smile; she gives me a half-grin. "I haven't experienced what you have, not exactly, but Machu Picchu...." I almost say: transformed me. But that sounds pretentious, even though Fio just used it and for some reason was able to get away with it. Now, why is that? Ahhhh, here's why: Jesus has more credibility than the Incas.

So I opt for: "Machu Picchu woke up a part of me that I didn't even know existed." Is it pretentious to speak of your own awakening? Yeah, well, tough. "Fio, I wouldn't trade places with anyone who's ever lived."

We gaze at one another, straining to make contact across a chasm that is seemingly a finger's length too wide. Then she recoils, as if she has tugged too hard against a tether, and it snaps her back onto safer ground. From her viewpoint, am I afraid to make the leap? Bereft of spirit? Duped by the machinations of the devil? Or just plain ornery?

She says, "You can't understand until you accept Jesus. No one can explain it to you."

"But someone must have explained it to you." She has no answer for that, which provides me not a shred of satisfaction. As Gracie has taught me, the goal of life, or love, has nothing to do with winning the debate. "Fio, help me with my search. I'm wide open." I stretch my arms far apart.

Her mouth smiles, if not her eyes. "Okay."

It's only noon, but I'm weary. I lie back, and she settles in beside me, nuzzling her cheek against mine.

She whispers, "I never want to leave this place."

The butterflies land and fold up their wings, rendering themselves invisible.

"Let's not go home, Theo."

We lie there at midday, and I mull over her proposal that we stay here. On the surface, it sounds sweet. As sweet as Inca Kola. But really, what she's saying is: If we go home, we'll have to face reality – let's find us a fantasy world.

I recall the jungle lodge's slogan: You Won't Come Back the Same. If Fio ran that company, their brochure would read: You Won't Come Back at All.

I pore over our conversation, imagining different turns it might have taken. There must be a sane way to approach this. If I could just say it better.... No, that's not right; if both of us could say it better, more clearly, more simply, more impartially.... No, if either one of us could say it better; it wouldn't matter which. Or maybe we need to listen better.

Cole feels the same frustration with Fio as I do, though the two of them agree on one point: In order to devote oneself to Christ, a part of us must die. They disagree, however, on exactly what part expires. Fiona would say the piece she sloughed off was human arrogance, the delusion that we can become spiritually whole without God's mercy, just as a snake will shed an outer layer of skin when it becomes too constricting.

Cole, on the other hand, believes that a Christian must relinquish the desire, or the ability, to self-critique the workings of her own mind. He might liken such a sacrifice to having a lobotomy performed by Incan doctors equipped with hand drills and minimally effective anesthetics.

Again it strikes me how differently they think, how differently they act and look. How different they are. Something Cole said comes back to me: "I wonder if Fi isn't my half-sister." And his uncle said Cole's mom had "a soft spot for a hard-on." And this Graham McHugh character – where does he fit in? Why would a stranger be sending them gifts? And then, from out of nowhere, one line plays in my head: "Yourrrr daddy ain't your daddy but your daddy don't know."

Add all this up, and it sounds like Graham McHugh might be a closer family member than suspected. Hijo de puta! Their family might be more messed up than mine.

I think Fiona is asleep, so she startles me when she says, "Tell me about your mother. You said you missed her."

I hesitate, just as I've hesitated before when the opportunity to talk about Mom has presented itself. I have no qualms about delving into the Duncan family's unseemly history; I've broached this matter with Cole and Gracie. But I am protective of my dogma-detesting mother, and the thought that Fio believes Mom is burning in hell is something I've been unwilling to face. Hasn't Mom suffered enough indignity? Nevertheless, Fio and I are now intimate, in a way I have never been – and have never imagined being – with anyone.

Fio waits. There's no getting out of this.

"Mom passed away," I say.

Exuding warmth and fortitude, Fio props herself up on an elbow and places a hand on my chest. My story tumbles out. She is silent until I finish.

Then she tells me, "She is lucky to have you as a son."

"*Is* lucky?"

"Of course. The soul is eternal."

Again, there's avoiding this. "Mom didn't believe in God."

"Yeah?" she says, expecting more. "So?"

"Well, where do you believe she is?"

"Oh, Theo, that's not for me to say. Your mother sounds like a wonderful woman, and if she...." Her eyes are suddenly brimming with heartbreak and horror. "You think I believe she went to hell. Don't you?"

"What else would I think?"

She falls silent, then says, "I can see why you'd think that. But, Theo, I don't know about hell, or heaven for that matter. Believing in Christ is all about how we live, here, today, and how we love."

This is an eye-opener for me, though it probably shouldn't be, because she said way back at Machu Picchu that Jesus' life is more interesting to her than his death. Her belief structure is more nuanced and fluid than I've given her credit for. She sees the world through eyes that are gray, not black and white. Though neither intentionally nor consciously, I have, until one minute ago, considered her Christian attitudes to be provincial and judgmental. Shoot, had I been asked this morning which of us was less tolerant, "Fio" would have been the obvious answer. But now? As Gracie chided Cole: You put up walls too.

Fio lays her head on my chest. "You are my Isle of He."

"Yo."

Her breathing changes. I wish her sweet, lovely dreams.

Fio and I walk down to the outdoor market in the early afternoon. Business is booming. Handicrafts and brightly colored textiles hang from pegs on makeshift walls. Acres of vendors offer vegetables, jewelry, fake shrunken heads, anything.

We stop at a stall that sells sheepskin rugs and sweaters made from llama wool. Fio holds up a brown and light blue sweater to my chest and tilts her head to one side. "These colors suit you. Feel how soft this is." She touches the luxurious material to my cheek, and I lean my face into her hand. She sets the sweater down and whispers, "Tell you what. I will buy you this sweater, but I want you to bargain for it. Deal?"

"Watch me operate." I put on my shades, smooth my hair back and wiggle my ears.

Fio nudges me with her hip. "Get on with it."

"Not to worry, lil' lady, I am too cool to fool."

The vendor stands with her back to us, helping another customer. I pick through sweaters and haughtily drop one from my fingertips, as if it has cooties.

"Don't lack much a'bein a bozo," says Fio. I look surprised, and she adds, "I love that saying. It's a wonderful way to keep Dixon in our thoughts."

The saleswoman approaches us, and I hold up the sweater Fio chose. "Cuanto cuesta?" How much?

"Dos cien mil." Two hundred thousand. Divide by 1400. About fourteen dollars.

I shake my head disdainfully. "Demasiado." Too much. The woman says nothing.

"Setenta mil," I say. 70,000 – five bucks.

She turns away and starts folding sweaters.

"Ochenta mil." 80,000 – six bucks.

She folds sweaters.

"Uno cien, um, mil, e, uh, ultima precio." A hundred, um, thousand, and, uh, last offer. She continues folding sweaters, though my butchery of her language is wearing her down.

"Uno cien mil...." Uh-oh, this is getting complicated. "E, uh, diez mil." 100,000.... plus, uh, 10,000. About seven bucks.

"Si," she says.

Yes! Mastering a foreign language is over-rated.

Fio asks me to put on the sweater. It's a bit large, but she nods and says, "We make a good team."

"My thoughts exactly."

We find a bench and Fio stretches a leg across my lap. We touch and speak in the manner of new lovers, treating each caress as a gift. Each self-disclosure is a treasure to be protected. Her teasing comments about my llama ears are delivered with a perfect mix of sass and intimacy.

Japanese women walk by, speaking with English accents. Black guys stand on the corner, conversing in French. Most pedestrians, however, are Otavaleños, indigenous people.

She asks, "Why have Indians fared so much better in South

America than North?"

"A lot of North American natives were nomadic, easy to push around. Here they were farmers; they owned land before Europeans arrived. People do better when they settle down."

She strokes my neck. "Would you settle down with me?"

"Yes, I definitely would."

"You said that people don't choose what they believe. I'd agree, and we also don't get to choose who we fall in love with. It would be easier if we did, but not better."

We wander the town arm in arm, aimless and content. I point toward the mountains and drawl, "Don't lack much a'bein' storm clouds."

Fio looks distraught. "I can't stop thinking about Dixon. If we hadn't followed him back to the canoe that morning, he would have paddled back by himself, and we might be the ones wandering around the jungle."

"Maybe so."

"Well, I feel awful about that. I was the one who insisted we follow him."

"Right. But you can't feel guilty about.... *caring*." I stop walking and place my hands on her shoulders. "Your intent was to make sure he wasn't alone."

"Yes, and look how that turned out. We're here to serve and save, Theo. And if we fail at that, what's the point of.... of.... What's the point?"

"Fio, he planned for us to follow him. He wanted us to. We did nothing wrong." But then I recall my conversation with Cole on the observation deck of the winged Madonna.

Fio catches the uncertainty in my eyes. "What?"

I shake my head and say, "Oh, nothing." But those steely eyes peer into mine and pull the truth from my body. I explain how we could have towed Dixon back to the lodge in the damaged canoe. "We are all guilty, I guess, guilty of being thoughtless. But it's not like we sinned. We made a mistake." She and I move on, walking slowly. "Dixon will find his way out."

She gives me a wry smile. "Sometimes I think your faith is stronger than mine."

We approach a brick church, topped by an elegant six-sided bell tower. Though not as grand as the cathedrals in Quito, the church holds a modest appeal.

"Theo, have you finished writing your song?"

"Pretty much, although I haven't figured out how to work in the phrase 'Mobius trails.' "

"Oh, I can't wait to hear it! But let's check out this church first." She grabs my hand. "How do you start writing a song?"

"A melody will pop into my head, all by itself, and then—"

"How does that happen?"

I've wondered this too. Is it magic? Or the voice of God? Is it a muse? An angel, humming in my ear? The subconscious mind, messing around on air guitar?

"I don't know," I say. "But the music always comes first – it's easy. Finding lyrics to match the melody is work."

We climb the stone steps of the church and enter the arched doorway. At the altar stand a tall redhead in a tux and a shorter Ecuadorian woman in veil and gown. The church is only a third full, with everyone packed forward, so we slip in and stand in the shadows along the back wall. The wedding ceremony is being conducted concurrently in Spanish and English.

A youngish American, standing to one side of the altar, strums his guitar and sings one of those vapid wedding songs purposely designed not to be unpleasant. As the last chord dies out, the priest acknowledges him with a compulsory nod and commences with the next part of the ceremony.

A Protestant minister then delivers its English equivalent: "Only in the spirit of Christ," the minister declares, "can two people truly be joined as one."

That line gets my attention, because Fio's hand clutches mine. My eyes have not yet adjusted to the dim light, but I sense her eyes on me. I shift my stance, making a scuffling sound that echoes off the stone walls. People turn to look, so we tiptoe out.

On our way back to the hotel, Fio is upset. When I ask if anything is wrong, she shakes her head.

"Only in the spirit of Christ;" those words echo in my head.

Eventually she says, "I woke up this afternoon, and thought about the talks we've had. One thought kept returning to me: If I could just say it better—"

"Yes, Fio! That was my thought too! Exactly!"

"Let me finish. If I could just say it in a better way, you

would accept Jesus."

"Hey, I'm just trying to find my way. You are trying to find *the* way for everyone."

"No, Theo. I've already found The Way, or at least My Way. And it's there for anyone willing to open his heart."

A Bible verse sounds in my head: No one cometh unto the Father but by me. I have never cometh unto the Father, and, apparently neither have the butterflies waiting on high alert in my stomach. Fio and I walk silently until it begins to rain, at which point we hightail it back to our hotel.

Back in my room, I get her a towel to dry her hair. When I exit the bathroom, Fio is holding my charango. She scowls and runs a finger over the dark, waxy image of lips on the instrument's face. "What is *this*?"

"Oh. Gracie kissed my charango the other night."

"She doesn't wear lip gloss."

"The other night she was."

"I'm not going to ask." She hands me the charango and takes a seat on the room's lone wooden chair.

Sitting cross-legged on the bed, I strum two chords and begin singing:

> Sadness etched in stone
> Strength I've never known
> Why and where did you go?
>
> Hidden well, our citadel
> Where mist and mountain meet
> No sound, in a ghost town
> A single llama roams the street
>
> The Sun God meets the Son of God
> No room for compromise
> How brutal, how beautiful
> And here the vanquished lie

Fio is crying. I am touched, but confused; this song is not really a tear jerker. I sing on:

Our climb was fast, our time will pass
Should we ever lose our aim
Any heart and mind, that we leave behind
The jungle will reclaim

Did we mistake our sacred dance?
Did we ever stand a chance?
Why and where did you go?

I re-sing that last line and set down my charango. Baffled by Fio's tears, I stand and pull her to her feet. She places her cheek against my chest and sobs, but she leaves her arms at her sides. Then it hits me: She thinks this tune is about us!

"My song is about the people who lived at Machu Picchu," I say, stroking her neck.

"Oh, Theo, I am so sorry." Her whisper is the wind of a passing ghost.

I have no idea what is happening, but I fear this will be the last time I hold her or smell her hair. I inhale deeply, breathing in her essence. I memorize the sensation of her body pressed against mine. This is so sudden, as sudden as a car crash: Where, oh where, can my baby be? The Lord took her away from me.

This cannot be happening; there's no sense in it. "Fio, let's give it time." My voice sounds whiny.

She suddenly seems frail. "This is not what I wanted." Does she mean that she doesn't want us to split up? Or does she consider it a mistake to have gotten involved in the first place? Or, is she saying it's not her intention to skewer my heart?

"Theo, it was wrong to make love with you. But I don't regret it." This is crazy talk.

"Fio, I don't have the same faith *as* you, but I have faith *in* you." She separates from me, and her eyes meet mine. I tell her, "I accept your beliefs as they are. Will you accept mine?"

She backs away. "What *are* your beliefs?"

Good question. "Music is the closest thing I know to truth. Sound, the beauty of music, means everything to me."

"But music and beauty are fleeting; they don't last." From what little I learned from Phil about eastern religions, Buddha would agree, though this doesn't seem quite the right moment to point that out.

She continues, "I want something lasting.... No, I've *got* something lasting. My relationship with Christ is eternal."

"I've had meaningful experiences, but I don't know how to interpret them. Yet. As Logan put it: Good luck trying to talk about it." My spiel sounds contrived and desperate. It occurs to me that if Fio Knows, then Maybe I Can Know.

"I have the melody, Fio. I just don't have the lyrics to match it yet." Too cryptic for her, I think. "Be patient with me. I'm not there yet."

"But, Theo, where are you headed? Are you just going to live and then die?"

It takes me a moment to respond. "I'm not sure, but the word 'just' is an effective trivializer. I am going to live and then die. Hopefully, I will be grateful for my time here." That line is something Cole would say, but that doesn't make it less true.

"That's clever, Theo, but cleverness won't feed your soul." Her eyes are lifeless, as they were that night we marched out of the jungle in triumph, only to be rebuked by Logan. "And like you said at Machu Picchu, you have felt lost for a very long time."

"Yes, but I haven't felt lost these last few days."

"I don't want to be.... your true north. Jesus is our...." Her eyes pop open, shining silver blue. "Jesus is my true north."

I look for vacillation, but find none.

She says, "I am going to sleep in my own room," and then she leaves.

Fio leaves me.

The rain lets up as the sun goes down, and I take a walk. Getting set to cross a street, my head swings back and forth, while I wait for a break in traffic. That listless swing of the head – where have I seen that? Oh right, Llove the Llama, wandering the maze that is Machu Picchu. Hmmm – maze, amaze.... interesting. No, not really.

I recall that morning at the ruins when Fio announced, "Here comes love!" Well, I can't say she didn't warn me.

I swing my head back and forth again, deliberately mimicking Llove the Llama, looking for my herd. No use; the sidewalks are empty. The one person in this universe with the inclination to love the llama has chosen to withdraw her love. Or maybe it was not a choice. She might pitch it as a realization that I would never be able to reach her core, that I lack the capacity to share her innermost joy. She could never be "joined as one" with a non-believer. From her perspective, I am not marriage material. Understandable, I guess.

What is wrong with me? Just believe, Theo. Accept that Jesus is your savior; it will make everything easier. Place your life in the care of a man whose language you don't speak. You've done it before, when Yachay led you out of the jungle, and everything worked out fine.

Jesus, forgive me. I accept that you died for my sins. I want to believe.

What now? Should I expect an immediate response? Do I wait? Believe, Theo, and in time you will Know. Jesus, help me believe. I accept your grace. Do I recite this until it takes hold? Lather, rinse, repeat. Am I on The List? Or does Jesus see through this kind of ruse? Verily, verily, that Duncan guy is just trying to get the girl. Yes, Jesus, that's part of it, but I want to believe, I really do.

An image of Francisco Pizarro flashes through my mind. As he lay dying from stab wounds, he used his own blood to finger-paint a cross on the floor of the Presidential Palace. Was that an act of devotion, or was he lobbying The Almighty to show mercy on him for slaughtering thousands of Incas? As the Grim Reaper is closing in, I imagine it's common for the faint of heart to pledge their undying allegiance to God. Still, you'd think they'd be nervous about Jesus seeing through such a ploy.

Should I run back to the hotel and pound on Fio's door, and yell through the keyhole that I'm trying? If I toss in a healthy dose of wailing and gnashing of teeth, will that help?

As for Christianity being True – capital T – who cares if it is or it isn't? Newton's laws of physics aren't true, yet they transformed our world in the most profound ways imaginable. And Isaac Newton is still an engineer's best friend. If Jesus' message holds the power to transform – and I don't doubt Fio has been transformed – shouldn't that be good enough for me? Maybe, but "good enough" will never be good enough for Fio.

Aw, who am I kidding? If I ever decide to pursue a god, or encourage one to pursue me, I'd do some research first. I'd go comparison shopping, rather than accepting my dad's meticulously crafted but warped religion, which had been bequeathed to him by his father.

It wouldn't be practical to study all religions, but I'd check out a fair number of them – Christianity, Buddhism and maybe Islam, as well as a few lesser known makes. Hold on, *makes*? Can't you just hear Cole?

Makes? he'd ask with a sardonic grin. As in "make and model?" As in "manufactured by somebody?" Well put, pally.

I'd begin my religious studies by interviewing adherents:

Yes, fill me in on your religion's military history.
Nice to meet you. Now, this business about eternal life....
Was your messiah kind? Did he sing or crack jokes?
What's your deal?

Why and where did you go? Fio thinks I wrote that song about us. I run through the lyrics: A single llama roams the street; no room for compromise; did we ever stand a chance; why and where did you go?

Hmmm, *did* I write them for her? See, there's the problem with language: You spend weeks crafting lyrics, seeking to capture a sense of both sanctity and loss, carefully choosing one pronoun over another, and then you come to find out that no one, not even you, the songwriter, is even able to discern the song's topic with any degree of certainty. Does that mean the lyrics are lame? Or evocative? Hell, ask ten people what "Hotel California" is about, you'll get ten different answers.

Maybe Meher Baba had it right, refusing to talk. Maybe I'll stick to writing instrumental tunes from now on, because the melody to my Machu Picchu song – which, for the record, pretty much wrote itself – evoked feelings in Fiona that she identified instantly: Machu Picchu was "so peaceful and sad and beautiful, like that song you were just singing." Her take on the Lost City at dawn echoed my melody precisely.

Getting back to those lyrics, maybe I did write them for Fio. Who knows? But, at this point, who.... the hell.... cares?

I caress the sleeve of the llama wool sweater she bought me. It's awfully soft, a souvenir of romance. The interweaving brown and blue hues teasingly hint at the union of Earth and Sky. I blink, and my right eye squeezes out a single tear that tickles as it trickles down my cheek. Wandering the wet, glistening streets of Otavalo, I find myself hoping Llove the Llama is faring better than I. Let's hope he's found a friend or a mate, maybe a new clan.

Nah, it's more reasonable to hope that he hasn't been eaten.

Chapter 22: Set for Life

Breakfast at the hotel restaurant is a dour affair. Rain has been falling all morning. Cole asks what's going on, but no one answers. Fio stares out the window. I feel the way I did in December, when we found out my mother was no longer with us.

Aw Jesus, Theo, don't pretty it up. Just say it: Mom *died*. And a piece of me died in December too. This morning it feels as if another piece of me, a smaller piece, is dying. My insides are numb; I don't even feel angry.

Gracie breaks the silence. "Fiona is going back to Barry."

"What?" Cole searches our faces in disbelief. "Whaaaat?" I give him a single nod. He looks diagonally across the table at his sister. "Fi, what're you doin'?"

"I need a man who shares my spiritual beliefs." She looks sorrowful, but doesn't sound like it.

I want so very badly to dislike her at this moment, but I am unable. All along, she has acted with integrity. Or am I being too easy on her? No, she may or may not have been honest with herself, but at every step along the way, she has told me her piece of the truth. She has acted erratically, but without malice. Still, this is maddening. Is the chasm between us really that wide? Wouldn't we find a way to bridge it?

Fio says, "I prayed about it. This is the right thing to do."

Cole asks, "Oh, you prayed about it, did you? Did you get a reply from God, saying, 'Dump Theo'?"

"Not in so many words."

"So many? Dump Theo – that's two words, Fi. Look, it's your life, but Theo is a better man than Barry, pure and simple. He's kinder, smarter, more curious, he respects you. I've seen how you look at him. I've *seen* it, Fi. Barry is.... he's a telemarketer, for God's sake! He sells cemetery plots over the phone."

I had not known that.

She speaks as if no one is sitting beside her. "Theo is a good man, but he does not share my faith." It strikes me that Fio cares more for me more than she does for Barry, but she loves

Jesus more than Barry and me combined.

"Fi, sister that I love, Barry treats you like a…. a girrrl." That last word is delivered as the ultimate insult. "And think about how you're treating Theo."

"*You* think about how you're treating him. He wasn't jaded until you got to him."

Cole is fuming. "He's anything but jaded, and he's a grown man. He can make up his own mind."

"He doesn't *stand* for anything – you said it yourself. And according to the Gospel—"

"Oh, JEEEE-ses, Fi! Have some humility."

Fio is here to serve and save. Today, she saves her best shot for last, and serves it up cold: "You are the one with the big head. Your cabeza is *enormo*." Her statement not only accuses him of being conceited; it also references his hat-buying venture and our hokey-pokey antics, thereby portraying our bar-hopping escapade as nothing more than exuberant buffoonery.

Cole bows his head and says, "This was a mistake." It takes me a moment to realize he's referring to their entire trip.

Boarding the bus to Quito, Fiona and Gracie take a seat near the back. Cole sits behind them, and I take the seat across from him. We're a subdued lot. There is no singing in harmony, no witty banter, no Endless Debate. The rain drums loudly on the roof. The women talk softly between themselves. Cole pulls a paperback out of his jacket. I ask what he's reading.

"Huck Finn. A birthday present from Graham McHugh."

What? Did I hear him correctly? He still has a slight lisp, distorting everything he says.

"Could I see it?"

He tosses me the book, and I read the inscription on the inside cover: If you read a lot, you're considered to be well-read. But if you're well-known, it doesn't mean you know a lot.

Underneath that, in block letters, is written:

>Save de planet
>Save de bliss

It's dated and signed Graham McHugh. I whisper the name

aloud. And then again. Well, I'll be damned! "Tell me about this McHugh guy." The three of them stare at me like I'm nuts. "Humor me," I say. "What do you know about him?"

"Like we told you," says Cole, "we met him when we were kids, I guess. Fi and I get presents – books – every so often."

"And I bet you've never seen a picture of him."

Cole and Fiona confer silently, then both reply, "Right."

"Did he send you any books by Robert Louis Stevenson?"

"Yes," says Fiona. "How did you—"

"<u>Dr. Jekyll and Mr. Hyde</u>?"

"Yes." Cole's forehead folds in on itself. "How could you possibly know that?"

"Any other McHughs in your family tree?"

"Don't know."

Fiona is getting annoyed. "Theo, where are going with this? I don't appreciate—"

I raise my hand. "Sorry, but please, bear with me. Was your grandpa ever diagnosed with Alzheimer's?"

"I assume so, but...." Cole stops and glares at me. "Hijo de puta!" This has become his favorite saying. "This is none of your business! The hell're ya doin'?"

"Let's play a round of Funetics." Ripping out a page from my journal, I write: Graham McHugh, Crampy Q. I hold out the paper and say, "Say these names aloud."

Fiona spits her response at me. "Theo, I am sorry for hurting your feelings, but you've got no right to bring this up! I don't play games!"

Cole takes the paper and quietly reads the names aloud. He repeats them and taps Fiona's shoulder. "Sis. Uh, sis?"

"Leave me alone!"

"Fi, do it! Say them aloud."

Fiona is livid, but she reads the names: "Graham McHugh, Crampy Q." She inhales and holds it. "My gosh! What...? What does that mean? Why...? They were the same guy?"

I say, "Not 'were.' Check out the date on the inside cover."

She opens the book and reads aloud: "February 17th, 1992."

Cole says, "This was my birthday present from Graham, last month. They *are* the same guy."

"Two sides of a Mobius strip," I say to Fiona. She doesn't

hear me.

"He's alive?" Her eyes widen. "Crampy Q is alive?" She stands, turns, and kneels on the seat. Cole leans forward to embrace her. I've never seen anyone cry as hard as they do.

I think about the journey they embarked upon seven years ago, after their grandpa disappeared. The changes in their beliefs were predicated on his death, and now that he's been resurrected, I wonder if they will revert to their previous positions? Will Cole all of a sudden be the one thumpin' me on the head with a Bible? Will Fiona embrace atheism? If so, there will be no reason for her not to come back to me.

Yeah, right.

When it comes to our most cherished beliefs, we act as if they were chosen rationally. But few of us have the clarity of mind, or the bravery, to hold our precepts up to the light and ask the simple question: Is this true? No, the process by which we adopt a belief system involves a series of random detours, routed through the deeply rutted backstreets of our reptilian brains. And once committed to an ideology, the human mind shores it up with a heady concoction of convoluted proofs, third-hand accounts, wishful thinking, anecdotes and whimsy – whatever's handy, basically – then we fix the whole thing in place using the cerebral equivalent of duct tape.

Which spurs me to ask: What is my cherished belief, the one that drops a veil over my eyes? And the answer is, of course: I don't know. Because if I did, I'd rip away the veil. At least I hope so.

To give my companions some space, I rise and walk up the aisle. The driver eyes me suspiciously in his rearview mirror, then glowers at the commotion in the back. I take an empty seat and stare out at the rain.

My trip is drawing to a close; it's time to resume my life in Tucson. I picture how it was, and how it will be: Open the door, there are my books, my guitar, my saggy couch. Fresh air and sunlight pour in through the kitchen window. My fridge is stocked with eggs and veggies, corndogs and ketchup. I am thankful to be a citizen of a country of such unbelievable bounty.

But my gratitude gives way to a crushing sadness. Over the past month, my heart has been broken in many ways: by the allure of Andean music and the remnants of a forgotten world; by the sight of destitute women selling toenail clippers on the street of an imploding city; by the image of Dixon limping through the proliferative rainforest, hoping to photograph his damn hogwar. Above all, I am crushed by my agonizingly short time with Fiona. The only upside is that such heartbreak temporarily eclipses the devastation wrought by losing my mom.

I wonder how Claire would weigh in on my.... my *affair*, she'd call it. I can just hear her: What did you expect, you ass cactus? She dumped that other sucker for you – did you all of a sudden expect your little vixen to be true blue? Dumb ass!

Thomas Jefferson said: Travelling makes you wiser, but less happy. As far as my trip is concerned, he got it half right – I am certainly no wiser. Until yesterday, however, I was willing to entertain the notion that my time in South America has been a transformative experience, an awakening, the first step on a path previously unimagined. And now? I'm about to have another meltdown, only this time it won't be an ecstatic one.

An ocean of rain is falling, bringing with it no miracles. There will be no parting of the seas. No ark will appear, offering to bear the pure of heart to safety. We won't even experience a changing of the tides. Hey, Pariaqaqa, go fuck yourself. Oh, I'm being irreverent, am I? Yeah, well, tough. Tough Titicaca.

And Fiona? She's a rogue wave, sweeping up whatever and whomever stands before her, washing away hope and delusion. Don't believe me? Go ask Barry.

The rain leaves me feeling neither buoyant nor born again. I am simply watching water vapor that has condensed into droplets heavy enough to fall.

A hand settles lightly on my shoulder. I awaken and turn at the sound of Gracie's voice: "Hey, you. Come join us."

The driver gives us a dirty look when I stand and follow Gracie down the aisle of the swaying bus.

"We have questions," says Fiona, her face red and puffy.

I have endeavored on several occasions to help my siblings sort through their issues, and I've failed miserably. Nonetheless, I hold out hope for the Quinn family.

Cole wipes his eyes. "How in holy hell.... Sorry, sis....

How did you figure out all this Graham McHugh stuff, Theo, when it's been right in front of us for years?"

"I wondered about that, and here's my best guess: The two names look nothing alike, and since you probably saw Graham McHugh's name on a package before you ever heard it, it wasn't obvious to you, whereas I heard the names before I saw them written down. Or maybe...." The rest of my response will likely fall on deaf ears, but I give it a shot: "Sound is everything to me. I trust it more than I do the written word."

Fiona turns away.

Cole says, "We put together a list of books Crampy Q sent us over the years. Have a look." He hands me a scrap of paper with a list of titles: <u>Dr. Jekyll and Mr. Hyde</u>, <u>One Flew over the Cuckoo's Nest</u>, <u>The Metamorphosis</u>, <u>On the Road</u>, <u>The Mysterious Stranger</u>, <u>Huck Finn</u>, <u>The Odyssey</u>, <u>Robinson Crusoe</u>."

I say, "Stories of split personalities, running away, travelling, being stranded, becoming someone else..... At least that's what the titles would suggest."

"He was feeding us clues all along," says Cole, looking humbled. "We were too dense to pick up on them."

"How long ago did he start sending you books?" I ask.

"As near as we can figure, about a year before he left."

"So his leaving was premeditated."

"Right, and when Grandma died, he took off."

Fiona adds, "When he thought he was no longer needed."

"Sad," I say. "But hold on. How has he managed to get by on his own with Alzheimer's?"

Fiona says, "Could it be that he didn't have Alzheimer's? Maybe his memory was deteriorating naturally, because of aging. He repeated himself, but maybe that was because Grandma had poor hearing. The villain in all this is Uncle Dick. I don't know how Becky puts up with him."

Cole sneers. "It was Dick who sold us on Crampy Q's feeblemindedness, by stealing from him. Crampy could never find his stuff, and it sounded like he was crazy. Dick was the one who suggested the idea of Dad getting power of attorney."

"Why would he do that?" asks Gracie.

"Not sure. To get Crampy to give up control of his estate? To drive him nuts? To make it look like he was nuts, get him into a nursing home, so he could move into Crampy's house?"

Gracie tells me, "I made Cole promise not to throttle Uncle Dick when we get back."

"I won't make any such promise," Fiona snarls. "Cole, you asked me last week if I had ever met the devil. The answer is: Yes, and he's a male that goes by the name of Dick."

Cole says, "Now we know why Dick was so riled up after Crampy disappeared. When he and Dad and Becky went through the estate, it was worth a lot less than expected. Remember, sis?" He manages a two-syllable chuckle. "I thought Dick's head was gonna erupt."

Fiona looks back and forth between Gracie and me. "Crampy Q cut his sons out of his will, because he thought our dad was stealing from him, and Uncle Dick would have wasted his inheritance on alcohol." She brightens up. "Crampy Q must have taken a pile of money with him."

Her smile is now doubly devastating. After today, I will never see her again. I stare at her, then close my eyes and attempt to etch her image onto the inside of my eyelids.

"Still," says Cole, "he left enough in trust funds to put us through college."

"I used the last of it to pay for this trip," says Fiona. "My trust is all used up."

Yeah, in more ways than one. Needing a distraction from her smile, I ask Cole, "Did your dad know your grandpa took off?"

Gracie says, "It would be hard to believe he didn't know."

Cole disagrees. "But remember, Crampy didn't trust Dad."

Fiona says, "I don't think Crampy Q wanted anyone to know he was alive besides you and me, brother. He assumed that as we got older and would be better able to keep a secret, we'd pick up on the clues he left."

"Speaking of clues," I say, "you wanna see my favorite?" I take the book from Cole, and hold it open for them to see. "Read the last part of the inscription."

Fiona says, "Save de planet, save de bliss. So?"

Gracie's eyes pop open, and she bends double with laughter. "Save de bliss," she wheezes. "Save de bliss!"

"*So?*" says Cole.

She stands, turns and launches herself over the back of the

seat, yelling, "Safety blitz!"

As we step off the bus in Quito, the driver glares at us and mumbles something that I suspect translates to: "May the fleas of a thousand llamas infest your armpits."

I ask to speak with Fiona. With our backpacks leaning against our legs, we stand amidst the racket and stench of poorly tuned diesel engines. From under the roof of the bus bay, I look out at the sheets of rain. Blues songs written in bus stations have always sounded corny to me. Never again.

"Fiona, you're unlike anyone I've ever met, and I love you. Whatever path you take, I hope it makes you happy."

Her swollen eyes have taken on the same dead cast as the featureless, steel-grey sky. "Theo, you are, and always will be, special to me." Special – not much of a consolation prize.

"If you change your mind," I say, "here's my address and phone number."

She sticks the slip of paper into her khakis without looking at it. "Good-bye, Theo. We changed our flight; we're going home tonight." Though there's no need to clarify who is meant by "we", she does anyway: "I called Barry last night."

"Yeah." It's devastating, knowing that I could not compete with that stiff, who was not even present. She is possessed.

"I am forgiven," she says.

Twenty-four hours ago, I would have asked: By whom? Barry? Jesus? Herself? Me?

Fiona stares at the pavement. "At Machu Picchu, I told you that a small part of me believed Crampy Q might still be alive. In here...." She pats her chest. "....I knew it all along." She lifts her eyes, and offers up a toned-down, used-up version of The Look, configured with harsh angles. "Even if it's a long shot, Theo, it's nice to believe." She touches my cheek with an index finger. "You helped me heal my relationship with Cole. I won't forget that. You have given me a gift." She walks away.

Staring out at the grayness, I whisper, "I'd have given you anything, everything." Had we been given another month, another day, another hour together, could we have reached one another? I don't know.

How disheartening. How humbling. Life has dropped me

at the corner of Mobius and I Don't Know. I left Arizona three weeks ago, convinced that Nobody Can Ever Know. Note the capital but silent K. It's a bleak outlook, sure, but at least we're all in the same boat. The same leaky boat. My agnostic certainty was then watered down – or moderated, an optimist could say – by my experience at Machu Picchu. Nobody Knows may have been a diminished position, but it held out a morsel of hope, allowing for the possibility that some of us might Know in the future. And then, the morning I woke up next to Fiona out in the jungle, she challenged me on the fixedness of my stance. To my credit, I saw immediately she was right; speaking about – or for – everyone is arrogant and simplistic. My position was not fair, and unfairness is the one attitude I've always considered to be.... well, unfair. So I further diluted the potency, if not the flavor, of my stance, to Nobody I know Knows, which only served to muddy the waters. Continuing my slide, it then occurred to me that Maybe Fiona Knows. And now? I am left with a humble "I don't know." Note the lower case, silent k.

If humility is an asset, I am set for life. I am going places. Woo-freakin'-hoo. Let's hear it for humility. Humiliation is more like it. A gust of wind blows a faceful of rain under the bus bay roof. Behind me, Fiona says goodbye to Gracie and Cole, then a car door opens and an accented voice asks something beginning with "donde." Where to?

Sinewy hands massage my shoulders. "Come in out of the rain, pally." We rejoin Gracie, and I ask about their travel plans.

Less buoyant than usual, Gracie replies, "Cuenca."

"What's a Cuenca?"

"It's a colonial city, south of here." She rattles off a litany of attractions: "Cobblestone streets, cathedrals, museums, artists, parks.... Will you come with us?"

"Count me in, although I'm flying home in three days."

It's good to know I'll be spending my last days in Ecuador with Cole and Gracie, though it now feels like I'm tagging along. But since getting dumped by Fiona – at some point I reverted to calling her by her full name – I do not want to be.... lonely.

So. This is what lonely feels like. It turns out that when I told Fiona at Machu Picchu that I'd never been lonely, I was speaking the truth.

Chapter 23: Call That Fair?

The next morning, I'm sitting behind the driver of a southbound bus, traveling through Volcano Alley. Gracie and Cole are seated across from me. The mountains, unfortunately, are veiled by mist and low-lying clouds. We pass through a series of Andean towns and cities, some run-down, some prosperous, and a few obscured by torrential rain, falling straight down.

A sodden numbness has replaced the warm ache in my chest. My brain is resolute in its need to rehash my days with Fiona, in an effort to reconcile her disappearing act with her declaration of endless love. She might claim that we did not connect deeply, but we did. Swear to God, I saw it in her eyes. Imagining the paths we might have traveled together, I re-write our future, over and over.

Gracie looks at me with a soft melancholy, offering to take on a share of my heartbreak as her own. Her everything-happens-for-a-reason doctrine has softened since Barry's money belt got snatched at Mitad del Mundo. I accept her solace and vow not to allow my grief to put a damper on these last few days with her and Cole. Hmmm, damper – a fitting word, given the 100% humidity. Or maybe "dampest" would be more apt.

A wind comes up, and the angle at which the rain falls begins to fluctuate wildly, as it rides chaotic air currents. I watch for a few minutes, then snap my fingers. "I know how that lady at Mitad del Mundo faked the Coriolis Effect. That basin had a big drain hole – it must have been four inches wide. And the larger the hole, the less swirling you get."

Responding to Gracie's confusion, Cole says, "Riiiight. Slick, imagine a basin with a foot-wide hole. The water would just dump straight out onto the ground. It wouldn't swirl at all." He cocks his head, and says, "But when she moved the basin twenty yards away, it did swirl, so.... Hold on, let me think about this." He slumps, bows his head and sets his forehead in his palms.

A minute later, Gracie cries, "Got it! The second time she ran the experiment, she poured the water in from.... let's see, to make the water spin counter-clockwise, she must have poured it in along the right side. And the third time she poured it in from the left. But how did she do it the first time? How can you make sure you're pouring it in the exact middle?"

I say, "She waited several minutes before pulling the plug. Remember? She explained the theory, and then she had us get our cameras out. She gave the water time to become still. But here's what I don't get: In the men's room, one time the water swirled one way, the next time it swirled the other. Why would it do that?"

"Chaos theory," says Cole. "Tiny variations in the initial conditions yield different outcomes. Microcurrents in the water made the results unpredictable."

Unpredictable – a cousin of my old buddy Unknowable. Ah, yes, we're back on solid ground, or at least familiar ground. And that's when the bus begins shaking. Is God coming to smite me for my agnostic ways?

We're surprised that the driver keeps going.

Cole says, "Feels like we're gonna drop a transmission."

The shaking stops, and the driver says, "That was our third earthquake this month. They're not so bad." His English is only slightly accented.

But the traffic comes to a halt in the next town, and our driver shakes his head. "Es muy mal." It's very bad. "It's been raining twice as much as usual. The road is probably blocked by a mudslide. Even a small quake can shake loose a hillside." He points ahead and off to our left.

I gesture toward the door. "Abierto, por favor?"

The driver opens it, and my friends and I step down into the chilly Andean air. A traffic jam stretches as far as we can see. The rain has let up, leaving the mountains and stucco buildings enshrouded in mist. I suggest walking ahead to see how far the road is blocked, but Cole ignores me.

"Come on," he says, and sets off at a trot, heading east, toward the clamor of sirens. Gracie and I follow. On a street parallel to the highway, a police car and fire truck rush by, toward the southeastern part of town. Pedestrians point up the hill, as a buzz of horror-stricken voices arises.

Cole says, "We gotta check this out."

"Our backpacks are on the bus." My protest falls on deaf

ears; Cole is already halfway down the block with Gracie on his tail. Ah, what the hell. That bus ain't goin' nowhere.

We run two blocks south before we see the problem: A hillside has given way, burying homes, cars, roads, people. The mud flows beneath a wooden bridge as a fast-flowing chocolate river, taking the path of least resistance, further eroding the hill's integrity. At the next intersection the slow-moving sludge, ten yards wide and two feet deep, swallows anything and anyone it encounters. Inhabitants of the neighborhood stagger out, covered with muck, gasping for air.

Those are the lucky ones.

We backtrack and head uphill, approaching the slide zone from the side.

Cole is tempted to charge into the mire, but he wavers. "The hill above us – we don't know if it's stable."

That's my first thought too, but it's immediately challenged by an impulse to plunge into the mud, to help those in need. My fear of drowning weighs in as well, and these voices duke it out for supremacy. My brain is swamped by a *whoosh* and a *whirl*, as a billion neurons fire with near simultaneity, demanding consensus. This all takes place in a span of seconds, and just like *that*, my mind is made up. I've had my fill of passivity. I'm here to serve and save. My choice is not so much a decision as it is a leap of understanding.

Or, maybe by this point, I don't give a damn.

I am more aware than most of the destructive power of water, and I vow to stand against it, to seek vengeance for the misery and havoc it has wreaked upon me. It may sound pointless to wage war against a liquid, but if I have anything to say about it, Pariaqaqa will claim no more victims today.

I wade into the cold, relentless ooze. It's so thick I have to lift my foot clear, then lean forward and set it down in what feels like quick-drying concrete. I call over my shoulder, "You're right; we don't know if it's stable. But we do know people are suffering."

That line of reasoning is good enough for my friends. They charge in after me. Cole is solidly built, so he's able to cover more ground than either Gracie or myself. He leans through the open window of a two-room house, and pulls out a bawling young boy or girl – it's hard to say which – and carries the little ball of mud to safety.

After twenty laborious steps, I step up onto the porch of a house, the walls of which are canted ten degrees right. I knock and put my ear to the door. A feeble voice replies. The door will not open – it's lodged in place by the tilted doorframe. I kick at it, but it holds fast. I take four steps back and foolishly ram it with my injured shoulder. The door splinters, and I stumble into the living room, ankle-deep in muck. An elderly man reaches out pudgy hands to me, and I help him outside. But he's unable to navigate the mire, and he falls, taking me down with him. A policeman wades over and helps me up. He's unhappy with me for moving the man without assistance. He and I drag the man by his armpits across the street and set him on a trash can.

Gracie appears from behind a house, a baby llama in her arms. It's bleating and kicking, but she holds on until they reach safe haven.

Dozens of people, some in uniform and some not, wade into the mud to help. A wild-eyed man grabs my arm and insists I follow him. One wall of his house is missing, and his ceiling has caved in.

"Mi esposa!" he cries. My wife!

A beam has fallen, pinning her to the floor on her stomach. The crazed man and I bend down and lift. It hardly budges.

He calls, "Uno vez mas!" Once more.

We lift until the veins in our necks bulge, and this time the beam moves enough for the woman to crawl to safety, but the movement causes her to scream. Against the man's protests, I go for help. I find a fireman and point to the house.

"Mujer, sangre." Woman, blood.

The rain starts up again in late afternoon, and a two-foot high mound of mud slowly muscles its way down a hillside, threatening to engulf a cluster of homes. My friends and I come upon an old man grappling with an upright piano, attempting to wrestle it through his front door. Gracie pleads with him to leave, but the man is adamant; he's not going anywhere without his piano. I climb through the living room window and push on the cumbersome instrument while Cole tugs on it from outside. Once we have the upright clear of the threshold, the four of us wheel it across a rocky yard, then turn it downhill. With mud lapping at our heels, others come to our aid. We lift the piano and lurch down the road as people gather to watch. Cole and I get our feet tangled, and we go down in a heap, with Gracie landing on top of us. I look up in time to see men hoist the piano up a flight of stairs and through the back door of a church.

My friends and I are lying on the ground, facing downhill, knowing the wall of muck is about to swallow us whole. I take a breath and hold it, as a voice calls out, "Gringos locos!" Bystanders erupt in laughter – a surprising reaction, given the disastrous events of the day – and the mud washes over us, cold and gritty. It takes all my will power not to open my mouth and scream. Only now do I recall nightmares I've had about drowning in dark waters, abandoned.

But we are not alone. Four seconds after our immersion, strong hands lift us to our feet and lead us out of the goopy torrent, to cheers and applause. Gracie's lustrous black hair gathers in lumps on her shoulders. Cole is coated in mud from head to toe, except for his eyeballs and grin.

My stitches have torn loose. I want nothing more than to get out of these filthy clothes, and change into....

Gracie is apparently thinking the same thing. "Our packs! We left 'em on the bus!"

We wave to the crowd and take off downhill. Gracie is limping. I ask, "Where's your other shoe?"

"I lost it, pulling my foot out of the mud."

"CHEEE-ses, Slick!" Cole is angry. "You could have cut it on glass, or stepped on a nail! You could've...." She shushes him by placing a muddy finger on his lips. He spits out the ooze, then bends over and sets his hands on his knees. "Climb on."

Not one to stay distressed for long, she takes five steps back, then runs and leaps, landing high on his back. "Giddy up!"

We enter Plaza de Armas at dusk, where people are rushing into and out of a towering cathedral – odd, given that this is a Wednesday.

Gracie asks, "What's going on over there?"

"Don't know," I say. "Let's go get our packs.

She slides off Cole's back. "Our packs won't go anywhere

in the next five minutes."

Cole gives me a shrug and jerks his head toward the cathedral. "Let's check it out, pally."

We look like creatures from the Black Lagoon, so we hesitate at the wooden doors and peer inside. The vast nave boasts vaulted ceilings and gold-gilded surfaces. The mood is anything but solemn, with people scurrying about, delivering food and medical supplies, tending to the homeless and injured.

A stern-looking nun exits, and I ask in Spanish what we can do to help.

She looks me up and down and replies, "Take a bath."

Gracie giggles, "I'm not sure what you were trying to say, Theo, but you asked how to improve yourself."

We are filthy, but no filthier than a lot of the people coming and going, so we enter the cathedral. The scale of human misery sobers us as we wander among the dazed, battered faces. They are being tended by doctors, nurses, fireman, nuns and clergy.

"It doesn't seem fair," I say, mostly to myself.

"You sound surprised," says Gracie.

"Well, if there is such a thing as God, you'd think he'd at least be fair."

"Why do you believe that?"

"Well, because it's...." That's as far as I get. "Don't you believe in a fair God?"

"Sure, some gods are fair, others not so much. A few are flamin' bitches."

"But that seems—"

"Unfair?" asks Gracie with a playful elbow jab. "Is there anything about life that seems fair? People come into this world hungry, unloved, limbs missing, whereas you, Theo, get to be.... you! Call that fair?"

Gracie jabs me again, pulling a reluctant smile out of me. While she may never lay claim to Knowing The Truth, she is a wizard when it comes to providing perspective. And she's right, of course. I have much to be thankful for.

Still, it occurs to me that my most cherished belief – well, one of them – involves a presumption that God is, or should be, fair. I find it distressing to realize that this longing for fairness – in a deity, in life, in family matters – is an affliction I share with

Barry. Fiona must be a sucker for guys who get seduced by their desire to believe in karma.

It's unsettling to entertain the notion that Fairness Incarnate is merely a human construct, *my* construct. Will my cherished belief come to feel constricting at some point? If so, let's hope I am brave enough to shed it, and that I'm able to view the loss as liberation.

There is a hollowness inside me, the cause of which, I tell myself, is not having eaten today. "Man, I could use a jumbo combo pizza right about now."

"Ditto that, pally. With mushrooms, pepperoni and grease, lots of grease."

"Pizza, in Peru?" Gracie asks mockingly. "Cheeses!"

"Yes," he says, leading us outside, "pile on the cheeses."

She stretches her arms around Cole's and my shoulders, and then jumps. He and I each catch a leg, then swing her back and forth while the nun looks on with distaste.

Carrying Gracie, we retrace our steps from this morning. Lucky for us, our bus is still stuck in a traffic jam extending endlessly in both directions. Cole knocks on the door and waves. Our driver, in a foul mood from sitting on his butt all day, opens the door, but he growls at us to stay where we are. I explain that we need our packs.

"You're not gettin' on my bus. Not like that you're not." He waits three seconds and bursts out laughing. "My name is Paz. I only have one Inca Kola, but you are welcome to it." He descends the steps with a bottle and pops the lid on the bumper, then hands the soda to Gracie. She and Cole each take a sip to express gratitude, whereas I guzzle the ultra-sweet drink.

Paz points behind us at a fountain, in the middle of which stands a ten-foot statue of an Incan warrior. He says, "It's frowned upon to bathe in there, but I don't think anybody would mind. I heard about what you did. Everyone is calling you Tres Gringos Locos."

Cole and Gracie jump onto the two-foot-high rim around the fountain. I set down the soda, and they give me a hand up. We salute the bus driver and join hands, counting, "Uno.... dos.... tres!" Together we back-flop into the waist-deep water. My lungs clench up instantly in the frigid water and I surface, gulping for air.

"CHEEE-ses!" Cole howls.

Gracie comes up gasping and giggling. When Cole and I make a move to get out, she says, "Not so fast!" Retrieving the Inca Kola, she says, "Kneel, heathens. Open wide and accept the holy water." We do as ordered and tilt our heads back. She pours the syrupy soda into our mouths and over our faces, making for a sweet baptism. She intones, "In the name of the Father, the Son, the Daughter...."

Cole grouses, "Hurry it up, witch!"

"Be silent, non-believer! Where was I? Oh yeah, the Mom, the Sun God—"

Shivering, I say, "The God of Shrunken 'Nads...."

Gracie dowses me again. "....Buddha, and the Goddess of Many Wings, I hereby declare thee baptized. Theo, may your heart heal quickly. Cole, you may now smooch the bride."

She hands me the bottle of Inca Kola, which I polish off. Cole, still on his knees, grabs her around the waist and kisses her, then he stands and deliberately tumbles sideways, re-dunking them both.

Gracie comes up sputtering. "Heathen! Sinner! Creep!"

She takes off her shoe and whacks him on his shoulder. He snatches it and flings it over his shoulder. It lands in the crook of the soldier's elbow.

I say, "Somebody's gonna find that shoe, and make up a story about how it got there." She and I climb out of the water, with Cole behind us.

He says, "They'll think it's a lost sole, left by a lost soul."

He's halfway out when Gracie and I yell, "Safety blitz!" We jump him, sending all of us back into the fountain. We pop out of the water, cussing and laughing. So, this is what family feels like – I'll take it. Tonight's baptism has been immeasurably more meaningful, and entertaining, than my first one twenty years ago.

I belong.

As we clamber out of the fountain, Paz chuckles and says, "Tres Gringos Locos." He hands Gracie a dingy towel. She dries her face and passes it along to me. I run it through my hair and toss it to Cole.

Paz retrieves our packs and leans them against the side of his bus. "You still look like a mountain fell on you. Follow me."

Cole hoists his pack onto his back and carries Gracie's pack in his arms. With chattering teeth, she walks beside him barefoot. Paz leads us to a hotel and holds the door open for us.

The small lobby has wooden floors and low-wattage lighting, but it's warm and clean. The clerk, a stocky man with bushy eyebrows and tufts of hair sprouting from his ears, takes one look at us and strides around the end of the counter.

"No, no, no!" he says gruffly, shaking his head and index finger. "Vamanos!"

Paz pushes past us and announces, "Tres Gringos Locos."

The clerk's eyes light up. "Tres Gringos Locos? Aqui?" Here? He pumps our hands, talking fast and loud, then he motions for Cole and me to remove our shoes.

My Spanish has improved enough to translate. "He has rooms for us, free of charge, and he'll be happy to get our clothes laundered."

We tell Paz and the clerk, "Gracias, gracias, gracias!"

Two hours and a hot shower later, we're scarfing down a pizza with onions, mushrooms and sausage, slathered with grease and cheeses. I'm wearing one of Cole's sweatshirts, which is a size too large, and Gracie has her long, wet hair tied up in a bun. Customers recognize us as Tres Gringos Locos, and the manager graciously picks up our tab.

After dinner, we return to the church and approach the same crotchety nun we'd seen earlier. Gracie asks if we can help. The woman is explaining what our duties will be, when a voice calls out, "Tres Gringos Locos!" We turn, smile and wave. The nun seems to know who we are, but she's unimpressed.

Cole, Gracie and I spend the next two hours tending to cuts and scrapes, and distributing Inca Kola. We dispense towels until they run out, then we collect them, take them out to plaza and wash them as best we can in buckets of swampy water. By midnight, families have staked their claim to bits of open floor space. Two hundred people bed down for the night.

Standing in the grand entryway, Cole gazes back down the nave. "It's a good thing this church is as big as it is." Realizing what he said, he looks at Gracie sheepishly.

She wraps her arms around his waist. "Been a lonnnng

day."
 "Amen to that, Slick."

Chapter 24: Bogeyman

The next morning we enter a cafe on the plaza. Our booth is upholstered in bright red vinyl that squeaks when we sit down. We all order trout with sides of something like hominy.

"Dixon's been resurrected," says Gracie. "Well, kind of. I called the lodge's Quito office to get an update. A woman from Yachay's tribe tracked a large, gimpy, nearly naked man with a monocle yesterday. He was talking to himself, and when this woman approached him with knife in hand, he took off into the jungle."

I slap my forehead.

Cole chuckles. "When you translate her description of him from Quechua to Spanish to English, it makes him sound like a noisy, chubby Cyclops. I bet that this is how fables and myths get their start. Maybe in five hundred years Dixon will be the subject of Quechua bogeyman tales. Can't you just hear it? Don't suck your thumb, Baby Yachay, or Icky Dixon will nibble it off when you're sleeping."

Gracie tries not to laugh. "At least Dixon's alive. I'll call again tomorrow. Hey Theo, we're heading up to the slide to help out. Wanna come?"

"Yeah, but first I need to confirm my flight for tomorrow night."

"I'm wearing mi bufanda rojo – my red scarf. I shouldn't be hard to spot."

"I had my recurring dream last night," says Cole. "The train was bearing down on me, but there was no tsunami. I was a goner. But get this: The tracks curved away in front of me, then the train stopped and a bunch of musicians got on. All this time I thought the train was coming for me. And I guess it was, kind of; it was coming to pick me up."

"Very cool," I say. "Do you think it means anything?"

As he ponders this, Gracie says, "Not to dig too deep, but music is the most powerful force you know, so it makes sense you'd represent it as a train. And music picks us up."

Cole smiles and spreads his hands. "There it is."

I say, "Well done, Gracious. Hey, before I forget, give me your address, okay?"

Cole grabs a napkin and starts writing. Well, I'll be damned! I'd forgotten he's left-handed, a trait he inherited from both grandparents.

"Cole, how did you know about your Uncle Dick stealing your grandma's jewelry?"

He regards me quizzically. "Becky admitted it to Fiona."

Fiona – the sound of her name skewers me all over again. I ask, "And nobody confronted Dick about it?"

"Right. Becky made her promise not to say anything."

"Uh-huh. Who first pushed for the reading of the will?"

"Aunt Becky. She said the family needed closure." His forehead crumples up. "What are you—?"

"This may sound like a dumb question," I say, "but what made you think your grandpa had Alzheimer's?"

"Well, it was obvious. Crampy Q repeated himself, and he was always looking for his keys and wallet."

"After your Aunt Becky cleaned house."

"Yeah…?"

"Is Becky left-handed?"

Gracie says, "No, we've played tennis; she's a righty."

"Your grandma had a left-handed banjo; why would she want Becky to have it? As you said, you can't just turn it around and string it backwards."

"You think she stole it? Along with Grandma's jewelry?" Cole rubs his temples, and we sit in silence, playing out various scenarios. Finally Cole bangs the back of his head on the vinyl padding. "CHEEEE-ses! It was Becky who pushed for her and Uncle Dick to move in with Crampy, saying they could expect 'compensation.'"

"Meaning what?" asks Gracie.

"She always said how much she loved that house. It had a great view of the Cascades. And before Dick finally agreed to move in, she pushed for Crampy to move into a nursing home. That would have been death."

I say, "You told us the other day that Dick wanted your dad to get power of attorney. What do you make of that?"

"Maybe he wanted to make sure the power of attorney didn't wind up in Dick and Becky's hands? Hard to say. Maybe he was trying to protect Crampy from her."

"Did a doctor diagnose him with Alzheimer's?"

"I assume so." Cole's eyes flit back and forth, scanning memories. "I'm not sure, but I remember Becky researched it, and said he had all the symptoms." He bangs his head again, harder this time.

"Sorry, but I gotta ask: Did you ever see Dick drunk?"

"Yes. Well, no, not exactly. But everybody knew about his drinking problem."

"How?"

"Becky told us." Cole bangs his head three times, then gives me a hard stare. "So Dick.... Uncle Dick is...."

Gracie finishes for him: "Apparently, not the devil after all."

I say, "The only unkind thing I know about Dick is that he laughed when your grandpa couldn't find his keys."

"Because he knew Becky had hidden them." Cole doesn't even bother to bonk his head this time. We sit in silence.

Gracie says, "Hubby, a couple days ago, you said something like, 'Now we know why Dick was so angry after Crampy Q left. There wasn't as much money in his accounts as we thought.' So he was complicit in Becky's plan, wasn't he?"

Cole shakes his head. "Maybe not. Maybe he was angry *because* Crampy Q left. Maybe he realized that he left because Dick and Becky were going to move in."

I'm not convinced. "Why would your uncle put up with all that from Becky?"

Gracie says, "I never told you this, Cole, but I danced with Dick at our wedding reception. He had a couple drinks in him, but he wasn't drunk, and he gave me some marriage advice. 'No matter what your man does,' he told me, 'you gotta forgive him. Take Becky now – she's meaner'n a skillet full of rattlesnakes, but I'd go over Niagara Falls for that girl.'"

"Which is where they got married," says Cole. "So, Uncle Dick took the fall for her. CHEEE-sus, I hope Fi doesn't kill him."

I call the Aeroperu office in Quito, and the woman tells me

my flight is now slated to leave tomorrow morning at ten, nine hours earlier than scheduled. I call the train station and discover that the only departure for Quito leaves daily at noon.

I pack, then go searching for my friends. The intersection where we first waded into the river of mud is unrecognizable. It rained again this morning, sending a new wave of mud, furniture and chimneys down the hill. Two blocks south, streets are ten feet underwater. They will be talking about this flood for a very long time. La Gran Inundación.

After searching for twenty minutes, I ask a policeman, "Donde esta la mujer con la bufanda rojo?" Where is the woman with the red scarf? I ask it three times, but he still doesn't understand me. After a month in South America, I understand Spanish pretty well, but it sounds like I have a bar of soap in my mouth when I speak it. I'm able to order beer and trout, but I lose my way after that.

Finally I try, "Donde esta Senorita Rojo?" Miss Scarlet?

"Si, si, si," says the cop, pointing back the way I came. "La Catedral."

On my way into the plaza, I gaze up at the impressive, imposing stonework of the church. I enter and immediately spot Gracie's red scarf, in an alcove near the altar.

She says, "We're staying here, Theo, in this church. We'll feed homeless people, and help them dig their lives out."

Cole gives me a wry smile. "Here I am, working and living in the Belly of the Beast. Who'd a'thunk?"

"Ah, sweet irony. But why? With the way you feel about The Church, why not work through some other agency?"

"That's just it. We've been talking.... well, Slick has been talking to people all morning; cops, firemen, volunteers. I wish you'd have been with us, pally; nobody believed we were Dos Gringos Locos. Anyway, everybody told us the same thing: 'Go to the church. That's where help comes from.' Regardless of whether there's a Guy with a White Beard in charge, this is a close knit community – they look out for each other. Catholic Relief Services are on the way with food and medical supplies. When people want to feel safe, they go to a church."

On a good day, The Church aspires to serve and save, just as it has done for two thousand years. This gets me thinking about

Fiona, who considered it her mission to serve by saving me. In her words: If we fail at that, what's the point? So, once she came to regard me as a lost cause, spiritually speaking, maybe it was time to move on.

I ask, "How long will you be staying in…? Wait a minute, where are we? What town is this?"

Gracie squeals with delight. "Isn't it great? We don't even know!"

Cole says, "We'll be here at least through the weekend. You're staying tonight, aren't you?"

I shake my head. "My flight changed. I'm catching a train out at noon."

Gracie takes my hands. "Oh Theo, I'm going to miss you." She hugs me in that bone-crushing, neck-wrenching, fabulous way that only she can.

"Same to you, Gracious. Are you guys looking forward to going home?"

She smiles and shrugs. "I could stay, I could go."

Cole says, "I can't wait to track down Crampy Q. I've been thinking about him and singing that line to your song."

He and I harmonize softly: "Why and where did you go?" Matching each other's timing precisely, our voices echo off the alcove's stone surface in a gloriously disorienting way, as if the glory is coming from everywhere, perhaps even from within us. Is this what people refer to as the Voice of God?

We sing that line over and over, until I realize it's caught the attention of the grouchy nun we encountered last night. I'm afraid she's gonna give us the boot, but as we sing, the tension leaves her face, and she bestows upon us a demure smile, tinged with sweet melancholy. When Cole and I begin singing again, the woman closes her eyes and allows her body to lightly sway. She does not understand my lyrics, though she identifies the feel of the music – peaceful, sad, pretty.

Grace adds her voice to the mix, an octave above mine, and the next time around, I settle in with another harmony line, sandwiched between theirs. They've brought my song to life in a way I never foresaw, and I can only hope my friends feel a sense of belonging that runs as deeply as does my own.

After singing that one line a dozen times, we've had our

fill, and Gracie says, "I want to hear that song when you finish it."

"Oh, it's done," I tell her. "I played it for Fiona."

"Hey, pally, don't give up on her. I predict she'll dump that stiff in a month or two."

"You're an optimist," I tell him. "That's your problem."

"Hey, Slick, ya hear that?"

"Yeah, I heard it."

"I keep saying I'm an optimist, but she never believes me."

Gracie whacks him in the stomach. "Come visit us, Theo. Promise?"

"I promise."

Cole gives me The Look, then wraps his arms around me. "Been a wild ride, pally."

Epilogue – three months later

The desert flora around Tucson is sparse. Consequently the soil retains little moisture, and during summer storms, rainfall is funneled into narrow canyons leading straight into town. Stream beds that are dry for ten months a year become inundated with a torrent of muddy water and uprooted trees.

Today I hiked up Sabino Canyon, through which flows a stream that's known to transform itself in a matter of minutes, from a trickle into a raging river. Fed by a watershed of thirty-five square miles, Sabino Creek will occasionally overrun its banks, rendering roads impassable. I was six miles out when a menacing bank of clouds rolled in, so I hightailed it out of there. I was lucky to make it home. Another hour and I'd have been stranded, up the damn creek without a paddle.

I open my mailbox, remove the single letter, and make a run for my apartment. I have not seen rain like this since my wonderful, excruciatingly short time in the Amazon. In Tucson, it's either drought or flash flood. I gotta get outta here.

I pull off the sweater Fiona bought me, wincing because of my sore shoulder. Though close to my heart, the wounds I received in Ecuador were far from mortal. I treasure my sweater, though it's now a half size too small and beginning to loosen at the seams. I will soon have to shed it, though not necessarily because I've grown. No, the sweater shrunk from an accidental washing in hot water.

The letter is postmarked Seattle; the name in the upper left-hand corner says "Quinn".

Theo,
I'm leaving for church in twenty minutes, but I wanted to get a letter off to you first. Let me apologize for getting annoyed with you on the bus ride back from Otavalo – I don't think I ever said I was sorry.

Barry and I have made our peace. He and I will never be close, but he has changed. He's learning about forgiveness. And who knows? Maybe I am too. He's been very understanding, more than I'd have been in his situation. And he finally realized what a jerk he's been.

I regret letting Dixon walk away. Yes, it was his choice, but each of us should act as our brother's keeper. I've been writing Logan. He says there were Dixon sightings until a month ago, but none since. Logan believes he hitched out on an oil truck. He'll let us know if they catch wind of him.

Gracie is pregnant! If it's a girl, and she's convinced it is, she wants to name her Thea. Nice, huh? As close as she can figure, she became preg-o-licious, as she puts it, on the equinox. I am excited!

Crampy Q rose from the dead. I talked to an aunt in Jersey who actually SAW him. We're hot on his trail. He officially changed his name to Graham McHugh and travels the country in an RV visiting college buddies. Thanks for helping us sort that whole thing out.

Remember that bar in Lima? You and I connected on "Can't Help Falling in Love with You." I want to explore what we began that night. And when you cut loose on "Losing My Religion," you weren't watching the audience. I was. They were possessed!

Speaking of cutting loose (nice segue, si?), maybe it's time you cut your fam loose. Step out of the vortex. It doesn't sound like you're doing them much good, and they sure as hell aren't doing you any favors. Move to Seattle! Yeah, it rains here, but nothing like the Amazon. Drip, ooze, slither, squawk (try saying THAT five times). You can stay here until you get your own place. Or stay here as long as you like – there's a spare room in the basement. It doesn't get a lot of sunlight, but hey, it's Seattle, NOBODY gets much sunlight once monsoon season hits.

You'll be surprised at the changes in my "spiritual" outlook. I'm proud to say that I'm more accepting of people with viewpoints that differ from my own.

Music update: Dread the Donkey is calling it quits – the bass player's wife doesn't like him getting home at dawn, smelling of smoke, disinfectant and beer. No accounting for taste!

Llove The Llama – Gracie says it's the best name ever for a band, especially if you can figure out how to amplify your charango. As a backup, she suggested "Barry the Hatchet." That girl's got her moments. By the way, her vote for 1992's Safety Blitz Award: Machu Picnic.

Bad news, pally: I was wrong about Fi cutting Barry loose. They're getting hitched in October. I had hopes of you and me being brothers-in-law. Hijo de puta!

Get THIS – I've sat in with the band at their church a few times. The preacher man has a hard-on for my soul, and he knows the only way to get me to church is by playing up-tempo, happenin' tunes. Don't lack much a'bein' a fair trade: I enlighten him musically; he gets his shot at saving me. It's a pain in the ass getting up Sunday mornings, but the people are cool, and Gracie likes how churches smell. I dig the whole scene – well, except for that religious stuff.

Hey, I haven't had that dream about the train in, what, two months? Three? Oh, I've lost track.... Safety blitz!

Let us know if – no, when – you're coming.

Cole

I play back my phone messages: "Phil here. Good news – I sold a painting, my fourth this year! A hundred and ninety bucks, cash. So next month you won't need to lend me as much...."

Fast-forwarding the tape, I come in halfway through the next message, from Claire: "Well, Ro's wiener-head husband gave her the boot – did I call that or what? And how about you? Are you still pining away over that wench you met in.... where was that? Portugal?"

I hit the STOP button and take another look at the letter. Until those last few paragraphs, I assumed Fiona had written it. Reading it again, I hear Cole's voice this time. Surprisingly, it makes sense either way. And it's not the least bit disappointing to discover that Cole wrote it. I might even prefer it this way.

Gracie is right: "Machu Picnic" should win the Safety Blitz Award. Which gets me to wondering how Llove the Llama is faring. At some point, will he pluck up the courage to leave the deserted city and continue his search elsewhere? I don't know.

I don't know – these three words call to mind an encounter with a customer who came in to buy a Fender Stratocaster today. He checked out a dozen instruments, but kept returning to a luscious sunburst Strat. Though smitten, he went about his business seriously, asking which models have rosewood fretboards, which have humbucker pickups, and so on. Being a Fender enthusiast myself, I answered his questions easily, until he picked up the sunburst and asked, "Are these American-made Strats better than the ones made in Mexico?"

How quick and sly are the workings of the human brain. In the span of four seconds, I auditioned two responses:

Yes, in my experience, they are.

That's the consensus.

Problem is, neither statement is true. First, I have never played a Mexican-made guitar. Second, American-made Strats have a rep of being built by superior craftsmen using better parts, which may or may not be a myth – part of the Fender legend – but which explains why American Strats cost twice as much as those made in Mexico, which doubles my commission, which should not affect which guitars I hype, but which sometimes does. I put a halt to this flood of "whiches" by remembering that we are here to serve and save, which today meant serving this customer by providing him a chance to save a bundle.

"I don't know," is what I told him. It only seemed fair.

That's when he smiled for the first time. Initially I thought it was a gotcha grin, like he had stumped me, but then he said, "I don't trust salesmen unwilling to say the words, 'I don't know.' " He clapped me on the shoulder and said, "I'll take the sunburst."

I don't know. That three-word admission has always struck me as a liability, a limitation. But today those words saved my credibility with that customer, and they served to validate all of my previous answers. Save and serve.

The descending arpeggio of the grey potoo plays in my head: G – E – D – B – G. And it still puzzles me: Do these notes imply a major chord, or minor? Or both. Or neither. It doesn't much matter. It's a catchy little tune – lovely, simple, ambiguous.

Such ambiguity calls to mind the photo taped to my fridge. The picture was taken with a six-second delay at Mitad del Mundo, and I take a moment to admire it. My friends hadn't yet shown up, and I had relinquished hope of ever seeing them again. My camera shutter opened one second after they'd called out, "Blue Muña!" My face in the picture is an emotional hash: anguish, joy, weariness, relief.

The phone rings, and I let my answering machine take it. "Ro again. How come you don't call back? Well, Claire just called; that porker told me *I* have a fat ass. Can you believe it? But, hey, that's not why I'm calling. Theo, I need a place to stay, as of this Tuesday. I hope you don't mind, but my sciatica is acting up, and your couch doesn't offer much support, so.... could I use your bed? Not for long, just a few weeks, a month or two at the outside. And, oh, just so you know, Howie, my new man – he's totally hot, by the way – is flying in for the week-end, and I won't be able to pick him up, so if you could...."

While she rambles, I flip through my phone book and find my landlord's number. The instant Ro finishes her monologue, I pick up the phone and dial.

I am getting out of here.

About the Author

Mel Conner taught mathematics for 32 years, in Australia and Kirkland, Washington.

He has written and recorded three CDs – <u>You Won't Come Back</u>, <u>Three Hands Clapping</u>, and <u>Iconnerclast</u>.

<u>Llove the Llama</u> is Mel's second novel. His first, <u>Your Child Left Behind</u>, chronicles the 25-year journey of Leo Haldini from hell-raising 9th grader, to offbeat teacher, to wasting-away administrator. It's a comedy and a tragedy.

Mel resides in Kirkland, where he is currently writing his third novel, <u>Committed to Memory</u>.

Made in United States
Troutdale, OR
03/18/2024